Spore Press

TARBABIES

a horror novel

TARBABIES

a horror novel

by

Allen R. Brady

SPORE PRESS LLC
LITTLE ROCK

TARBABIES
Allen R. Brady
Copyright Allen R. Brady 2013
Published by Spore Press

ISBN: 978-0615861227

SPORE PRESS LLC
6916 Incas Drive, North Little Rock, AR 72116, USA

PRINTING HISTORY
Spore Press eBook/ September 2013
Spore Press Paperback / September 2013

For information, address: Spore Press Marketing,
6916 Incas Drive, North Little Rock, AR 72116.

http://www.sporepress.com

Spore Press Books are published by Spore Press LLC
SPORE PRESS and the "Spore" design are trademarks of Spore Press

Dedication

To Lisa, who for some reason has stuck with me.

"One day atter Brer Rabbit fool 'im wid dat calamus root, Brer Fox went ter wuk en got 'im some tar, en mix it wid some turkentime, en fix up a contrapshun w'at he call a Tar-Baby…"

JOEL CHANDLER HARRIS
Uncle Remus and the Legends of the Old Plantation

I

I like to think that it all started with the thing that was a duck.

I know. It's ridiculous to suggest that something as comprehensive as the end of the world could be traced to a single, neat, underlying cause, and anyone who's still alive to read this has already heard a thousand theories about exactly what the tarbabies are and where they came from. Perhaps you don't call them tarbabies. Perhaps you prefer Goopy Guys, or Slow Walkin' Joes, or Sticky Toffee People, or another of the three dozen epithets the pundits have tossed around. But the thing that was a duck came close to being where my story ended, so the romantic in me likes to think that's also where it started. And that's not even considering what it did for Pixie.

It's correct to say that the thing *was* a duck, because not long ago, it *had been* a duck. It's also true that the thing was *trying to be* a duck, and in that it met with varying degrees of success. It could more or less walk like a duck, but it could not quack like a duck. It was shaped like a duck, but no one who looked at it twice would mistake it for a duck. And while it knew what a duck did, it did not know why it was doing it. It could float like a duck, for example, but it would never understand that the primary purpose of flotation was keeping the head above water.

In my dreams, I see the thing, which was a duck floating in that filthy pond. Its head brushing occasionally against the slimy muck at the bottom and its feet pointed up toward the sky, had the sky been visible through the thick canopy of trees. In my dreams the thing that was a duck waits. It does not know what it is waiting for, nor how long the wait will be. But something tells me it can wait for a very long time.

And the romantic in me thinks it was waiting for me.

2

My first exposure to the tarbaby plague came three-and-a-half minutes into Gavin Gouligan's monologue on a Monday night in May. Like you, I get the bulk of my news from late-night comedy shows, though I admit Gouligan's show, *Going to Bed with Goulie*, tended to be less informative than his competition. Gouligan was an abysmal interviewer, but I liked his sketches about the constipated Terminator robot, and sometimes there was a guy who brought on monkeys, so I watched. Libby thought he was a tool, and it's hard todisagree.

"And if you think that's nuts" was Goulie's go-to segue in his monologues. He had just finished a joke about some bimbo socialite's recent appearance on *So You Think You Can Type* when he said, "And if you think that's nuts, wait'll you hear what's going on right here in New York City. The city so nice they named it thrice. Ain't that right, Geronimo?"

Goulie's jokes required a lot of set-up. Geronimo Colstadt, conductor of the *Going to Bed* band, owed his paycheck to his penchant for keeping his boss's riffs alive. "Thrice, Gavin?" he replied, in that smooth jazz baritone of his. "I thought they named it twice."

"That's 'cause it doesn't like to use its Hebrew name: Mordechai."

"Mordechai, huh?"

"Yep. New York Mordechai New York. You heard it once at the bar mitzvah, then never again." That's how the show went. Goulie had about five bits per show, so each one had to be milked for about eight minutes to round out the show. In this case it took him four minutes to trot out every cliché he knew about Jewish culture before he remembered what point he was trying to make. "Anyway, it turns out we've got our very own monster."

"A monster, huh? Like a Godzilla monster or a Bigfoot monster?"

"They're calling it the Port Authority Bogeyman," continued Gouligan, but I got distracted when my wife Libby came out of the bathroom. She was brushing her teeth, which is a skill I greatly admire in her. Toothbrushing has for me always been a sloppy, frothy affair, best performed with one's head stationed squarely above the bathroom sink. Libby has a dainty, ladylike brushing style, and never drools a drop. She's petite (is *waifish* a word?) and a full head shorter than I am, with auburn hair she cuts like a boy and a pale complexion just this side of translucent. Think "elf" and you would not be far wrong. Anyway, she wears this old t-shirt to bed that she just thinks of as comfy, but which has worn thin enough over the years that... well, Goulie simply can't compete. That t-shirt was the reason I thumbed the power button on the remote that night, thereby missing the pre-game show to the end of the world.

That's twice I've used the phrase "the end of the world" now, and I confess I'm not being entirely accurate. The tarbabies may very well represent the end of humanity, possibly the end of life as we know it, but the planet is no doubt going to keep spinning any way, oblivious to what may become of us tiny specks of carbon that have been clinging along for the ride. Still, for the sake of establishing the scope of the problem, "end of the world" makes a convenient shorthand.

It was four days later before the subject came up again. I work in Search Engine Optimization, which is when you help companies make sure their websites show up first in the list of search results at sites like Yoohoo or Bingle. If you're lucky enough to still have Internet access, you can find me online at Heaney SEO. That's my name, by the way—Josh Heaney. Pleased to meet you. If you exist.

The work I do is exactly as tiresome as it sounds, but it means I can work from home, which is good if you're as lazy as I am. Like most who work from home, my day alternates between staccato bursts of work-related activity and long stretches of killing time on the Internet. On this particular Friday, I got an email link from some guy I don't know. It linked to a video called *In Search of ShadoMan*, which featured a pack of Bridge and Tunnel jugheads stalking the rampways of Port Authority Bus Terminal, searching for whatever it was their hero Gavin Gouligan had been talking about.

It was a terrible quality video, both because of the low light conditions of the Port Authority bus ramps and the fact that it was shot by Bridge and Tunnel jugheads. The video consisted of just over four minutes of nearly solid blackness, punctuated here and there with shaky close-ups of spotty faces and a couple of seconds of accidental clarity. One of the pack was noticeably taller than his compatriots, with a fondness for shouting "Goulie!" while jumping up and failing to slap the overhanging beams that supported the ceiling, but otherwise the kids were so indistinguishable that it was difficult to tell even how many there were.

The payoff came at about the two-and-a-half minute mark. Peering over the edge of the 41st Street overlook, one of the jugheads became apoplectic about a shadowy figure on the ramp below them. The silhouette was man-sized, and just barely lighter than the shadow of the parking structure surrounding it. At first glance it seemed to be nothing more than a shadow itself, but the only strong light source appeared to be the daylight above. The jugheads spent the next forty seconds trying to figure out how to get down to the next level. By the time they gave up and returned to the overlook, the shape was gone.

I was going to reply to the email, but couldn't think of anything particularly clever to say about the video. In the end, I deleted it and forgot about it until three days later, when Libby actually met the ShadoMan.

It was Monday morning, axx week after Goulie's Bogeyman bit. Libby was in the shower when I poked my head in to impart some important commuting tips. "Are you going into work today, Pixie?" I asked her. I suspect the primary reason Libby married me is because as soon as I met her, I called her "Pixie." Her given name is Liberty Belle Rimbeau, and there is no permutation of that name that she likes. She hates that her last name sounds like "Rambo," she hates that her first name is inevitably shortened to either Bertie or Libby, and she hates that her first and middle names together betray the fact that she was born on the Bicentennial. But her parents are like that. You'll meet them later, by the way.

"That's the plan," she replied, slathering a half pound of conditioner over a quarter pound of hair.

"Port Authority's been shut down."

"Seriously? How come?"

"Some kind of police action. They've got the whole building cordoned off."

Libby and I live in the town of Otterkill, New York, some sixty miles to the north of Manhattan. Her commute into the city is long, but when everything is running properly, it isn't particularly stressful. On the picturesque Palisades Parkway, it's an hour's drive to the George Washington Bridge, and another fifteen minutes puts us into midtown. Buses are plentiful, and have always been Libby's preferred method of travel, but they all terminate at Port Authority. Her least favorite option is the train, since the frequent stops make the ride longer than the bus, and the fact that they come into Grand Central Terminal leaves her with an extra half hour walk to get to her west-side office.

What makes the long commute bearable is the fact that she only has to do it three times a week. Libby temps as a legal proofreader for a midtown law firm. The work is insipid, the lawyers are boorish and demanding, but the pay is good, and she can effectively set her own hours. This particular week she was scheduled to work the noon to midnight shifts Monday, Wednesday and Friday, which meant she avoided the rush hour completely.

I drove Libby to the train station in time for the ten o'clock local. She plugged in her headphones and settled into her latest audio book, a thriller about a mystery writer who murders other mystery writers to try out story ideas. As she listened to the protagonist drop veiled, incriminating witticisms for the benefit of the investigators, she watched the Hudson River roll past her window, peppered along its length with tiny pleasure craft.

Since this was an off-peak train, it hit every stop along the route, from the remote northern villages of Cold Spring and Garrison to the affluent bedroom communities of Westchester. As the stops piled up, the train's motion, the heat of the morning sun, and a particularly lengthy description of the murderer's typewriter all conspired to make Libby drowsy. She was nodding off by the time they reached Ossining and sound asleep by Tarrytown. It wasn't until they reached Manhattan that she opened her eyes again. The train was stopped by signals near the 153rd Street Station, a brand new stop built specifically for the new Yankee Stadium.

On most days, this station is deserted as trains only stop there when games are scheduled. Since Libby's commutes had never coincided with game-day arrival times, she was surprised to see someone on the far platform, apparently waiting for a northbound train.

She missed him at first. The platform initially appeared to be empty except for the sign board on which the train schedules were posted. But as she leaned her head against the glass of the window and found her gaze drifting down the platform, she caught the faintest trace of movement out of the corner of her eye. The figure was mostly hidden in the shadows, and she was unable to distinguish any of his features. She guessed he was a man based on his height, but could tell nothing about his race, or age, or even if he was facing her. Whoever it was appeared to be dressed all in black, and his skin was dark enough that he easily blended in among the shadows.

It's unlikely Libby would have given the stranger a second glance if it hadn't been for the legs. There was nothing particularly unusual about them, except that there were more of them than there should have been. Above the waist, there was a head, a pair of shoulders, and a single set of arms. But by the time the shape hit the platform, Libby was counting one, two, three, four feet.

She knew it was an optical illusion, of course. There must have been another person standing on the other side of the sign, with only his legs visible. It just *looked* like all four limbs were on the same side, hanging down from the same waist. Or perhaps she was just seeing his shadow from an odd angle. It didn't *look* like there was anything there to cast a shadow on, but there must have been. Maybe a mirror? Or was that a jacket tied around his waist, with the sleeves hanging down?

When the signal finally released and the train surged forward again, Libby's interest in the stranger faded as soon as he had slid out of view. She flipped back through the tracks on her music player, trying to remember where she had dozed off.

While Libby was off working, I was doing the next best thing—loafing and getting paid. I've never been the model of diligence, but I'm fast at the work I do. I likely average a little less than two hours a day of actual work, but since the things I do are things my clients haven't yet figured out they can do for themselves, I can still command a good rate for my modest efforts. Libby tells me if I were ambitious, I would also be rich. As things stood, I was content to earn enough to pay the mortgage on our humble two-bedroom cottage.

One of those bedrooms serves partial duty as my office. Given my appalling work ethic, the last thing I need is a TV to distract me, so of course that was the first thing I put in there after we moved in. On most days, my routine consists of fifteen minutes of checking search result pages, followed by a few adjustments to some crucial keyword positioning, rounded out with a half-hour lounge on the day bed, snacking and flipping channels. I'm a hair on the north side of six foot three and have always tended to lankiness, but I know my metabolism can't fight off this kind of lifestyle forever. I guess that's the upside of having a severe lifestyle change thrust upon you.

On this particular day my channel surfing had an actual purpose. I was trying to find out what was going on at Port Authority. Though each of the local networks had cameras on the scene, there was very little to see on the outside of the station. They were making heavy use of footage captured earlier in the day, which was mostly shots of police coordinating an early morning evacuation of the station and blocking off the surrounding streets with powder blue sawhorses. One tantalizing shot showed half a dozen officers in hazmat suits filing in through a side entrance.

The news anchors zeroed in on the hazmat suits and gleefully conjectured we were dealing with a chemical attack. Perhaps anthrax, perhaps bird flu, or perhaps the fan-favorite "dirty bomb." The fact that there had been no explosion did not dissuade teams from three separate stations from speculating on the impact of a "dirty bomb" at every opportunity, each time pausing just enough to make it clear that they were surrounding the term in verbal quotation marks.

The channel that specialized in New York news tried to keep a level head about the situation, offering the possibility that the problem might be something as prosaic as a gas leak or chemical spill. That explanation fell apart in the early afternoon as reports started coming in of similar police actions at three other locations throughout the city.

The first of these was the Herald Square subway station, just half a mile south of Port Authority. At two o'clock, the Eighth Avenue trains had been ordered to skip the 34th Street Station. Half an hour later, the order extended to the Seventh Avenue trains as well. By three, service on both lines had been suspended throughout all Manhattan. Interviews with transit workers described dozens of police officers searching the tracks on foot, though no one could say exactly what it was they were looking for.

The subway shutdown was what made me nervous. The 34th Street subway stations are at the entrance to Penn Station, home of Amtrak, the Long Island Railroad and PATH train commuter lines.

With Port Authority already out of service, shutting Penn Station down would cut off two major arteries out of the city, potentially stranding hundreds of thousands of commuters. By three-thirty, a cordon had been thrown around the Times Square Station. The focus of the investigation this time appeared to be the S train, also known as the Crosstown Shuttle, the most direct route between Port Authority and Grand Central Terminal, which was Libby's ride home.

I called Libby's cell phone shortly after four. The staff weren't supposed to take personal calls while on the job, but she picked up immediately. "Hey babe," she answered, "you watching the news?"

"Yep," I replied, because I was. "This is turning into a major transit headache. You may want to consider getting out while you still can."

"Half of the staff has left already. Everyone who lives in New Jersey is afraid they're going to shut down Penn Station, so they ditched."

"They'd better hurry."

"Not much they can do. With the subways down, they're going to have to hoof it. And with both Port Authority and Herald Square cordoned off, they're probably going to have to cut all the way over to Tenth Avenue. It could take them an hour to get there."

"Are you coming home?"

"Ugh," she groaned. "I hate the thought of Grand Central at rush hour. Especially with the overflow from all the bus riders."

Against my recommendations, Libby decided to stick it out. Her instincts about the pending rush hour mess were on target. Penn Station was indeed shut down, right at the height of peak travel.

With Port Authority out of the picture, thousands of commuters swarmed the docks of the ferry terminals to begin the long wait for boats across the river to New Jersey. Long Island residents had to make their way to Brooklyn, in hopes of picking up the LIRR there. And, as predicted, thousands more crowded onto trains at Grand Central, hoping at least to get out of the city, then worry about how to cross the river later.

It was after eight when Libby finally decided that the Grand Central crowds might have subsided enough to chance leaving. The sun was setting when she left her office, sending fingers of brilliant orange light down the canyons of Manhattan's streets. Seeing how crowded the streets of the West Side were even at this hour, Libby avoided the Times Square area and headed instead for Grand Central's northern entrances. As she approached Madison Avenue, twilight had fallen, and the blazing orange of the setting sun had been overwhelmed by a strobing sea of red and white. The flashing lights of a dozen emergency vehicles surrounded the 47th Street entrance.

Fearing the worst, Libby quickened her pace and continued on to Park Avenue. This entrance was still open, but she knew that might not last. The schedule board showed that the next Hudson Line train wasn't departing for another forty minutes. Rather than wait, she opted to take the first train that would get her north of the Bronx and rely on me to retrieve her.

She checked the board again. A train bound for Croton-Harmon was scheduled to depart in seven minutes on one of the upper-level tracks. She could make that if she hurried, despite the mini-labyrinth she would need to run. Down one escalator, past the ticket machines and customer service office, down a second escalator, down one hallway, up a staircase, down another hallway, down a second staircase and up a third, and she was on the track with three minutes to spare.

Or so she thought. Her watch said 9:10, and the schedule had said the train left at 9:13, but there was no train waiting for her. Instead, there were only a few hundred confused commuters, all peering down the tracks like an enormous colony of meerkats to see if anything was coming for them.

Libby walked up the platform toward the main terminal to see if there was anything else heading north. Her last spark of hope faded the closer she got to the terminal, where she saw the throngs of travelers piled up at the platform gates—gates that were now being locked by MTA workers flanked by armed National Guardsmen.

At Libby's size there was no way to see over the crowd, but she did manage brief glimpses of what was causing the commotion. A cadre of rescue workers were gathered in a semi-circle around a pair of figures on the floor of the Main Hall. One was easily discernible as an EMT worker by his bright yellow vest and green trousers. The paramedic was prone, and seemed to be lying on top of the second figure, with his head at about the level of the other's chest, as though he were listening for a heartbeat. About the second figure, she could tell almost nothing. All she could see for sure was that it was the right size and shape for a man, and that it appeared to be a uniform black from head to toe.

Engrossed by the scene, Libby flinched when the station's public address system blared to life. "Ladies and Gentlemen," announced a voice utterly bereft of confidence, "due to a medical emergency, no trains are permitted to enter the terminal. Please make your way to the nearest exits in a calm and orderly fashion. Until further notice, Grand Central Terminal is closed."

3

Libby was just getting out of Grand Central when her phone rang. Leaving the station was taking a lot longer than entering it had. The police had closed off the main exits by now, and hundreds of commuters who were still inside were now forced to file out the smaller Park Avenue exit. The opening chords of Duran Duran's "Union of the Snake" told her it was me calling. It would have been "Wild Boys" if I had still been home, but I was on my mobile at this point.

"Josh? Where are you?"

"In the car. I'm coming to get you." There's nothing I enjoy more than riding to the rescue, so I had been monitoring the situation at Grand Central to see whether it was in danger of closing like Penn Station. The news networks had no information, and Metro-North's website was inaccessible due to network traffic, so it was a New York commuter forum that first confirmed something was up.

At 8:41 p.m., a poster calling himself Suffern Succotash left a message reading, "gremlinz @ GCT—xpect shutdown soon."

"Confirmed," replied RamapoRailRider. "Inbound 7:50 fm Croton stuck at Marble Hill. There not letting us in & their not letting us out."

"Big trouble," agreed Suffern Succotash at 8:55. "Paramedic down. Nat Guard called in. Machine guns everywhere. NO TRAINS."

With that, I concluded that Libby was not getting out on her own. I grabbed my wallet, phone and keys, hopped into our Focus hatchback, and pointed it south. Once on the Palisades Parkway, I thumbed the speed-dial key for Libby's phone, but got only a recorded message that all circuits were busy. This came as no surprise, as cellular service is habitually spotty in New York during times of crisis. Text messages usually have a better chance of getting through, but I'm neither dextrous nor dumb enough to text while driving, so I engaged my phone's auto-redial function, switched on the radio, and tried to tune in a news station. Ten minutes later, as I was passing the Bear Mountain Bridge, my phone chirped, alerting me that I had a connection.

"You're on the road already?" asked Libby. "How did you know?"

"I got mad browsing skillz. Are you at Grand Central?"

"Yeah. There's army guys here, and something's going on in the Main Hall."

"Army guys?"

"Lots of them."

"You mean soldiers?"

"Whatever."

"I think a paramedic got attacked. Grand Central may not be safe. You should get away from there."

"Where are you now?"

"Bear Mountain. I should be at the Bridge in about forty minutes. Where do you want to meet?"

"As far uptown as possible." Libby was walking north along Park, calculating in her head. "Midtown is really gross right now. Shall we try for Lincoln Center?"

It was a good spot. Libby could easily make it there by the time I arrived, and it had its own drop-off and pick-up lane. "Lincoln Center it is. Call me when you get there."

After the requisite exchange of smoochies, we signed off. My speedometer told me I was doing sixty-five, a little above the Palisades' posted limit. Hoping the police had too much on their plates tonight to worry about traffic enforcement, I nudged the Focus up to seventy.

Half an hour later, the lights of the George Washington Bridge were in sight. My phone chirped again as I rolled through the toll booths.

"Pixie?"

"That's me!"

"Are you at Lincoln Center?"

"Above it now. Coming up on 70th. Where are you?"

"Just getting on the Bridge."

"Stay off the West Side Highway. I can see it from here, and its logjammed. I haven't seen any cross-town traffic since Columbus Circle. I think they're trying to keep cars away from Port Authority."

"How's Amsterdam?"

"Wall to wall emergency vehicles. I'm going to get as far north as I can. I don't know how far you'll be able to get."

From the Bridge I could see a good distance down the West Side Highway. It was nothing but tail lights, and they weren't moving. "I'm going to try Riverside. Can you get over there?"

"I think so," replied Libby. "Tell you what, if we get cut off, we'll meet at Riverside and 80th." She turned left at 72nd Street, heading west. "So, do you have any idea what's going on?"

"Not really," I admitted as I left the Bridge and exited onto Riverside. "The news channels were obsessed with the idea of a terrorist attack, but I think the police are looking for someone. I've seen the word 'bogeyman' used about four times today on different message boards."

"Bogeyman? That's kind of vague."

"One guy claims he saw a Shadow Man."

This struck a chord with Libby. That's when she told me what she had seen on the train that morning, as well as what she had glimpsed at Grand Central. In turn I told her what I could recall from the day's news broadcasts. It was hard to remember what parts were fact and what had been pure speculation, but the upshot seemed to be that there was something in the subway tunnels, and it was spreading.

By the time Libby reached 80th Street, I was passing Grant's Tomb up in the 120s. With 40-odd blocks to go, I would be at her location in less than five minutes. Libby told me she was going to cross to the west side of the street. Riverside was a rarity in Manhattan—an avenue with two-way traffic. Since I was coming from the north, it made more sense for her to be near the downtown lane, so I wouldn't have to turn around to meet her.

The crosstown light was red at the corner of 81st, so Libby stopped to wait for it to change. To her immediate left was a bus shelter, within which a young woman was rocking a stroller back and forth. Scattered around her feet were a dozen white plastic shopping bags. A man paced outside the shelter, craning his neck to peer down Riverside.

Noticing Libby, the man called out to her, "you seen any buses?"

"No, I'm sorry," she answered.

"Twenty minutes we're waiting," he continued, in a thick Dominican accent. "They closed the trains, so we're stuck."

"Yeah, I heard that. Sorry." The walk light came on, and Libby started across the street. As she stepped off the curb, she turned her head to wish them luck, and noticed there was someone behind her.

Coming along 81st Street, about a quarter of the way down the block, was… someone. Just as with the figure at Yankee Stadium, Libby was unable to tell much about the person who was approaching. He was short, perhaps even shorter than Libby. He was heavy too—round enough that Libby could only guess at his gender. She was entirely unable to discern specifics like race and age, because like the figure at the train station, this person appeared to be solid black from head to toe. But at that range, in the dim orange glow of the overhead sodium lights, it was difficult to determine anything for sure.

"Where are you now?" she asked into the phone once she was safely across Riverside.

"A hundred and sixth. I'm at a light."

Twenty-five blocks. Two minutes away, maybe three if I hit another light. Libby looked back down 81st. The Dark Guy was closer to Riverside, but not by much. He was definitely moving, but at a plodding pace. Even if she stood still, it was unlikely he would get across the street in another three minutes. If she continued at a moderate walking speed, he could never catch up to her.

The Dominicans at the bus stop were another story.

"I'm moving again," I reported, because I was.

"Do we have room for some passengers?"

"Umm… sure. Where we going?"

"Not sure yet. I'll tell you in a second." Libby crossed back over Riverside. As slow as the shadowy figure was progressing, she was confident she was in no immediate danger, but walking toward him still put her on edge. She did a quick count and determined there was the length of eight parked cars between the Dark Guy and the intersection.

"Excuse me," she said as she neared the bus stop again. "My husband is coming to pick me up. Can we give you guys a ride somewhere?"

"Really?" asked the man, at once hopeful and suspicious.

"You're headed uptown, right? It wouldn't be out of our way. And I really don't know if any buses are coming."

"Sure, sure. That would be great." The man turned and said something in Spanish to the woman who may have been his wife, who exhibited the same misgivings he had. Libby guessed they didn't get many offers for free rides on the Upper West Side. Her eyes flicked briefly back up the street, where the Dark Guy was now passing the sixth car.

The young woman hesitated for a moment longer, then relented. "Está segura?" she asked.

"Sí," said Libby, straining to recall her year of high school Spanish. "No está problema."

As the couple began gathering their shopping, Libby checked the figure's progress. There were just five cars left.

"My husband's coming from uptown," said Libby, "so we should cross the street."

"OK," the man said. "That's no problem." The woman began prepping the stroller, taking the brake off, adjusting her child's hood, and hanging bags off the handles. The man waited patiently for her to finish, doubtless having been through this routine before.

"Sir?" asked Libby as the young woman went about her organizing. "Does your wife speak English?"

"Not so much. How come?"

"I think we should hurry." She nodded down the block to the approaching figure. There were now just three car lengths between the Dark Guy and the bus shelter. The Dominican's eyes followed hers, then narrowed as he tried to make sense of what he was looking at.

At this distance, Libby could hear the Dark Guy's footsteps. They weren't the normal clicking or shuffling sounds usually created by shoes on pavement. Instead, they were moist, slurping sounds— a gentle *splut, splut*—as if the man were wearing sopping wet sneakers.

The Dominican exchanged a quick glance with Libby, then snatched up half a dozen shopping bags. "Vámonos," he said to his wife, "rápidamente." Libby grabbed a few bags herself, but left one hand free for the phone.

"Josh? Where are you?"

"Eighty-seventh. I'll be there in a sec."

"We'll be at the corner of eighty-first. And Josh, we may need a quick exit."

I paused before responding. "Hang on. I'm almost there."

The young woman appeared puzzled by her husband's sudden urgency, but did her best to keep up. The man started to cross Riverside, and almost walked into an oncoming car. Looking back, Libby saw the Dark Guy had reached the last parked car.

As the young woman turned her head to see what her husband was staring at, the figure raised his arms, as if reaching out for them. It was only twenty feet away, and the light was against them.

4

Standing on the corner of 81st Street, with her back to the Riverside Drive traffic, Libby got her first unambiguous look at the thing that had shut down the New York City transit system. He was indeed shorter than she, standing just a hair over five feet tall. He was also quite pudgy, though that impression might have been biased by his plodding way of moving. He staggered forward with what seemed to be exhausting effort, each labored step accompanied by that wet, sucking *splut*, but aside from the sound of his footsteps, the Dark Guy was entirely silent.

He was also hard to look at. A uniform shade of black from head to toe, he was discernible as human only by his silhouette. Libby's eyes kept trying to discern distinct facial features, but there was nothing there—no eyes, no mouth, perhaps the barest hint of a bump where his nose should be. Whenever she attempted to look at what she presumed must be some kind of surface detail, she found that she was actually focusing on a spot an inch or two beneath his skin. Although the man was dark, he also appeared to be translucent.

He was still advancing, arms held out directly in front like a cartoon Frankenstein's monster as he took another awkward step toward the quartet on the street corner. Both women took an instinctive step backward, but forgetting for a moment where she was, the Dominican woman stumbled over the back wheel of her stroller. She tumbled sprawling to the pavement, and Libby grabbed the stroller to keep it from going over with her. She succeeded in keeping it upright, but in doing so left herself vulnerable to the approaching figure.

To her relief, the husband's sense of chivalry kicked in immediately. Rather than retreat with them, his instinct was to step between his wife and the Dark Guy, directly inserting himself in harm's way. With his hands full of shopping bags, he was unable to grapple their pursuer directly. Instead, he came in sideways, holding his elbow up at the level of the guy's face to ward him off.

The intruder did not stop. Another half step, and the Dark Guy was upon the husband, grabbing at his arm with both outstretched hands. The Dominican attempted to shake free, but his attacker held fast. Frustrated, he swung at the Dark Guy with the shopping bags in his free hand. The bags sailed in a quick, tight arc, scoring a direct and potent hit on his assailant's head.

Splut.

The Dominican pulled his arm back again, preparing for a second strike, but found himself clutching nothing but a few strands of plastic. The handles of the bags had torn off in his hand, while the bags themselves were stuck to the Dark Guy's head.

As he watched, the two plastic bags sagged slowly to the side, spilling their contents. Most of the items that fell out clattered directly to the pavement. A jar of grape jelly exploded like a firecracker, splattering a sweet mess over more than a square yard. A handful of items didn't make it to the sidewalk. Instead, they stuck fast to the Dark Guy's body as soon as they made contact. A tube of toothpaste came to rest on his shoulder, a bunch of plantains affixed to his hip, while a bag of pinto beans spilled out along the length of the man's leg, coating him like scales on a fish.

Feeling the first twinge of panic, the young man attempted to backpedal away from his assailant. The Dark Guy held fast to the sleeve of his jacket, maintaining a tight grip no matter how hard his victim yanked his arm. That's when it first became clear that the Dark Guy might not be a guy at all.

As Libby watched the struggle, she could see the Dark Guy's hand begin to change. His fingers were becoming flatter and thicker, as though they were melting. Before the trapped Dominican's eyes, the hand was collapsing into a dark, viscous goo that began to overspread his sleeve. Panicked, the man flailed his arm back and forth, but could not pull free.

"Your jacket!" yelled Libby, as she helped the man's wife to regain her feet. "Take off your jacket!"

The man spun, momentarily putting his back to his attacker. He flapped his trapped arm, yanking it free of his jacket. Continuing his spin, he freed his other arm and left the jacket dangling empty in the Dark Guy's grip.

That's when I arrived, pulling the Focus to the curb on the opposite side of Riverside Drive. The light was changing, and Libby and her new friends charged across the intersection, leaving a trail of spilled groceries and plastic bags behind them. Libby saw me and sprinted to the car's passenger door, beckoning to the others. The man threw open the rear door, yelling at his wife in Spanish.

"Oh, hi! I'm… uh, Josh," I said, because I am.

The couple struggled to free their baby from the stroller. It wasn't a difficult process, but there were buckles to undo and arms to pull through straps, and their coordination was hampered by their panic. Only when the father triumphantly hoisted his son onto his shoulder did they steal a glance back at their attacker.

The Dark Guy was still following them, but had barely moved. He had advanced only two or three steps off the curb, the jacket still hanging limply from his arm, a shopping bag still stuck to his head as if stapled there, and a trail of groceries still dribbling down his side.

My new passengers did not waste time packing up. After his wife had clambered into the back seat, the Dominican threw their remaining groceries on top of her, then tucked his squirming child under his arm like a football and fell in place beside her. Libby hauled the unfolded stroller into the front seat with her and slammed the door shut.

"Hiya Babe," she said. "These are… some people."

"Ramón," the man volunteered. "This is Gabriela. The boy is also Ramón."

"Libby. And that," she added, pointing to the lumbering figure across the street, "is the Bogeyman."

As I pulled the car away from the curb, Ramón looked back wistfully. "I really liked that jacket."

ſ

Considering it's an island, Manhattan is a remarkably difficult city to quarantine. You can blockade the George Washington Bridge and seal up the Lincoln and Holland Tunnels easily enough, but that still leaves five bridges and two tunnels leading into Long Island. Cordon off those and you now need to worry about the seven bridges spanning the Harlem River to connect Manhattan to the Bronx. The Army National Guard made an admirable effort, establishing a presence at all major points of exit within twenty-four hours of the quarantine order, but they had two significant strikes against them. First, they were a lot more experienced in evacuations than in quarantines, and turning panicked civilians away from their barricades did not come naturally. Second, they had no field guide for how to turn back refugees who had no fear of being shot.

We counted ourselves fortunate to be watching the quarantine efforts from the outside. After dropping Gabriela and the Ramóns off in Washington Heights, we were surprised to find an exceptional amount of traffic waiting to get onto the George Washington Bridge. We hopped on the Henry Hudson Parkway instead, crossing the river up at Bear Mountain. Radio reports confirmed that traffic on the lower Hudson crossings was stalled in both directions, as National Guard units performed searches on all vehicles going in or out.

Early the next morning those routes were closed entirely. The first reports hinted at some kind of viral infection at work, but too many people had seen the effects of the alleged infection firsthand for that theory to last long. By lunchtime, some disturbing video footage was beginning to circulate around the network news channels. The clip of the Brooklyn Bridge standoff was on nearly continuous loop on every cable news program during the first days of the crisis. Libby and I first saw it on Channel One, where a news team was covering the National Guard's efforts to secure the river crossings. No one knew what they were dealing with at that point, and the Monday-morning quarterbacks had yet to emerge. Like the Guard, most of us watching thought the concrete crash barriers they had dragged across the roadway would be enough to keep them safe.

The Channel One cameraman spotted the trio of shadowy figures emerging from the nearby City Hall Park well before the Guardsmen did. His clumsy attempts at focusing on the shapes were impeded by the early morning light as much as by the fact that he had no idea of what he was looking at. The figures went unnoticed as they plodded toward the bridge, and it's possible they would have made it all the way to the barricades undetected had the news crew not alerted the Guard to their presence.

Specialist Kim of the 69th Infantry Division is the only one of those men whose name I remember. He was the first to engage the trespassers, stepping out from behind the barricade with his palms open, indicating that the bridge was off-limits. The figures kept walking, and Specialist Kim, discerning no weapons or threatening gestures, continued out to meet them. He got within fifty feet of the intruders before he saw something he didn't like. That's when he first called back to his comrades for assistance.

The cameraman still wasn't having any luck focusing. No matter how he adjusted his lens, he could not get any better resolution on the advancing figures. They appeared to be nothing more than solid masses of black, with no discernible features and a comical lack of grace. They didn't walk so much as trudge, as though the simple act of movement was a labor and every step required a concentrated effort just to get their feet off the ground.

Every action the Guardsmen took would have been appropriate if the trespassers had been human. Even once the figures were close enough for him to see there was something seriously wrong with them, Specialist Kim tried to warn the advancing shapes to turn back. To this day we have no idea whether they could have understood what he was saying, and they certainly gave no sign at the time. And when Kim finally raised his weapon on the lead figure, there was no way he could predict it would just keep walking until its chest bumped gently against the gun's barrel.

I'm sure you've heard as much speculation as I have on exactly what Kim was trying to do next. A number of commentators have tried to attribute his backward tumble to the pavement as panic, or simple clumsiness, but I don't buy it. From what I've seen in the video, I think he went to the ground on purpose. I think that, once he realized that he was unable to pull his weapon free from his attacker's chest, he was trying to throw the creature off. And yes, it's kind of weird that he didn't simply open fire, but we all know that wouldn't have made a dime's worth of difference anyway. So he tried to somersault—to use his attacker's own momentum to roll him over and off of him. With no knowledge of what he was facing, there's no way he could have realized that this was the last thing he should have done.

The other Guardsmen would also have reacted differently if they knew what we know now. But with poor Specialist Kim pinned on his back, unable to shake off the shadowy form that had dropped on top of him, grabbing the intruder and trying to drag him off seemed like a natural enough reaction. I know those of us watching at home were equally surprised when they found themselves unable to let go.

"They're stuck!" cried Libby, as she watched the soldiers trying to shake their hands free. "They're stuck to it just like those shopping bags last night, and Ramón's jacket!"

For the first few seconds after the soldiers grabbed the creature, they panicked like rats on a glue trap. They pulled and jerked and yanked their arms, but made no progress. And when they suddenly just stopped their gyrations, we allowed ourselves to believe that everything was all right again.

That's when the two remaining Guardsmen opened fire on the other intruders. Their shots were precise and focused, and later analysis of the video footage proved that every last one of their bullets slammed directly into their targets' chests. There was no reaction. The things did not pause a moment, but merely continued toward the soldiers at the same plodding pace.

In the commotion that followed, the cameraman chose to focus on exactly the wrong thing. I'll admit it was very dramatic footage, what with the Guardsmen vaulting behind the barricade, switching their weapons to full automatic fire, and letting all hell thunder down on the advancing shapes. But after the hundredth round had ripped into the creatures without even slowing them down, he should have realized that this was not the real story. He did shift his focus back to Specialist Kim and his comrades momentarily, but since the scene there was so quiet, he failed to appreciate the importance of what was happening. All three of the soldiers had stopped struggling. The would-be rescuers were standing with their heads bowed forward slightly and their weapons lying discarded on the roadway beside them. It was difficult to tell considering the distance and the fact that they were still wearing their helmets, but they actually appeared to be smiling.

If the cameraman had lingered on the shot for just a moment longer, he might have noticed that the black substance composing the creature's body was now covering each man's hand up to the wrist. Only on the still-frame replays could we see that the thing's body looked as if it were deflating—sagging and spreading out over the man pinned beneath him. Kim's face was hidden from view at this point, but he didn't seem to be moving.

Since their mission was the non-lethal containment of a friendly urban population, the Guard had not been equipped with heavy artillery. The unit on the bridge had little in the way of options other than opening fire or falling back, and in the ensuing firefight, the news crew was forced to abandon their position. A news chopper was on the scene shortly to get a bird's eye view of the situation, but by then the remaining Guardsmen had retreated to the relative safety of their Humvees. At some point, the three invading creatures had been joined by three more, all of which seemed intent on getting to the trapped soldiers. Oddly enough, they made no attempt to break in. Their preferred strategy seemed to be simply to surround the vehicles in the hopes their prey would eventually come to them. After a long period of inactivity, the copter crew panned down the bridge to the site of the original conflict. Where the initial struggle had occurred, there was now only a scattering of weapons and empty shell casings.

"What happened to the soldiers?" asked Libby, though I had no answer for her. "Are they OK? Did someone get them out of there?"

We pondered this question as the camera panned back to the soldiers holed up in their Humvee. No one was moving.

"You don't suppose those things… ate them? Like… dissolved them?"

In fact, I didn't. I had a far stupider idea. I couldn't help but notice that the situation had started with three bogeymen and three soldiers, and somehow ended with six bogeymen and no soldiers. I shared this observation with Libby, but it took her a moment to catch on. "You think some of those things used to be… people?"

Kind of. I thought *all* of those things used to be people.

The news teams took a little longer to commit to that conclusion, but as the amateur video began pouring in, the consensus was that these creatures were not killing their victims, but rather transforming them.

It took a lot longer for them to come to a similar consensus on what to call these things. The News 4 Action Team was the first to offer a name, relying on precedent and going with the safe but uninspired "Shadow Men." Channel 7's News at Noon responded with the slightly more poetic "Shadow Walkers," but their attempts suffered from inconsistency. The different field units all elected to try out their own variations, and within the space of an hour, audiences heard the creatures referred to as "Shadow Stickers," "Shambling Men," "Sticky Shadows," and the promising but short-lived "Gummi Men." This one seemed to be gaining in popularity until a Cease and Desist order was issued by Sauerbrächt Confections, makers of the popular GummiMenschen candy line. News 6 went completely over the top with "Darknight Demons", a label the on-air talent were committed to using, because their parent company had the foresight to trademark the phrase as soon as the outbreak started. They came up with a really cool animated logo too, though it was a little hard to read.

The name that would ultimately resonate most with the public was one that the news channels vehemently shied away from. In one of News 4's talking head segments, they interviewed Michele Thomas, a representative from Manhattan's Fifteenth Congressional District. Congresswoman Thomas related a story she had learned from her grandfather, which turned out to be part of the Uncle Remus collection of folktales. In the story, Br'er Fox had built a doll out of tar and turpentine and left it lying in the road. Soon, Br'er Rabbit came by and attempted to engage the doll in conversation. When the doll didn't respond, Br'er Rabbit became angry and punched it in the head, only to find his paw stuck fast. So he punched it with his other paw, and his other paw also got stuck. He kicked it, and his feet stuck. He head-butted it, and his head stuck. Only when his prey had been completely immobilized did Br'er Fox emerge from his hiding place to claim his prey. The doll he used as his snare, Thomas explained, was what Br'er Fox called a Tar-Baby.

Because of the term's racist connotations, no reporter who valued his job wanted to be the first to use the description. Nevertheless, the points of comparison between the folktale and the monsters that were now overrunning Manhattan were too obvious to be lost on the general public. For better or worse, "Tarbabies" was the name that stuck.

It was Tuesday evening when the first tarbaby escaped the cordon, and Manhattan's crisis became the world's problem.

6

"Banjo! Come!"

This was not the first time I had awoken to those words. The clock on my bedside table read 6:20, at least two hours before I normally get up. Banjo was the Spillers' dog—a dim, high-strung cross between a Collie and an Italian Greyhound who lived opposite our house on Ichabod Lane. The voice belonged to Norman Spiller, Banjo's master, if by "master" you mean the guy who picked up his poops. We were accustomed to the dog's early morning theatrics, along with his mid-afternoon dramatics, late evening histrionics, and hourly fit-pitching, so I rolled over, pulled the pillow over my head, and tried to go back to sleep.

"No, Banjo! Leave it! Leave it! Come!"

Norman yelling at Banjo. Perfectly normal Thursday. Was it Thursday? Friday. Perfectly normal Friday.

"Come!"

Bad Banjo. Naughty doggy.

"Come, Banjo! Come!"

Nothing strange about that.

"Leave it!"

Except Banjo wasn't barking.

There was an established pattern to this ritual. Banjo sees something, or imagines he sees something, or fails to see something he was hoping to see, and the alarm is raised. Norman steps out onto the porch and yells at Banjo. Banjo ignores Norman and continues his tantrum. Norman walks out onto the lawn and drags Banjo back into the house. Repeat as needed.

Except Banjo wasn't barking. And Norman wasn't going out to get him.

I rolled out of bed and peeked out the curtain. There was Banjo all right, prancing in a wide circle, tail pointing straight up, head bobbing frantically as he sniffed the air. At the center of the circle stood Norman...

"Come!"

Hold the phone. Norman was still on the porch. So who was that on the curb?

I scooped up a t-shirt and pair of cargo shorts on my way out the door, dressing as I descended the stairs. I think my shirt was on inside out, but I had bigger worries.

"Wuzzat?" asked a sleepy voice from the bedroom.

"Tarbaby!" I called as I slipped my feet into a pair of sneakers. "Banjo's caught a Tarbaby!"

"Wuzzat?"

I threw open the front door and dashed across the lawn, shoelaces flapping free behind me. The object of Banjo's scrutiny was standing in the shadow of a willow tree just to the east of the Spillers' mailbox. It would have been easy to mistake for nothing more than a man in the shadows, but as Banjo revolved around it, the thing took an occasional step in his direction. When it stepped out of the shade of the tree, it brought the darkness with it.

When Norman saw me stepping out into the street, he called a warning. "Look out! I think that's one of those Shadow Guys from the news."

I crossed into the Spillers' lawn on the other side of the mailbox, keeping it between myself and the creature. "Hey, Banjo!" I called. "Come here boy."

Banjo greeted me with an impatient chuff, then returned his attention to the intruder. He still made no sound while circling, but sniffed the air warily. Seeing that I wasn't interesting enough to serve as a distraction, I abandoned any hope of being clever. I walked up to Banjo, hooked a finger into his collar, and dragged the dog back up to the porch, where I turned him over to Norman.

Embarrassed that he hadn't thought to do that already, Norman stammered, "Oh, thanks. I didn't want to get too close to that thing."

"I saw one in Manhattan. They're pretty slow."

As if illustrating the point, the tarbaby took a clumsy step closer to the porch. Norman put Banjo back in the house and shut the door behind him. The dog's conical snout soon appeared in the living room window, nudging the curtains aside and fogging the glass in his efforts to keep an eye on the intruder.

"So what's up with Banjo?" I asked. "He barks his pointy little head off at chipmunks, but a bona fide monster doesn't get a peep out of him?"

"It's weird," Norman admitted. "I've only seen him act this way once before. We were on the Jersey shore, and some kids had a bonfire going. Banjo couldn't have been more than two years old at the time, and I don't know that he had ever seen fire before. I expected him to go ballistic, but he didn't bark once. He just kept walking circles around the fire, sniffing the air the whole time. He didn't get close to it, but he didn't run from it either. It was like he knew the fire was dangerous, but hadn't quite figured out whether he should be afraid of it or not."

"Dogs are weird all right, but you know what else?"

"What's that?"

"I think that thing is coming this way."

The shape was fully out of the shadow of the willow and was advancing methodically toward the porch. At its stumbling pace, it would take the better part of a minute to close the gap. Norman pulled the screen door open, and without a word, backed into the house. Though I hadn't been explicitly invited, I followed. Banjo was standing on the couch, his nose leaving a cloudy smear on the living room window. Norman closed the front door, and we peeked out from the small windows flanking the entrance.

"It's still coming," observed Norman.

"Yep."

"So what do we do?"

"I'm trying to think of what they do in the movies. This is a lot like *Night of the Living Dead*."

"OK, OK," prompted Norman, "that's good. So what did they do?"

"They all died."

"Oh."

"So we won't do whatever they did. It's kind of like *Halloween*, too."

"Did they all die in that?"

"Pretty much. People do really stupid things in movies."

"OK, so we won't do what the people in the movies do. What does that leave?"

That one took some thought. The best I could come up with was "Call for help? They almost never do that in the movies."

"Right. Good. I'll call the police." Norman snatched a cell phone off the coffee table and flipped it open. He looked at the handset for a moment, then back at me. "It's dead."

"Crap! They always do that in the movies too!"

"Oh, no, sorry. I mean the battery's dead. It's OK, I've got a landline in my office."

"Ah. Well, good. You call the police, then. I'm going to warn the neighbors." I threw open the front door and stepped out, directly into the creature that was now waiting on the porch.

To the end of my days, I will remain forever grateful for screen doors. My own house doesn't have one and I now see the reason for one It keeps you from walking into monsters on your porch and sticking to them. The screen door hit the creature with a metallic *WHANG* and stopped. Not expecting this, I kept going, driving my face into the screen mesh, bringing it in contact with the face of the thing on the porch—or at least the black void where a face should have been.

I flinched backward in time to avoid touching the creature directly, but even through the screen I could feel the thing's stickiness. My face peeled away with a flare of pain similar to a band-aid being ripped off, leaving my cheek flushed with heat as though I'd been slapped. For its part, the screen door was now stuck fast to the tarbaby, and I couldn't pull it closed. I slammed the main door again and flipped the lock. Just for good measure, I put the chain on as well. "Son of a bandicoot!" I exclaimed, or something to that effect.

"What's wrong?" asked Norman, emerging from the office with a phone receiver on his ear. "What happened?"

"That thing's on the porch. I'll have to go out the kitchen."

"Why not just stay here?"

"Because my wife's out there too."

Libby was on our own front stoop, wondering where the dashing young rogue she had married had gotten to. She yawned as she peered up and down the street, puzzling over my last statement. "Pancho's got a tarp, baby," was what she had heard, which didn't sound like a problem that required running out of the house at dawn. To the best of her knowledge, we didn't know anyone named Pancho, and she'd never known me to get that excited about a tarp before. She had another look around and was about to go back in when she spotted me, tearing around the corner of the Spillers' house, yelling her name at the top of my voice.

"Who's Pancho?" she called as I sprinted into the street. I still hadn't taken the time to lace my sneakers, and I lost one as I came off the curb. I didn't bother to pick it up, but instead skipped the last ten yards onto our lawn and up to the stoop.

"Who's what?"

"Pancho. You said Pancho's got a tarp."

"No I didn't."

"Well that's what I heard."

I had to think a minute. It was awfully early, so it was possible I really had told her about Pancho's new tarp. Then it hit me. "No, I said 'Banjo's caught a Tarbaby.'"

Libby squinted. "You need to enunciate better."

"It's six o'clock in the morning. I don't enunciate until nine."

"Anyway, I still don't know what that means."

I pointed to the Spillers' porch. Libby followed the gesture.

"What am I looking at?"

"On the porch."

She took a step forward and squinted again. After a moment, her hand went to her mouth. "Is that…?"

"Yep."

"What are we going to do? We've got to warn the Spillers!"

"Norm's calling the police now. I'm thinking we ought to tell the rest of the neighbors what's going on."

Libby gasped and looked at her wrist. She hadn't put on her watch yet, of course, so she put her wrist away and looked around for a clock instead. She didn't find one, but I knew it had to be a little after six-thirty.

"The buses are coming," she said. "The high-school kids have to be there by seven-thirty. Their bus usually comes through here a little after seven. The little kids don't get picked up until after eight."

"OK, who's got kids in high school?" Yes, I know. I'm home almost every day—I should know this kind of stuff.

"Courtney Daniels is in ninth grade. Brandon Mathis is graduating this year. The McAphee twins are sophomores, I think."

"Great," I said, looking up and down the street. "Do I know any of these people?"

Libby sighed. "The Mathises are at number Seventeen. The house with the Rottweiler. You go tell them. The Daniels and the McAphees are up the street—I'll take care of them."

Libby tightened the belt on her robe and set off north. I jogged across the street and fetched my lost sneaker, then took a moment to tie my shoes. The tarbaby was still on the Spillers' porch, and appeared to still be stuck to the screen door. Because of its lack of features, it was difficult to say for sure which way the creature was facing. I assumed it had its back to me, but wondered if it might be able to see me anyway. I jogged on to the Mathis house, sneaking glances over my shoulder the whole time.

Number Seventeen was an enormous three story colonial, with a wraparound porch circling three sides of it. It was clear the Mathises had money, and I made a mental note to ask Libby what they did sometime. We never talked about the Mathises much, mostly because "Mathises" was kind of hard to say. I padded up the porch steps and paused at the front door. I couldn't remember ever having rung a doorbell this early in the morning, and felt a little self-conscious. Hoping I wasn't waking anyone, I pushed the button. The first ten notes of "Turkey in the Straw" rang out before the porch began to vibrate. I looked around for signs of attack, but I was still alone. Whatever was causing the rhythmic thudding was coming from inside the house, and was approaching fast.

The figure that opened the door was as oversized as the house he lived in. At least six foot five, and probably weighing in near a deuce and a half, he made me feel scrawny by comparison. By a happy coincidence, I really am kinda scrawny, and therefore didn't feel put out.

"Hiya… Brandon?"

"Yuh. 'Sup?" Brandon was wearing a loose fitting New York Jets jersey, but the sheer weight with which he moved gave me the impression of substantial masses of muscle sliding about underneath.

"Hiya," I said again. "I'm Josh Heaney. From number Twelve?"

"Yuh." Brandon may not have been a morning person.

"Have you been watching the news lately? About the quarantine in Manhattan?"

"Nuh-uh."

"Oh. Well, have you heard of the tarbabies?"

Brandon's eyes lit up, and he woke up enough to offer something close to full words. "The Slow Walkin' Joes!" This was a euphemism I hadn't come across yet, though I instantly liked it. "You think they're real?"

"I would have to say so. There's one a couple doors down right now."

"Shyuh?" Brandon stepped out onto the porch.

"Yeah, the Spillers' dog, Banjo, found it this morning."

"Brandon, who is that?" asked a scratchy female voice from inside.

"Dude from down the street. Says there's a tarbaby at the Spillers'."

"No way!" exclaimed a third voice, and a blur of pre-adolescence streaked past us and down the stairs. This was Logan, Brandon's little brother, who was eleven years old and invested with all the natural delight in monsters and freaks appropriate for that age.

"Logan, get back here!" Helen, the Mathis clan matriarch, now made her appearance. Amply filling her denim culottes and New York Islanders shirt, Helen was blessed with the stout genetic stock necessary to give birth to a giant like Brandon.

"Hey, kid!" I called to the younger Mathis boy as he trotted across the lawn, "that thing could be dangerous!"

"No it's not," answered Logan, with the kind of arrogant certainty you only find in eleven year-olds.

"I got him," said Brandon, and loped off after his brother, leaving me to figure out what happened to my plan to be helpful.

"What's going on?" asked Helen.

"Um, one of those tarbaby monsters showed up a few doors down. I was hoping to get everyone to stay inside until the police got here."

"Oh," said Helen, returning to the kitchen. "Good luck with that."

When I got back to the Spiller house, Brandon and Logan were standing at the curb, staring at the creature that was still stuck to the screen door. From up the block, I could see Libby returning as well, accompanied by an older and much skinnier woman wearing a bright red kimono. If I had been able to remember the name of the people Libby said she was going to visit, I would have assumed she was one of them.

"That's the most awesome thing I've ever seen," said Logan.

"Yuh," Brandon confirmed.

"I've seen the Transformers movie eight times, and this is still the most awesome thing I've ever seen. Did you know that if you touch that thing, it'll stick to you, and you can never get loose? Not ever?"

"That's what they said on the news," I agreed.

"And did you know if you get stuck, it turns you into one of them?"

"Pretty horrible, all right."

Logan pondered this for a moment. "Dare me to touch it?"

Should have seen that coming. "No, I dare you to stand right here and not do anything stupid."

"Oh for the luvva Mike. Where the holy hell did that thing come from?" This came from the woman whom Libby had escorted down the street, and who was now fishing a pack of Newports from the pocket of her kimono.

Libby made the introductions. "Josh, this is Melissa Daniels, Courtney's mom. Hiya boys."

"'Sup," Brandon answered.

"Courtney's mom. Right. Pleased to meet you." I did a quick headcount to confirm that whoever Courtney was, he or she wasn't here at the moment.

"So are the cops coming?" Melissa thumbed the wheel on her disposable lighter and fired up the first poison of the day.

"Norm was calling them," I replied. "They should be here any minute."

"Heh. You've never had to call the cops before, have you?"

"Um, I guess not."

"Don't hold your breath. We'll be lucky if they show at all."

"Would it help if we all called?" suggested Libby.

"Don't cost nothing. What's the kid doing?"

I looked at the empty patch of lawn where Logan used to be. I looked back toward the Mathis house. I looked back at my own house. That was the end of the list of places Logan could possibly be, so I turned back to face the Spillers' house, where the boy couldn't possibly be, on account of the monster. Everyone else had beaten me to it. Sure enough, Logan had mounted the first step on the porch, and was poking the tarbaby with a stick.

"Logan!" I shouted. "What the hell are you doing?"

"Poking it. It's gooshy."

"You really think that's a good idea, kiddo?"

"It's like poking a bag of snot."

I tried switching to Dad mode. "Little Mister! You get back here this instant!" No one present expected that to work, least of all me.

"You're not my dad!"

"No, I'm the guy your dad's going to murder if his kid gets turned into a walking bag of snot!"

"I got it," said Brandon, as he slouched his way across the lawn. Reaching the base of the steps, he hooked a mammoth arm around Logan's waist and hoisted the smaller boy over his shoulder like a bag of rice. As he turned around, he felt a small tug. "Leggo the stick."

Reluctantly, Logan leggo the stick. It clattered to the steps, but did not fall. The other end was still stuck to the tarbaby's leg. Brandon began walking back to the curb, then froze at the sound of a screen door slamming.

"Uh-oh," said Logan. To my surprise, Brandon had the presence of mind not to turn around, but simply quickened his pace, depositing his little brother on the pavement before turning back to the source of the noise.

That source was a shock to no one. Whether it was because of his poking or his retreat, Logan had succeeded in attracting the creature's attention. It had released its grip on the Spillers' screen door, and was now attempting to follow them down the steps. The literal stumbling block to this plan was Logan's stick, which was still stuck to the thing's leg, but also trapped in the spindles of the staircase banister. Once the tarbaby took its first step down, its back leg was unable to follow. The thing pivoted forward slowly, reached a tipping point, and then toppled forward. It slammed into the steps face first, breaking the stick in half as it fell. For a long moment, the creature lay still.

"We killed it!" exclaimed Logan triumphantly. A wet flapping sound from the porch ended his celebration. The monster was rocking back and forth, trying to right itself, but was unable to extricate its legs from the staircase.

From up the street came the sound of an approaching engine. Certain that the school bus had arrived early, I began trotting in the direction of the noise, waving my arms to catch the driver's attention. To my relief, the approaching vehicle was actually an

Otterkill Sheriff's Department patrol car. When the driver spotted me, he flipped on the dome lights. I motioned for him to follow, and returned to the Spiller's yard.

"Cheezit, it's the fuzz," chuckled Melissa. She dropped her butt onto the pavement and ground it out with the toe of her slipper. The patrol car rolled to a gentle stop, angling itself across the street to prevent traffic from passing. The door opened, and a squat, solid man about my Dad's age emerged, wearing a crisp blue uniform with creases sharp enough to slice fruit. The nameplate on his right breast pocket read "Keane."

"Howdy folks," he said as he closed the door. "You still smoking, Melissa?"

"That's me," replied Mrs. Daniels as she fished a fresh cigarette out of her pocket. "Still-Smokin' Melissa. How you doing, Andy?"

"Livin' the dream. What's the attraction here?"

As one, the assembled group pointed toward the flapping mass of goo on the Spillers' front lawn. With its feet resting on the second to last stair, it had almost managed to shake itself free. "That one of them things from the news?" asked Officer Keane.

"Looks to be," said Melissa.

"One of you folks the homeowner?"

"No sir," I said. "Norman Spiller is still inside. He's the one who called you."

"Does Mr. Spiller have a family?"

I started to answer, then looked to Libby for backup.

"There's four of them," she said, after the subtlest eye-roll you've ever seen. "Norman's wife is Carrie. They have a boy and a girl. Five and seven, I think?" All of this sounded plausible, so I nodded an enthusiastic confirmation. "That's them up there," said Libby, pointing to an upstairs bedroom window. Two young children with hair the color of wheat were peering down at the strangers in their front yard. The boy gave a timid wave. Logan and Officer Keane waved back. The bedroom curtain parted, and Carrie Spiller appeared behind her children, looking confused.

"Stay right up there, ma'am," Officer Keane called to her as he approached the front porch. Logan tried to follow him, but was yanked back to the curb by his brother's strong hand. With a final thrust of its legs, the creature shoved itself off the stairs, falling flat on the lawn. Officer Keane stopped ten feet away, his right hand resting casually on the butt of his gun. "Hello there," he said to the monster. "How are you feeling today?"

Slowly, the thing began to fold itself backward, as though it were attempting to do yoga. It drew its head back to its knees, then sat back and gently rolled its torso upward. As it settled into a kneeling posture, its head lolled to the left, as if pondering the significance of the group in front of it.

"Can you understand me?" asked Officer Keane. "If you can hear me, I need you to stay right where you are."

The patrol car was beginning to attract the rest of the neighborhood. Half a dozen people were now standing on their lawns in various stages of dress. No one was attempting to approach yet, but that wouldn't last long.

"Sir, you need to stay down." The tarbaby either didn't understand Officer Keane's instructions, or didn't care. Holding its arms in front of it for balance, the creature lifted its knees off the ground, then slowly rose. "Aw nuts," said Andy, as it straightened itself to a standing position once again. "All right, last chance. Stand right there!"

The creature took a step forward, prompting Andy to draw his weapon. If I were Tom Clancy, I would tell you it was a service-issue, .78 caliber Glockenspiel Comanche with breech-loading gravity feed and automatic redial or somesuch. As it stands, all I can say for sure is that it looked loud. Angling back to the crowd at the curb, he stage-whispered, "You know, I'm not actually allowed to shoot anyone who isn't pointing a gun at me."

That's when a gravelly voice from the north end of the street called out, "Hold on a minute!" I didn't know the name of the man who was limping toward us, but I recognized him as the sole occupant of Number One Ichabod Lane. Fifty years ago, Number One was the only house on the street. It hadn't had a coat of paint since then. The man himself looked like he had just fallen out of bed, though if that were the case, it seems that he slept with a pistol strapped to his thigh. I don't know what kind that was either, but it was an enormous silver revolver that must have been a foot and a half long.

The newcomer was apparently known to Officer Keane. "Morning, Carson. You really need to be carrying that blunderbuss around at this hour?"

"The Second Amendment can't read a clock, Andy. I'm just preparing to defend the homestead is all. Y'all are welcome to go first."

This exchange had given the tarbaby time enough for another couple of steps, so Andy backed up and reset himself. Not wanting to fire toward the house, he flanked the creature instead, assuming a shooter's stance five feet to its right.

"Last warning!" he yelled. "Stop where you are or I will shoot!"

The tarbaby took another step. Andy swore in frustration at having his bluff called. He holstered his pistol and shooed us all back across the street.

"Dang it Andy," croaked Melissa Daniels. "Stop horsing around and put that thing out of our misery!"

"Sorry Melissa, but I can't shoot somebody just because they look funny."

"You seen what these things did to them soldiers down to the City."

Officer Keane sighed. "Yeah, well, I'm also not allowed to shoot somebody just because they look like somebody else who's causing trouble."

"This ain't even a problem," said Carson, drawing his pistol as he stepped onto the lawn. "You go write somebody a parking ticket, and I'll get business took care of."

"Put it away, Carson. I can't let you go shooting people without cause either."

"We still ain't got a problem. 'Cause that ain't people, and I got cause."

"Doesn't this count more like Animal Control?" asked Melissa.

"Yeah!" agreed Logan. "My Dad had to shoot a rabid raccoon in our backyard once. This is practically the same thing."

Carson liked this idea. "Practically the same thing," he confirmed, sharing a conspiratorial wink with Logan.

Officer Keane was less than convinced. "Look, there's no way I can let you discharge a weapon on someone else's property without the homeowner's consent…"

"Shoot it!" came a muffled voice from inside the house. "I'll sign whatever you need, just get that thing off my lawn!"

Carson raised an eyebrow. "Good enough?"

Officer Keane sighed again, and waved us all back another ten feet. "Just don't miss."

"Hell, Andy. You seen me hit stop signs from a hunnert feet when I was lots drunker than this."

Following Andy's example, Carson obligingly stepped out to the creature's side to avoid firing toward the house. He fished a pair of yellow-lensed eyeglasses from his shirt pocket, hooked his left thumb in a belt loop, raised the cannon steadily in his right hand, and called out "Firing!" He squeezed off a single shot, and even from a distance we could see the thing's chest deform, cratering like it had been hit by a meteor. After a few seconds of silence, it took another step.

"Huh," grunted Carson, then once again yelled "Firing!" This time he snapped off three shots in rapid succession. Again the creature's chest dimpled from the impact. Again it paused for the briefest of moments. And again it resumed walking forward.

"You using hollow points?"

"'Course I'm usin' holler points, Andy," answered Carson as he holstered his sidearm again. "Can't have slugs flying out the other side, can we?" His assault had failed even to distract the creature, much less stop it. The tarbaby continued its ponderous trek across the lawn, and even Carson had the sense to back away this time.

"Officer," said Libby, "we're a little concerned about the time. The school bus is going to be rolling through here any minute.

Andy checked his watch, then marched to his car. Unclipping a key ring from his belt, he leaned into the police cruiser. When he emerged again, he was already loading shells into a short barreled shotgun. He chambered a round and strode back across the lawn, this time planting himself directly in the tarbaby's path.

"You've got to shoot them in the head," suggested Logan.

Carson slapped himself in the forehead. "Aw, hell yeah. Everybody knows you gotta go for the headshot. What was I thinking?"

Officer Keane looked skeptical, but he leaned in closer, bringing the shotgun's barrel to within inches of the creature's head. When he pulled the trigger, the thing's head expanded to half again its size, then slowly deflated back to normal. Andy chambered another round, pushed the barrel directly into the creature's face, and fired again. Again the head ballooned, and again it deflated, but the tarbaby did not fall.

Andy stepped back, but the gun did not come with him, as the barrel was stuck to the tarbaby's face. Andy tugged, but only succeeded in dragging the creature closer to him. It raised its arms, and Andy leapt back, releasing his grip on the shotgun. The weapon fell, adhering instantly to the creature's chest with a wet *splut*.

The front door of the house opened, and Norman stepped out onto the porch. "Did you get it?"

"Working on it," yelled Carson. In the distance, from the south end of Ichabod Lane, the sound of a large engine was growing in volume.

Officer Keane grimaced at the noise. "Hell's Bells," he hissed. "Right on time. All right folks, listen up. I have to go detour this bus. I'm going to need all of you to get yourselves indoors, and don't come out until this situation has been dealt with. I'll be right back." We watched as he returned to his patrol car, executed a neat K-turn, and sped off back the way he had come.

The tarbaby had reached the street, with the shotgun still stuck to its chest and face. Carrie Spiller joined her husband on the porch, while the rest of us formed a loose semi-circle around the advancing monster.

"So," said Libby, "I guess we should get inside." The tarbaby took a step off the curb into the street, heading directly toward her. She took two steps backward in response.

"Nuts to that," replied Carson. "We got a problem needs dealt with."

"This is one problem you're not going to be able to drink away" said Melissa. The creature continued its methodical advance on Libby, who was checking over her shoulder every few seconds to ensure that the path back to the porch was clear. Logan and Brandon were slowly approaching the thing from the rear, hoping to get a better look.

"Mebbe so," cackled Carson. "But mebbe I know something better." With that, he struck a sloppy about-face and began walking back home.

"Oh," said Libby. "OK then." She took another nervous step backward as the tarbaby passed Ichabod Lane's halfway mark. "We should probably do what the officer suggested, don't you think?"

Logan danced around the shambling shape in the street, daring it to catch him. "Why bother? Look how slow it is." He lunged toward the creature, then dashed around to the other side of it.

"Brandon," I said, "would you say Logan is a particularly graceful young man?"

"Pfft." Brandon scoffed.

"And if he trips and falls into that thing, who's going to catch hell for it?"

Brandon sighed, and his massive shoulders slumped. "C'mon squirt," he said as he turned and headed for home. Logan gave another loop around the tarbaby, then ran to catch up to his brother.

"All right," said Melissa, "that thing is seriously creepy. I'm going inside."

"Sounds like a plan," agreed Libby. "Melissa, the McAphee twins are going to be heading out to the bus stop any minute. Could you let them know what's going on?"

"Soon as someone tells *me* what's going on. You folks are going to be keeping an eye on that thing, right?"

"We'll call you if it starts heading your way," Libby promised, as the tarbaby took its first step onto our lawn. We ran up the front stoop and inside the house, then closed the door behind us, locked it, and just for good measure, ran upstairs to the bedroom. Peeking out the curtain, we saw that the Spillers had followed suit.

For the moment, the street was empty except for the monster that had just stepped onto our lawn and was advancing toward the front door.

"Crap. It's still following us."

"Do you think we should try to lure it away from the house?" wondered Libby.

"I dunno. I kind of want to keep it where I can see it." As the thing mounted the steps of our front stoop, I pressed my face against the glass of the bedroom window to keep track of it. When it had finally gained the top step, the creature finally paused, standing motionless before the front door as if unsure what to do next.

"Do you think it's going to try to get in?" asked Libby, but I had no reply for her. After another minute or so, I was forced to pull my face away from the window again. The sun had risen above the Spillers' roofline, and was now shining directly in my eyes.

I lay back down on the bed and was considering going back to sleep when Libby announced, "It's going away."

"Really?" I rolled out of bed again and looked down into the lawn. The tarbaby was indeed on the move. Long minutes ticked by as the creature trudged to the curb, then across Ichabod Lane, finally coming to a stop beneath the same willow tree where Banjo had encountered him earlier.

"It's back under the tree," I noted. "Why would it leave us to go back there?"

Libby shielded her eyes with the flat of her hand and squinted down into the neighbors' yard. "Is it the sun? Is it trying to avoid the sun?"

"Weird. It wouldn't leave the Spiller's front door earlier."

"They have a porch. It could still get shade there."

"True, but it did come out eventually."

"But that was only when there was prey around."

We considered this possibility in silence, as we regarded the monster beneath the tree. Before long, without any apparent provocation, the thing started walking again.

"What's it doing?" I wondered. "Is it leaving?" I flattened myself against the window again, trying to see as far down the street as I could. "Ah jeez. And here I thought Logan was going to be the problem."

Libby opened the window and stuck her head out to get a better view of the approaching figure. Carson, our new acquaintance and, as far as I knew, long-time neighbor, was striding purposefully down Ichabod Lane. In each hand he held something long and dark.

"That's not… He doesn't have…"

I could only shrug.

"Is that dynamite?"

7

By the time we got downstairs, the tarbaby had shambled its way past our property. Carson had stopped ten paces in front of the creature. With his legs spread wide on the asphalt, he tucked several of the sticks he was holding into his back pocket. I took a few hesitant steps off the front stoop, debating how to address our neighbor without attracting the monster's attention.

"Hey there, Mister... um... Carson," I tried. Carson returned a small salute before he began fiddling with the stick in his hand. "So, how's it going?"

"Don't worry, son. The situation is under control." Carson unscrewed a small piece off the top of the stick, transferred it to his other hand, and then struck the two pieces together abruptly. A bright magenta light hissed into life.

When I was finally convinced that I hadn't been blown up, I straightened and spoke over my shoulder to Libby, who was still standing in the doorway. "It's OK," I told her. "It's just road flares."

"And what is he planning to do with them?"

I turned back to the street in time to see Carson lob the lit stick at the tarbaby. The flame spun end over end in a lazy arc, finally smacking against the creature's shoulder. The flare continued to blaze dramatically, and I could see its diffused glare even through the thing's head. At no point did the flame come into direct contact with it, however, and the creature appeared to be oblivious to its presence as it continued its slow march up Ichabod Lane.

Carson stood his ground, muttering a small "whoops" as he unscrewed the igniter cap on his second flare. He struck the cap, and another magenta flame erupted. Instead of tossing it, he stepped forward to meet the creature, holding the flare out at arm's length, as if to ward the thing off. The tarbaby lumbered onward, taking no notice of the flame. When the creature raised its arms, Carson ducked just within its reach, stabbing the flaming end of the flare into its side. The flare penetrated less than an inch beneath the surface of its translucent skin, but that was enough to cause it to stick fast. The flame blazed brighter for a brief second, then flickered and went out completely.

Carson ducked to avoid his pursuer's grasp, then spun around and retreated a few paces. As he pulled another flare from his pocket, he winked at me. "Third time's the charm!" he hollered. The third flare blazed to life. This time, Carson limped a tight circle around his target, slapping the flare on its back before it had time to turn around. Rather than sticking the hot end into the creature, he opted to lay it flat against the thing's back, ensuring that the naked flame would touch its gelatinous skin.

Nothing happened. The flare continued to spout fire, but didn't seem to be causing the creature any discomfort. Carson continued circling it, looking for any signs of damage.

"Now what?" I called.

"That was all the plan I had," replied Carson. "Spooky here looked so much like creosote, I figgered he'd go up like a roman candle. Maybe when Andy gets back..." He was interrupted by a sharp *FWOOSH* as the tarbaby's back and head erupted into flame. As plumes of fire danced across its shoulders, Carson gave a short victory whoop and pumped his fists in the air. "Now that's more like it!"

"Good job," I muttered. "Now, instead of a creepy, sticky swamp monster, we've got a creepy, sticky swamp monster on fire."

"All we need's some marshmallers!" It had not yet dawned on Carson that, while the creature was indeed going up quickly, it wasn't slowing down at all. The flames had engulfed the entire top third of its body, completely obscuring its head and shoulders, when the flare on its shoulder was consumed in a sudden, spectacular geyser of fire. Carson jumped back to avoid the sparks it threw off. "Jesus please us," he croaked.

Carson backpedaled as the heat of the walking inferno washed over him. The tarbaby followed at its usual cumbersome pace, undeterred by its condition. The flames continued their march down its body, soon reaching the third flare that was still stuck in its side. This one also blazed magnificently, spouting flames like a miniature volcano from the creature's ribs. It was this that ultimately drew Carson's attention to the final thing he hadn't considered. Stuck fast to the tarbaby's chest was Officer Keane's shotgun, and it was still loaded.

"All right. I mebbe ain't thought this through a hunnert percent."

"Is there anything I can do?" I asked.

"I say we let him burn. Long as we keep clear, he's gonna peter out sooner or later."

"Yeah, I guess." I backed up and whispered to Libby. "Have we got a fire extinguisher?"

"I remember buying one," she said. "I'll check the kitchen. You look in the garage."

Our garage was small, just barely big enough for the Focus, and detached from the house. I squeezed past the car and rummaged through the cabinets. I couldn't imagine what would have ever prompted us to store a fire extinguisher outside the house, but I've learned not to question Libby about such things. So search I did.

Several minutes later I remembered where I had seen the extinguisher last. I bolted from the garage, almost running down Libby, who was holding the object of our search above her head triumphantly. "It was in the pantry," she said.

"Behind the Pringle's," I confirmed. "Why did we think that was a good place for it?"

"Where's Carson?"

I stepped into the street and peered up Ichabod Lane. The tarbaby was still marching onward, covered from head to toe in a thick cloak of orange flame. Carson, on the other hand, was nowhere to be seen. "You don't think he went back inside, do you?"

"Why wouldn't he?" asked Libby.

"Because that thing is still following him." I grabbed the extinguisher and sprinted off after the tarbaby. It was not even half a mile to Number One Ichabod Lane, but the monster had gained a lot of ground during the hunt for the extinguisher. By the time I caught up, the creature was mounting the steps of Carson's house, leaving smoldering footprints behind in the peeling paint of the stairs.

I pulled the pin on the fire extinguisher. It didn't budge, so I flipped the canister over and began reading the instructions. The first line told me that Step 1 was pulling the pin. I pulled again, and again the pin refused to move. I tried twisting it instead, and felt it give just the slightest bit.

The front door flew open and Carson stepped through, holding a saucepan full of water. With a shrill yelp, he threw the contents of the pan into the tarbaby's torso. Rather than dousing the fire, the water only caused it to flare higher, as if he were spritzing a grill. The flames reached high enough to lick at the ceiling of the porch, singeing it and prompting small blossoms of fire to sprout. Carson dropped the saucepan and scanned his foyer for something that might help him. He settled on a small wooden chair, which he snatched up, thrusting the legs into the creature's blazing midsection. He tried to push the tarbaby back off the porch, but didn't have enough leverage. Leaning in closer than he wanted to, Carson put his shoulder against the seat of the chair and shoved.

That's when the shotgun shells exploded. The brunt of the blast was directed up the barrel, spraying past the creature's head and peppering the porch roof with shot. But the shells in the back chambers exploded outward, catching Carson square in the face. He screamed, clutched at his face and dropped to his knees, scrambling to get back inside the house. The blazing figure standing over him leaned forward, then dropped like a stone.

Without thinking, I vaulted up the porch steps, still tugging at the fire extinguisher's pin. It was turning in its hole, but not coming free.

"Get it off me!" Carson pleaded. "I can't see!" He also couldn't move. The tarbaby lay across him, pinning him to the porch with both its own mass and the chair that was now affixed to its torso. Its legs were touching Carson's, and his blue jeans were now ablaze. Carson screamed again, and this time I joined him. With a final, violent yank, the pin came free, taking a tiny chunk of my finger with it. I squeezed the lever on the extinguisher, releasing a feeble stream of white foam. Ignoring the pain in my finger, I tightened my grip, and the stream strengthened. I hosed down Carson first, focusing primarily on his flaming legs, then sprayed the tarbaby until the canister ran dry.

Though most of the flames on the creature had subsided, I was unable to extinguish them all before running out of foam. Its chest, hands and the top of its head still burned with a weak, blue flame, while the timbers on the porch roof continued to char. Worst of all, Carson was still trapped, and still screaming. I could see no way to extricate him without lifting the tarbaby off of him. His pants were charred black and smoking, and I could detect the faintest whiff of cooking meat.

Still blinded from the shotgun blast, Carson was flailing wildly, trying to throw his attacker off. The tarbaby had started melting. Its legs were thinning out, spreading over its victim's blackened jeans. Its hands rested on Carson's shoulders, growing both larger and thinner as they oozed over his upper arms. Its head drooped forward, inching lower toward Carson's exposed face.

"Carson," I yelled, "you need to lie still!" I scanned the porch for something I could use to protect his face.

"It hurts! It hurts! It hurts!" screamed Carson, oblivious to my warning.

Finding nothing of use in the immediate vicinity, I stripped off my shirt. "Keep your head down! We can't let that thing touch your skin!" I started up the stairs, looking for a good angle from which I could get my shirt over Carson's face.

"Get it OFF ME!" With that, Carson bucked forward, his feet and head both jerking off the floor. His face collided with the drooping mass that formed the creature's still flaming head, and he screamed for the last time.

8

Andy Keane had not expected re-routing a school bus to be the most challenging task of his day. The driver had been on this particular route for over fifteen years, and claimed to remember the name of every child she had ever picked up. A single swamp monster, she argued, was not about to keep her from fulfilling her responsibilities to the district. Andy had sympathized extravagantly, commending her on her sense of duty. In the end, he could only send her away by promising to deliver every single child on Ichabod Lane to their respective schools personally. This was a promise he would not deliver on.

Driving the mile-and-a-half from the turnoff of route 301 back to the Spillers' house, Andy was learning firsthand just how many kids that would have been. He still had half an hour before he needed to worry about the elementary school bus, but the residents of Ichabod Lane were out in full force, aware that something unusual was going on. There was even activity at the Friendly Haven Assisted Living Center on the corner of Ichabod and Gun Club Road. It was normal for the occupants of Friendly Haven to be up early, but they seldom ventured out of doors until after breakfast. Today a half dozen seniors were clustered at the edge of the driveway, peering down the road. They would have no doubt waved at the passing patrol car (they waved at everyone), and if I'm reading Officer Keane right, he would have waved right back.

It wasn't until he got to the Spiller house that Andy felt the first twinge of annoyance. Though he knew the lookie-loos would make their appearance sooner or later, he had hoped the people he had spoken to directly would have followed his instructions for at least fifteen damn minutes. But there in the middle of the street was the short, pale girl from number Twelve. She was staring off toward the north end of the street, but turned around when she heard his car approaching.

"Ma'am, I really think you ought to stay inside," he began as he pulled alongside her, but Libby didn't give him a chance to finish.

"That weird guy from down the street set that creepy thing on fire!"

"Carson? Aw, you've got to be kidding me."

"My husband went after him with a fire extinguisher. He was afraid it was going to burn the guy's house down!"

Andy sighed and put the car back into gear. "All right, I'll handle this. You get yourself inside." He pulled out, and was not surprised to see Libby following him at a discrete distance.

By the time he reached number One, the roof of the porch was blazing away furiously. I stood at the foot of the staircase, shirtless, without a clue as to what I should do next. In the open doorway of the house, a tangle of man and monster was billowing clouds of dark gray smoke.

Andy thumbed the button on his radio. "Dispatch, this is unit eight, requesting emergency response. We have a house fire at number One Ichabod Lane. That's at the corner of Ichabod and Irving."

The dispatcher confirmed the call, and Andy got out of his car. Walking around to the rear of the vehicle, he saw that Libby was still approaching. He popped the trunk release, and pulled out a fire extinguisher—a mammoth canister that left my own depleted little tube feeling wholly inadequate. As he slammed the trunk shut again, he called back to Libby, "You have got the strangest definition of 'inside'." Libby shrugged, but kept walking.

I scampered out to the street to meet them. "That thing's got Carson," I said. "He's hurt pretty bad."

"Stay right here," said Officer Keane as he quickened his pace. He yanked the pin on his extinguisher and foamed down the two figures on the porch, quickly putting out the last of the residual flames. He likewise took care of a few smoldering patches on the porch itself. He looked up at the roof, but the fire up there was too much for his extinguisher. He tossed the canister down onto the grass, then stooped to examine the mass in the doorway.

Both figures looked to be in bad shape. The tarbaby was badly malformed as it continued to ooze out over its victim. Its skin was also ashen and flaky, like the residue on the side of a charcoal grill. Carson was not moving, but had burns visible over much of his legs and what remained of his face. The tarbaby had covered almost a third of his head by now, including his left ear and eye as well as most of his scalp. "Carson?" asked Andy. "Can you hear me, Carson?"

Carson's exposed eye sprang open. "That you Andy?" he said in a far more chipper voice than I was expecting.

"Yes, Carson, it's me. I'm right here."

"Can't see too good right now. Purty much shot myself in the face."

"You hang in there. We'll have an ambulance here shortly."

"Dumbest thing I done all day," Carson chuckled. "Course it's early yet." It was difficult to tell with one eye covered, but I'm pretty sure he winked at this point.

"That is really strange," I told Officer Keane. "He was screaming in pain from the burns not two minutes ago."

"Could be shock. Carson, do you feel cold?"

"Cold? Nah. I'm good."

"Are you in any pain?"

"Funny thing about that. I was in a world of hurt just a minute ago, but it just kind of… went away. Tell you the truth, Andy, I can't remember ever feeling better."

"I think we need to get you out of here."

"Can't see why. I don't know any place I'd rather be right now. I had a doozy of a hangover this morning. Prob'ly shouldn't have been carrying, if you want the honest truth. It's gone now, though. I got my face shot up and my legs burnt up, and don't neither of them hurt a bit. I say we let well enough alone." The gummy mass of the creature's head was now covering Carson's nose, making him sound like he had developed a bad head cold, and was starting to spill over his mouth. His single exposed eye fluttered closed again.

"Carson? Stay with me, buddy!"

The eye opened again. It was badly damaged, with burst blood vessels evident all around the iris. But it looked squarely at Officer Keane. "Really, Andy," said Carson, without a hint of fear in his voice. "You don't need to worry about me."

The tarbaby's ooze dripped over Carson's mouth, and he did not speak again.

Officer Keane stood up and backed away down the steps. Libby stepped up to meet him. "Is he a friend?"

Andy shook his head. "Carson's been a piece of work since the day he was born, but still..." He surveyed the top of the house. Flames had engulfed the second story and were licking at the roof. He glanced around at the junk scattered on the porch and side lawn, then waved us back toward the street.

"This place isn't safe. I want both of you out of the yard right now." We stepped back to discover the curb had become considerably more crowded. The smoke was beginning to attract the neighbors. A dozen residents of Ichabod Lane's north end were milling about, either in the street or their own yards, and more were now sidling up from the south. I could see the Mathis boys at the head of the pack, both of them now sporting matching sweatshirts. Even from that distance, Logan appeared to be chafing at having to wear the thing and his entire body language seemed to decry the unreasonableness of mothers everywhere. Still, when on an expedition to inspect the neighborhood monster, it was important to guard against early-morning chills. The Spiller family followed close behind.

Conspicuous by their absence were the Otterkill Volunteer Fire Department, of whom there was still no sign. Libby and I retreated to the curb outside number Two, which belonged to the Robinsons, an older empty-nest couple. I was on a wave-in-passing basis with them, but don't remember ever having met them in person. I knew that they owned a thirty year-old RV that I had never seen leave their yard, and that was about it. Libby, of course, greeted them without hesitation.

"Hi Celia!" she called to the woman, who was watching the fire from her porch, wearing a lavender housecoat and slippers. Her husband, a heavyset man with a neatly trimmed salt-and-pepper mustache, sat on the porch swing in sweat pants and a v-neck undershirt. On his lap sat an ancient cocker spaniel, who may or may not have been named Peaches. I waited patiently for Libby to clue me in on Mister Robinson's name, as well.

"Quite a ruckus," answered Celia. "Any idea what started it?"

"Yep. We've got our very own Shadow Man." I could see that Officer Keane had returned to his patrol car, where he was currently talking on the radio and looking annoyed.

"We've got a what now?"

"One of those things from the news," explained Libby. "Those monsters that were overrunning Manhattan."

"A tarbaby," I offered in an effort to be helpful and neighborly, and immediately regretted the gesture. Mr. Robinson stopped skritching Peaches behind the ears, Celia arched an eyebrow, and Libby hauled back and belted me. "Ow!" I protested, rubbing my arm. "What's the gag?"

"That's a term you want to be careful with," suggested Mr. Robinson, returning his attention to Peaches. "There are folks who would be inclined to take offense."

"To what? Tarbaby? Ow!" Libby slugged me again, and I was beginning to suspect it had something to do with the Robinsons being black. That's probably something I should have mentioned earlier.

Celia suppressed a laugh. "It's a word I haven't heard in quite a while. Time was, it was what you'd call a pejorative."

"Oh, sorry." The apology was on general principles, as I had no idea what she was talking about.

"An epithet," explained Mr. Robinson.

"Ah. Got it." I hadn't.

"A *racial* epithet."

"Oh. It's just… 'cause they're sticky… like tar…"

"And they're black. Like tar."

I looked at the fire for a moment as I considered this. "So, what do you guys call them?"

"Haven't called them anything yet," said Celia. "This would be our first."

Officer Keane was back out of his car, watching the burning house and considering his options. Carson's house was now almost entirely obscured by thick walls of smoke. Here and there pockets of flame flared through the haze. The bodies on the porch were no longer visible.

"The news teams have all kinds of names for them," said Libby. "Shadow Men, Shadow Walkers…"

"GummiMenschen," I added.

"Gummi?" asked Mr. Robinson. "Like the candy?"

"Yep."

"Well that's just stupid."

I agreed. "Yeah, that's why I like 'tarbaby'." I hopped to the side to avoid getting punched again. "Well it fits! If you touch them, you stick to them, and you can't get loose! That's how they get you! That's how they got Carson!"

"Carson?" asked Celia. "Roscoe Carson?"

So Carson was his last name. You live and you learn.

"They got him? He's dead?"

I had to think about this one. "Well, not exactly. He set the thing on fire, and then he got stuck to it. It was trying to… do whatever it is they do, but I don't know if that means he's dead."

A commotion among the onlookers drew our attention back to the Carson house. The porch was still obscured by smoke, but it was apparent that something was moving within. A dark shape emerged, plunging its right foot heavily down onto the top step. Its left foot followed, and the creature was now visible to all. The charred remains of a shotgun were still affixed to its chest, and a light dusting of white ash still clung to it, but the chair Carson had used to defend himself was gone. Perhaps it had simply burned away.

By the time the creature reached the third step, it was clear that it was not alone. A second figure stirred in the gray haze of the porch, resolving into another human shape. In color and texture, it looked identical to the creatures we had seen already, but its silhouette was unmistakably that of Roscoe Carson.

"Well," I said, "there they are. So, what do you want to call them?"

Mr. Robinson set Peaches down on the porch and leaned forward to get a better look at the monsters descending his neighbor's porch steps. "I'm withholding judgment."

9

"What do you mean, they're not coming?" hissed Melissa Daniels. "They're the Fire Department! They have to come when you call them! That's how it works!"

While he considered it important to keep the public informed, Officer Keane was keeping one eye on the smoking figures that were shambling across the lawn toward the crowd in the street. Now was not a good time for a press conference. "It's a volunteer fire department, Melissa. They've got exactly one pumper truck, and right now it's committed."

"I sent them twenty dollars last year!" Melissa complained.

"They've had an unusually busy morning."

"This isn't the only one, is it?" asked Libby. "There's more of these things in Otterkill, aren't there?"

Andy sighed. "There's been at least a dozen sightings in the county this morning. And where they go, people get stupid."

"So how are we esposed to put the fire out?" asked the guy who lived at number Three . I don't know a lot about him, aside from the fact that he used words like "esposed," but I'm pretty sure his name was Tony. When we first moved onto Ichabod Lane, Libby and I made an effort to introduce ourselves to our new neighbors. Somehow, every man we met was named Tony. The women had more diverse names, ranging from Kristen to Kristin to Kirsten. After a while I gave up on trying to remember them, preferring to identify my neighbors by characteristics I could more easily remember. The house at number Three always had a Fiero parked in front of it, one of those lower-middle-class sports cars that Pontiac hasn't produced for twenty years, so this particular fellow became Tony Fiero.

"We're not," answered Officer Keane, scrutinizing the progress of the fire more closely. The flames had by this time advanced all the way down to the foundation, and it was clear the house could not be salvaged. "We're going to let it burn."

"Whoa whoa whoa!" protested Tony. "That's my house right next door!"

"You're a good two hundred feet away, and there's no wind. A bucket brigade wouldn't be enough to put out that blaze, even if we didn't have to worry about dodging these monsters. Right now those things are more of a danger than the fire, so we're all going back inside until we've dealt with them."

"And how are we esposed to do that?"

In lieu of a reply, Andy waved everyone back a few yards. The tarbabies had almost made their way across the lawn. At the pace they were plodding, they seemed about as much of a threat as a tiger in a zoo. It was easy to forget there was nothing protecting us from them other than distance.

"You can't kill them," noted Tony Fiero. "You can't even touch them."

"Can't you put them in jail?" This suggestion came from young Logan, who was currently swinging like a monkey from his older brother's massive arm.

Andy chuckled. "I doubt we're going to get them down to the courthouse."

"But maybe we could trap them somewhere," observed Libby. "Someone's garage, maybe?"

"Dog run," mumbled Brandon Mathis.

"Sorry?"

"We got a dog run," Logan explained. "Behind our house. We could use that like a jail, right?"

"Five foot chain link," added Brandon. "These freaks don't climb, do they?"

"Not that we've seen," Andy admitted. He didn't seem to like the idea much, but he was clearly stuck for other ideas. "That might be worth a shot."

"These guys live all the way down the street. How are you esposed to get those things down there?"

The first tarbaby, the Original Recipe version, stepped into the street, with the thing that used to be Roscoe Carson just a couple paces behind it. Except for minor variations in shape and size, the latter creature was largely indistinguishable from the thing that had spawned it. It was only out of a perverse sense of symmetry, and not any discernible physical differences, that I would come to think of this second monster as the Extra Krispy version.

"I don't see that being a problem." Officer Keane turned to the assembled crowd. "Everybody inside! I need every last one of you in your homes right now. I'm going to lead these things down the street and get them fenced in. We don't want to offer them any other targets!"

The order seemed reasonable enough, but the residents of Ichabod Lane bristled anyway. Part of that was our normal human resistance at being told what to do, but mostly it was our disappointment at missing the show. Despite our reluctance, we dutifully retreated. The Robinsons, who had never left their porch, went back inside, and Tony Fiero crossed back onto his own lawn. The rest of us sidled slowly down the lane, trying to eke out as much entertainment value as possible.

Once he was satisfied the civilians were out of harm's way, Andy took a few steps closer to the monsters, hollering and waving his arms. He then trotted a few dozen feet to the south, turning to make sure they were following him.

They weren't. The tarbabies continued plodding across the street, seemingly oblivious to the policeman's antics. He tiptoed as close to them as he dared, then shouted directly into the place on their heads where their ears would be. They paid no attention. He looked about for something he might use as a club, but saw nothing close to hand. In frustration, he scooped up a handful of gravel from the street and threw it in the face of the closest creature. The stones stuck, but the monster kept walking. Andy could only watch as the things continued into the Robinson's yard, heading directly toward their front door.

"Crap in a hat," muttered Andy. He looked back to the audience in the street. "Keep an eye on the bad guys. I'm calling for backup."

As Officer Keane returned to his patrol car, the residents of Ichabod Lane conferred.

"How come they don't go for the cop?" wondered Tony Fiero. "Should we make some more noise?"

Melissa Daniels lit another cigarette. "Who sez those things can even hear?"

"So how else can we distrack them?" I'm not embellishing. He really did say "distrack."

"How did you get them off of my porch?" asked Norman Spiller.

I answered this one. "That was actually the Mathis boy, Logan."

"That the squirrely kid?"

"Yeah, he went up and poked the thing with a stick."

"He poked it?"

"Yeah."

"And you let him?"

"Well, see, he's… squirrely. The point is, the stick stuck to the thing, like everything else does, and when Logan started tugging on it, well, he got its attention."

Tony scratched his stomach as he watched the tarbabies cross the Robinsons' impeccably manicured lawn. The lead creature had almost reached the immaculately painted porch steps. "So you think we oughtta poke them with a stick?"

"How about a net?" asked Libby.

"Who's Annette?"

"No," corrected Libby, enunciating more precisely. "A Net. Or a lasso maybe."

"A lasso?" Norman mulled this over. "The squirrelly kid wouldn't be a junior rodeo champ, would he?"

A stream of muffled profanity was approaching, followed close behind by its source. Officer Keane was returning at a fast clip, mumbling under his breath as he crossed the street. "This is about the worst day I've had all day," he said as he joined us. The Original

Recipe tarbaby had mounted the Robinsons' porch steps and now stood motionless in front of their door, as if waiting to be invited inside. "We're not getting any backup. Not right away anyway."

"This ain't a priority?" asked Melissa.

"Apparently, this day is chock full of priorities. Otterkill's got eight full-time police officers, all of whom are currently engaged. I'm on my own until the state steps in."

"No offense, officer," said Libby, "but if bullets don't work against these things, is there anything the state police could do that we can't?"

"That's a fair point," Andy conceded. "Any ideas?"

"They were thinking of having a rodeo," said Tony.

"That's not far off," I admitted. "We were thinking we might be able to try some kind of lasso."

"Or a net," added Libby. "Really anything that will encourage them to move in our direction again."

"Huh." Andy considered this for a moment, then looked back up toward the north end of the street. "How far do you think it is to that dog run?"

"It's like ten miles," offered Logan.

Brandon put one of his enormous hands over his brother's face. "Half-mile. Tops."

Andy studied the creatures on the Robinson's porch. Original Recipe was standing patiently at the front door, doing not much of anything, while the Extra Krispy version of Roscoe Carson stood directly behind it on the top step.

"So, who's up for some bogeyman burritos?"

10

"You be careful with those," called Celia Robinson from the upstairs bedroom window. "Those are Egyptian cotton."

"Don't worry, ma'am," Officer Keane shouted back. "We'll replace anything that gets damaged."

"Oh no you will not," shouted Mr. Robinson from within the house. "She's got a closet stuffed to busting with nothing but sheets, shams and frilly business. The more we can get rid of, the better."

That was just as well, since it was unlikely anyone would want to sleep on these particular sheets after what Andy had planned. After securing a quick donation of linens from the Robinsons, the residents of Ichabod Lane were busy unfurling a dozen queen-sized sheets across the lawn. The tarbabies had yet to react to any of the activity behind them.

"All right folks," shouted Officer Keane, gathering us into a loose semi-circle by the mailbox. "The objective here is to make these things safe to touch. We're looking for containment first, then disposal. We want them completely covered, head to toe. Tony, whenever you're ready."

Tony Fiero had been the second to volunteer for Andy's plan. The first was Logan Mathis, who was disqualified on the basis of being insufferable. Their target was to be the tarbaby on the top step—the one that an hour ago had been Roscoe Carson. Each took a corner of a fitted seafoam sheet with an embossed shell pattern and tiptoed up the porch stairs. The creature ahead of them showed no indication it was aware of their presence. Once in position, Andy did a slow three count, and they tossed the sheet gently over the thing's head. Their aim was ideal, and the sheet billowed as it descended, neatly enveloping the tarbaby in its center. By the time the fabric settled, only the thing's feet were still visible.

"Nice!" called Brandon, who was to be my partner in the second team. Our task was to cloak Original Recipe, at which point we could turn our attention to yanking the creatures off the porch. We pulled a sheet the color of orange sherbet off the lawn and moved toward the front door. We were just about to ascend the first stair when Andy called out, "Hold up! We've got movement!"

Extra Krispy had finally figured out that something had changed. It began thrashing its arms in an attempt to remove the sheet that was covering it. These gesticulations only served to wrap the sheet around it tighter, as more of the surface area was brought in contact with its body. The creature stepped backward, and Brandon and I retreated to a respectable distance. The tarbaby continued to flail about in its linen cocoon, and was losing its already tenuous balance. It took a second step backward, and this time its foot found nothing but empty space behind it. It plummeted the eight inches down to the next riser, and landed with a loud thud. The creature teetered precariously, then gravity took over, and the tarbaby fell hard.

Andy pounced. "Wrap it up! Wrap it up!" he called. Brandon and I threw our sheet over the fallen creature's exposed legs, and Tony Fiero moved in to help us secure it. "Watch the one up top!" Libby cautioned. "He's moving!"

She was right. Original Recipe's curiosity had been piqued, and it was slowly swiveling toward us. Brandon knelt down beside the prostrate form on the lawn and gave it a forceful heave, rolling it away from the porch. The orange sheet swirled about its legs, enveloping them both back and front. I wrapped my arms around the creature's knees while Tony grabbed the thing by the shoulders, but the slick material of the sheets made it difficult for him to get a decent grip. Andy and Brandon rushed in to help, cradling the cocooned tarbaby while Tony readjusted.

We hoisted our bundle just as the crashing began behind us. Perhaps sensing that the shortest route to its prey was a direct plummet, the creature on the porch was tumbling down the steps, arms extended directly outward. We began moving immediately, but encumbered as we were by our load, we didn't stand a chance. Original Recipe tagged Tony on the back. "He's got me!" he yelped.

"No!" called Andy. "You've got him! This is what we want!" Officer Keane backpedaled toward the street, while pointing at another of the sheets scattered across the lawn. "Drop him over there! Tony, walk toward me!"

Tony Fiero was a short man, but he was burly. He lowered his shoulders and advanced toward Andy like an ox in the yoke. The creature attached to his back was heavy, but Tony was motivated. A dozen ferocious steps later, he had dragged his passenger halfway across the lawn. When he reached a sheet with a yellow floral pattern, Andy stopped him. "OK, lose the shirt!" Sal unbuttoned his shirt and shrugged out of it, and Original Recipe flopped awkwardly to the lawn.

Under Andy's direction, Tony, Brandon and I each grabbed a corner of the sheet the creature was lying on, twirling it around our hands to improve our grip. We hoisted the wriggling bundle up off the ground and shuffled to the street. The tarbaby redoubled its efforts to writhe its way out of its cocoon.

"Right," said Andy. "Half a mile. We can do this."

We stepped up the pace, breaking into a slow trot. As we gained more confidence in our load, we increased our speed. By the time we passed house number Seven, we were managing a quick jog, the wriggling figure between us causing the makeshift litter to sway back and forth wildly. Logan sprinted ahead of us, eating up the distance to his house in short, bounding strides.

Turning to verify we were still behind him, Logan jogged backward into his driveway, then continued into the back yard. In the far corner of their lot was a rectangular pen measuring twenty feet by thirty, surrounded by a five foot chain link fence. Inside was a four foot igloo made of white plastic, from which protruded the salt and pepper muzzle of an antique Rottweiler. The only evidence that he was aware of Logan's approach was a slight flaring of his nostrils.

"Hey Bacco," said the boy as he flipped open the catch on the pen's gate. He swung the gate open wide and invited the dog to join him outside. "C'mon dog. Gotta borrow your crib for a bit." The Rottweiler raised his head slightly, sniffed the air, and yawned as the four of us made the turn into the Mathises' driveway.

"C'mon Bacco" he repeated. "We gotta go." The dog stretched its forepaws out, then lowered its head again. We thundered into the back yard, coming to a halt at the gate. All of us except Brandon were sweating profusely, and my arms felt like cooked noodles.

"What's going on?" asked Tony, struggling for breath.

Brandon set down his corner of the sheet and strode into the pen. "Gotta get Big Tobacco out," he said. "Don't want Goopy there getting his hands on my Rotty." Squatting and stretching his arms as far as they would go, Brandon gripped the igloo's base in his right hand and the entrance in his left. Straightening his legs, he stood upright again, lifting both doghouse and dog several feet off the ground.

"You need a hand with that?" asked Andy, as Brandon staggered toward the gate.

"Nah, s'cool," replied Brandon, lugging the igloo through the gate. Once outside, he gingerly lowered the house back down to earth. Big Tobacco promptly stepped outside, shook himself, and lay back down on the lawn to continue his nap. The rest of us positioned ourselves in front of the entrance and began swinging the sheet between us.

"One!" called Andy.

"Two!" echoed Tony.

"Three!" we all shouted, and pulled the sheet taut. The body inside was launched half a dozen feet into the dog run, landed squarely on its head, then crumpled to the ground, where it continued its attempts to wriggle free from its wrappings.

Logan shut and latched the gate. Behind him, a window opened, and his mother's voice called out. "Logan? What's going on back there?"

The boy looked back at the men gathered around the dog run, including three grown adults who were just now beginning to realize that perhaps they should have sought permission beyond that of an eleven-year-old. "Mom?" he called. "Is it OK if the cops keep a monster in Bacco's yard?"

II

By the time we got back to the Robinson house, Libby and the rest of the neighbors had wrapped Original Recipe up nicely. It was a disturbing sight—a figure the size and shape of a corpse enveloped in a pastel floral shroud, writhing methodically from side to side as it struggled to free itself. "Welcome back, boys," called Libby. "How'd it go?"

"Carson's squared away in the dog run," replied Andy. "The Mathis's aren't real happy about our turning their back yard into a swamp monster gulag, but hopefully this is just a temporary fix. Unless these things can climb chain link, I think it'll hold them."

Mr. Robinson considered the possibility as he watched the first creature flop about at his feet. "Doesn't seem likely," he concluded. "These pinheads are persistent, but none too spry."

"So, we doing the litter again?" asked Tony, who had the foresight to hold onto the sheet we had used on the first trip. With a quick flick of his wrists, he snapped the sheet open, allowing it to flutter back down to the lawn beside the wriggling thing.

"Might as well," answered Andy, as he rolled the creature onto the sheet with his foot. "Who's up for another trip?"

Tony and I agreed to go again, and since Brandon was busy catching an earful from his mother, Norman Spiller took his place. Each of us grabbed a corner of the improvised litter and hoisted the tarbaby off the ground. The sense of urgency we had felt during the first run had passed, and this time we elected to maintain a reasonable walking pace. "So," said Norman as we stepped back into the street, "you have any better idea as to what these things are?"

"Wish I did," admitted Andy. "They're unusual. That's for damn sure."

"There's no more room in Hell," said Tony, solemnly.

"Oh knock it off," chided Andy.

"Don't you go mocking my religion."

"Religion my hindmost. That's from *Dawn of the Dead*. 'When there's no more room in Hell, the dead shall walk the Earth.'"

"Yeah," Tony admitted. "I didn't think you'd seen it."

"That the one in the mall?" asked Norman. "With Ving Rhames?"

"That's the remake," I observed. "The original's from the '70s."

"Don't matter," said Tony. "The line's in both of them. But whatever these things are, they ain't zombies."

"You ever see *the Blob*?" asked Norman. "This kind of reminds me of that."

"The original or the remake?" I asked.

"I don't know. Are they different?" No one answered, as none of us had seen both of them. "Anyway, the Blob kept absorbing people, like these things do. That's how it kept growing."

"But these things don't seem to grow," observed Andy. "They transform their victims into something just like them, but the victim remains a separate individual."

"So what does the tarbaby get out of it?" I wondered. "If it's not eating its prey, what's the point?"

"Spreading the faith?" suggested Norman. "It doesn't eat its victims; it converts them."

"So they just want everyone else to be like them?"

"It's like evolution," offered Andy. "The objective is always to spread your DNA as far as you can. In the end, you're just making copies of yourself." At this, Andy winced and drew in a sharp breath. He stopped, letting the breath out slowly through his clenched teeth.

"You alright, Chief?" asked Tony.

"Ow. Back spasm. It happens when I get tense." Andy doubled over, letting his corner of the litter fall to the street. The rest of us let down our ends as well. Original Recipe's flailing had loosened the sheets that were wrapped around it, and now a gap in the material exposed about four inches of the creature's dark form.

"We've gotta get a move on," I said. "This guy's not going to stay wrapped up much longer." We had almost reached our house by this point, so I knew we didn't have much further to go, but the effort of lugging our wriggling bundle over half of Ichabod Lane was proving to be more exhausting than any of us had expected.

"You think you can handle the feet by yourself?" asked Norman, moving to the front to take up Andy's corner.

"I can try." Although the creature was heavier than it looked, it wasn't just the weight I was concerned about. The problem was leverage. None of us wanted to come into direct contact with the tarbaby, even through a couple layers of linen. With four men on the litter, keeping a safe distance was easy. To lift the legs by myself, I would need to center myself directly over the thing's feet, bringing me uncomfortably close to striking distance.

Libby solved the problem for us. "You guys want some help with that?" she asked, trotting up the road to meet us.

"Grab a corner and join the party!" I said. Libby took up the position Norman had vacated, while Officer Keane stood with his hands on his knees.

Reinvigorated by the brief rest and the fresh pair of arms, we hoisted our parcel and set off once again. "Have you guys figured out what these things are?" asked Libby.

"We've decided they're like zombies and the Blob put together," offered Tony. "Other than that, we've got nothing."

"Where do you suppose they came from?"

"Manhattan," grunted Norman.

"Well, sure, but not originally, right?" Libby snuck a quick peek inside the sheet. "Do you suppose this is some kind of alien plague, or maybe a government experiment gone wrong?"

"Or maybe a government experiment gone *right*," I suggested. Libby fell silent for a moment as she entertained this new possibility.

"So is this dog pen going to hold these things?" asked Norman.

"Gosh, I sure hope so," answered Andy, as he limped along behind us, trying to straighten up.

"What do we do if they get out?"

"Put them back in again, I guess." From the south end of the road Brandon and Logan came to meet us. "So," Andy asked the boys, "is anyone minding the prisoner?"

"Big Tobacco's on the case," answered Logan.

"Oh good. You left the dog in charge."

"I think we should try burning them again," offered Norman. "That first one went up pretty good. As long as it's confined, it ought to burn itself out eventually."

Andy shook his head. "I don't know, Mr. Spiller. Roscoe's first try at that went about as bad as you can expect. I'd be hesitant to make any more human torches until we're sure we can control them."

"You also might want to give some thought to their rights," suggested Libby.

"Their rights?" asked Norman. "These things have rights?"

"Officer Keane just called them 'human torches.' I don't think there's any doubt that the tarbabies used to be human. Are we sure they're not *still* human? Legally speaking, I mean?"

"They're walking snot piles," protested Tony. "If you're worried about their civil rights, just look at them."

"All I'm saying is that a police officer can't afford to be cavalier about killing, especially if he's killing something that might be somebody." The tarbaby's head briefly scraped the pavement. I hoisted my corner up to shoulder level to compensate. "These things are essentially people who have been infected by… whatever this is. Some kind of mold, maybe?"

"Would you say the same thing about a zombie?" countered Norman. "Or a vampire? They used to be people too, right?"

"I was thinking more along the lines of a leper. You know, something that actually exists?"

"Leprechauns don't exist!" protested Tony, then immediately reconsidered his objection. "Do they?"

"Lepers. People with leprosy. It's an actual disease, not like vampirism."

Norman shook his head. "No, it's no fair saying zombies and vampires don't count just because they're not real. A week ago, these things weren't real either. Now they are."

"Yeah," admitted Libby, "that's actually a good point." The speed with which she conceded the point made me suspect she was tiring. I looked ahead and was relieved to see that we were less than a hundred yards from the Mathis house.

"Besides, lepers don't try to kill people, far as I know."

"What about that one in *the DaVinci Code*?" asked Tony.

"Albino," I said. "That's something different. But there's another problem. Are these things really killing people, or are they just... infecting them? Is Roscoe Carson dead, or is he in the Mathis's' dog run? If you burn up the thing in the dog run, are you murdering Roscoe Carson?"

"Dude," said Tony. "He's a walking jello salad."

"Look, just imagine what happens if Officer Keane actually does kill this thing, and then next week somebody finds a way to cure these guys? To turn them back? When things go back to normal, what kind of trouble is he in?"

We walked in silence as we approached the Mathis's' driveway. "Still, these things are clearly a threat," said Andy.

"They're a threat when they're loose, or when they come knocking on your front door. Are they still a threat when they're confined?"

"'Bacco!" Logan raced ahead of us, sprinting toward the back yard. Halfway down the driveway, we stopped, silent except for the sound of rustling linen as the tarbaby in our midst struggled to free itself.

"Yeah," said Norman at last. "I'd say they're still a threat."

The door to the dog run stood wide open. Just outside the entrance stood the thing that was Roscoe Carson. Sitting before the creature was Big Tobacco, his tail thumping merrily, and his paw in Carson's hand.

12

"Geez, look at him," said Brandon, as he pulled his younger brother back to the house. Logan had made a valiant effort at freeing Big Tobacco from the tarbaby's grip, but when tugging on his collar failed, there wasn't a lot left to try. When it became evident that the dog was making no effort to separate himself from the creature, Brandon retrieved the boy before he got himself stuck as well. As he was pulled away, Big Tobacco gave Logan a generous faceful of slobber, but did not attempt to follow him. "I haven't seen him this happy in a long time."

Indeed, the dog was not merely content to sit before the tarbaby—its inky, gelatinous form slowly oozing over his outstretched paw—he seemed to be thoroughly enjoying himself. His tail bounced rhythmically against the ground, his face wore a hearty doggy grin, and his eyes held a sparkle that had long been dulled by cataracts. He looked the very picture of a dog that was exactly where he wanted to be.

"It's true," said Helen Mathis, who had emerged from the house once the commotion started. "He's fourteen years old. Older than Logan, even. In the last year he's really gone downhill. He sleeps eighteen hours a day. He doesn't play anymore. I honestly didn't think he would make it through the summer. But look at him now. He looks... happy."

This was undeniable. Even Logan was having difficulty maintaining his distress in the face of the unbridled doggy joy that was radiating from Big Tobacco. His enormous head swiveled about as he took in all of the humans assembled around him. He looked thoroughly pleased with himself, and happy to be the center of attention. When his gaze returned to the creature that was slowly enveloping him, his look was one of unabashed adoration.

"How the deuce did he get out of there?" asked Andy. "I saw the kid latch that gate. I'm sure I did."

"I guess Gumby there unlatched it," suggested Tony.

"Is that possible? Could they figure out how to work something like that?"

"They used to be human," noted Libby. "Who knows how much they remember?"

We pondered this as we watched Extra Krispy spread out further over the Rottweiler. His lifted paw was now completely covered, and the goop was creeping up his leg toward his red nylon collar. "You suppose they could figure out doorknobs?" Norman wondered. No one cared to speculate on that.

In the driveway, Original Recipe was gradually loosening its wrappings. "So what are we going to do with this guy?" I asked.

Andy looked at the squirming bundle on the pavement, then the dog, then the gate. He ran a hand through his hair and sighed. "Unless anyone's got a better idea, we stick with the plan. These guys go back in the pen. Only this time, we'll padlock it shut."

"Shouldn't we do something about the dog?" asked Norman. "Before it's... y'know... turned?"

"Do something?" Brandon parroted. "Something like what?"

"Yeah," sniffed Logan, "something like what?"

"You don't mean..." said Andy.

"Well, no," replied Norman. "I mean, yeah. I just mean, maybe we should... y'know... put him out of his misery?"

Brandon looked back at Big Tobacco, who was watching a squirrel cavort on a tree branch directly overhead. His big pink tongue lolled sloppily out the side of his mouth. "He looks miserable to you?"

"No," sighed Norman. "No, I guess he doesn't."

"You're not shooting my dog," said Logan, and that was the end of that. We watched in silence as the tarbaby flowed over the Rottweiler. Within minutes, the goop covered Big Tobacco's head and muzzle entirely. It seemed impossible that the dog could either see or breathe, but still his tail pounded joyfully against the ground. Without a word, we returned to the work of disposing of Original Recipe, who was now almost free of his shroud. Since Extra Krispy was standing in the gateway to the dog run, we couldn't bring the other creature in that way. Instead, we bundled it up again, carted it around to the side of the enclosure, and heaved it over the side. It landed with a bounce, and rolled for several feet. Immediately, the creature began to pick itself up off the ground, the linens sloughing off its body like dead skin.

At the rate the dog was being consumed, the change would be complete in another ten minutes. We needed to get all three creatures inside the fence, with the gate closed and locked, before that happened.

Andy considered the situation, then addressed the Mathis family and the small crowd of onlookers that were still gathered in the street. "Listen up, folks! We can't have anyone outside right now. If these things see people wandering around out here, they're going to go straight for you. If we're going to contain them, we need to get them to stay put." Turning to Helen Mathis, he continued, "Ma'am, if you could find us a padlock, that would be a big help."

"I got one," said Logan, and wiping his nose on his sleeve, he shuffled into the house. His mother followed, and the crowd in the street began to disperse.

Andy walked around to the side of the dog run opposite the gate. "I need you four to get out of sight. Once those things are mobile again, I'm going to jump the fence. When I get their attention, and they come after me, I need you to close the gate and lock it. Then I'll scoot on out again."

"You're going to jump the fence?" I asked. "You can barely stand. I'll do it."

Officer Keane shook his head. "I can't ask you to do that." He tried to straighten up, and winced.

"So don't." I walked around to the opposite side of the enclosure and took up my position. Andy made no further protests.

"C'mon," said Brandon, "we can watch from the kitchen." They entered the house through the side door, leaving me alone with the monsters. From my new vantage point, it was hard to see how much of the dog had been consumed. It looked like the tar had spread down to Big Tobacco's shoulders, but it was difficult to tell against his fur. I leaned my elbows against the chain link fence and listened to the rhythmic thumping of the dog's tail.

Original Recipe had regained its feet. I hadn't been keeping track of the creature's position, and had no clear idea of whether it was facing me or the house. I lifted a hand and waved experimentally, but the creature did not react. I opted not to press my luck and held my position.

I don't know if this is a personal flaw, or a statement on human nature in general, but I've never encountered a situation so novel or intriguing that I couldn't eventually get bored. The exertion of hauling two bodies a half mile down Ichabod Lane was taking its toll, and despite the fact that sticky, goopy death stood less than ten feet away, I was soon startled by my right elbow dropping off the fence. A ribbon of drool dangling from my lips told me that I had nodded off, and I grabbed at the fence to keep myself standing.

Everything looked the same, but something was different.

A couple of things, actually, and both took a moment to register. I first realized that the thumping had stopped. The former Roscoe Carson, who had been leaning forward as he absorbed the dog, now appeared to be standing fully upright. Big Tobacco was just a large black mass at the first creature's feet, and it was difficult to tell whether the two were still joined or had separated. In addition, Original Recipe was a step or two farther away, and was heading for the gate.

"Hey!" I shouted. "You're going the wrong way! I'm over here!" I hoisted myself up onto the fence and swung a leg over. For some reason the top of the fence was coated with drool, and my hands slipped as I descended, making for an awkward landing. I managed to keep my feet, and was gesturing wildly to the retreating shapes the moment I regained my balance. "Hiya creepy! Come and get me!" The creature paid no attention, but continued lumbering out toward the Mathises' yard. The thing that used to be Big Tobacco was now also moving, but even more clumsily than the human figures. The Dog-Thing seemed to be having difficulty figuring out how to get its legs under it, as though it had already forgotten the most fundamental elements of being a dog.

I moved toward the gate, taking big, lunging steps and swinging my arms in great, sweeping circles. I continued to taunt the creatures as best I could, without knowing whether they understood anything I was saying. "Where you going, lumpy? Aren't I good enough to join your creep club? You ain't yella, are you?" As I exhausted my small and feeble arsenal of taunts, I found myself hoping that the things really couldn't understand me, and that the people watching from inside the house couldn't hear me. I stepped as far around Original Recipe as I could, then dashed to the gate. Extra Krispy was only a couple feet from the enclosure's entrance, but I wasn't certain how I might be able to lure it back inside. I looked for the sheet we had carried Original Recipe in and saw that it was still wrapped around the creature's right foot.

The screen door to the Mathises' kitchen slammed open, and Brandon burst forth, screaming at the top of his voice. Andy was out the door a second later, shouting "Get back!" Brandon was heading toward the dog run at a full sprint, holding out something that appeared to be a large plastic trash bag. It took him only a few seconds to close the distance from the house, giving me barely enough time to spin away from the gate. Ten feet from the fence, Brandon launched himself into the air, vaulting his former dog, and hit Krispy in the chest, with only the trash bag between them.

The creature bent backward at the waist from Brandon's momentum, yielding almost a full ninety degrees. A human spine forced to that angle would have snapped, but the tarbaby simply floundered for balance, toppling backwards as Brandon hit the ground behind it. Brandon took the impact on his shoulder and continued rolling, a graceful move that carried him safely out of his target's reach. Unfortunately, the subsequent somersault sent him careening directly into Original Recipe.

Brandon had just enough time to throw his right arm up between the creature and his face. His forearm hit the thing's gooey leg with a soft smack, and the sleeve of his hooded sweatshirt stuck fast. Stunned by the impact, Brandon was uncertain what to do next. After glancing about the yard for inspiration, he settled on pulling his hood over his head for extra protection. I was by his side a moment later, struggling to convey a set of coherent instructions.

"Off! The shirt… thing… this thing! Get it off!" The word I was reaching for was "hoodie," and I yanked the sleeve of Brandon's off of his left arm to demonstrate. With a nimble roll to his left side, he was free of the sweatshirt.

Both of the humanoid tarbabies were now well inside the fence, leaving only the doggoid to take care of. I looked behind me to determine Big Tobacco's current location, and nearly tripped over it. The Dog-Thing had shuffled back inside the run, and was silently stretching its muzzle toward my legs.

I leapt forward with a manly squeak and an elegant pinwheeling of my arms. I dashed to the fence and flung myself over in an adrenaline-fueled spasm, just as Brandon slipped out the gate. Once the boy was clear, Andy slammed the gate shut and secured the latch.

I let out a nervous laugh that combined both apprehension and triumph, then did a quick recount to confirm that all three tarbabies were now inside the perimeter. Satisfied that I was safe, I took a step backwards and collided with the thing that had been lurking behind me.

My laugh ended in a croak. I'm dead, I thought. We missed one. There was another one floating around that we didn't know about, and now I'm dead. And I never even got to ride on the Space Shuttle.

"'Scuse you," said Logan as he slipped around from behind me, holding up a large padlock. "You guys still want this?"

13

It was after lunch before I had relaxed enough to leave the house again. Libby had fed me grilled cheese sandwiches until I calmed down. She had hoped to pass the afternoon in the company of her favorite daytime drama, *My Life Is Mine,* but the show had been pre-empted. The series taped in Manhattan, and production had been halted a few days ago by the quarantine. In its place, the network was showing live news coverage from around the Northeast.

It wasn't a surprise to learn that the tarbabies were no longer confined to New York City. Dozens of the creatures had been spotted on New Jersey's eastern shore, and a smattering of sightings had been reported in upstate New York and Connecticut. Local residents were being urged not to confront the creatures, but instead to leave their disposal to trained professionals.

"Trained professionals?" asked Libby. "Who exactly has been trained to deal with these things?" Not the police, that was certain. Andy Keane had been recalled to the Otterkill Police Substation, where the Sheriff was struggling to cobble together a plan to keep the town's new problem contained. Andy promised he'd be back as soon as he got instructions on how to deal with the creatures, but that was the last we ever saw of him.

With little concrete information to work with, news coverage had largely devolved into an endless string of eyewitness interviews. The stories all followed the same inevitable rhythm. Someone had seen a tarbaby. Someone had challenged it. Someone had done something foolish. Someone had gotten killed. Or absorbed. Or converted. Or whatever it was that was happening to them.

It was early evening when the first tangy hints of barbecue came wafting into the house. Looking out the living room window, I discovered that the Mathis house had become the scene of an impromptu block party. "Feel like mooching off the neighbors?" I asked.

Libby slipped into her sandals. "I could mooch."

Armed with a six-pack of a local microbrew, we sauntered across the street. Banjo was dozing on the Spillers' porch and lifted an ear in acknowledgement of our passing. The welcome was warmer at the Mathis house, where close to two dozen neighbors had gathered. Herb Mathis, the clan patriarch, was home from work, and was using the incident as an excuse to fire up the grill. He waved a pair of greasy tongs as we rounded the corner into his backyard. Norman Spiller and Mr. Robinson were both at the grill with him, consulting on the optimal flipping times while their wives chatted with the crowd around the dog run. The little Spillers were there as well, sitting at a picnic table with Melissa Daniels, who was trying to teach them how to play canasta.

I deposited our beers into a plastic trash can full of ice, fished one out for myself, then joined Libby at the fence. The tarbabies were no longer as intimidating as they had been when loose, and the onlookers craned forward to get as close a look as possible. The two human shaped creatures were in constant, albeit slow, motion. They wandered the perimeter of the dog run, raising their hands tentatively whenever they came anywhere near an audience member. In response, their targets kept relocating, moving a few feet further down the fence. Only the former Big Tobacco was motionless. The dog-shaped mass was sitting patiently against the gate, with what used to be its snout pressed firmly against the chain link. From the outside, I could see that the black gelatinous substance was bulging outward.

Logan was hunched in front of his former dog, watching him with rapt fascination. "I think he's trying to get out," he concluded. "I think he's trying to ooze his way through the fence."

"Do you think they can do that?" asked Carrie Spiller, squatting down beside the boy.

"You might want to come away from there," admonished Celia Robinson, "until we know exactly what they can and can't do."

"It looks like a big mass of pudding," noted Carrie. "I can't see any reason why it couldn't just flow right through."

"Don't they have bones?" wondered Libby.

"Not that I can see." Carrie scooted a few inches to the left. "Come take a look at this. Get the dog's head between yourself and the setting sun."

Libby knelt beside our neighbor and peered into the tarbaby's black face. When the sun was behind the creature, its head glowed a dull and uniform orange. The effect was like looking through darkly smoked glass. It was clear there was no skull in there to block the light.

"See that?" asked Carrie. "They're nearly translucent. You can almost see right through them."

"But if they don't have any bones, how are they keeping their shapes?"

"I'm not so sure they are." This answer came from a thin, bespectacled man standing a few feet down the length of the fence. I recognized him as one of the neighborhood Tonys.

"Hi Anthony!" chimed Libby. "You remember Josh, don't you?"

"Of course," he answered as we shook hands. "We met at the Fourth of July fireworks, remember?"

"Sure," I lied. "You're at the blue house, aren't you?"

"Nah, I'm at the Cape Cod. You're thinking of the Grogans." I was thinking of no such thing, but I went along with it. "Look at this guy here." Anthony with the Spectacles indicated the creature that a few hours ago had been Roscoe Carson. "Take a look at his ears."

It was difficult to make out details in the dark mass of the creature's head, but if I stood in the right light and squinted, I could indeed discern the curves that used to be the thing's ears. "They look like ears," I offered.

"Now check out the other guy." Anthony led me around the corner of the dog run to get closer to Original Recipe. I leaned in and squinted, but this time I could only make out a small bump on the side of the creature's head.

"I can't really see them very well," I said at last.

"Me neither," confirmed Anthony. "And I think it's because they're not there anymore."

"So, what, the thing is… melting?"

"Dunno. Maybe. We know this thing has been… whatever it is… longer than the other two. I think it's gradually losing cohesion."

I popped open my beer and took a small sip as I considered this. "So as time goes on, they become less detailed? Like a statue eroding?"

"Something like that."

"Maybe it's forgetting what a human being is supposed to look like," suggested Celia Robinson.

Original Recipe appeared to be taking an interest in us. It took a cumbersome step toward us, and we backed away from the fence.

"Maybe so," said Anthony. "Or maybe it's just too much effort to hold onto details it doesn't need. In any case, I'm betting these two will be indistinguishable in a few days."

"What about the dog?" wondered Carrie. "Do you suppose it's going to keep its dog shape?" She rocked forward onto her knees, trying to peer deeper into the creature's body.

"Careful!" cautioned Libby. "Don't get too close."

"Look at that." Carrie was pointing to the Dog-Thing's neck. "Is there something inside it?" Logan and Libby both leaned forward to get a better look. "Was the dog wearing a collar?" asked Carrie.

"Yuh-huh," replied Logan. "Bacco's worn a collar for as long as we've had him. He gets a new one every year on his birthday."

"Did it fall off when he turned into... this?"

"I didn't see it anywhere."

Carrie looked deeper into the creature's goopy flesh. "I think it's still inside there," she suggested.

"Really?" asked Logan. "Where?"

"Look into its neck. There's a darker patch, like there's something in there. And I think there's something reflecting light." Carrie leaned back slightly and called to her husband. "Norman? Come take a look at this!"

Splut.

"Be careful!" shouted Libby. But the mistake had already been made.

"Lady! Look out!" yelled Logan, as he tugged at Carrie's wrist.

"Oh, don't worry," replied Carrie. "I'm fine. Norman! Come have a look!" Carrie Spiller may have indeed been fine, but she was also now stuck to Big Tobacco. The act of leaning back and turning her head to call her husband had shifted her balance ever so slightly. The effect was minimal, but it was enough to move her outstretched finger forward, bringing it in contact with the Dog-Thing's snout. As Carrie waved for Norman's attention, she was unaware that she was touching it, or that the viscous darkness was now flowing up her finger.

"What's up, hon?" asked Norman as he sauntered over, carrying half a hamburger on a paper plate. Carrie continued waving him over with her right hand, as Logan pulled desperately at her left.

"Lady! Let go!" screamed the boy. All eyes were now on Carrie, as Libby joined Logan in attempting to free her from the pitch oozing up her finger.

"Hon?" Norman's burger fell to the grass as he stood in numb horror, watching his wife wave to him happily, a wide grin splitting her face as she was consumed.

"You dropped your sandwich," said Carrie, and for a brief moment, her expression turned to one of puzzlement. She looked at her husband's trembling jaw, then slowly swiveled her head around, finding the same reaction on every face she encountered. At last, she brought her gaze back forward, and looked at her finger.

"Oh," she said after a moment. "Oops."

"Mommy?" The Spiller children were the last to notice something was wrong. As their father fell to his knees, wrapped his arms around their mother, and began tugging with all his strength, Melissa grabbed a child in each hand and led them out of the yard. The kids walked backward, trying to see what was going on. When the young boy fell, Celia rushed to Melissa's aid.

"Come along now, children," she said, picking the boy up and flinging him across one broad shoulder. "Mommy and Daddy need some adult time."

"Honey, you're being silly." Carrie was offering no resistance to anyone at this point—not to the Dog-Thing, not to Logan or Libby, and not to her husband, who was kicking against the fence, flinging himself backward as hard as he could in a futile attempt to free his wife from the creature's sticky grip. "Really," she assured him, "I'm fine."

The only thing approximating a weapon within view was a battered croquet mallet. I grabbed it and ran to the gate. Not wanting to risk jumping the fence with three of the creatures inside, I instead hauled myself up until my waist was even with the top of the fence. Balancing myself with my left arm, I swung the mallet in a ferocious overhand arc, then brought it crashing down on Big Tobacco's head. The handle splintered with the impact, and I fell, scraping my stomach and chest roughly against the top of the chain link. As I fell back down to the ground, I could see the shattered croquet mallet perched jauntily atop the Dog-Thing's head.

Norman planted both feet against one of the posts supporting the gate, wrapped his arms tightly around his wife's chest, and thrust himself backward, laying out to his full length against the grass. The chain link pulled away from its support posts, and a sharp crack rang out as Carrie's body twisted violently to the right. "Stop it!" cautioned Libby. "I think you dislocated her shoulder."

Carrie just smiled at her, rolling her eyes slightly. "I'm fine," she insisted. "But you're sweet to worry."

"Didn't that hurt?" asked Logan.

Carrie turned her head to face the boy. "Sweetie, I've never felt better."

"We've got to do something," moaned Norman from beneath her. "What can we do?"

"Has anyone tried chemicals?" asked Anthony Spectacles. "Something to dissolve it, maybe?"

Norman wriggled out from underneath his wife. "What? What would work?"

"Well, I don't know." Anthony turned to Herb Mathis. "Have you got any drain cleaner? Maybe ammonia?"

"Maybe," answered Herb. "I know we've got bleach."

"Anything's worth a try at this point." As Herb scurried into the house, Anthony addressed the assembled crowd. "Um, everyone? We're trying to find something that will hurt these things! We need to find anything caustic, or acidic… heck, anything in a bottle."

"How about lighter fluid?" suggested an older woman cradling a hot dog.

"No fire!" I yelled.

"Just grab what you can!" shouted Anthony, before bolting out of the yard. After a brief hesitation, others followed, with various levels of confidence in what they were looking for. I was taking a mental inventory of our household chemicals, wondering what effect weed killer might have, when I turned back to Libby. She had given up trying to free Carrie, but remained by her side. Logan had joined his father in his search for monster poison, and the two women were now alone.

"Where's Norman?" I asked.

Libby looked around uncertainly. "I'm not sure. Did he go into the house?"

"You should go inside too," suggested Carrie. "Honestly, don't worry on my account." Her hand was now completely enveloped in the inky goo of Big Tobacco's snout. Her left arm appeared longer than normal, with the shoulder distended at a sickening angle.

"Oh, Carrie," moaned Libby, "how can that not hurt?"

Carrie considered her own shoulder for a moment, and her brow furrowed. "It really should, shouldn't it?"

"Here we go! Here we go!" Herb Mathis came trotting back out from his kitchen, a large plastic jug in each hand. "I've got bleach and drain cleaner!" Behind him trailed Logan and Brandon, each with an armload of aerosol cans.

"Drain cleaner might work," I said. "It's acid, right?"

"Alkaline, dude," corrected Brandon. "It's a base."

Herb fiddled with the jug for a few seconds, then handed it off to Logan, who smacked the cap with the heel of his hand, popping it off. "Whatever it is, you all need to stand back." Herb took the jug back from his son, then took stock of the situation. Big Tobacco's head was slightly more conical than previously, as much of his snout had sloughed through the fence to the other side. Otherwise, he had not moved. Attracted by the commotion at the gate, Original Recipe and Extra Krispy had taken up positions a few feet on either side of the Dog-Thing. Pouring the contents of the jug onto the creature's head from the other side of the fence while remaining out of the reach of the other two would not be easy.

Herb looked to Brandon, who was a full head taller than his father. The boy accepted the jug without a word, then leaned forward, upending the contents of the bottle onto his former pet. The results were immediate and impressive. Wherever the liquid hit, a bright white foam bubbled enthusiastically, followed by a thick gray smoke. As the vapors rose, Brandon jerked his head back and fell away from the fence.

"Ho! What a reek!" he moaned, massaging his sinuses. His eyes were tearing up, and his nose was beginning to run. "Don't..." he gasped, "do NOT breathe that crap." Brandon dropped to his knees, alternately retching and blowing streams of snot into the grass.

As Herb and Logan retreated to help Brandon, the pungent funk of the bubbling foam hit the rest of us. The chemical smell of the drain cleaner was familiar, but there was a much thicker aroma overlaying it. I had once destroyed the transmission of a twenty year old Dodge Colt on a summertime trip through the Catskills. The reek of burning clutch that filled the car was similar to what was now emanating from the wounded tarbaby, only this smell was far more concentrated. Libby gagged and turned her head away, but stayed at Carrie Spiller's side. Carrie appeared not to notice the stench.

Once the chemical volcano started to subside, Libby coughed and asked, "did it do any good?"

I peered over the fence from a respectful distance. The smoke had thinned to a gentle mist, through which I could see a film of white still sizzling and popping feverishly on Big Tobacco's head. While the drain cleaner's effects had been dramatic, there was no indication the creature was in any way distressed. "It's hard to say. Maybe if we had a bathtub full of the stuff..."

Before I could finish the thought, I was distracted by a loud sobbing. I assumed it had to be coming from Brandon, and indeed the teenager was in bad shape, still leaking several flavors of fluid from his head. He was suffering in silence, however, and was not the source of the wracked spasms that were approaching.

I turned and discovered Norman returning to the yard. He was weeping copiously, his face dark red and dripping wet, and in his hands he carried an enormous pickaxe. The tool was intended for heavy-duty landscape gardening, and its broad end was nearly a foot wide to help in moving large volumes of dirt. He was heading for the dog run's gate.

I raised a hand in a tentative greeting. "Hey Norman, whatcha got there?"

Norman snuffled. "It was all I could find."

"Well, it's worth a try," I said, as Norman positioned himself in front of the gate, "but be careful. If a bullet can't hurt these things, I don't know if... Heywatchit!" I ducked as my neighbor reared back without warning, swinging the pickaxe over his head.

"I'm sorry!" screamed Norman as he brought the broad blade of the tool down hard on Carrie's outstretched arm. The pick rebounded violently, and I scrambled out of its way. Carrie's arm undulated like a snapped rubber band, and the links of the chain fencing rattled in sympathy. The impact had almost certainly shattered the bones of her forearm, but her expression remained one of aloof bemusement.

"Honey," she told Norman, "you're being silly."

With a shriek of frustration, Norman brought the blade down again. His aim was off, and the blade only caught the side of her arm, opening a cruel gash just below her elbow. Carrie giggled as the wound blossomed bright red.

"Stop it Norman!" Libby threw up a hand to ward off another blow, but retracted it when she saw that another blow was coming anyway.

Norman sobbed as he swung the pickaxe again. "It's the only way," he moaned. The blade thudded down for a third time, this time catching Carrie with a clean, solid blow. She fell back into Libby's arms, her left hand and most of her forearm still dangling from the Dog-Thing's elongated snout.

Norman dropped the pickaxe and sank to his knees. Carrie stared at the stump of her arm, which was beginning to pump blood onto the grass. Her expression changed from amused detachment to confusion. She did not yet seem concerned that her arm was gone, but something was clearly not going to plan.

I fumbled at my belt buckle. "Tourniquet!" I shouted. "We've got to… there's too much blood!"

"We can cauterize it!" suggested Herb. "We've got the coals from the grill!" He started to clamber to his feet, but Logan was far faster, and had already snatched up the barbecue tongs.

My head was swimming, and I was starting to feel nauseated. Carrie must have been in an astonishing amount of pain already, and burning the wound certainly wouldn't help that. As I pulled my belt out of the loops in my jeans, I asked Libby how the injured woman was doing.

Carrie had not taken her eyes off the stump, but she was now trying to stand. "I think she's in shock," said Libby. "Carrie? Sweetie? We need to get you to a hospital." Carrie's face blanched as Libby helped to her feet, and for a moment I was sure she was going to faint. Instead, she took two hesitant steps toward the driveway, with Libby holding her tightly around the waist. I stepped in to assist, but flinched from the stream of blood issuing from her severed arm.

Carrie stopped, then turned to her husband, who was still kneeling in the grass. His body was shaking from the force of his weeping, and he looked to be just seconds away from throwing up. Still, he met his wife's gaze, and his breath caught in his throat when he realized she was smiling.

"That was very sweet of you," said Carrie, "but really, it's OK." With that, Carrie blew her husband a kiss, pivoted out of Libby's grip, took two bounding steps back toward the fence, leapt into the air, and wrapped an arm and a half around the nearest tarbaby.

14

It took a little less than twenty minutes for the creature to absorb Carrie Spiller. She had managed to get a solid grip on Original Recipe, and both arms and her face were in direct contact with it as soon as she hit. In just five minutes, the black goop had enveloped her head, shoulders and arms. The flow of blood from her injured arm slowed to a trickle from the moment she touched the tarbaby, and stopped completely once the gooey black mass had coated the wound. After ten minutes, the syrupy substance was covering her to the waist, and it was difficult to tell where the tarbaby ended and Carrie began.

I found it strange that the sticky black goo flowed over Carrie's t-shirt and jeans, but not her sneakers. Instead, the mass oozed into her shoes, and after a minute or two, they fell off into the grass. Soon after that, the thing that used to be Carrie began sliding down the length of the fence as it sloughed off of Original Recipe.

Norman made no further attempts to rescue his wife. His brief bout of frenzied mayhem had left him drained. He remained kneeling in front of the gate, watching as his wife's severed arm was absorbed into the ever-expanding snout of Big Tobacco. Even after the arm was gone, he stayed immobile, staring into the black goo that was seeping through the fence.

Except for Brandon, no one left the yard. The boy's eyes had swollen shut, and he was having difficulty breathing through the river of mucus streaming from his nose. Helen Mathis, who had been in the kitchen when the accident happened, had come out to shepherd her son back into the house.

Very few of the neighbors who had gone in search of chemical weapons returned to the yard. Most chose to lock themselves in their houses and hope that someone else would come up with a solution. Melissa Daniels elected to remain with the Spiller children, which drastically improved my opinion of her, while the Robinsons came back with a bucket full of cleaning supplies. Anthony Spectacles showed up a few minutes later, carrying an educational chemistry set.

"Oh, sweet Lord," moaned Celia Robinson, when she saw what remained of Carrie's body attempting to separate itself from the fence. "How did...?"

"She jumped," sighed Norman, still with his back to them. "She was free. I got her free, and she jumped right on top of that thing like she was celebrating a touchdown."

"How did you get her free?" asked Anthony. His question was directed at me, but it was Norman who answered.

"Cut her," he said softly. "I cut her damn arm off. This thing took it, and that one got the rest of her."

No one could think of an appropriate response to this, so we simply stood in a loose semi-circle for a while, watching Carrie's slow slide down the fence. After a few moments, Norman continued. "It's got her ring."

"Her ring?" asked Libby.

"Her wedding ring. I can just barely see it, floating around inside this monster's nose." Norman wiped his face with his sleeve. "I guess they can't absorb diamonds. Or gold."

The thing that was Carrie Spiller had succeeded in extricating itself from the fence and now stood separate and whole—

excepting half of its left arm—on the Mathises' lawn. When it took its first tentative step into the yard, everyone but Norman took a step back in response.

"You should come with us," suggested Libby. "It's not safe here."

Norman continued to stare in silence for a moment, then said, "this one's getting out."

"What's that?"

"The dog. It's still oozing out of the fence. I think it's figured out it can get out that way."

The thing that was Carrie lurched forward again, so I eased her husband to his feet. "We've got to get out of here," I whispered. "Your kids need you."

As I led Norman home, Anthony asked, "do you still want to try any of these chemicals?"

By this time the sky had darkened to the color of a bruise. "The sun's down," I replied. "I don't want to mess around with these things in the dark."

"We're not just going to leave them back here, are we?" asked Herb. "I can't have monsters running loose in my backyard!"

"I'm sorry, Mister Mathis," I sighed, "but I just don't know what else to do right now."

"Should we get the cops back here?"

"Cops ain't coming back," said Mr. Robinson. "Cops got their hands full tonight."

"Just stay inside," I suggested. "If we all stay inside tonight, we'll be fine. If these things try to get into your house, just call us. We'll come running, I promise."

A few phone numbers were exchanged, and the party broke up. We escorted Norman back to his house, where Melissa Daniels was entertaining the children. We offered to stay with him for a while, but he waved us away. "I've got to tell the kids about their mom," he said. "You don't want to be here for that."

I had been hungry when we left the house that evening, and despite the recent events, by the time we returned home I was ravenous. After a few minutes of aimless puttering around the kitchen, we decided to go for the easy solution of frozen pizza. As the oven was heating, I dialed the number of the Otterkill Sheriff's Office. There was nothing but a recorded greeting, inviting callers to leave a message or, if this was an emergency, to hang up and dial 911. I hesitated for a moment, concerned that I might be tying up emergency resources for people who really needed them, but in the end I dialed the number anyway, mostly out of curiosity.

After five rings, a very tired voice came on the line. "911 emergency dispatch," she yawned. "Are you calling about the swamp monsters?"

Somewhat shocked that I was not talking to a machine, it took me a moment to stammer out, "uh, yes. The monsters. We've got three of them. No, wait. Four. We've got four. One's a dog."

"A dog?"

"Yes ma'am."

"That's a new one. What's your name and address?"

"Josh Heaney. Twelve Ichabod Lane in Otterkill."

"Ichabod Lane?"

"That's right."

"Seriously?"

The smell of pizza cooking in the next room gave me sudden incentive to end the conversation as quickly as possible "We're off of Route 301. Near the Friendly Haven Old Folks'... um... I mean Retirement... Assisted Old Folks' Retirement Home?"

"Ichabod Lane, off of 301. Four swamp monsters," confirmed the woman on the other end of the line. "One's a dog. Got it."

"Great. Are you going to be able to send anyone out?"

"That's really not looking likely anytime soon, sir." I could hear phones ringing in the background. "All police, fire and EMT units are currently on assignment."

"ALL of them?"

"Everyone we could reach, anyway. You've got to understand, these sons of bastards are turning up everywhere."

"Do you have any tips on getting rid of them?"

"Don't even try. Just stay out of their way. Stay inside and keep your TV on. If anyone figures these things out, it'll be on TV."

Half an hour later, the pizza was eaten and night had fallen. Aside from a handful of streetlights out by Friendly Haven, Ichabod Lane was dark. The only illumination came from a moon that was just over a quarter full and the odd porch light. Everywhere were patches of deep blackness large enough to hide an army of tarbabies. I flicked on our own porch light. It contained a compact fluorescent bulb which, while energy-efficient, took several minutes to warm up to full brightness. The light it cast now barely revealed the front steps.

"There could be a dozen of those things on our front lawn," I told Libby, who was on the sofa browsing the Internet on her laptop. "We'd never be able to see them in the dark."

"Probably a good idea to stay in then," she replied. I closed the blinds and joined her on the sofa. "Do you think we're safe for the night?" she asked.

I glanced at the front door to make sure it was locked. "Safe as we can be, I guess. Those things don't seem to be particularly ambitious. I can't imagine them breaking the door down."

"What about the windows?"

To this I could only shrug. "To be honest, I don't know what to think. They're so slow and awkward; it seems like we should be able to avoid them easily."

"And yet we've gone from one of them to four in just sixteen hours."

The math was hard to ignore. "Jeez, the problem's quadrupled in just one day. How long before they take over the world?"

Libby brought up her computer's calculator and typed in a few numbers. "Eighteen days," she said after a moment.

"Say what?"

"If you start with one, and quadruple every day, you hit four billion by day seventeen. There's about seven billion people on the planet, so the last of them would be getting rounded up by lunchtime on day eighteen."

"So we've got eighteen days until the end of the world?"

"Well, no," said Libby. "We're well past Day One." She brought up a news website and angled the monitor so I could see. "The current estimate is that there's more than ten thousand GummiMenschen in Manhattan alone."

"Ten thousand? Already?"

"And maybe half that many in the surrounding suburbs." Libby tapped out a few more calculations. "That would put us at about Day Eight."

"So ten days until the end of the world?"

"Maybe a little longer. I'm not sure the dog counts."

I fished the remote control out of the sofa cushions and turned on the TV. A panel of talking heads was discussing whom to blame for the monster epidemic. I flipped channels until I found a non-news station. It was a home design show, where an enthusiastic young woman was demonstrating how to ruin furniture with hot glue.

"Well," I posited, "maybe Roscoe shouldn't count either. He was dumb enough to attack the thing."

"And Carrie just got careless."

"So barring carelessness and orneriness, how else can these things get at us?"

A high-pitched squeal drew my attention back to the TV, but the home show host didn't seem to be the cause. Puzzled, I hit the mute button. The squealing continued, and could now be placed as coming from outside the house. We sat frozen for a moment, trying to make out what the screaming voices were saying. Both of us stopped breathing when we realized the word being shouted the loudest was "Mommy."

I got to the door just ahead of Libby and struggled with it briefly before I remembered the deadbolt had been engaged. I twisted the latch and threw open the door, revealing the same ocean of blackness I had seen through the window. The feeble amber glow from the porch light did almost nothing to cut the gloom of the front yard. With Libby's hands on my shoulders, I descended the front steps.

The grass prickled my stockinged feet as I scanned the immediate vicinity. Within our yard I could see nothing. There appeared to be something in the street, but I couldn't make out any details. The commotion seemed to be coming from across the street, but although the Spillers' front door was open, I could not see far enough into the house to determine what was happening. I turned back to my wife, who was still at the top of the steps. "Get the flashlight!" I whispered, and Libby retreated into the house.

A high-pitched shriek made me flinch. From out of the Spillers' front door shot a tangle of arms and legs enveloped in a white cotton nightdress. "Mommy!" screamed the Spiller girl (and I cringed at the thought that I still did not know her name) as she tore out her house and across her lawn, heading straight for the street. In that instant, I understood what the shape in the road had to be.

Barely a second after the girl cleared the porch, Norman Spiller was out the door behind her. "Emma!" he screamed. "Get back here!" Norman's heel caught on the top step, and he slipped, thudding down the porch stairs on his tailbone. By the time he hit bottom, I was moving. Though I still could not see more than a few feet ahead of me, I sprinted toward the street, hoping to intercept

Emma before she could reach the dark shape she was hurtling toward.

Norman didn't have a chance. By the time he regained his feet, Emma had almost reached the curb. He seemed to be having difficulty finding his balance. I wasn't certain whether that was due to pain, fatigue, or something more medicinal, but I knew I had a much better shot at catching the girl. Though I was farther from the street, my strides were four times as long as Emma's, and I was covering the distance between us much faster. If I could just avoid whatever was in the street, I could scoop her up with seconds to spare.

I peered through the gloom as I ran, attempting to fix the exact position of the thing in the road. Had I been watching the ground in front of me, I might have spotted the dark shape on our own lawn. As it was, the collision knocked my feet out from under me, and my momentum was enough to carry me rolling into the street. I gasped as my forearms scraped against the curb and pulled my arms against my chest for protection. This only caused me to tumble faster, and I thrust my legs out to stop myself. With a muffled *splut*, my right foot struck the thing in the road, and I shuddered to a halt.

Despite the chaos of the last several seconds, the scene in front of me bordered on idyllic. The thing that several hours ago called itself Carrie Spiller was on its knees in the middle of Ichabod Lane, its arms spread to its sides in a welcoming posture. As one arm was substantially shorter than the other, the welcome appeared somewhat lopsided. On her right was a young boy of perhaps five, whom in the darkness I could only assume was Carrie's son. He stood with his arms wrapped around the creature's neck and his forehead nestled softly against its shoulder. That portion of the boy's face that wasn't already covered in the sticky effluence of his mother's former body wore an expression of perfect, beatific joy. I knew nothing about the boy, not even his name, but the child's face told me he was exactly where he wanted to be.

He was also exactly where his sister wanted to be. I heard the quiet slapping of bare feet on pavement, then felt the thud as the girl slammed into her mother, throwing her arms around both the mother-monster and her little brother. The impact rocked the tarbaby backward by an inch or two. The girl giggled happily, then let out a sigh of profound contentment, and nestled her chin against the tarbaby's left shoulder. As she settled down to be smothered in the inky goo, her eyes met mine, and she smiled.

I stared at the child's face for several long seconds, until Norman Spiller staggered into the street, his jaw hanging slack and his hands on either side of his head. The sight of him snapped me back to awareness, and I realized my foot was still stuck to the Carrie-Thing's back.

I yanked my leg back, and was shocked when my foot slipped free easily. I scrambled back onto the relative safety of my own lawn. Something hot and wet was thrust in my ear, and the lights came on.

"Josh, are you all right?" asked Libby, who had found our emergency flashlight—the big one that took six C cells which we kept around for blackouts. By its stark purplish light, I could see my new assailant, a ball of wetness and hot breath. Banjo was hunkered beside me, bathing my face in slick slobber. The dog must have been what I had tripped over in my race to intercept the girl. He either slipped out of the house during the confusion, or was never brought back in after the ill-fated barbecue. Now his tail was tucked between his legs, and while most of his attention was focused on greeting me, he kept shooting furtive glances at the scene in the street.

"Oh, Emma," croaked a voice from the street. "Emma, why do you never listen?" Libby swung the flashlight beam into the street, where Norman stood, swaying softly. His eyes were red and puffy—his voice hoarse and raw.

"It's mommy," said the girl quietly. "She's back."

"M'mmy b'ck," agreed the boy, though his words were slurred by the black goo filling his mouth.

Emma's voice lowered to a whisper. "She wants us all to be together again."

The light flickered as Libby's hand started to tremble. The look in her eyes told me she was trying to figure out how to fix the problem—to tell Norman what he needed to do next. But her lips quavered soundlessly, as she rejected every word that came to mind.

"I couldn't stop them," Norman explained to no one in particular.

"I know," I answered.

"They were out the door before I knew what they were doing."

"We saw." I held up my bloodied forearms. "I tried to stop her."

"But she's so FAST!" Norman said this with sincere admiration, as though her speed were an attribute that would serve her well in the future.

Ichabod Lane was quiet. A lone cricket in the driveway, the hum of a neighbor's air conditioner, and the soft slurping of Banjo as he bathed my face were the only sounds I could hear. No neighbors came to investigate. Either they had not heard the commotion, or they had had enough of monsters for one day. The thing in the street was utterly silent as it oozed over the Spiller children. After several minutes, the silence was split by a deep sigh as Norman dropped his hands. For the first time since leaving the house, his gaze fell upon me and Libby.

"Can you take care of Banjo for me?" he asked, as he walked to his family.

Libby finally found the right words. "No, Norman," she said quietly. "Don't do it."

Norman paused a moment, weighing her words. "But they're so happy," he said as he knelt down. "I want to be happy with them." Then he slipped his arms around his children and kissed his wife on the head.

Libby sat down on the curb next to me, with Banjo nestled between us, and the three of us watched the thing that used to be Carrie Spiller engulf her family. Libby set the flashlight on the pavement, and the light came to rest on the creature's back, where we saw a long white streak that had not been there before. I looked down at my naked right foot—my sock had stuck to the tarbaby when I ripped it free. On my left foot, I found four toes safely swathed in white cotton, and one thrill-seeking piggie sticking through a hole in the fabric. I felt my dinner rising in my throat when I realized that, had I struck the creature with my left foot instead of the right, that exposed toe would have come in direct contact with the thing's skin. That hole would have been all I needed to join the Spiller family in eternal stickiness.

The conversion process took far longer than had Roscoe Carson's, or Big Tobacco's, or Carrie's. The tarbaby was absorbing three people simultaneously, and though two of them were substantially smaller than any of the previous victims, it was still well past midnight before the four figures separated and stood upright again.

I considered crossing the street to close the Spillers' front door, but in the end Libby and I simply stood up, walked back inside, locked the door and drew the curtains. Though he had not been specifically invited, Banjo followed us in, and when we turned out the lights and retreated to the safety of our bedroom, he shoved his way underneath the bed and curled himself into a tight ball. I could hear his ears twitching as he slept.

15

The room was bathed in the soft pink light of sunrise when I awoke. Libby was already up and peeking out the window. I had expected to be sleeping late today, but the clock said it was just after six.

"Wussgon?" I muttered.

"Something's happening out there. I think they got someone else."

I pulled the covers up over my head. It seemed the only appropriate response. If one monster could become seven in the space of a day, our eighteen day window was going to get a lot shorter.

"I'm going to take a look," said Libby, stepping into her jeans. Banjo shimmied his way out from under the bed and padded softly behind her as she left the room. I heard Libby's footsteps on the stairs, followed by the click-clack of the dog's toenails. The front door opened, then closed again immediately. More footsteps and toenail clacking followed, after which I heard the door to the back patio sliding open and shut again.

I could also hear voices from outside, and they sounded combative. I slid the covers aside reluctantly and swung my feet to the floor. I was too tired to undress properly the night before, and the tattered, twinless stock was still clinging to my left foot, the hole now exposing the little piggie who had roast beef. I stood, yawned, and pulled back the curtain to see Libby crossing the lawn with Banjo trotting along after her, but no one else. Whatever was going on was happening further up the street, in the direction of Gun Club Road.

After slipping on some clothes, I shuffled downstairs, opened the front door and nearly stepped out into the arms of the tarbaby that was waiting patiently on the porch. "Ah," I said, then closed and locked the door just as I had heard Libby doing, and made my exit by the back patio.

I was past the Mathis house before I found the source of the voices. A group of about ten figures was clustered in front of the Cape Cod at number Twenty-two, which I vaguely remembered as being Anthony Spectacle's house. As I approached, I saw that Anthony was indeed among the group, and was currently the most animated of the bunch. Libby was there as well, with Banjo nervously sniffing at her feet. Some other neighbors I kind of recognized were out, as were a handful of older men and women I had never seen before. At the center of the loose circle of people was a skinny old woman holding hands with a child. I laid a hand on Libby's shoulder as I stepped up behind her. Anthony was shouting by that point.

"Because it's not safe!" he yelled. "People live here!" Anthony's complaint was directed at a large man of perhaps eighty years of age. The stranger wore a floppy fisherman's hat, a short-sleeved button-down shirt, grey sweat pants and slippers. The casual footwear indicated the man lived nearby, so I guessed several of these people may have been residents of the Friendly Haven Assisted Living Center.

"Gladys lives here too," replied another man, taller than the first, wearing Coke-bottle bifocals and a lush broom-bristle mustache. He had tennis shoes on, but they had no laces, as he presumably didn't have far to walk. "She's probably lived here longer than you."

At his side was a short, plump woman on a motorized scooter. "She ain't hurting nobody," she pointed out as she leaned against the handlebars. "And I guarandamteeya that whatever's going on there, it ain't illegal."

Whatever was going on there appeared to be nothing more than friends holding hands and enjoying the day. The center of attention, whom I guessed must be Gladys, was an ancient, wizened woman who looked like she would never again see fewer than a hundred candles on her birthday cake. I marveled that the woman could even stand. Her exposed shins and forearms were rail-thin, and her skin was almost transparent, revealing a network of bright blue veins interrupted by the occasional dark purple bruise. Her unbrushed hair, mostly white with yellow patches throughout, hung in tangled knots down her back. She wore a tattered flannel bathrobe over a polyester nightdress, and her feet were bare.

When I approached, I had assumed that the woman was holding hands with a child, and undoubtedly the thing standing before her had once been a child, probably as recently as the night before. Now it was the smallest tarbaby I had yet seen—a tarbaby-baby that had to reach up to grasp the woman's hands, which were already engulfed past the wrists in the dark viscous fluid of the monster's body. From the size of the creature, it had to be the former Spiller boy. There was currently no sign of the rest of the family.

Anthony Spectacles had worked himself up into quite a lather. His hands were balled into tight fists, and spittle flew from his mouth when he spoke. "She's hurting *herself!*" he screamed. "And when she's done with that, she's going to be coming after us!"

"What do you say Gladys?" asked the man in the fishing hat. "You hurting yourself?"

The old woman turned her head and beamed a bright, toothless smile back at us. "Don't talk foolishness, Clancy. I can't remember ever feeling better!"

"Yeah, we get that part..." protested Anthony, but was interrupted by Clancy.

"See, the thing is, there's a whole lot of things Gladys can't remember. The poor woman was diagnosed with Alzheimer's, you see."

"Sorry to hear that..." Anthony began, but was interrupted once again.

"Twenty years ago."

"That was long before any of us showed up to the Old Folks' Home," added the mustached man. "Miss Gladys is something of an institution at the institution." The mustached man chuckled at his joke. No one joined him.

"And none of us has ever heard her say a word," said Clancy. "I've been at Friendly Haven nearly a decade now..."

"It's only been eight years," said Gladys, still smiling brightly. "I remember it was after those buildings fell down in New York. Terrible thing, that."

"That's right, ma'am," Clancy confirmed. "And do you know who you are?"

"I do!" she exclaimed. "I'm Gladys Weaver Hoffspring, widow to Rodney George Hoffspring, who passed to his reward in 1986. He died on the very same day that space ship exploded, though I don't mean to suggest the two were related." Gladys winked at Libby when she said this. Libby smiled politely in return. "I used to be a potter," she continued, "but I'm currently a resident of the

Friendly Haven Assisted Living Center." She gazed off into the distance for a moment before continuing. "You know, I don't believe I know the address. I don't believe I've *ever* known the address. Is it on Ichabod Lane?"

"Yes, ma'am," answered Libby.

"Oh, that's nice," said Gladys. "Otherwise it would have to be on Gun Club Road." At this Gladys laughed long and loud. "What a silly name for a street!"

"Especially since there's no gun club," agreed Libby.

"Oh, but there used to be!" continued Gladys. "Right where Friendly Haven is now. It finally shut its doors in 1979, round about the same time that power plant in Pennsylvania went on the fritz."

"I don't believe many people 'round here know that," said Clancy. "Miss Gladys, did you know you have Alzheimer's Disease?"

Gladys sighed. "I do. Everything's been... foggy... for so very long." The old woman's voice quieted, but her smile did not dim.

Clancy continued. "Did you know you haven't spoken to anyone for as long as any of us have known you?"

"And I do apologize for that," giggled Gladys. "It wasn't bad manners, honestly! Just a touch of brain damage!"

"Did you know you've got bladder cancer?" asked the woman on the scooter. "Had it two years now?"

"Don't forget the arthritis," chuckled Gladys, "plus cataracts, low blood sugar, fallen arches, and chronic tinnitus in my left ear. I'm a proper wreck and no mistake!"

"And how do you feel now?" asked Clancy softly.

Gladys gave some thought to this before she replied. "When I was just ten years old, I took part in our school's spelling bee. And while the Lord hates a braggart, I have to confess, I was inspired. Every single word I was asked, I could see in front of me like it was literally written in the air. It felt like I knew every word that ever was. I won first place—got a blue sash out of it. The winning word was 'synecdoche.' S-Y-N-E-C-D-O-C-H-E." She turned to face the diminutive black shape in front of her. "Well, I feel like that now, only not just about spelling. I feel like I know everything I ever knew. Better yet, I know every*one* I ever knew."

"And physically?"

"Nary an ache nor a pain. I feel like I could fly."

Anthony stepped closer to Gladys, though he remained wary of getting too close to the creature in front of her. "Ma'am? How did you get out here?"

"I walked. I was in my chair this morning, looking out my window. Seems like that's all I've been fit to do for the last few years—sit and look out the window. And I saw this little fellow walking by, and I had to go to him."

"Why?" asked Anthony. "Why did you have to go to him?"

"He needed me," answered Gladys. "Or he needed someone anyway. He looked so… lonesome. I couldn't find my slippers—can't remember the last time I had to put them on myself—but I knew I had to go to him anyway." Gladys turned to face Anthony. "It took me a while to catch up, I'm afraid. This little guy's slow, but I might just be even slower. Leastways, I was. Things have changed."

Anthony scratched his head, wondering whether to persist in his questioning. Ultimately, his need to know outweighed his sense of tact. "Do you know… were you aware that you're going to…"

Gladys finished his question for him. "Join these things? I don't think I did, at first. But I do now."

"Aren't you frightened?"

Gladys laughed. "My doctors say I'll be dead by Christmas. They don't think I can understand them when they talk about me. Most of the time, they're probably right about that. But the cancer's inoperable. I'm going to die, and it's going to hurt." She laughed again. "That is, I was *going* to die, and it was *going* to hurt. Now… well, now I'm not too sure. What I do know is that I've got no pain, and I can think again. And maybe, just maybe, this is for keeps."

Anthony sighed. The black goop had oozed its way up near Gladys' elbows. It would take the better part of an hour for the little monster to consume her entirely. Had she not been so emaciated, I would have wondered whether it could have turned her by itself.

"What do you think you're going to do… after?" asked Libby.

Gladys lifted her head, and let the morning breeze play over her face. "I think I'm going to walk," she said at last. "I've spent the last twenty years in a chair in my room, watching the world through a window. I want to see it all again."

"See?" said the woman in the scooter. "She ain't gonna hurt no one."

"I wish I could believe that," said Anthony. "But we've got four of these things on the street already…"

"Seven," I said.

"What?"

"This one here?" I pointed to the small black figure before us. "I think that's Norman Spiller's boy. Last night, the whole family... turned."

"What? How did this happen?"

"They wanted to be with their mother," said Libby. "How do you stop something like that?"

Anthony stammered in confusion, then looked around nervously. "Where's the rest of them?"

"We're not sure," I said, "though I think Norman's on our porch."

Clancy cleared his throat. "There's something you folks should probably see." With that, he and the mustached man started walking back toward Friendly Haven. Their companion swiveled her scooter nimbly and circled around them. As she drove off, I could see a bumper sticker on the back of her scooter, reading "To hell with the Grandkids, ask me about my soaps."

The residents of Ichabod Lane paused to pay their respects to Gladys, then followed Clancy to Friendly Haven. Aside from Anthony, the only other neighbors I recognized were a middle-aged couple I had come to think of as Tony and Kristen Gardenweasel (long story) and a pair of women who may or may not have been sisters. It was a short walk to the Retirement Center from our current location. The Spiller family had gotten there ahead of us.

I have no idea how many people lived at Friendly Haven, but I would have been very surprised if any of them were still inside the building. The front of the facility hosted a semi-circular driveway and small parking lot, about what you might find at a mid-sized chain motel. Half a dozen benches flanked the main entrance, all of which were now occupied by a platoon of senior citizens in various arrangements of sleepwear. At two of those benches were the missing members of the Spiller family. At a third sat Big Tobacco, his paw raised into the hand of a small bald man with a severe hunch in his back. The man's face was pointed down at the pavement, but I could still see the corner of a smile peeking around.

The tallest of the tarbabies, the one who used to be Carrie, sat in the middle of the next bench. Two elderly women flanked her, with their arms draped lovingly around her neck and chest, and their heads cradled on her shoulders. I couldn't tell if these women were smiling or not, because their faces were entirely obscured by thick black goop.

Past the large automated sliding doors that led to the Reception Area, the thing that used to be Emma Spiller stood before a third bench. She was holding hands with a fat woman in a pink terrycloth robe. The tar had already oozed up the woman's forearms, and was now hidden in the sleeves of her robe. Two more women sat on either side of her, chatting happily as they awaited their turn.

"What the devil are they thinking?" demanded Anthony. He scanned the twenty or so faces outside the building. "And where the hell are the attendants?" Anthony stormed through the loose crowd, and the reception doors slid open at his approach.

"This is insane!" said Tony Gardenweasel with more volume than was strictly needed. "They're just feeding themselves to these monsters!"

This was met with a hearty round of laughter from the assembled residents. "Ain't no such thing as monsters," replied one of the women at Emma's bench. "Your mother should've ought to told you that."

"But they're trying to kill you!" protested Tony, though he did not appear to be certain that this was true.

"These people ain't dead," noted Clancy, gesturing toward the Spillers. "Fact is, far as we know, they're gonna live forever."

"Oh come on! You think these freaks are immortal?"

Clancy pulled off his hat and ran a hand through his hair. "The army has spent the better part of the last week trying to figure out how to kill one of these fellers," he said. "Near as I can see, they haven't got one yet."

"And you can stop talking about them like they're something alien," added the woman in front of Emma. "Because they're not. They're us."

Her friend on the other side of the bench nodded her agreement. "They're angels."

"Well that's just stupid," protested Tony, but his wife interrupted him.

"What's so stupid about it?" demanded Kristen Gardenweasel. "The tarbabies take away your pain, and they make you immortal like them. That sounds like angels to me."

"You tell him, dear," agreed the woman on the bench. "When you've lived as long as I have, you know a blessing when you see it. God's sent these blessed souls to free us from our earthly shells."

"One touch, and we'll live forever," confirmed the woman at the other end of the bench. "It's the Rapture."

Tony tried to stammer a reply, but no words would come. His jaw bobbed as his brain systematically rejected every response that came to mind.

"Only it's better than the Rapture," suggested Clancy, "because everyone's invited. Ain't that right, Herschel?"

The small man holding Big Tobacco's paw looked up briefly and waved. "Herschel's Jewish," explained Clancy, "but these fellers don't seem to discriminate."

Libby and I followed Anthony into the Reception Area, where I was surprised to find another dozen residents of Friendly Haven, none of whom showed any inclination to venture outside. A handful of staff members were there too, and Anthony had cornered them.

"How can you not have a doctor on staff?" he shouted at a short, tired-looking woman in purple pants and a multi-colored smock. "These people are all sick! There must be a doctor around!"

"Not at night," said the desk nurse. "Unless there's an emergency, the night shift only staffs nurses and attendants."

"And you don't call this an emergency? Your patients are dying out there!"

"No they ain't," said a tall black man in mint green scrubs who was sprawled across a faux leather sofa. "Whatever it is they're doing out there, it ain't dying."

Anthony began massaging his temples. "Fine," he said at last. "What time does the doctor get here?"

"She was supposed to be here a half-hour ago," said the desk nurse. "She hasn't shown up, and she hasn't called in."

"None of the day shift has called in," added the man on the sofa. "You ask me—I don't expect they're coming."

"All right, this is ridiculous," protested Anthony. "You have to get those people back in here. Restrain them if you have to. Sedate them if you have to, but get their asses back in here!"

"Sure," sighed the desk nurse. "Which one of our patients are you related to, anyway?"

Anthony hesitated. "Umm…"

"You must be related to someone out there. You wouldn't be telling us how we should be treating our patients—you wouldn't so *presumptuous* as to demand that we forcibly medicate our patients— unless you were next of kin, right?"

"Look," began Anthony, but he had clearly lost the momentum.

"'Course he wouldn't," said the man on the sofa. "Otherwise, he'd just be trespassing."

"So that's it?" asked Anthony. "You're just going to let those people die out there?"

"They ain't dying," repeated the man on the sofa.

The desk nurse elaborated. "Those patients went outside of their own free will. They're not prisoners here. We have no legal authority to hold them against their will. And they're not hurting anyone."

"Not yet, anyway," said Anthony. "What happens when they try to get back inside?"

The woman in purple stared out the front window for a long time. "We lock the doors," she said at last.

"No, Alice," said a wheezy voice from a chair near the window. "*We* lock the doors. *You* get home to your kids." The voice belonged to a leathery man who could have still been in his sixties. He still sported a full head of hair, but had it cropped in a severe buzz cut the exact same length as his mustache. A slender plastic tube hung from his nose and connected to a pair of metal canisters on a wheeled trolley beside his chair.

"The Major's right," said the man on the sofa. "Your kids will be up by now. You need to go."

Alice finished up some unnecessary filing. "I can't go until the day nurse gets here. Or Doctor Talbot."

The man on the sofa sat up and swiveled his feet to the floor. "Doc Talbot ain't coming. I don't think anyone on the day shift is coming. Two orderlies called out already. Said there were roadblocks on Route 15. The rest we ain't heard from, but if they haven't shown by now…"

"Hillary would call if she could," Alice protested.

"But she didn't, so she likely can't."

"We're not all idiots, you know." This comment came from the Major, and it took me a moment to realize it had been directed at me.

"Pardon?"

The Major directed his gaze out the window. "We're not all as eager to die as those morons outside. There's still a few of us geezers who don't intend to surrender to those devils."

"Devils is what they are, all right." The agreement came from a spherical woman several feet to the Major's right. Despite the early hour, the woman was fully dressed in a hunter green pant suit that nicely offset her unnaturally maroon hair. The thick stripe of crimson on her lips and the cluster of pearls on each earlobe confirmed that, if the Rapture was indeed upon us, this woman would meet her maker suitably attired.

"Some of the folks outside seem to think they're angels," noted Libby.

"Hogwash," tutted the woman in green.

"The folks outside are idiots," continued the Major. "They were born idiots; they lived their fool lives as idiots; and now they're going to die idiots. I just want you to understand that we haven't all gone nuts. We may be old. We may be infirm. But we aren't stupid."

I resisted the urge to salute. "Yes sir. We'll remember that."

"So what are you going to do?" asked Anthony. "Are you evacuating?"

"Where to? We've got food here. Medicine too. We've got beds, TVs, phones, toilets. And we can lock the doors. What more do we need?"

"But what happens when your food runs out?"

"I'd say we've got at least a week. By then, the government will either have this situation under control, or they won't. If they don't, running out of pudding cups is likely to be the least of our worries." The Major turned to face Alice. "But you need to either go home to your kids, or bring them here. Either way, you should get a move on. There's more of those things springing up every hour."

"Devils is what they are," repeated the woman in green.

Alice still seemed reluctant to leave her post. "What about you, Jasper?" she asked the man on the sofa. "Are you going home too?"

Jasper shrugged. "I'm better off here. Got no cable at home, and no air conditioning. I don't even have much groceries in."

"There's going to be plenty of open beds after today," the Major noted. "You folks should consider staying as well. Once we lock this place down, it's likely to be more secure than your houses."

"That's… actually not a bad idea," said Anthony.

Alice had gathered up her jacket and purse. She pulled a ring of keys from her smock pocket and brought them over to Jasper. "Remember," she told him, "you can't just lock the doors. You have to turn off the sensors first. That's behind the desk."

"I've locked up before," he assured her. "Now get going."

Alice took a last hesitant look around at the remaining residents. Her eyes met the Major's. "I'll be back," she promised.

"Not if you've got any sense."

We walked out with Alice to find that the other residents of Ichabod Lane had retreated to the opposite curb. Alice cupped her hands around her mouth and addressed the crowd around the benches. "Good morning, people! I need your attention, please! In a few minutes, Jasper is going to be locking the main doors. If any of you want to return inside, where it's safe, you need to do so right now!"

No one moved. A few of the seniors nodded at her and smiled, but all seemed content where they were.

Disgusted, Anthony shouted, "come on, people! This is silly! Your rooms are inside, and all your stuff! Plus there's TV in there, and food…"

"They got a cure for diabetes in there?" asked an obese man in a teal track suit.

"No," I confessed, "but I hear there's pudding."

16

We passed Gladys again on the way home. She was still smiling, but she did not offer us a wave, as her arms were now totally engulfed in sticky, black pitch. She nodded cheerfully, and I guessed she had no more than ten minutes before she would be unable to do even that. Libby smiled in return, but we picked up the pace to avoid having to watch as her head was consumed.

The maybe-or-maybe-not-sisters peeled off without a word at number Twenty-Seven, and the Gardenweasels said their goodbyes across the street. As we passed Anthony Spectacle's house, I noticed a heap of blankets on the Mathises' porch. Closer inspection revealed a pair of legs sticking out the bottom. Libby and I crossed the street, trying to make nervous look like nonchalant. The figure on the porch stirred at our approach.

"'Sup," said Brandon, though it was unclear whether he actually recognized us, or was simply falling back on his default greeting. The blanket in which he was swaddled fell back from his face, revealing a sickly fish-belly white pallor. His thick black hair was plastered to his head, but though he was sweating profusely, he was also trembling. A crust the color of cigarette ash ringed his nostrils and the corners of his mouth, and a sticky, wet cough issued from his throat as he clutched the blanket tighter around his body.

"Jeez," I said. "You don't sound too good. Shouldn't you be in bed?"

"He should be in the hospital," said his mother, emerging from the house carrying a small blue duffel bag with the words

"Otterkill Badgers" stenciled on the side. "But just try to get a friggin' ambulance."

"You tried 911 again?"

"About a dozen times. They're not even answering anymore."

"'M fine, Mom," moaned Brandon, wiping a bead of sweat from the tip of his nose.

"You look like you've got a fever, sport." I instantly regretted calling the boy "sport," a term I would never use in less stressful circumstances.

"I wish," said Helen as she descended the front porch. "A fever I'd know what to do with. He's cold as ice. His temperature's gone down half a degree every hour since he breathed in that poison. He's down to ninety-two, but he's still sweating like a swine."

Herb Mathis joined his wife on the porch, with young Logan shadowing him. Brandon wobbled precariously as he struggled to his feet, but soon corrected himself, and was able to navigate the stairs with his mother's help. Logan dashed ahead to open the passenger-side door of their enormous SUV.

After loading Brandon into the front seat, Helen and Logan clambered into the back, while Herb took his place at the wheel. Otterkill didn't have a hospital, so the nearest emergency room was thirty miles away. It would take the Mathises an hour to drive there. Brandon's eyes remained locked on the backyard dog run as they backed out of the driveway and sped off toward Gun Club Road. I soon realized what it was that held his interest.

"They got out," I said, and Libby and Anthony came forward to confirm that the dog run was empty, though the large brass padlock was still securely in place.

"So where are they?" asked Anthony, his eyes darting from bush to bush like a nervous squirrel.

I turned and started once again toward home. "Oh, I expect they'll turn up."

There was no sign of the former dog run inmates on the short walk to our house, but the thing that I assumed was once Norman Spiller was still waiting patiently on our front stoop. It hadn't gotten bored and wandered off, as I had hoped. It hadn't taken a seat. I don't even think it had turned around, though it was often difficult to tell which way these creatures were facing.

We circled around to the back of the house and entered through the sliding glass doors. The kitchen clock said it was just after eight o'clock. On a normal day, I wouldn't even be up this early. I yawned and opened the pantry door to consider our breakfast options. We had three boxes of cereal, two of which were already open, a little over half a loaf of bread, some crackers and peanut butter. On a lower shelf, there were a few cans of soup and some miscellaneous tinned vegetables. "How much food do you suppose we have?"

Libby opened the refrigerator and took a quick inventory. "Some. Maybe half a gallon of milk. A few eggs."

A muffled click-clacking was coming from the back patio, and it was a few seconds before I recognized the sound as toenails. I had forgotten that Banjo was following us and had shut the door on him. I slid the door open and he trotted in, a reproachful look on his face.

"He must be hungry," I said, taking a seat at the kitchen table. "Have we got anything he can eat?"

"Not much. We should probably go shopping. If the stores are open, that is."

"The Spillers must have some dog food. Should we go over and have a look?"

"You mean just break into their house? Has the looting started already?"

"He did ask us to take care of his dog," I reminded her. "And, the situation being what it is, I doubt they're going to object."

Libby remained reluctant, but when she saw Banjo peeking at her expectantly from under my chair, she relented. "OK, but let's do it quick, before the neighbors see us."

We left through the back door again. This time, Libby was armed with a folding shopping trolley.

"You weren't kidding about the looting."

"Have you ever seen how dog food is packaged? Those bags weigh more than the dog!" She reached down and gave Banjo a quick scritch behind the ears. "Besides, we should empty out their fridge too. We don't want to let anything spoil."

The street looked clear. We trotted out to the front yard with Banjo close at our heels. The thing on the stoop was still the thing on the stoop. The dog whined as we passed and stole glances back to make sure the creature wasn't following. It was one of those backward glances that caused him to plow into my legs when I stopped at the road.

The door to the Spillers' house stood wide open. Neither of us had the presence of mind to close it after last night's catastrophe, and we both failed to notice it in our dash out of the house this morning.

"What do you think?" asked Libby. "Is anyone home?"

I looked up and down the street. A bend in the road hid the crowd at Friendly Haven from view. There were no other signs of life. "Only seven or eight ways to find out."

We crossed the street and the Spillers' lawn at a quiet trot. Libby and I paused at the porch steps, but Banjo scampered right up, his toenails making a happy racket on the stairs. He padded inside the house, then turned back to ensure that his new friends were following.

I peered inside the house and called out softly. "Hello? Is anyone here?" When no one answered, I whispered to Libby, "stay here while I check this out."

"No thanks." She stepped inside and closed the door behind us. After a moment's consideration, she locked the deadbolt for good measure.

My whisper was more urgent this time. "There might be someone in here!"

"There's definitely someone out there," Libby said, pointing back to our house. "And if he gets it in his head to come over here, I want a couple inches of door between us. Where's Banjo?"

The Spillers' house was carpeted, which afforded the dog more stealth than our laminate floors. He poked his head out from the kitchen, issued two quick barks, and then retreated again. When we caught up to him, he was licking the inside of a blue ceramic dish on the floor.

"Gotcha. Breakfast it is." The floor of the pantry was dominated by a gigantic bag of kibble. I scooped out a serving with a little plastic shovel and dumped it into Banjo's bowl. "Go to town."

Banjo looked at his bowl, then looked at me, then looked at the pantry, then looked at his bowl again. After a moment he put his head down, selected a single piece of kibble, and picked it up. He didn't chew it, but simply sat with it in his mouth, looking as though he had been kicked.

"That good, huh?"

"You forgot the best part," said Libby as she reached past me to a higher shelf. She pulled a small tin from an open box, peeled back the top, and found a spoon in the sink. Banjo started a bouncy, waggy dance as she upended the tin over his dish and scooped out the pungent quasi-meat inside. She barely had time to pull her hand out of the way again before the dog thrust his muzzle into the dish and began devouring the contents. "It's not breakfast if it doesn't stink," she said as she deposited the can and spoon into the sink.

I pulled the case of tinned dog food from the pantry and placed it in the bottom of the shopping cart. The bag of kibble went on top of that, nearly filling the cart to the brim. Libby turned her attention to the refrigerator as I scanned the rest of the pantry shelves. "Huh. They weren't big on prepared foods. We've got flour, condensed milk, oatmeal, baking powder. Lots of ingredients, but nothing…you know… edible."

"Oatmeal's food," said Libby as she deposited a gallon of milk on top of the cart.

"If you want to get technical. I was hoping for something with marshmallows and a cartoon mascot."

Splut.

Something thudded against my leg, and both Libby and Banjo froze at the sound. I looked down at my feet, and guffawed when I saw what was pressed against me. "It's just the cat," I chuckled. "I thought for a minute..."

No one else was laughing. Banjo took half a step forward, then chuffed.

The thing at my feet used to be a cat—that was certain. Now it was a boneless bag of stickiness, and I watched in dumb shock as it wrapped itself around my left leg. I lifted my foot off the floor and gave it an experimental shake, but succeeded only in losing my balance.

"It's... uh... it's heavy," I said, looking to Libby for suggestions.

"Pants," she said.

"Pants," I agreed, without comprehending.

"It's not stuck to you yet. It's stuck to your pants."

I popped the fly on my jeans and slid them down to my knees. Kicking off my right shoe, I drew that foot free, then braced myself against the kitchen counter and lifted my left foot again. Careful to keep my hands safely within the fabric, I pushed against the weight of the Cat-Thing. It slid a few inches, but wouldn't move past my shoe. Pushing harder caused my feet to slide on the vinyl flooring, and I ended up sitting on the kitchen floor, my pants still wrapped around my left ankle.

While I was not in the best position to judge time objectively, I was certain this tarbaby was flowing much faster than any of its predecessors. It was noticeably flatter than it had been when it first made contact and had already formed a complete circle around my leg. The inky black tendril of its tail was now probing around the loosened waistband of my jeans.

In a flutter of yellow, the Cat-Thing vanished. Libby had wrapped the creature in a dish towel and was now tugging experimentally at the mass of fabric. With surgical patience, she slipped her fingers beneath a flap of towel and untied my remaining sneaker. We pulled, the sneaker thumped to the floor, and the pants came free of my leg. Libby held the bundle of pants, towel and monster at arm's length, then pitched the entire wad into the pantry, slamming the door behind it.

Three seconds later, she yanked it open again, snatched a box of dog biscuits off the top shelf, and slammed the door shut.

"They got the cat," I puffed from the floor.

"Yeah. It was a really pretty cat, too." She tucked the biscuit box on top of the shopping cart and helped me to my feet. Banjo resumed eating, though he kept both eyes locked on the pantry door.

I scanned the floor as I pulled my socks up, on the lookout for more kitty monsters. "So, did it just wander in after it… turned?"

"I think it lived here." Libby returned to the refrigerator and rooted through the freezer compartment. Two pints of ice cream, a box of waffles and a bag of frozen pierogis joined the heap in the cart.

"You don't suppose it got monsterized in the house?"

We peeked into the dining room, which contained nothing more threatening than economical Danish modern furnishings.

Beyond that was the living room, which was likewise free of movement. I turned back to the kitchen, but Libby caught my arm. She pointed, and I followed her gaze back to the living room.

She was pointing at an overstuffed recliner just inside the archway that separated the dining and living areas. The chair's back was to us, and since it was upholstered in faux black leather, it was difficult to see the solid black limb that was draped across the armrest.

With great care, Libby backed the grocery cart out of the kitchen and into the main hallway. She wheeled it back to the front door and out onto the porch. From the kitchen Banjo watched us in confusion, his breakfast not yet finished. I snapped my fingers, and the dog scampered down the hallway, slinking between Libby's legs as he left the house.

I risked a peek into the living room. Sporting a built-in cup holder and remote control caddy, the big black chair in the corner was designed for professional-grade TV viewing. From the front, with the lights off, it was difficult to see the thing that used to be Norman Spiller slumped down in its leathery bowels, with its head resting at a gentle angle against the pillowy top. I couldn't tell if it was looking at anything in particular, but the focal point of the room was a 52-inch, wall-mounted flat screen TV. I tiptoed into the room, just far enough to press the power button on the monitor's side. The set flared to life, displaying a high-spirited cooking show. I backed out of the house and shut the door behind us.

The tarbaby on our own front stoop was still maintaining its silent vigil. I had assumed it was the one that used to be Norman, but that was when I thought the others were safely locked away. Now, I guessed it was probably Original Recipe—the one we had seen in the Spillers' front yard just the previous morning, before there were quite so many of them. That would leave the thing that used to be Roscoe Carson unaccounted for. I wondered if that one had wandered back up to Roscoe's house. If that place hadn't burned up, perhaps he would be sitting in his own favorite chair right now.

Or perhaps it would be hunting.

I remembered I had no pants on, and we went home.

17

"They were all lined up, just waiting their turn." As I got to work preparing breakfast, Libby recounted the morning's events to her mother on the phone. "They all thought it was going to make them immortal or something. This one lady even claimed it was the Rapture."

I broke the seal on the frozen waffles and dumped them out onto the counter. "No, the Rapture," continued Libby. "You know, the end of the world, when all the good little boys and girls get to go to Heaven?" She tapped on the toaster to get my attention as I dug a frying pan out of a cabinet.

"I don't know. They seemed to think the tarbabies are angels." I held up the frying pan proudly. Libby pointed at the toaster. "Mm-hmm. One of the ladies inside said the same thing."

She pointed at the waffles, then at the toaster again. Disappointed, I put the frying pan back in the cabinet. I had never used it before, and was looking forward to the opportunity.

"Yes, some of them decided to stay inside. They're going to lock themselves in and wait the whole thing out." I was trying to load the waffles into the toaster. Libby pulled them out of my hand and unwrapped the plastic packet.

"Why would they want to stay here?" Libby gave me her "my mother's crazy" look. I pushed the plunger down on the toaster and nodded sympathetically. "But they've got their own rooms there. And food. And their... old folk stuff."

When the first pair of waffles popped up, I applauded with delight, then slid them onto a plate and started the next batch. By the time Libby had finished her conversation, I'd toasted all six, providing me with an enormous sense of accomplishment. "Do we have any syrup?" I asked, scanning the contents of our own pantry.

"I don't think so," answered Libby, as she returned the cordless phone to its charging cradle.

"What else works on waffles?"

"Fruit?"

I checked the fridge as a formality, though we both knew it was an empty gesture. "Nope."

"Ice cream?"

"Really? For breakfast?"

"Who's gonna know?"

"Awesome." I pulled a pint of Chunky Monkey out of the freezer and daubed a liberal scoop onto each waffle stack, then handed a plate to Libby with a superfluous flourish. "Check it out! I cooked!"

Banjo yapped from beneath the kitchen table. He had nestled himself under a chair and was staring fixedly out the sliding patio doors. I couldn't see anything that might capture a dog's interest. "What's the matter, boy?" I asked. "Is there a squirrel?"

Libby stood on tiptoe to get a better look out the window above the kitchen sink. "That's not a squirrel," she replied before taking a seat at the table. I moved to the table as well, and stared out the window again.

I carved off a liberal chunk of waffle and a proportional glob of sweet, sticky goodness and shoveled the mass into my mouth. As I chewed, I continued to scan the yard. "Where is it"?

Libby swallowed. "Behind the pine tree."

I leaned forward, then back again as far as I could, then scooped up another mouthful of breakfast. Libby was right—there was something out there, but it was still difficult to spot. It stood in a patch of shadow in front of the tree line that marked the end of our property, and was partially obscured by a small ornamental pine tree about thirty feet from the house. It would have been impossible to distinguish from the background shadows if not for its feet. Only by leaning my head forward far enough could I see the twin stripes of the thing's lower legs under the tree. If the sun had been a little lower, I would have missed it entirely.

"This is really good," said Libby through a mouthful of poor nutrition.

"Is that the one that was on the porch?"

Libby leaned backward in her chair and peeked into the living room. She could still see the shadow of the tarbaby on the front stoop through the frosted glass. She settled back in her chair and scooped up another bite. "Nope. He's still there."

"So we're being boxed in."

"Looks like."

"That's a handy thing to know." I set my plate on the floor, and Banjo obligingly cleaned it for us.

We didn't put our imprisonment to the test until the honking started. Noon had come and gone by that time, and after a morning spent scanning news reports to see if anyone had a handle on how widespread the tarbaby problem had become, I was giving sober consideration to a nap. That's when we heard the first shrill blasts of a car horn coming from down the street. I toyed with the notion of ignoring the sound, but it had been a while since Banjo had gone out. Also, I was confident that whatever was going on was happening near Friendly Haven. More trouble there we didn't need.

The backyard tarbaby hadn't moved since that morning, so it was easy work to slip past it. Banjo did his business as soon as we had left the house, and the look of defiance he directed to the creature behind the pine tree made it clear that he wasn't simply relieving himself. He was marking boundaries.

Libby gave a wave to the Robinsons when we reached the street. The elder couple was standing in the middle of the road, staring down toward the retirement center, but choosing to venture no closer. Aside from them, we encountered no more of our neighbors until we reached Friendly Haven.

The intersection of Ichabod Lane and Gun Club Road was a disorienting mix of calm and chaos. Most of the figures present were standing about perfectly still, or plodding very slowly in pursuit of a fresh victim. I counted eighteen fully developed tarbabies before I was interrupted by a car running me down. That at least was the impression I got when screeching tires and a blaring car horn coincided with a sharp impact in my back. As it happens, that impact had come from Libby, who had obligingly shoved me out of the way of the Mathis family's SUV. By the time I figured out which way the car had gone, it was already around the corner and out of view.

From the look of the tire tracks on the road's narrow shoulder, the Mathises had just navigated their car around the enormous coach-style tour bus that was now blocking the south end of Ichabod Lane. Outside of the bus was a congregation of several dozen people, one of whom was screaming and gesticulating like a monkey dancing on a hotplate.

That was Anthony Spectacles, who was arguing with anyone who would listen, but primarily dogging a large woman wearing a dowdy gray suit and shoes so sensible I would trust them to do my taxes. The woman was trying to get people organized, but was having difficulty making herself heard over Anthony's tantrum.

"But why do you have to do this *here*?" screamed Anthony. "People *live* here!"

"We're not here to bother anyone," replied the woman in gray. "We'll be out of your way in no time."

Anthony spotted us and gestured frantically. "Tell them!" he shouted. "Make them go away!"

Libby approached the woman in gray tentatively. "Excuse me," she said, "could you possibly tell us what you all are doing here?"

The woman beamed the broadest, most sincere smile Libby had seen in a long while on the face of someone who wasn't being absorbed by a monster. "Of course, my dear. I'm Sister Teresa, and this," she said, indicating the crowd at large, "is the First Universal Church of the Most Precious Blood."

"That's the church up by the highway, isn't it? Next to the buildings where they store the road salt?"

"That's us!" Turning to Anthony, Sister Teresa added, "We're practically neighbors."

"They're a cult!" fumed Anthony. "They're all here to turn themselves into... into... THOSE!"

Sister Teresa held up a placating hand. "We are here to view the miracle for ourselves," she said. "Each member of the Church is welcome to participate according to the dictates of his or her own conscience."

"Where'd you get the bus?" I asked.

"We chartered it a few days ago. We had been planning to drive down to Manhattan, but when the Lord saw fit to bring his blessings up into our own backyard, He made His intentions clear. So we loaded everyone up and came out here."

"And now you can load everyone back up and leave!" shouted Anthony. His face was red as a beet, and he trembled as he spoke, his hands balled into fists held stiffly at his sides.

The tarbabies at Friendly Haven's entrance appeared to have finally noticed the newcomers. A handful of them were trundling across the parking lot toward the crowd in the street. In response, several of the more intrepid crowd members inched forward to get a better look.

"Wow," said a young man near the back of the bus, wearing a button-down shirt of a shade that I think might be called periwinkle. "They really are beautiful, aren't they?" He stepped up on onto the curb that marked Friendly Haven's perimeter.

"Aw, nuts," I moaned. "You people don't think these things are angels too, do you?"

Sister Teresa graced me with a Sunday-school smile. "From what we've heard, those they touch are cured of disease, freed from care or misery, and transcended to a higher state. As far as we know, they can't die." She took my hand in her own and looked directly into my eyes. "Can you really be certain that they're *not* angels?"

I studied the creatures advancing from the parking lot. "Well... yeah," I managed.

"And why is that?"

Anthony answered for me. "Because they're gross!" he bellowed. "Because if angels did exist, they wouldn't look like something a coal miner coughed up!"

The man in the periwinkle shirt chuckled from his place at the curb. "You need to open your mind to new possibilities, bro." With that, he advanced confidently to intercept the nearest of the tarbabies.

"You knock that off right now!" demanded Anthony.

"It's the only way to be sure," replied the man, as he placed his hands firmly on the head of the nearest creature.

Splut.

Aside from those tarbabies that were already in motion, no one moved. No one spoke. No one breathed. The only sound was the soft *splut, splut* of the creatures' feet on the asphalt.

The man in the periwinkle shirt threw his head back and laughed. "This... is... AWESOME!" he bellowed to the sky.

The crowd behind him laughed in relief, then broke into applause. In twos and threes, they dribbled forward to join their colleague. Banjo was not at all pleased with this movement, and darted through the mob, yapping at random strangers to indicate his displeasure.

"Are you going to do it?" I heard one woman ask of another. "Heck yeah," was the reply. "I'm not sitting out the Rapture."

"I got dibs on the dog," laughed a heavy, middle-aged man as he trotted past.

"I hardly think you need to call dibs," chided Sister Teresa. "The last shall be first and the first shall be last. There will be enough to go around."

"I didn't even know there were dog angels," added a skinny young woman who, I saw with mounting horror, was cradling an infant in her arms.

"Hey, wait a minute," I said, moving to intercept the young woman. I turned to Anthony and Libby for support, but Anthony was no longer there. Libby saw my concern and confronted Sister Teresa.

"Surely you're not going to allow that woman to endanger her baby," whispered Libby.

"I'm not going to *allow* anything," replied Sister Teresa, with just the faintest hint of exasperation encroaching upon her kind smile. "It's not my place to allow or forbid. These people wanted to see the miracle, and I brought them to it." She folded her arms as she watched the crowd continue to advance on Friendly Haven's parking lot. "What they do from here is between them and their Lord."

"But you're endangering *us*," continued Libby, with all the calm she could muster. "These things don't just wait for people to come to them. Once your parishioners have been converted, we're going to have a hundred of these things on our street, looking for whoever is left over."

Sister Teresa sighed, but her smile did not falter. "I am sorry if this is an inconvenience for you," she said, "but as I see it, what's happening here is either a very good thing, or a very bad thing. If it's a good thing, and my heart tells me that it is, then I can hardly feel much regret for bringing the agents of the Lord to your doorstep."

"And if it's a bad thing?" asked Libby.

"Then won't we look foolish!" Sister Teresa laughed at her own words. "And you'll have the satisfaction of being right. But honestly, where is the danger? If you want to avoid these… persons, then you just walk away from them. They're not going to catch a healthy young girl like you."

Libby would have told Sister Teresa about Roscoe Carson, and about Carrie Spiller. She would have told her how these two had been converted against their will, through simple acts of carelessness. But as the thoughts were forming in her head, she was interrupted by a commotion in the crowd.

Anthony Spectacles had returned, and in his hands he held Norman Spiller's lethal pickaxe. Spots of Carrie's blood were still visible on the blade, to anyone who was close enough to look. And several members of the First Universal Church of Redemption were getting a closer look at that blade than they cared for, as Anthony waded into the crowd, swinging the pick in wild, random arcs.

"Get BACK!" he screamed at the crowd. "Get back on your damned bus, and go get yourselves killed somewhere else!" The mob gasped as one wild swipe brushed against a woman's arm. She shrieked and grabbed at her elbow as she scurried out of Anthony's reach.

I snagged Banjo by the collar to prevent him from lunging at Anthony and pushed forward, while still attempting to remain outside the reach of the lethal gardening implement. I held my free hand up in a placating posture and told him, "Come on Anthony, this isn't the way!"

"You're ruining it for everyone!" shouted someone in the crowd, and there was a general murmur of assent.

"Then GO!" he screamed at them. "Go do this someplace where you're wanted! Just leave us ALONE!" He punctuated this last by slamming the pickaxe down into the street. A mouse-sized chunk of pavement flew up and struck a nearby man in the leg.

"You're making a fuss over nothing," said a remarkably calm voice. Fifty heads turned as one to the man in the periwinkle shirt, whose hands were now covered in the inky goop that flowed from his new friend's head. He turned to smile at Anthony. "No kidding, bro. Don't knock it 'til you've tried it."

The crowd laughed. Anthony looked them over in disgust, then turned back to the man in the periwinkle shirt. He pushed his glasses back up the bridge of his nose, then shouldered the pickaxe and strode to the spot where the man was happily embarking on his new career as an abomination.

I followed. "Anthony, think about this. Remember what happened with Carrie…"

Without a word, he let the pick fall from his shoulder. In a single fluid motion, he brought it back up again in a high swipe that ended at the man's head. The pointed end of the tool hit just above his left temple, and its momentum buried it four inches into the man's skull. The man uttered a soft "oh" and his legs wobbled, then collapsed from underneath him. His knees hit the pavement, but with his hands still trapped in the tarbaby's head, his body hung slack from the gelatinous creature's frame. Anthony abandoned his grip on the pickaxe, which jutted from the side of the man's head as a tide of crimson seeped into the periwinkle fabric of his shirt.

For an absurdly long moment, no one moved or spoke. The crowd watched in dumb horror as the black goop retreated from the dead man's hands. With a *splut*, the tarbaby detached itself from the man in the periwinkle shirt, and his body collapsed to the pavement like a rag doll.

The spell was broken. The crowd surged forward like an avalanche, accompanied by shrill cries of "Murderer!" Anthony made a half-hearted attempt to backpedal, but he was exhausted, confused, and not at all certain what he intended to do next. He made no effort to escape the mob that slammed into him, carrying him back into the monster he had just deprived of a victim.

Splut.

Propelled by the momentum of the crowd, Anthony hit the creature high. Standing face to face, the tarbaby would have looked directly over the smaller man's head, but the enthusiasm of the crowd had deposited him high enough that the back of his head hit where the creature's nose should have been. Once he was released, gravity and the thing's natural adhesion struggled briefly for control, before arriving at a temporary truce. Anthony's body sagged against the creature until he came to contact with the ground again, on the very tips of his toes.

Anthony's jaw hung slack as his eyes scanned the crowd. "Holy crap," he said softly. His eyes met mine, and he smiled. "You guys gotta try this!"

The corpse at Anthony's feet lay forgotten by human and tarbaby alike as the mob watched Anthony's absorption with rapt fascination. Seeking to avoid an invitation to participate similar to what Anthony had received, Libby and I slipped silently out of the crowd. As we backed out of their reach, Sister Teresa gave us a chipper wave. "If you change your mind, you'll know where to find us!"

Our instinct for self-preservation told us to keep our eyes on the congregation, which left us oblivious to the monster that was approaching from behind. The First Universal Church of the Most Precious Blood might have lost interest in us, but the thing that used to be Gladys Weaver Hoffspring found us fascinating. Transfixed by the scene in front of us, neither Libby nor I saw the Gladys-Thing coming, still draped in her tattered flannel bathrobe, with both arms raised to her sides as though she were determined to get both of us at once. As we backed away from the bus, puzzling over Sister Teresa's parting words, the jolly woman in gray raised an admonitory finger. She then pointed that finger downward and made a quick circular motion. The meaning of the signal was entirely lost on me, but it prompted Libby to take a glance over her shoulder. She gasped, shoved me to the side, and the two of us spun around either side of the Gladys-Thing, evading her touch by scant inches. Our steps quickened to a run as we hurried up the street, and by the time we looked back over our shoulders, Sister Teresa was lost among the crowd.

We didn't slow down until we passed the Cape Cod at number Twenty-Two, at which point I paused to open the lid on Anthony's mailbox. As we had seen no mail trucks in the last two days, I was not surprised to find it empty.

"Looking for something?" asked Libby.

I shrugged and closed the box. "I was just wondering what his last name was."

The Mathises were nowhere to be seen, but the family SUV was parked more or less in the street in front of their house. Only one tire had made it into the driveway, and three of the car's doors hung open. Vowing to avoid the same mistake we had made with the Spillers, I closed the doors before we left.

The tarbaby on our front stoop was still on duty, so we walked around to the back door. The backyard monster had relocated, and was now standing directly in front of our patio doors. Getting in through the doors meant going past one of them.

"What do we do now?" asked Libby.

I considered the ground floor windows, but they would all be locked from the inside. Even if we got them open, it would be difficult to get the dog through that way. I looked around to confirm Banjo was still with us, and sure enough the dog was at our heels, looking up with his customary look of confusion.

"The old Okey-Doke," I said at last, heading for the garage. Banjo followed and, a moment later, so did Libby.

"The old what?" she asked, as I rooted around among the gardening supplies. "Is that a thing?"

"It's a zombie thing," I said, producing a pair of canvas gloves and a rake. "We get one of them to follow us, then run around the house and come in from the other side." I pulled on the gloves as I stepped out of the garage. "There may be a lot of these things, but they're not getting any faster."

Banjo yapped, then stepped toward the street and threw a doggie tantrum. He barked as ferociously as he could manage, turning circles to punctuate his frustration. The object of his concern was across the street, but it wasn't a monster this time. We watched as Herb Mathis exited the Spiller house, closing the door gingerly behind him. Though he could not have helped but here the dog's barking, he did not look in our direction as he crossed the Spillers' lawn to the street, his head down and his hands in his pockets.

"Herb?" called Libby. He stopped and nodded to us, then continued on his way.

"How's Brandon?" she asked, and Herb stopped again. "Is he in the hospital?"

"We never made it to the hospital," said Herb. "We tried to get to Goshen, or Middletown, but the roads are... all messed up. We even tried crossing the river, but the bridge was a logjam. We didn't know what else to do, so we just... came home."

Libby hesitated, certain she knew the answer, but asked anyway. "So where's Brandon?"

Herb's only reply was to look back to the Spiller house.

Libby tried to ask the question, but couldn't decide what words would be least painful. "Is he still... is he going to...?"

Herb shook his head. "I don't know. It's up to him now." His voice began to quaver. "He's dying. That crap he breathed in is killing him from the inside out. There's no way he's coming back from this."

"Unless..."

"Yeah. Unless." Herb started walking again. As we watched him wander off down the street, I found myself of two minds about what he had done. Inevitably, this was going to result in yet one more monster to deal with. On the other hand, this was his son, and if the choice was between him dying as a man or living forever as one of those things...

Living forever.

I looked to the Spiller house. Banjo was already back on our lawn, and was clearly ready to return to his new home. Libby was also looking to me, uncertain as to what we were waiting for. For my own part, I had no desire to return to my neighbor's house, but I knew I had unfinished business inside.

"One sec," I said. "There's something I need to do." I crossed the lawn and mounted the stairs, with Libby following close behind.

"Something to do? What are we doing?"

Even under these extraordinary circumstances, I was reluctant to open the door to someone else's house without permission. I knocked softly, neither expecting nor receiving a reply. "It's the cat," I explained.

"The cat?" asked Libby, unsure as to when we had gotten a cat.

I left my rake leaning against the door frame, then turned the knob and let the door swing inward. "Hello?" I muttered. "Is anyone home?"

"The cat? The tar cat?" Libby had followed me up the stairs and was now peeking over my shoulder into the house. Banjo had also joined us, though he would come no closer than the bottom of the porch steps. "The thing that stole your pants?"

There were voices coming from the living room, one of which I recognized. The TV was still on, and I could hear Judge Geordi admonishing a young woman for her sub-standard customer service skills. From what I could tell, the case involved hair extensions or nail tips or some such vanities, and the notion that somewhere in the world—indeed, somewhere in our own country—people were still spending their days squabbling over such trivialities left me momentarily disoriented. It was the coughing that brought me back to my senses and reminded me what I had come for.

I stepped inside the house, leaving the door open behind me. Though the light inside was dim, I could see that the thing that used to be Norman Spiller had not yet left his recliner. Brandon Mathis sat on the sofa next to him, swaddled in a heap of colorful quilts and fighting for breath.

"Brandon? How's it going there, buddy?" It was a stupid question, of course, but I felt a powerful need to address him, to confirm that I recognized he was still a human being, and no other words seemed appropriate. "Can I get you anything?"

His only reply was another fit of coughing. Satisfied that Norman was showing no interest in me, I backed out of the room with all the stealth I could muster and tiptoed down the hall to the kitchen.

"What are you doing?" whispered Libby from the doorway, still refusing to enter the house.

"I just need to let the cat out."

Libby wasn't whispering anymore. "Are you out of your mind?" she called. "That thing tried to kill you!"

"It rubbed up against my leg, Pixie. It's what cats do. It's a sign of affection." I had reached the pantry by now, but had still not worked up the nerve to touch the doorknob.

"Yes, these things love you! We've established that! Now leave it alone!"

I took a breath and put my hand on the knob. Though I knew how slowly these things moved, I still had visions of a streak of black lunging for my face the moment I opened the door. "It's in a closet, babe. This thing may live forever, and it's trapped alone in the dark. And I put it there."

"Josh, I really don't know about this..."

"Pixie, what if it's lonely?" I knew that this would be enough to convince her, but I pressed the point anyway. "What if it's afraid?"

I tightened my grip on the doorknob. "I wouldn't leave a real cat trapped in a closet, and I won't leave this thing either."

"Just hurry up," said a quiet voice from the porch.

I turned the knob and jumped backward into the kitchen. I could see a blob of black at the bottom of the pantry, but the light was too dim for me to tell whether it was looking my way or not. Under the circumstances, I felt compelled to say something to it. "Nice kitty" were the only words that came to mind, so that's what I said.

As I turned to leave the kitchen, I spied a familiar logo on one of the pantry's upper shelves. Careful to keep my feet well away from the creature inside, I leaned in and snatched up a brightly colored box before trotting back up the hallway.

There was one last thing that needed to be done. I saw that the remote control was still in its caddy on Norman's chair, and I didn't dare get that close. Instead, I located the cable box and fiddled with the buttons until I had located the channel selectors. It took about fifty clicks to cycle up to the twenty-four hour sports network. They were showing stock-car racing, and I was once again astonished by the normalcy of the moment. Just a few hundred miles away, dozens of men had no greater worries than driving around a circular track for several hours.

"Good enough?" I said to the room, and though he did not have enough breath to answer, Brandon's right hand emerged from his quilted cocoon, and his thumb pointed skyward.

Content that my job here was done, I returned to the porch, retrieved my rake, and closed the door behind me. Libby did not speak, but she did take my hand as we descended the steps.

"What's that?" she asked, noticing the box in my hands. I proudly held up my prize for inspection—a box of limited edition Banana Chocolate Fudge Toaster Pastries. Twenty-four count.

"That's instant karma," I explained, before I was interrupted by an enthusiastic round of yapping from the front lawn.

"Cool it, doggy," I admonished, before I realized Banjo was facing the wrong way. His attention was now fixed on Original Recipe, who had left his post on our front porch and was now lurching across the lawn toward us. "Oh... I mean... good doggy!"

It looked like my Okey Doke maneuver was going to be unnecessary, as the creature had now left us with an opening. When it had taken a half dozen steps we moved, jogging in wide circles around either side of him. We met at the stoop, ten luxurious feet out of the thing's grasp, and ascended the stairs.

The moment she touched the doorknob, Libby knew what she had forgotten. "Did you bring your keys?" she asked.

I jiggled the knob for myself. Libby raised an eyebrow at the unspoken implication that perhaps she just wasn't using the doorknob right.

The tarbaby was not yet on the steps, but it had closed most of the distance. It would only need to raise its arms to block our path.

We could have gotten in by breaking one of the thin glass windows flanking the door, but memories of Big Tobacco squeezing out through the chain link fence told me this would be a bad move. I gripped the rake with firm resolve. "The back door it is."

I descended the stairs at a run and planted the broad end of the rake in the center of Original Recipe's chest. The creature stopped, but although I leaned forward with all my weight, I was unable to budge it backward. Instead, the rake's tines sank slowly into the monster's chest. Within seconds, they had disappeared several inches into the muck of the thing's torso.

I shifted my grip. Instead of pushing the rake into the creature, I shoved the handle out sideways, toward the lawn. The monster pivoted in that direction, and as it lost its already tenuous balance, I squeezed past. Once on the lawn, I gripped the rake again, and attempted to pull the tarbaby away from the porch. I couldn't budge it, but the creature was disoriented enough to allow Libby and Banjo to slip by as well. After a brief and fruitless tug of war, I dropped the rake in frustration. We returned to the backyard, where a replay of our strategy eventually got us back inside, this time at the cost of both my gloves. I managed to hang onto my Toaster Pastries though, so there was that.

When the thing that used to be Gladys finally found our front lawn, we made our decision. Libby called her mother, and we packed our bags.

18

Even with the benefit of hindsight, it's hard to say whether our decision to wait until the next morning to leave was prudent. Traveling at night would have been dangerous, given the tarbabies' tendency to all but disappear in the dark. On the other hand, the delay gave a dozen of the creatures' time to find our house. From the upstairs windows I counted three on the front lawn, another two in the backyard, and no fewer than nine in the street in between our lawn and the Spillers'.

"How much should we bring?" asked Libby, hovering over the suitcase she had opened on our bed. We had spent much of the previous night preparing our "Go-Bags," which contained only the most essential gear. Libby's was a sturdy, well-constructed nylon hiking backpack, boasting a dozen handy pockets and pouches, including dual caddies for water bottles, as well as a waist strap and cross-support braces for ease of carrying. It was brand new, and still smelled of the "do not eat" silica packs that had been scattered at the bottom. I had received it three years before as a promotional gift from a client, and it's possible I would have used it before now if it hadn't featured the logo of the Summer's Mist Feminine Hygiene product line in bright pink embroidery across the back. Libby insisted it was magenta, but I know pink when I see it.

For my own Go-Bag, I selected the same worn canvas duffel that had served as my primary travel bag for the last decade. Where the words "Hudson Valley Community College" had once been visible there was now just a darkening smudge, though it was still possible to pick out "nity Coll" if the light was right. Into this I stuffed a few pairs of socks and underwear, a couple of t-shirts, my toiletry bag, a Swiss Army knife, and a small hatchet that had been in the garage when we bought the house. We don't usually keep bottled water on hand, but we fished half a dozen twenty ounce soda bottles out of the recycling bin and filled them from the tap. Libby had two tucked in her backpack pouches, and I put the rest in my duffel.

We packed whatever food we could comfortably carry. A box of granola bars, my prized Toaster Pastries and some individually-wrapped cracker packages went into the Go-Bags; everything else that wasn't perishable got stuffed into a cardboard box. The dog food went into a plastic trash bag.

"We've only got the two suitcases," I noted in response to Libby's question. "Whatever we can't fit in there is going to have to stay. These guys aren't going to let us make more than one trip."

"These guys, huh?" Libby joined me at the bedroom window. "They've gone from 'those things' to 'these guys' in just two days."

"It's tough to think of them as monsters when you know where they came from." I pointed at a figure in the street. "Look, Gladys still has that damn bathrobe on."

"Hi Gladys!" shouted Libby, waving cheerfully. The thing that had been Gladys did not react.

By the time we finished packing, little had changed. The sun was a bit higher in the sky, and the tarbabies shifted position to find the shade, but they showed no inclination to leave. Original Recipe was still minding its post on the front stoop, and the one at the back door wasn't budging either.

"How are we going to get out?" asked Libby.

"We could try the old Okey-Doke again. Open one of the doors, lure the thing inside, and then slip past it."

Libby shuddered. "I'm not keen on the idea of letting those things run loose in my house. I'd like to think we'll be coming back."

I thought for a moment, then opened up the bedroom window, which overlooked a small section of roof that sloped down toward the front lawn. "We could jump."

"Seriously?"

"It can't be more than a ten foot drop to the ground. And it's just grass."

"What about the dog?" Banjo was standing on his hind legs, with his nose poking out the window, trying to see where I was going. The little dog might have been able to make the jump, or he might have ended up with four broken legs.

"Yeah, OK," I conceded. "So just me then. I'll go out and get the car. Try to get these guys to come after me. Then you and fuzzface can make a break for it."

I crawled out onto the roof, then leaned back in so Libby could hand me the first suitcase. I crab-walked to the side of the house and dropped the bag onto the narrow strip of lawn that separated the house from the garage.

Libby winced at the crunch of the impact. "You're not going to try that with the groceries, I hope."

"Let's strip the bed," I suggested. "We should bring some blankets and pillows with us, anyway."

Libby emptied the linen closet of all of our winter blankets and comforters, plus our meager supply of spare pillows. I dropped them into a pile next to my suitcase, then considered the drop again.

"Do you want the mattress too?"

"Nah," I said. "It won't fit in the car."

"You have a plan?"

"Not much of one." I dropped my Go-Bag over the side of the house, held my breath, and followed after it.

It wasn't a big drop at all really, and I could have made it without injury. But I didn't. I was fine when I hit the ground, but when I stood back up again, my right foot rolled on a pillow. I wobbled and fell, then yelped as a sharp stab of pain shot up my leg.

Libby scrambled out onto the roof. "Are you all right?"

The sudden pain gave me the clarity to see the hundred things we should have packed, but hadn't thought of. "Get some aspirin!" I yelled. "And ibuprofen! Band-aids! Just empty the medicine cabinet! We'll sort it out later." I took a few tentative steps, wincing as I brought my right foot down. When the pain had subsided, I turned toward the garage. On the first step my ankle buckled, and I collapsed face-first onto the grass.

Libby had crawled to the side of the house and was preparing to take the plunge after me when I rolled onto my back. I saw her poised on the roof's edge and held up a hand to stop her. "Get ready, and meet me around back!" I sat up, extended my arms behind me, and scooted backward toward the garage. After a few awkward attempts, I soon found myself able to move nearly as fast as the tarbabies that were now shambling toward me from the front lawn. Libby waited until I was at the garage before ducking back inside.

She had wrestled the other suitcase downstairs when she heard my first scream. It wasn't a scream of pain, nor was it terror. It was a tone she knew well, just at a louder volume than she was used to. This was a scream that indicated the screamer was unable to comprehend how he could be so pitilessly stupid. Libby looked to the front door and immediately spotted my keys hanging from a hook by the light switch.

"Libby!" I screamed for the third time. "Keys!" It was a minor miracle that I realized my mistake before I got into the driver's seat. Instead I was on the ground by the car's rear bumper, trying to gauge the speed with which the monsters on the lawn were advancing. I had thrown open the hatchback, and was about to haul myself into the back when I remembered the keys. At the rate they were moving, I had less than a minute before the creatures would be upon me.

Curiously, not all the monsters were heading my way. The two that had been on the side of the lawn closest to the garage were eagerly shuffling toward me, their upper bodies swaying precariously as they attempted the closest thing they could manage to haste, and one of the shapes in the street was advancing as well. The others all maintained their positions, as though they were consciously trying to keep their distance from one another. I wondered if they were spreading out on purpose, creating some kind of web to maximize their range.

"Heads up!" came the cry from the roof. I looked up just in time to see the ball hit me in the face before careering into the car's open hatch. "Sorry!" yelled Libby. I rubbed my nose in annoyance, but discovered I was not injured. The ball had been a pair of rolled-up socks, into which Libby had stuffed my keys.

I planted my hands against the car's bumper, shoved off, and landed with a flop in the hatchback's cargo area. A quick scramble forward put me in the car's back seat, where I found the sock ball. Feeling marginally less exposed, I checked on the progress of my pursuers. The closest was only a half-dozen paces from the garage. I reached back to close the hatch behind me, but in my current position, I could find nothing to grab hold of. I opted to move forward instead.

My first attempt at climbing into the front seat resulted in a searing pain in my ankle. As green dots swarmed before my eyes, I grabbed the seat in front of me and hissed through my teeth to keep from passing out. Trying to swing my left leg through the cracks between the front seats, I had put too much weight on my injured ankle. Shifting my weight back to my left foot, I tried passing my right leg forward without success. It was a comically tight squeeze, and I could picture all manner of ways I might get myself stuck in the attempt.

With no easy way to get my feet through the gap in the seats, I saw no other option than to go through head first. Hissing a stream of colorful invective under my breath, I peeled the socks from around the keys and crawled forward, hauling my upper body into the front seat. I jammed the key into the ignition and twisted, and the Focus purred to life. Holding down the brake pedal with my left hand, I shifted into Reverse with my right, then quickly grabbed the steering wheel. As I released pressure on the brakes, the car began to roll backward. With my face pressed against the driver's seat, I could not turn my head far enough to see behind me, but my peripheral vision was enough to tell me when I had cleared the garage. The moment I saw daylight, I spun the wheel hard to the right. The Focus cut a sharp circle, carrying it away from the house. A loud crunch told me I had clipped off the passenger side mirror in the maneuver, but at least I was out of the garage.

Splut.

The interior of the car darkened as the lead tarbaby collided with the driver-side door. I had hoped to get the car out of the way before the thing caught up, but at least now there was a pane of glass between me and the monster. I took a moment to rehearse my timing, exhaled slowly, and then put the car into Drive.

Nothing happened. The car lurched a bit, but did not advance as I expected. The weight of the attached tarbaby appeared to be enough to prevent the Focus from rolling forward. On a solid concrete pavement, it might have proven impossible to dislodge the creature, but our driveway was nothing but gravel on dirt. I leaned forward again and pressed down the accelerator pedal. The front tires spun ineffectually for a moment, kicking up gravel into the car's undercarriage. Then all at once they were moving, and moving fast.

I mouthed a silent prayer to the gods of front-wheel drive. Without it, I would have surely careened into the side of the house. Instead, a single jerk of the steering wheel was enough to correct our trajectory, threading the Focus neatly between the house and garage. I jammed down the accelerator once again, then craned my head to the left to check our progress. The moment we cleared the house, I pulled the wheel to the left.

The car thudded, slowed, and then thudded again. I yanked the parking brake, then sat back to see where we had ended up. My goal had been to bring the car as close to the sliding patio doors as possible, and in that I had succeeded. The momentum of the car had been sufficient to knock the Backdoor Monster away from the patio. It was now doubled over, its arms spread out over the hood of the Focus. The Hitchhiker was still affixed to the driver side door, only now it was also pinned to the glass of the patio doors. From her position inside the kitchen, Libby saw the dense black sludge of its body flattened against the glass, as though the world's largest Jelly Baby were peeking in. Over the creature's shoulder she also saw me, frantically signaling for her to come out.

Libby threw up her hands and pantomimed pulling at the door. Clearly, she was not going to be able to slide it open with the creature attached. I thought for less time than I probably should have, then released the parking brake. The car began to roll forward again, smearing the creature against the glass. Libby flicked the lock, and the door slid open.

Banjo was outside like a shot, barking at the car as he looked for a way in. It was a tighter squeeze for Libby, encumbered as she was by our luggage, but she managed to dump her suitcase and the boxes and bags of groceries in the back, then slammed the hatch and ran to the passenger door. Banjo snuck in ahead of her, heading for the driver's seat. I grabbed him by the collar and pulled him into the back with me. "You'll have to drive," I told Libby. "My ankle's hosed."

Libby crawled over the gear shift with far more grace than I had managed and settled into the driver's seat. She applied gentle pressure to the accelerator. The engine purred, but we went nowhere. She pressed harder, and the engine roared. But the Hitchhiker was now wedged between the car and the door frame, and was not budging.

"Try reverse," I suggested. Libby shifted gears and gunned the engine. The car leapt backward, and the patio door exploded into a thousand tiny shards of safety glass.

"Son of a crap!" she screamed, banging her fist against the dashboard.

"Can't do anything about it now, babe."

"But they're going to get into the house!"

"If they want to. But that's a problem for another day. Right now, we've got to go."

Libby paused to offer a very unladylike gesture to the creature stuck on the driver side door, then put the Focus in Drive again. "Are we going to be able to get anywhere with these things on the car?"

"We're going to get crap mileage. What's the gas look like?"

"Half a tank. A little over."

That was six gallons, maybe seven. On the highway, we averaged thirty miles to the gallon. Round that down to twenty-five to account for the extra weight, and that gave us a range of a hundred and fifty miles or more. Albany was eighty miles away. "We'll make it," I concluded. "If we can find gas, we'll fill up. If not... we'll make it."

Getting out to Ichabod Lane turned out to be a navigational challenge. There were two tarbabies in the driveway, one of them centered between the house and garage, blocking our escape route and forcing Libby to stop by the side of the house. I took the opportunity to lean out the passenger side and retrieve my dented suitcase and an armload of blankets and pillows. Banjo immediately claimed the pile of linens as his own.

With the driveway blocked, Libby steered the car out around behind the garage, then drove across the side lawn, where she flattened three ornamental shrubs in an effort to weave around yet another creature we hadn't spotted before. While they had seemed reasonably spread out from the viewpoint of a pedestrian, the car could just barely fit through the gaps between them. Libby pointed the car toward the street, then held her breath until our front tires finally clomped up over the curb. She spun the wheel to the right, and the car swiveled south onto Ichabod Lane.

"No!" I shouted. "Left! Left!"

Libby hit the brakes. "But the thruway's down here."

"So is Friendly Haven, and however many friends of the Precious Blood found religion out there." I leaned forward to peer down the street. "There's no telling how many of those things are down that way now, or whether they ever moved that damned bus."

From every point of the compass, a half dozen tarbabies converged on the Focus. Libby executed a sloppy K-turn, aiming the car north again. As she maneuvered, the creatures on the passenger side advanced steadily, yet those on the driver's side hesitated. As before, only those things that were closest to the car showed any real sense of purpose. Those behind them stayed put, as if politely waiting their turns.

Libby threaded the Focus through the web of creatures with deliberate care. They were more spread out the farther north we went, but enough of them had wandered into the street to keep her cautious.

"Once we make it to Irving, they should have thinned out. There aren't many houses at the intersection there…"

"Do you hear that?" Libby interjected. I quieted, but could only hear engine noise. "Is that us?" Libby added.

It took me a moment to determine what she was talking about, but eventually I heard it. There was a higher pitch to the engine than normal, almost as if it were straining to shift into a higher gear.

"How's the engine temperature?" I asked, leaning in to peek at the dashboard.

"There aren't any lights on." The tachometer needle was resting at a reasonable 2000 rpm, but the revving sound was getting louder.

"Son of a mother!" shouted Libby. I looked up and saw Libby's eyes staring back from the rear view mirror. Without warning, she mashed the accelerator pedal down, throwing me backward in my seat. I turned to look out the rear window, and saw the reason for her panic.

A wall of beige was hurtling toward us, doing better than thirty miles an hour. Based on its size I assumed it was a truck, but there was no windshield, no grill, and no obvious place for a driver to sit. And while it was weaving madly, it was doing a miserable job of avoiding the tarbabies. As we sped forward, I saw the thing hit two of the creatures dead-on, plastering their gooey bulks to its beige front. When it swerved, I caught glimpses of more black shapes clinging to the vehicle's sides.

With the help of our adrenaline-inspired burst of speed, we had nearly cleared the residential portion of Ichabod Lane. Up ahead to our right was the blackened husk of Roscoe Carson's house. On the left was the Robinsons'.

"Ah nuts!" I hollered as I realized what was chasing us. I had seen the ugly thing just about every day for the last five years, but never from the rear. I certainly had never seen it driven at high speed or, for that matter, backward. "It's the bloody RV!"

The bloody RV, the Robinsons' perennially grounded camper, showed no signs of slowing down. On an open road, the Focus could have easily outrun it, but there were too many monsters shambling in the street for Libby to risk it. She judged the distance left to Irving Street against the speed at which the camper was advancing on us, and concluded that she didn't like our chances. When we came to Carson's driveway, she turned the wheel hard. The Focus thumped over the curb, then coasted to a stop on the front lawn.

The Hitchhiker hanging on our driver side door obscured much of the view, but there was no missing the thirty foot recreational vehicle as it lumbered past. As soon as it had passed far enough for the driver to realize we were there, he jammed on the brakes. Twin strips of smoking rubber shrieked from the road's surface, and the RV lurched backward onto the Robinsons' lawn, taking their mailbox with it. The enormous vehicle shuddered to a stop, and through the windshield we could see the shocked faces of the Robinsons gaping at us. Mister Robinson was staring straight ahead, his fingers locked into claws around the steering wheel. Celia was yelling in his direction, but didn't appear to be angry with her husband. Her inaudible tirade seemed to be directed at the tarbaby that was now plastered to the RV's driver-side door, peeking in at them. Only the top of its head could have been visible from her vantage point.

"Should we get out?" asked Libby. "Can we help them?" She climbed across into the passenger seat, but stopped when the RV's horn blared. The Robinsons were shaking their heads theatrically, and waving their hands in a prohibitive gesture. They did not appear to want Libby to be taking any risks. She pointed at them, then made a circle with her thumb and index finger, to ask if they were OK.

Celia nodded and waved a hand dismissively. Her husband gave us a double thumbs-up.

I jerked a thumb back to the south end of the street, then raised my hands palms up, hoping to inquire what was going on at the other end.

Even from this distance, I could see them rolling their eyes. Mister Robinson pointed at the tarbaby at his window, then held up all his fingers, as if counting. Ten, then hands closed. Ten more, then hands closed. Ten more, then hands closed. Celia joined the act, and between the two of them mimed at least two hundred. I was sure they were exaggerating, but the intent was clear. There was no getting out that way.

Libby scooted back into the driver's seat and fastened her seat belt. She turned the car until it was facing the street, then put on her right turn signal. Mister Robinson gave her an expansive "after-you" sweep of his hand, and she pulled out into the street again.

As she made the turn onto Irving, Libby considered the RV in her rear-view mirror. "Jeez. I thought that thing was ugly from the front."

19

Gun Club Road would have been the shortest route to the thruway. We could still get there from Irving, but it meant a detour through the Town of Otterkill. It was a quiet day in town, which is not to say the Otterkillians weren't out enjoying the early summer weather. They were simply enjoying it as shambling mounds of black goo.

The concentration of tarbabies in town wasn't nearly as high as what had amassed around Friendly Haven. Libby still had to weave around the occasional stray shambling monster, but as we were the only vehicle on the road, she had plenty of room to maneuver.

As we passed the four-sided clock outside the combination Town Hall and Library, Libby glanced at her rear-view mirror. "Still no sign of the Robinsons," she said.

I leaned back to look out the rear window. "They might not be coming this way," I suggested. "They could be heading west."

"Celia's got a sister in Atlanta. Maybe they're trying to get there." I marveled at the kind of things my wife managed to commit to memory. I had a difficult enough time keeping track of my own family's whereabouts without worrying about anyone else's.

"Going anywhere near New York would be suicide," I replied. "If they're going south, I hope they do it by way of Pennsylvania."

"Should we try filling up?" A combination gas station/convenience store at the end of town was dark and appeared to be closed for business. They had a pay-at-the-pump system, but I doubted that would be running with the store closed.

"Doesn't look open. We'll probably have better luck on the thruway."

The detour through Otterkill took us five miles out of our way, but the trip was uneventful. I did see a few other human beings, but they were all peeking out from their houses, apparently hoping to wait this thing out. No one was outside, and no one aside from us was attempting to drive. "At least traffic will be light," chimed Libby.

The entrance to the thruway was next to the Highway Department storage depot, which was dominated by a garage full of snow plows and mountains of salt stored up for the winter. The tollbooth was unmanned, but the automatic lane was functioning, and we rolled through.

"I wonder if salt would have any effect on these things," I mused as Libby guided the car onto the northbound on-ramp.

"You mean like with slugs?"

"It might be worth a try. We could just drive into the storage area and…" I fell silent, then banged on the back of Libby's seat. "Stop the car! Stop the car!"

Libby plunged the brake to the floor and the Focus squealed to a halt. I shoved Banjo out of the way, then fumbled for the door latch.

"Where are you going?" asked Libby as I climbed out of the car and unfolded myself onto the pavement of the on-ramp. My ankle did not feel broken, but it still hurt to put any weight on it. A moment later Libby was out of the car and following me up the ramp. Banjo hopped out as well, taking the opportunity to relieve himself on a concrete sound baffle.

With the tarbaby blocking the driver's window Libby had been unable to see the actual thruway. What she saw now was a parking lot. In the northbound lanes, the late morning sun reflected off a sea of red tail lights. Nothing was moving. The southbound lanes were faring a bit better, though all of the cars on that side were heading the wrong way as their drivers picked their way around abandoned vehicles and the occasional tarbaby shambling along the road. In the median ditch separating the lanes were dozens of cars that had tried and failed to navigate the steep incline that would bypass the tangle of traffic congesting the northbound side. Half a mile up, an overturned bus stretched diagonally across both of the northbound lanes. Beyond that, I could see nothing but smoke. It was the same charcoal color I had seen billowing from the monster that Roscoe Carson had ignited.

Amid the chaos, the tarbabies were difficult to spot, but the longer we watched the scene in front of us, the more creatures we discovered. Some were wandering among the stalled traffic, others were scattered along the shoulders or median strip. A good many more were attached to cars, blocking doors and windshields, just as the two on our Focus had done. I made a cursory attempt at counting the things, but gave up when I hit fifty.

There were people on the highway as well—more people than we had seen in one place in many days. Armed National Guardsmen roamed the shoulders of the road, each with a string of tarbabies plodding along behind him like baby ducks. Though every soldier had a rifle slung over his shoulder, none seemed to have found any use for his weapon. Instead, they patrolled back and forth, attempting to assist stranded motorists while simultaneously evading their clumsy but determined pursuers. Two helicopters buzzed overhead, while a third hovered over the site of the disabled bus.

There were civilians everywhere. Many had abandoned their vehicles and were slogging up the highway on foot, carrying whatever they could salvage from their cars. A few determined drivers were still attempting to navigate around the snarl, or hop the median to get into the southbound lanes. And in some cases, people simply sat in their cars and waited. This may have been because they had little other choice. Just twenty yards from where Libby and I stood, a silver BMW was still occupied. A man and woman sat inside, and a child's safety seat was visible in back, though at this distance we couldn't tell if it was occupied.

The car had been flanked on either side by tarbabies. One stood patiently at the driver's door, and another two waited on the passenger side. There were cars both in front of and behind the Beamer, and though the driver likely had enough room to maneuver his way out of the traffic, he could not do so without touching the monsters beside them. And so they waited. On the side of the road, three Guardsmen conferred, evidently trying to come up with a scheme to lure the tarbabies away. They weren't being given much time to think, however, as a half-dozen other creatures converged on their position, requiring them to retreat from the vehicle for fear of making the situation worse.

One of the Guardsmen glanced up at the overpass and saw us looking down on them. He stopped and waved his arms back and forth to indicate we shouldn't come any closer, then pointed back to the toll booth from which we had come. We waved our thanks and returned to the car.

The tarbabies were still glued to the Focus, so we were obliged to enter through the passenger side again. Riding in the front seat gave me a bit more leg room, so I was able to take the shoe off my injured foot and survey the damage to my ankle. It was tender and swollen, but there didn't appear to be any permanent damage. Libby backed the car up the ramp, and we returned to the side roads. On our way out, we paused at the Highway Department storage garage. With a small plastic shovel I found in one of the snowplows, I dumped a few scoops of salt onto the creature stuck to the front of our car. It did not react. I scooped a few more shovel loads, until the thing resembled a giant, man-shaped nonpareil. When it still did not move, we continued on our way.

In the lower Hudson Valley, heading north is relatively easy. If the thruway is unavailable, there are still a half-dozen reliable north-south routes that will take you as far as New Paltz in Ulster County. These are all two-lane local routes, however, and when the roads are peppered with the occasional monster, the going can be slow. It was close to noon by the time we reached New Paltz, which was our next opportunity to try the thruway.

Things were a bit better organized than they had been down in Otterkill. We still couldn't get onto the thruway, but at least we discovered this before going through the toll booths. The National Guard had established a roadblock and were turning away those few cars that were still trying their luck.

A thin young man in fatigues stood beside a concrete barricade. He wore a holstered sidearm, but was not carrying a rifle. Libby pulled the car over, and I rolled down my window. "I guess the thruway's out of commission?" I asked.

"Yeah, it's every flavor of crazy down there," replied the soldier, whose name tag read "Anderson." His insignia was a single chevron over a pair of crossed rifles. I wasn't sure what that meant, but for the sake of argument, let's call him a corporal. "Did you know you've got a giant Sno-Cap Man on your hood?"

"Yeah. You know how salt makes slugs shrivel up? Turns out these things aren't slugs." Behind the toll plaza, thick columns of black smoke rolled up from the highway. "What's with all the smoke?"

Probably-Corporal Anderson looked back toward the road. "Once they figure out they're stuck, a lot of people are trying to fight these things. Most of the time, the most dangerous thing they've got in the car are road flares or butane lighters." He looked up into the darkening sky. "It's a really bad idea. These buggers go up easy enough, but once they're lit, they stay lit. Far as I can tell, they can burn for hours, and it don't seem to bother them."

"Try not to breathe the smoke. A neighbor of ours got really sick that way."

"I'll do my best."

"So, what do you do if one of those things comes after you?"

"Walk away," replied Probably-Corporal Anderson. "We've got standing orders not to engage the Gummies under any circumstances."

"You're calling them Gummies?"

"Last I heard. What do you call them?"

"Tarbabies."

"Ain't that racist?"

"Maybe. We're still not sure."

Through the partially obscured driver's side window, I saw another vehicle approaching. It was a black SUV, big enough for eight passengers. It bore no markings, but the tinted windows gave it an air of authority.

Probably-Corporal Anderson surveyed the two monsters hugging the Focus. "If you're trying to get north, you're going to have to get these things off your car. Greene County is still Gummy-free, far as we know, and they're trying to keep it that way. They won't let you past Kingston if those guys are with you."

The black SUV pulled in front of our car, angled enough so that we could not advance around it. A pie-faced man in his late fifties emerged from the passenger side, wearing the same uniform as Probably-Corporal Anderson. The latter offered a sloppy salute. "Afternoon, Major."

The Major's return salute was crisper than Anderson's but his aim was off. He was inspecting our car critically. "What's going on here, Corporal?" he asked without looking at his fellow soldier.

"Got some folks trying to get north," replied definitely-Corporal Anderson. "I already told them they can't go up the thruway."

"Can't go up any way," said the Major, leaning down to the car's open passenger-side window. "I'm afraid we can't let you go any further with these things on your car."

"I thought we were OK as far as Kingston," I protested. I wasn't sure why it hadn't occurred to me before now, but it really was ludicrous to assume that we would be allowed to transport dangerous creatures into uninfected areas.

"Sorry," said the Major unconvincingly, then addressed Libby. "Ma'am, I need you to pull your car into the Visitors' Center behind you. Do you live near here?"

"No, Sir," said Libby. "We're about fifteen miles back, in Orange County."

"You're in luck. We've set up a refugee center at the state college here. We'll find you a place to stay until you can arrange for transportation home." Spotting Banjo in the backseat, he added, "We'll have a quarantine facility for your dog, as well."

Libby paused, unsure she had heard correctly. "A refugee center? We can't stay here. We need to get to my parents in Albany."

The Major shook his head. "If you can get the swamp monsters off your car, you can go anywhere you like. Until then, we need to impound your vehicle and get you to a secure area." He pointed back to the Visitor Center. "Just pull in here. We'll have a shuttle bus coming by shortly."

The Major returned to his vehicle, but did not get in. Instead, he stood just off the vehicle's bumper, making it clear that we would not be going forward.

"Sorry folks," said Corporal Anderson, who seemed to mean it, "but we'll have to insist."

Libby sighed, then backed the car up and turned into the Visitor Center parking lot. There were already some two dozen vehicles in the lot, each with a tarbaby attached somewhere.

The Visitor Center was a clean building, though sparsely furnished. We made use of the restrooms, then mingled with the rest of the refugees who had already been assembled.

"Been waiting long?" Libby asked a woman with an infant on her lap. The child looked bored, and the mother weary.

"About forty-five minutes," said the mother, sighing. "I'm only five miles from my house. I could almost have walked there by now."

While Libby made new friends, I scanned the tourist posters and brochures scattered around the lobby. The room was dominated by an enormous table, six feet wide and twice as long, the surface of which was covered by a topographic relief map of the Hudson Valley. Around the perimeter of the table was a series of buttons set below small glass windows. Two young girls were circling the table, happily stabbing buttons and giggling at the results.

I pushed the button in front of me, and a foot long line of yellow LED lights lit up in the middle of the table. The window above the button lit up at the same time, explaining that the lights depicted the hiking trail to Gertrude's Nose, a scenic rock formation in the nearby Mohonk preserve. As I was reading the details of the hiking conditions on this trail, a bright white line blazed to life down the middle of the table, spanning its entire length. I looked up and saw that the girls had pressed a button at the corner of the table. The younger of the two had to stand tiptoe to see the results. She laughed, and they ran around the corner to the next button. The bright white line went dark.

I walked to the corner the girls had vacated and pressed the button again. The white line flared up, and a helpful window illuminated to tell me that I was looking at the Long Path. According to the text, the Long Path was a continuous stretch of trails that extended from Fort Lee, New Jersey—right at the base of the George Washington Bridge—all the way up to Albany, a distance of some hundred and forty miles. The severity of the trail had been rated as "variable."

The girls giggled again and pushed another button, but this time just a single light burned—a bright red one near the center of the table. It represented our current location: New Paltz, New York. Only sixty-five miles from Albany.

From outside came the sounds of a large vehicle engine and raised voices. The shuttle bus had arrived, but not without complications. A tarbaby had attached itself to the bus's back bumper and was now being dragged over the asphalt of the parking lot in an attempt to knock it loose. The thing was in an awkward seated position, with its shoulders at bumper level and its body blocking the vehicle's exhaust pipe. The Guardsmen would not be able to run the bus safely until they got the creature off.

I returned to the information counter and picked out a handful of brochures, then found Libby chatting with her new friend. "Can I show you something?"

I handed her a pamphlet that folded out into a map. "What's this?" she asked.

"The Long Path. If I'm reading this right, it passes right by here. And it goes all the way to Albany."

Libby examined the map more closely, not understanding. "You want to go hiking?"

"It may be our best chance at getting out of here."

"Seriously? You want to walk a hundred miles to Albany?"

"It's only about sixty-five from here." I did some crude mental calculations. Four miles an hour, I thought. I was pretty sure that I had heard four miles an hour is what a human being can average on foot. I couldn't remember where I had heard that, but I suspected it involved Tommy Lee Jones somehow. "That's like sixteen hours on foot. We could do that in two days."

Libby looked out the front window. "There's a lot of those things out there..."

"There's a lot of those things where people are. You've been on the Appalachian Trail before. How often do you see people? Once an hour? Less?" It was true. Even on the busiest weekends, New York's hiking trails were sparsely populated. With most of the state hunkered down awaiting rescue, the Long Path was likely to be deserted.

"Do we have enough supplies?"

"We only need to get through one night. I think we can do this. And I definitely like it better than the thought of a refugee camp." I looked at the scene out front. Three tarbabies had entered the Visitor Center parking lot, attracted by the commotion at the bus. The Guardsmen surrounding the vehicle fanned out to keep the creatures from fixating on any one spot. Despite their efforts, one of the monsters appeared to be heading for the Visitor Center. I concluded my sales pitch. "If we don't go now, we may miss our chance."

"Come on," sighed Libby, "there's another exit by the rest rooms."

Leaving by the rear exit was a lucky break. We were closer to the car, farther from the tarbabies out front, and temporarily out of sight of the Guardsmen. The Hitchhiker on our car door had not moved at all, but the one on the hood appeared to have slid down a foot or more, as it slowly sloughed its way to the ground. I opened the hatchback and handed Libby her Go-Bag. I slung my own duffel over my shoulder, then considered the rest of our cargo. "How much should we take?"

"The blankets, definitely. We can't be sure we'll be sleeping indoors."

"How much food can we carry?" Libby spread one of the blankets out on the pavement, then rummaged through the grocery box. Anything dry and light went on the blanket, including boxes of granola bars, cereal and crackers. Whenever possible, she dumped the contents onto the blanket, then tossed the empty boxes back into the car. Anything tinned or that required cooking was left in the box. She folded the corners of the blanket over the center of the pile and tied them together, creating an oversized bindle.

"Can you carry that?" she asked. I slung the pack over my shoulder. It couldn't have weighed more than ten pounds.

"No problem." Libby dumped out most of the dog kibble and wrapped what was left in our other blanket.

"What about the suitcases?"

Libby looked at her bag longingly, but shook her head. "Not for sixty-five miles. We'll have to make do."

I slammed the hatchback shut, then thumbed the lock button on the key fob. I kissed Libby on the forehead, and with Banjo click-clacking behind us, we made our way across the parking lot toward a large wooden information sign. A web of arrows pointed the way to a network of hiking trails. The arrow for the Long Path was turquoise.

None of the Guardsmen noticed our departure. A loose group of a half-dozen tarbabies had circled the bus and were resisting the soldiers' attempts to lure them away. From the direction of the thruway, I could see at least another ten creatures slogging their clumsy way toward us. A Humvee was trying to navigate its way around this crowd without much success.

We headed in the direction indicated by the turquoise arrow. Ten minutes later, we were on the Long Path, and all alone.

20

"This is nice. I'm so glad we thought to try this." This was the closest I could get to bragging with Libby around. She had a low tolerance for any kind of self-aggrandizement, so I usually avoided taking credit for my best ideas. If I was going to pat myself on the back, the easiest way would be to imply that this was as much Libby's idea as my own.

If she was going to get credit for someone else's idea, this was a nice one to get saddled with. The trail was gorgeous, flanked on both sides by giant poplars and beech trees, all sporting a healthy crop of spring foliage. They provided a consistent shade in the lower elevations, making the weather at the forest floor ideal. The temperature was in the low 70s, and in the direct sunlight it could have gotten unpleasant after too much exertion, but after an hour of hiking we still felt vital and refreshed.

Banjo was having the time of his life. The Spillers never walked him, so he was making the most of this opportunity to broaden his horizons. For every step Libby and I took, Banjo took forty. On the straight paths he would bound ahead of us, then stop at the next bend in the trail and run back, tail thumping and tongue lolling. He chased every chipmunk that poked its curious head out of the underbrush, and caught none of them. And if there was an occasion to pee, he took it. It was the first time in all the years that we had known him that the dog had appeared unreservedly happy.

Navigating was easy, too. The brochures I had snagged at the Visitor Center told us the Long Path was maintained by the New York-New Jersey Trail Conference, and they did an admirable job. The trees that had fallen during the winter had been cleared out, and the aquamarine swatches that marked the path every hundred feet or so had been recently repainted.

We had broken into the food already. Nothing extravagant, just some crackers and peanut butter so far. Banjo got a share as well. As long as we didn't go overboard, I was confident our little cache could last us two days.

I was less optimistic about our water. We each had three twenty-ounce bottles, which seemed like it should be enough to get us through that day. We hadn't figured on the dog, though. Banjo was exerting a lot of energy and building up an impressive thirst. The first time I opened a bottle to take a swig, Banjo looked up at me expectantly, his tongue hanging out the side of his mouth like a dead worm. I dug the measuring scoop out of the kibble bag and filled it with water. Banjo slurped greedily, emptying the scoop and looking up for more. By the time he was satisfied, the bottle was almost empty.

Still, there was little cause for alarm. We were heading into the mountains, and even this late in the season I knew the winter snows at the higher elevations would still be melting. We would find water when we got a little higher up. I was looking forward to the climb, as I expected the views to be spectacular.

What I didn't realize yet is that, once you start going uphill, you never stop. The Long Path doesn't skirt the Catskills, it goes smack dab through the heart of them. Mountains in this portion of the range peaked at around 3,500 feet—two-thirds of a mile—most of which was scaled an inch or two at a step. Reaching a summit could require traversing four to five miles of horizontal travel, punctuated by the occasional escarpment of bare rock, which had to be clambered over using both hands and feet.

And then there were the false summits—rocky outcrops that offered both breathtaking panoramas of the valley below and false hope. Moving off of one of these photo spots inevitably started us heading downhill, and gave us confidence that the next few miles would be easy ones. Then we would turn a bend and find another, steeper rise ahead of us.

For two hours, uphill followed uphill. And the higher we went, the more shade we lost. The day was still not a hot one, but the sun beat down continuously on the rocks we were climbing over, and we started to sweat.

By four o'clock, my water bottles were empty. Libby still had a full bottle left, but I refused to dip into her supply. Banjo did not share my sense of chivalry, and soon the full bottle became half a bottle.

"There's going to be water up here, right?" I asked, scraping a handful of damp hair off my forehead.

"There's got to be a stream or something somewhere," replied Libby. "Just look at all the greenery up here. There'll be water."

But there was no water. Not on this pile of rock, anyway. Then the downhill began. We had assumed the downhill portions would be easier than the uphill, and to a certain extent we were right. It required marginally less effort to go downslope, but if it was less strenuous, it was no less painful. The trail was littered with debris, from gravel to leaves and pine needles, and even the occasional remnants of last season's acorns. When we were going uphill, the footing seemed secure. On the downslope, it felt treacherous, as if advancing too fast would send us sliding down the rocky trail. And the rock outcrops that had to be scaled on the way up had to be jumped on the way down. Each drop was only a few feet, but the impacts tortured our already weary feet and shins. We proceeded with caution, and our legs ached.

The trail was finally leveling off again when I first noticed my fingers tingling. I adjusted my pack, thinking that the shoulder strap might be cutting off circulation in my arms. It was then that I felt the muscle cramps in my shoulders. I had grown accustomed to the stiffness in my legs already, which made any other pains in my body seem negligible.

"I think I'm going to have to lighten my pack," I told Libby. "It's... uh... it's cutting off..." She looked back in concern as I trailed off. "I think my hands are falling asleep."

Libby stopped me and held a hand to my forehead. "You're not sweating."

"That's good."

"No, that's bad. You're dehydrated." Libby dug her last water bottle out of her pack. It was less than a quarter full. "Drink this. Right now."

I drank. My throat had dried up, and the water choked me as it went down. I coughed, then took another sip. The bottle contained less than an inch of water when I handed it back to Libby. "We should have brought our bikes."

Libby started walking again. "They wouldn't fit in the car. Besides, what would we do with Banjo?"

We plodded on for a moment in silence. "Where is he, anyway?"

Libby stopped again. "Huh?"

"Where's Banjo?" We were on a reasonably level stretch of path now, but it was heavily wooded. With all the bends in the trail, we couldn't see more than fifty yards ahead or behind at any time. The dog was not on the path with us.

"When was the last time you saw him?" asked Libby. I had no idea. The constant walking, combined with fatigue, had robbed me of any sense of time. I knew the dog had been with us on the last downhill section, since I had almost tripped over him more than once. For the last hour, it hadn't occurred to me to look for the animal.

"Banjo!" I shouted, or tried to shout. It came out a hoarse croak, which devolved into a coughing fit. Libby dug out the water bottle again, but I waved it off. "Should we go find him?"

"No," said Libby. "Let's find some water first. He's a dog. We're the only ones out here. He can find us if he wants to." We set off again at a listless pace, and for a long time neither of us spoke.

We found the cistern an hour later. Beyond an overgrown access road we discovered the ruins of what appeared to be an old farm. The foundation of one building was almost entirely intact, revealing posts for a dozen smaller compartments. Libby guessed they were milking stalls, and that this may have been a dairy farm back in the nineteenth or early twentieth century. But of far greater interest than the buildings was the cistern. It was an enormous stone circle, perhaps twenty feet in diameter that resembled a well for a race of giants. The rim was as high as Libby's waist, and when we peered over the lip, we could see that there was indeed water down there, and plenty of it. It was a good ten feet down though, and in the early evening gloom, it was as black as tar.

"Can we get down to it?" I wondered. There were no indications of access points in the stone walls—no iron rungs or pulleys for buckets. Just a circle of stone holding a swimming pools worth of water.

"Do we want to?" responded Libby. "Does that stuff look drinkable to you?"

"Right now, to be honest, yes it does." As our eyes adjusted to the gloom, more details appeared. Here and there branches protruded up from the water's surface, the remains of tree limbs that had fallen from the canopy above over the last century. And there was something on those branches. Something small and round.

"Did you bring a flashlight?" asked Libby, though she knew I had. I have something of a fetish for flashlights, and am rarely caught without some kind of light source on my person, even if only an LED pen light on my key chain. I dumped my Go-Bag on the ground, grateful for the opportunity to have its weight off my aching shoulder, and rummaged inside until I found two oblong plastic objects that bore no small resemblance to phasers. Pulling a tab on one of them released a small hand crank. I wound the crank furiously for about thirty seconds, then folded up the tab and handed the unit to Libby.

"No batteries required," I said, wearing my favorite I-did-something-clever grin. Libby thumbed the button on top, and three bright white LEDs blazed to life. She pointed the beam into the cistern, and after a moment she was able to figure out what was looking back at her.

"Turtles," she said. I trained my own flashlight beam down into the water and confirmed that not only were there turtles, there were a *lot* of turtles. At least half a dozen slid off the branches they had been occupying to escape the harsh light of the LEDs. We counted no fewer than twenty more, plus a handful of bullfrogs, before turning off our flashlights again. "Lots and lots of turtles."

"Yeah, I don't want to drink that," I conceded, mostly because I couldn't figure out a safe way to get down to the water anyway. "Still, if they built a farm here, there must be a water source somewhere."

We surveyed the surrounding area, trying to determine the most likely direction water might come from. But the farm had been built in a kind of natural depression. The ground sloped upward on three sides, none of which looked particularly promising.

I sighed, and Libby shushed me. She closed her eyes and swiveled her head back and forth while keeping her body motionless. I closed my eyes as well and tried to hone in on whatever she was listening for. I heard nothing but the leaves rustling overhead, and the occasional chirrup of a frog.

"Do you hear something?" I asked, and was enthusiastically shushed once again. Libby took half a dozen steps away from the cistern, then stopped again and opened her eyes.

"Maybe," she said at last, and began climbing the slope in front of her. The path she had chosen was not a marked trail, and the underbrush was thick. She climbed carefully, relying on the surrounding trees for support. I followed as best I could, but my height proved a disadvantage, as I had to stoop to avoid low-hanging branches.

Several minutes later, Libby let out a squeal of delight. "Found it!" she shouted, as I lagged behind some fifty feet downslope. I scrambled to catch up with her, invigorated by her triumph.

"Where?" I said, once I realized I had no idea what it was she had found.

"Right there," she said, pointing to a dark patch on the ground in front of us. I stared, not comprehending what my wife was trying to show me. With a sigh, Libby walked forward, stood over the dark patch, and pointed straight down. "Right there. On the ground. Where I'm pointing. With my finger."

I advanced hesitantly, suspecting this might be a sadistic prank. It wasn't until I was on top of the dark patch that I saw what she was pointing at. The patch was indeed water—a thin puddle perhaps a quarter inch deep, extending a length of some three feet. It was really more wet dirt than the river I had been hoping for.

"I'm don't know how to drink that," I began, and was shushed for a third time. Libby was listening again, only this time I could hear something too. I closed my eyes to confirm it. A very faint trickling sound was coming from our right. When I opened my eyes again, Libby was already heading toward it.

We found the stream behind a group of small boulders. It was tiny, no more than six inches across at its widest spots, and we could only see about twenty feet from the point where it emerged from beneath the rocks to where it disappeared again. But it was bubbling merrily, it was wet, and although the dimming early evening light made it difficult to tell for sure, it looked clean.

I uncapped one of my empty water bottles and knelt beside the tricking stream. The rivulet was extremely shallow, and it was difficult to find an angle that would allow much water into the bottle. Eventually, I succeeded in trapping a few inches of liquid, which I scrutinized with the aid of a flashlight.

"What do you think?" asked Libby.

"It's pretty clear." The water had just a hint of brown cloudiness to it, like a coffee cup that has been rinsed but not washed. I swirled it around, checking for sediment, then took a sip. The water was cool and felt exquisite against my dry lips and tongue, but it had a distinct earthy flavor to it. I spit out the water and ran my tongue over the roof of my mouth. It felt slick, as though I had been drinking canola oil.

"There may be some algae in there," I concluded. "But we're hardly spoiled for choices." I drank again, draining the contents of the bottle in a single swallow. When I failed to die I repeated the process, coaxing another four or five ounces into the bottle at a time. After a dozen repetitions, my hands finally stopped trembling. To compensate, my head was beginning to ache.

"Do you want to go on?" asked Libby, checking her watch. It was past eight. The sun had set behind the mountains, and the residual light wouldn't last long. "Or should we call it a day?"

We opted to camp at the ruins of the farm that night. None of the buildings had a roof, but it still provided a semblance of civilization. We dined on toaster pastries and crackers, then stashed our remaining food on top of the highest wall that was still standing, then built a nest. The sky was crystal clear, and though the day had been warm, we knew temperatures would plummet overnight. Neither of us had thought to pack matches, so a fire was out of the question. Instead, we emptied our Go-Bags and put on every piece of clothing we could find. We each donned triple layers of socks, as well as several extra shirts, then pulled up the hoods on our sweatshirts and cinched the drawstrings tight. Libby curled into a ball, and I wrapped myself around her, pulling both the blankets tight around my body.

"How long did we walk today?" I asked, fatigue slurring my words.

"Something like seven hours."

I yawned. "So figure we've gone twenty-five miles? Maybe thirty?"

"Mm." Libby wished she had thought to grab the portable GPS unit from the car. She wished she had thought of a lot of things, but she had not anticipated that our two hour drive would turn into a multi-day hike.

"If we start at dawn," I continued, "we should be able to make Albany by sundown."

"Go to sleep, baby. You need your strength." Under the blankets, half a dozen layers of clothing and her husband's arms, Libby shivered. She knew as well as I did that we hadn't been averaging the four miles an hour I had been counting on. During the uphill stretches, it was unlikely we were managing even one. And we certainly weren't headed in a straight line toward Albany. Even if we had walked as much as twenty miles that day, we might only be fifteen miles closer to our target. Maybe even as little as twelve.

I pulled my head further under the blankets. Tomorrow, we would need to find some landmarks.

21

In my dream, I was smothering. I was inside the tarbaby, enveloped irretrievably in its inky blackness, and could not breathe. I was drowning in sticky darkness, unable to move. But while my rational mind declared that my attacker was sticky, another part of my brain insisted that it was wet and slippery, and smelled powerfully of bacon.

The tarbaby licked my face, and I knew that wasn't right. I opened my eyes, and was surprised to see that the sun was still setting. This was good, because I desperately needed sleep, but I had a vague recollection that the sun had already set when we had gone to bed. I also had the notion that we were currently facing east, which is quite literally the last place the sun should be setting. Also, the tarbaby was licking my face again.

Banjo yapped his joy at the sight of us regaining consciousness, then ran back to the pile of kibble at the base of the wall to continue gorging himself. Lesson learned. The top of a seven foot brick wall is not a secure place to store food in the wilderness. Libby wrestled a hand free from the blankets she was swaddled in and checked the time. She was surprised to discover it was past six, and startled at how cold the air felt. She soon realized that the air wasn't the problem. In fact, it had been stifling under the blankets.

Libby pulled back the covers. One glance at me explained why our little nest had been so hot. I was curled up tight, my arms clutched to my chest, and sweating profusely. The hood of my sweatshirt was damp, and the skin of my face was warm and wet.

She pulled the hood off my head and shook me. "Baby? Wake up, baby!"

"Hnmh? Wzzat?"

"Baby, you're sweating. We can't let you get dehydrated again." Libby unzipped my sweatshirt and began pulling it off of me. I pulled my arms tighter across my chest.

"Sick," I replied, grimacing. "Gda slp."

Banjo came to the rescue. He thrust his snout into the cowl of my hoodie and licked the sweat off my face with the joy of one who is doing exactly what he was born to do. I tried to shoo the animal away, but my enthusiasm was no match for the dogs. With a wince, I sat up and blinked my way back to consciousness.

"I feel awful," I said, and Libby saw nothing in my face to contradict that.

"We need to get you some more water. You ready to walk?"

I rose slowly to my feet, but did not stand fully upright. I remained hunched, with my arms crossed over my abdomen. "Stomach's cramping," I mumbled.

"Do you think you can eat something?" I shook my head, but Libby handed me a cracker anyway. I nibbled at it obediently, but found myself unable to swallow. I offered the rest to Banjo, who sniffed it with suspicion, but gobbled it down nonetheless.

In the daylight we discovered the stream was not nearly as far as it had seemed last night. It still took us the better part of ten minutes to reach it, as I shuffled along many yards behind Libby, unable to even lift my head fully. This was not going to be a day for making good time.

When we at last reached the stream, I sat down heavily on a small boulder while Libby filled a bottle. Banjo splashed into the middle of the stream and began lapping it up. In the daylight, the water looked murkier than it had the night before, but it was all we had, and Banjo drank greedily, oblivious to my stomach cramps. I accepted the bottle from Libby gratefully, though I could only manage small sips. I finished off half of the contents, then bathed my face with the rest. Only then did I realize that Libby wasn't drinking.

"You're not going to try it?"

"In a bit," she replied as she filled our other bottles.

"Waiting to see if I drop dead?"

"Of course not. I'm waiting to see if you puke."

I dried my face on the sleeve of my sweatshirt. "So far so good," I said, just before doubling over and vomiting on my shoes. My stomach continued to spasm even after emptying its contents, and I curled up on my side until it subsided. Libby handed me another water bottle, which I used to rinse and spit.

"Are you going to be able to walk?"

"Not much choice," I groaned as I struggled to a sitting position. "How far do you think it is?"

"Last night, you seemed to think we were halfway there."

I tried another sip from the bottle. Though the water was thick and oily, it still felt cool on my raw throat. "Did you believe me?"

"Not so much."

"Smart girl." I rose to my feet, then sat back down again, my vision swimming. I tried it again, more slowly this time, and managed to stand upright without fainting. "Still, we can't make any money here."

Though the slope of our path was nowhere near as steep as what we had encountered the day before, our progress was still glacially slow. The stream followed our path, even crossing it in several places, and Libby periodically sampled it to see if it was getting any clearer as we went further upstream. It wasn't. In fact, it seemed to be getting shallower the higher up we went, as well as wider, frequently spreading out over the trail until it was little more than a stagnant puddle. Every few minutes, I risked another tiny sip, and to my relief I seemed to be holding it down.

By the time the sun was overhead, the trail had plateaued. There were still periodic ups and downs, but we had not needed to use our hands to climb all morning. Instead, we now found our progress being slowed by the very thing we had been desperate for the day before—water. The stream we were following became no deeper, but was instead spreading out, making the ground spongy and marsh-like in places. The trail soon became so damp that the mud squelched beneath our shoes, and the footing became precarious. Wherever possible, we picked our way across exposed rocks to avoid the mud. When the stepping stones ran out, we risked leaving the path to find more secure footing off-trail.

Just before mid-day, these dry spots ran out, and we found ourselves slogging through ankle-deep mud. On either side of the path lay an expansive bog of brackish standing water, coated with a thick film of algae. I watched as a plump bullfrog gave a lazy kick with its back legs and plopped heavily into the marsh, leaving a frog-shaped hole in the algae. I stared at the water, then looked back at the direction we had come from. Although the trail was comparatively level, it was clear that we had been gaining in elevation since that morning.

"Oh, gross," I muttered.

Uncertain as to whether the comment was directed to her, Libby glanced back. "What's wrong?"

"I think this skunk water is what I've been drinking."

"What? No. That stream was miles away."

"Miles downhill. I think all the mud we've been sloshing through is run-off from this swamp. I think that stream is just more of the same."

Libby hopped onto a fallen tree to avoid a particularly deep puddle. The nearest dry patch was more than two yards away. "But when it goes underground, it's going to get filtered, right?"

"By what?"

Banjo did not scruple with such niceties as stepping stones, tromping instead down the middle of the sodden path. A thick layer of mud coated his feet and underbelly, but he did not seem to recognize this as a problem.

"By... I don't know, the dirt. The earth." Libby jumped from the tree and almost cleared the puddle. Her left foot splashed down into the water, and slipped out from under her. She hopped forward with the right to compensate, and landed neatly on the path again. "I'm sure the ground filters out anything that's living in the swamp."

"And who knows what it picks up on the way?" I was trying to follow Libby's route across the flooded path, but was having trouble finding a safe perch on the fallen tree. I grabbed at an overhead branch for additional support. "The water I drank has probably been through every earthworm, slug and toadstool on this side of the mountain."

The fallen tree snapped while I was preparing to jump. I was still standing when I hit the ground, but my feet slipped with the impact. I grabbed a low hanging branch from another nearby tree, but that only served to swivel me sideways, sending me splashing off the path entirely. When I finally gave up on trying to keep my balance, my fall was slow and reasonably controlled, if lacking in grace. I sat down gently in water that came up to my armpits.

"This was my idea, wasn't it?" I asked as I struggled to regain my footing. Libby walked back and offered her hand.

"Look on the bright side," she said as pulled on my arm, "the scenery's got to be more interesting than the SUNY gymnasium."

I managed to get my feet underneath me, but had difficulty standing. My duffel was dragging in the water and appeared to be caught on something. I tugged tentatively and confirmed that it was moving. I pulled harder, anticipating the sound of tearing stitches, but the bag held. It was just heavier than it should have been.

"This thing must be waterlogged," I said. "It feels like its twenty pounds heavier…"

"Drop it!" shrieked Libby as she let go of my hand. When I looked to see what was wrong, she had already retreated several yards up the path. I scanned the area, trying to see what had upset her, but she seemed to be pointing directly at me. "Drop it!" she screamed again, wagging her finger for emphasis. Banjo had returned to the water's edge, with his hackles raised and his teeth bared.

Still uncertain as to what was causing their panic, I slipped the bag's strap over my head. Moving with exaggerated caution, I held the satchel out at arm's length. At that distance, the added weight of the bag was immediately apparent, even if the source of the extra mass was not. It was only when I rotated the bag on its strap that the black glob attached to the side came into view.

The thing did not have a readily discernible form. It was vaguely comma-shaped, with most of its volume concentrated in a blob the size of a loaf of bread. It was this mass that had affixed itself to my duffel. From there dangled a single appendage, a thick tail of some sort that swayed from side to side.

"Drop it!" Libby repeated. "Throw it back!" I was tempted, but the Go-Bag held all that was left of my rapidly dwindling possessions, and I didn't want to risk losing it. I also found myself curious as to what this new creature could be.

"What the hell is this thing?" I asked, swiveling the bag back and forth on its strap to view the creature from all sides.

"It's a tarbaby, and it's disgusting, and it's going to kill us!" insisted Libby. "Now throw it back!"

I gently lowered the bag to the ground. The long, tail-like section landed on the trail with a sound like a wet towel. Laid out at its full length, it resembled a giant tadpole. I was beginning to wonder if the creature had been some kind of fish, when I noticed the ears—or at least what I presumed to be ears. Two thin flap-like appendages were sticking out from the top of the creature's primary mass.

"I think it's got ears!" I called to Libby as she and Banjo continued their slow retreat up the path. "Or maybe gills. They kind of look like... ACK!"

The movement had been small and slow, but my nerves were frayed to the point that overreaction was inevitable. While I was examining the appendages, the creature had extended its ear-gills toward me. They now stood out from the thing's body on thin, twig-like stems some four inches long. As they reached for my face, I could see the delicate webbed membrane flexing across it. Immediately my perspective reversed, and I at last knew what I was looking at.

"Oh gross. It's a duck."

"A duck?" asked Libby.

"Yeah, we were looking at it upside-down. That's not a tail, it's his neck." As if confirming this, the Duck-Thing curled its head up off the ground. If it had eyes, it would have been staring directly at my face across its overturned belly.

Libby, who had always been fond of ducks, sidled up behind me to get a better look, though Banjo chose to stay put. "Poor thing," she said. "I wonder how it got… like that."

"That's a good question," I replied, scanning the surrounding marsh with a new sense of trepidation. Up until now, our primary concern had been human-sized tarbabies. Nothing as big as a man would be able to sneak up on us easily in all of this brush. But if animals could be changed, the woods might be full of a thousand unseen dangers. There might be an army of tar-birds, squirrels or chipmunks waiting for us in the forest shadows. "Oh, crap!" I added, after a reflective pause.

"What?"

"The skunk water! If this thing has been floating around in this pond, who knows how much of that sludge has been absorbed into the water? What if it was in the water I drank?" I gagged at the thought.

"Calm down babe. It's nothing to get worked up over."

"I've been drinking this monster's bath water!" I collapsed onto my hands and knees and began coughing over the trail, trying to expel the water in my belly without success.

Libby knelt beside me and stroked my hair. When that failed to calm me, she clipped me on the ear instead.

"Ow! Quit it!"

"Quit it yourself! OK, so you drank monster juice. We're just going to have to deal with it!"

"I am dealing with it!" I insisted as I attempted to retch once again. "I've got that muck inside me! It may be turning me into one of those things from the inside out!"

"It's not!" shouted Libby, as she hauled me to my feet.

"How do you know?"

"Because if you were turning into one of them, you wouldn't be such a baby about it!"

I took a deep breath, ready to shout back my reply. After a few moments, I exhaled again. She was right. Everyone we had seen transformed before now had appeared entirely unafraid, and reported feeling magnificent. It seemed unlikely that I could be turning if I still felt this wretched.

I sat back down on the trail. Banjo walked to my side and shook himself vigorously, flicking his coat of mud all over my right side. "I've still got an upset tummy."

"I know you do baby."

"So you shouldn't yell at me."

"I like yelling at you."

"And you definitely shouldn't hit me."

"We'll see. Now come on. I think that thing is figuring out how to walk."

The Duck-Thing had rolled over and seemed to be finding its feet. This was no easy trick. The spindly duck legs were not well suited to a body made of a uniformly dense bag of gelatinous goo. The creature listed from side to side unsteadily, before finally planting its head on the trail to steady itself. The resulting tripod wobbled precariously, and I took its hesitation as an opportunity to retrieve my bag. It was still heavier than it should have been, and a quick look inside confirmed that most of my clothes had been soaked in the fall. Our food bundle was likewise soggy, though we didn't have time to take an inventory.

"Come on," said Libby. "Let's get away from that thing." We resumed our trek up the path, leaving the Duck-Thing behind to figure out how its peculiar feet worked.

Just before we left it out of sight, the creature whipped its head forward, hitting the trail with a sharp *splut*. The thing paused like this for a moment, then quickly padded forward on its inadequate feet to catch up to its extended head. It was still for a few seconds, then slapped its head forward again, and padded forward to catch up. It was a woefully inelegant form of locomotion, with each undulation carrying it barely half a foot, but it was movement.

Splut.

Pad pad pad pad.

Splut.

Pad pad pad pad.

The chase was on.

22

"It's still behind us."

I nodded, pausing to wipe sweat out of my eyes before lifting my head to confirm what I already knew. Libby was right; the Duck-Thing was indeed plodding along the trail after us, its regular tedious pace hampered even further by its need to hop awkwardly over the stray tree branches and boulders that littered the path. It was easily the funniest thing that had ever tried to kill me.

"Can you go on?" asked Libby. She had been trying to let me rest as much as possible, but the Duck-Thing's proximity was disturbing. If this ridiculous little creature had managed to catch up to us with its clumsy hops and stumbles, there would be little hope when something a bit more graceful found us.

With Libby's help, I managed to rise from my haunches, though my knotted stomach still wouldn't allow me to straighten up fully. "I can try," I replied, dragging a stray lock of hair off of my sweat-soaked forehead, "but I really need to lie down."

"Soon, babe. I promise."

Over the course of more than three hundred miles, hikers on the Long Path are treated to a jaw-dropping variety of scenery. Starting off with views of Manhattan, the Long Path runs first along the shores of the Hudson River, which has been favorably compared to the Rhine in terms of both beauty and majesty. Some forty miles later, the Path turns inland, crossing through three separate state parks before terminating at Thacher Park in Albany. In the Shawangunk Mountain range, hikers can see into four separate states, and are treated to breathtaking views of white stone cliffs and some of the most stunning waterfalls in the northeast.

Regrettably, we weren't on that part of the Path. At the moment, we were in the thick of the Catskill Forest Preserve. Spanning three hundred thousand acres spread across four counties, the Preserve boasts scores of attractions and hundreds of scenic overlooks. It also features thousands upon thousands of acres comprised of nothing but rocks and trees and, on this occasion, us. Though we were ostensibly climbing a mountain at the moment, the canopy was thick enough that we could see nothing beyond a couple dozen yards before and behind us, and trees to either side. It was impossible to tell exactly where we were, or how far we were from the summit.

"Criminy Christmas," I wheezed. "Have these people never heard of downhill?"

One of the perils of being unable to pinpoint your location is the number of false summits you come across. On more than a dozen occasions that day, we had clambered upward onto a reasonably level section of path, convinced that we had finally arrived at the crest of the mountain, and it would all be downhill from there. And on more than a dozen occasions, I had lifted my head to find the path was still sloping upward.

The stretch we were on now was particularly daunting. It wasn't even fair to call it a path at this point, as the next bit was almost entirely vertical. The climb wasn't huge, barely fifteen feet, but it would definitely require using our hands. In my current condition, those fifteen feet would be exhausting.

Libby waited at the base of the outcrop, watching the path for any sign of the Duck-Thing as I began my ascent. My climb was awkward, as my stomach cramps kept me doubled over in a tight crouch. To compensate, I climbed backward, sitting whenever I could and scooting upward a couple of inches at a time. Several rocks were covered in moss, so I took extra time to make sure of my footing whenever I needed to shift my weight. Toward the top, I was able to grab hold of a small sapling growing out of the side of the hill, throw a leg over the top, and roll to solid ground.

Once I was confident I wasn't going to roll back down again, I peeked over the side to see if Libby needed a hand up. This turned out to be a mistake, as Banjo had chosen this moment to make his own ascent. He crested the outcrop at a single bound and thumped me square in the mouth with his head as he alighted over the top. He yapped his indignation and shook himself out as Libby clambered up, taking a seat on the rocks, with her legs dangling over the edge.

I moaned, more out of despair at seeing how easily the dog had managed the slope than from any real pain. To give Libby more room I rolled onto my other side. This prompted another moan, once I had time to take in the steep upward slope that now lay before us.

"You OK, babe?" asked Libby, taking another scan for the Duck-Thing.

"Uphill. It's always uphill. How can it always be uphill? Hills can't go up forever, can they?"

"How's your stomach?"

"Disgusting. Something nasty is going to happen soon, and I haven't decided what end it's coming out."

Satisfied that our pursuer was nowhere to be seen, Libby consulted her watch, and glanced briefly at the sky. What she could see was a deep blue—not quite indigo yet, but that was just minutes away. The moon wasn't visible yet, and the shadows from the surrounding trees were long and dark. Libby pulled a tattered map from her back pocket and tried to gauge our position.

"Well," she announced, "I've got good news and bad news."

"I could go for some bad news. The day's been going far too well so far."

"That's it for today," she continued. "It's going to be dark soon, and as narrow as these paths are, it's going to be too dangerous to try to walk much further."

"Dangerous. Don't want that."

"I really don't know if we're going to find a better place to stop for the night."

"So what's the good news?"

"Pretty much the same thing. We're done. You get to rest."

"I like the sound of that. What about the Devil Duck?"

"I don't see him. And to be honest, I don't know if he'd be able to make it up that last rise."

"He's a tenacious little sod. He'll find a way." I sat up and shrugged off my Go-Bag. Sweat had soaked through my t-shirt, plastering the canvas of the bag to my back. I peeled it loose with a grimace, then dug out my sweatshirt. With no clouds in the sky, the night was going to get cold very quickly. "At this point, I'm not even sure if that would be a bad thing."

Banjo had been sniffing around the pack that contained the sad remnants of our groceries, so Libby fished out the bag of kibble. It was light, with barely more than a cup of food remaining inside. Banjo devoured it hungrily, oblivious both to its soggy texture as well as to the fact that this was the last we would be able to offer him before we reached civilization again.

"Don't tell me you're planning on Going Goopy now, too?" asked Libby as she inventoried the rest of our supplies.

I chuckled weakly. "No, I'm not crazy yet. I'm just wondering if it could fix my stomach."

"I don't believe they actually fix anything. I think they shoot you a quick dose of some painkillers, maybe some hallucinogens—just enough to keep you dopey while they take over."

"Right about now, dopey sounds pretty good."

Libby yawned. Her eyelids were drooping, but she was still in nursemaid mode. "Do you think you can eat anything?"

"Sure can. I can puke it up again, too. Have we got any more of that skunk water?"

"You are not drinking any more of that swill."

"No, I just want to wash up some."

Libby handed me a bottle, half full of water the color of weak tea. I poured some onto a sock, then swabbed my face and neck. It was the first minor pleasure I had taken in far too many hours.

"Do you think it could actually convert us?" asked Libby as she wrapped a blanket around herself. "We've never seen anything so small try to change something as big as a person. I wonder if it would have enough mass."

"My goal is to remain ignorant of that for at least one more night." Libby was having trouble keeping her eyes open. I didn't think my stomach pains were going to let me get to sleep, so I figured at least one of us should be comfortable. "Rest up, babe," I told her. "You need some sleep."

"Maybe for a little bit, but wake me in a couple hours. You're going to need some rest, yourself."

"Will do." I leaned over and kissed her on the lips.

"Blech. You taste like skunk water."

"Deal with it, Pixie. I'm the only game in town."

As the sky blackened overhead, Libby's breathing deepened. Banjo turned three complete circles, then settled down at her feet, resting his muzzle on her thigh. She still looked cold, so I lay down beside her and threw my blanket over both of us. The ground was rocky and uncomfortable, but being off my feet still felt sublime.

"Lying down is a bad idea," I thought, as my eyelids began to flutter. "I need to sit up if I'm going to stay awake." The logic of this was so compelling that I resolved to sit up three separate times before I finally drifted off to sleep.

23

A vicious leg spasm shocked me into full consciousness. There was still some light in the sky, so the sun must not yet have gone down fully.

Except I could have sworn I had been looking at the stars a few seconds ago.

I checked my watch, but could make no sense of what I was seeing. There were three hands. That shouldn't be, should it? Wait. One was a second hand. Don't look at that one; look at the other one. The hour hand was on the two, and the minute hand was on the five. So it was 2:25. But it was light out. It's not light at 2:25. Or is it? When was the last time I had been up at 2:25?

Which was the hour hand again? The big one. No. The little one. I had been reading it backward. So it wasn't 2:25 at all. It was 5:10. In the morning.

It was morning? Had I overslept? What time was I supposed to get up? Was I supposed to have gone to sleep at all? Why not? What was I waiting for?

Not waiting. Watching. The Duck-Thing was still following us.

Libby. Where was Libby?

Libby was right where I left her. She was curled into a ball with her blanket wrapped tightly around both herself and Banjo, who had insinuated his way up into her arms at some point. She looked cold, but she was still human.

I exhaled slowly, calming myself. All three of us had fallen asleep, which could have been fatal, but everything was all right now. We had all gotten much-needed rest that would have been denied us if we had spent the night on watch. Now we were safe, it was morning, and we could go on as soon as I figured out what that odd noise was.

Splut.

Shluuurp.

I wanted it to be water dripping, but I knew there was no water near.

Splut.

Shluuurp.

I wanted it to be frogs cavorting, but I knew we were too high up.

Splut.

Shluuurp.

I wanted it to be Banjo hiccupping in his sleep, but I could hear his steady breathing just a couple of feet away. This new sound was coming from further off.

Splut.

Shluuurp.

It was coming from over the edge. From the direction we had come.

Splut.

Shluuurp.

From the direction the Duck-Thing would be coming.

I eased closer to the edge, straining to see the base of the rock outcrop we had scaled the night before. There was still not quite enough daylight to penetrate the shadows of the cliff. I found my Go-Bag and dug out my hand-powered flashlight. Giving its handle a few quick spins to charge it, I returned to the overlook and peered over the drop-off.

I could see nothing on the ground, which did not surprise me. None of the tarbabies we had encountered so far had made this kind of noise while walking. My suspicion was that this one had figured out something new. Dropping to my hands and knees, I shone the light over the rock wall, listening for the wet, arrhythmic sound that had alerted me.

Splut.

Shluuurp.

Closer than I expected. Less than five feet down, and about ten feet to my right. As its body was entirely black, it was hard to pick out amongst the shadows of the rock face, but I found it. My assumption had been that the Duck-Thing was simply walking up the rocks, relying on its unnatural stickiness for traction. The truth was a lot sloppier. Perhaps the tarbaby did not have enough structural integrity for it to hang all of its weight on its spindly bird legs, or perhaps this was simply another symptom of their natural awkwardness. Whatever the reason, I counted us fortunate that the Duck-Thing's climbing skills were substandard.

The creature had flattened itself against the rock as much as its bulk allowed. To ascend, it let its neck fall backward, then whipped it forward and up, slapping it into the rock wall as hard as it could. With its head plastered against the cliff face, it wriggled the rest of its body upward until it could release its head and start the process again. It only gained a couple of inches with every effort, but it was unquestionably making progress. I guessed we had no more than fifteen minutes before it dragged itself over the top. I walked back to Libby and gently nudged her.

"Wakey, wakey. Eggs 'n' bakey."

Banjo was immediately at attention, but Libby didn't even open her eyes. "Don' wanna. Go 'way."

"No can do, Pixie. We got troubles."

"Duck troubles?"

"Well, former duck troubles, anyway."

Libby rolled onto her back and rubbed her face. "What time is it?"

"Just after five."

That woke her up. "In the morning? You stayed up all night?"

I take pride in the fact that I have never lied to Libby, no matter how dire the circumstances. "You needed to sleep," I replied, congratulating myself on the evasion. I was already calculating how much I would be able to capitalize on my implied all-night vigil.

Libby wrestled a hand free of the blanket and rested it against my forehead. "How are you feeling?"

"Tell you in a second." I wandered off to a large thicket of bushes about a dozen yards up the path. Banjo tried to follow me, but I waved him off. The distance was more for my wife's benefit than out of any sense of modesty, but I knew this wasn't going to be a pleasant start to the morning. Libby moved to the overlook to monitor the Duck-Thing's progress, finding its labored splutting sounds less disturbing than the symphony of exotic noises currently emanating from her husband's innards. The Duck-Thing was less than three feet from the top. A dozen more spluts, and it would be upon us.

"Five minutes, babe," she called. "Then we're out of here."

I only needed another minute to finish voiding my body of whatever nastiness the skunk water had planted inside me. The cleanup took a little longer and required the sacrifice of yesterday's t-shirt to the greater cause of personal hygiene. "Pixie," I said, "If you love life, you will avoid those particular bushes for the rest of your natural born days."

"Feel any better?"

"Much. I can stand up again. A little woozy, though."

"You're still dehydrated, and you haven't eaten in more than a day. We'll try to take it easy, but we've got to get moving." To punctuate her point, the Duck-Thing's head slapped up over the lip of the rock wall. Banjo flinched backward and yapped at the interloper.

"So he's learned a new trick," I noted. "That's sweet."

"I was thinking we might try a new trick ourselves. I think we ought to consider getting off the path."

"Really? Is there an alternate trail?"

"Not really, but it looks like we've still got a lot more uphill. With you sick and us out of water, it's not going to be long before we're both exhausted. I say we head downhill."

"Back the way we came?"

Libby pulled the map out of her bag. "Only a little way. If we head due west, I think we'll hit Route 28 in just a few miles. That's got to improve our chances of finding water, and maybe even a safe place to hole up for a while."

"I thought we were trying to avoid the major roads."

"I'm not sure any of the roads in this area qualify as major. We're trying to avoid population centers. The Catskills aren't exactly famous for population density."

With a wet flop, the Duck-Thing dragged itself over the lip, then rolled back and forth in an attempt to right itself. Banjo turned a nervous circle, then looked to us, as if waiting for us to make the call.

"Decision time," said Libby. "What do you think?"

"Any plan that involves the word 'downhill' sounds good to me. Shall we?"

"Let's let ducky get a little further from the edge there. Then we'll flank him and head down."

"Ooh, you said 'flank him.' You're Rambo."

"No, I'm Rimbeau."

I pulled my last cleanish t-shirt out of my bag and slipped it on while we waited. It was still damp from the dunking it had taken yesterday, and it smelled musty. I vowed to retire it at the first opportunity, though the same could probably be said of my entire wardrobe at this point.

As soon as it was on its feet the Duck-Thing resumed its monotonous hunt. In the soft glow of the early morning light, we got our clearest look yet at our pursuer. Like the other tarbabies we had seen, it was at once dark as pitch and nearly transparent. A TV commentator had described the creatures as resembling obsidian glass, but this one didn't look anywhere near that clean. "Charcoal Jell-O" did a much better job of capturing the monster's wobbly consistency. It undulated when it moved, illustrating its lack of any kind of skeletal structure. In addition, there were visible particles floating within it, like marshmallows or fruit floating in a Jell-O mold.

The Duck-Thing was not quite as duckish as it had been yesterday. The head and beak were no longer as distinctly defined, and the legs were shorter and thicker, as though more of the creature's mass had flowed down to help support itself. Perhaps the climb up the wall had stretched it out some, or perhaps it was simply forgetting what it looked like back when it was an actual duck.

When the tarbaby had trudged about fifteen feet from the drop-off, we moved. Banjo and I went left, Libby right, giving the monster plenty of room as we circled around it. By the time the creature had turned itself around again, we were already beginning our descent. I prostrated myself on the rocks, scooting down in much the same way I had gone up. Banjo and Libby both took a more direct route, leaping most of the way, and they hit the ground first.

"You're really getting into this jungle-woman shtick," I noted, dusting off the seat of my pants.

"Want to be my monkey sidekick?" she asked, readjusting her pack and continuing on down the path.

"Why yes. Yes, I do."

We had progressed about fifty feet from the base of the outcrop when we heard a solid, wet thud behind us. Looking back, we discovered that the Duck-Thing had learned its second new trick of the day. Foregoing its awkward splut-walk, the creature had mimicked Libby, and simply dropped the fifteen feet down to the path.

Banjo trotted ahead, Libby picked up her own pace, and I labored to keep up.

24

Our progress downhill was slow at first. We were on the southwest face of the mountain, and the sun had not yet climbed high enough to cast much light into our section of forest. But while our vigilance to ensure we were on safe footing slowed our pace, the Duck-Thing was only gaining speed.

The tarbaby was not as concerned with avoiding injury as its quarry. Instead of picking its way carefully over downed tree limbs or small boulders, the creature just flopped over them. Instead of slowing down when the slope steepened, the Duck-Thing got reckless, bouncing down the path in an awkward series of splats and tumbles. It wasn't pretty, but it was making good time.

"OK," said Libby after we had gone about two miles from our campsite. "Do you see where the trail bends up ahead? If I'm reading the map right, that's the closest spot on this side of the mountain to Route 28. If we head due west from there, we can probably make the highway in an hour or two. You up for it?"

"I don't have a better plan," I admitted. "Let's do it."

"It looks pretty clear over there." Libby nodded at the trail ahead.

"Where?"

"That section there," she repeated, pointing toward a reasonably treeless patch ahead.

"On the left?"

"Yeah."

"Isn't that east?"

"What?"

"We're heading south, aren't we? If we want to go west, don't we have to turn right?"

"Oh, hell," said Libby as she stopped and turned around. East and west had confused her for as long as she could remember. The only way she could get them straight was to visualize a map of the United States in her head. "OK, we came from the north; that's Canada. We're headed south, toward Mexico."

"More toward Florida."

"Hush. So New York is that way," she said, holding her right arm out to her side, "and California is that way." This time she held out her left arm.

"And California's west."

"So west is to the left. Isn't that what I said?"

"Yep, but you were facing the other way when you said it." I spun her around and pulled her left arm down, leaving her right arm pointing outward.

"Oh."

Behind us, the Duck-Thing took another tumble. It couldn't have been more than a hundred feet away.

"It's still a good plan," I reassured her, as I plunged into the brush on the right side of the road. Sensing the plan, Banjo bounded ahead, and was lost among the underbrush at once. With a brief glance over her shoulder, Libby followed.

Our first few steps off the path were torturously slow. The vegetation lining the trail was low enough to see over, but it was dry and prickly, catching on our pants and tangling in our shoe laces. The occasional rustle from ahead told us that Banjo was making far swifter progress than we. Trying to follow his lead, I used my greater mass to force a narrow path that Libby could more easily squeeze through. After a hundred feet of this, the underbrush let up, replaced by scores of downed trees, victims of an ice storm the previous winter.

Though the morning was cool, I was soaked with sweat after just a few minutes of clambering over the shattered trees. It took us about ten minutes to reach a spot clear enough for us to see where we were going. Banjo was nowhere to be seen, but we refrained from calling to him out of fear of revealing our position to our pursuer.

"It looks like it's mostly pine trees over there," I observed, scanning the forest ahead. "That should mean lots of needles on the ground, so not much undergrowth."

We headed in the direction of the pine trees, and got our first good news of the day. The forest floor was indeed reasonably clear, and as we had hoped, it was downhill for as far as we could see. We began jogging in an effort to put a bit more distance between us and our pursuer.

After a quarter hour of relatively comfortable travel, fortune smiled on us again. A small stream intersected our path, bubbling happily over a bed of fractured shale. I dropped to my knees and slathered the water over my head and neck. It was icy cold and blissfully refreshing on my overheated skin. After cooling myself off, I took a few tentative sips.

"Careful," warned Libby. "That's what got you sick in the first place."

"No choice," I replied, shrugging off my pack. "If I don't rehydrate, I'm not going to make it." I pulled out a plastic bottle, filled it with water from the stream, and gulped it down. "If I get sick again, I'll deal with it."

I drained the bottle dry and refilled it, this time dumping the contents over my head. Against her better instincts, Libby also refilled one of her bottles and took a reluctant sip, ready to spit it out. The water tasted clean, so she too drank her fill, then topped off the bottle.

A crash from behind froze us in place. After a few seconds of rustling, a second crash followed, then a third. I stood up and shouldered my pack once again, straining to find the source of the noise in the distant gloom.

"Duck?" asked Libby.

I nodded, then took a step back. "Oh crap. It's rolling."

Libby stood up to confirm what I was seeing. The Duck-Thing was no longer much of a duck at all. It had rolled itself into a ball, slightly larger and considerably lumpier than a bowling ball. Its imperfect shape caused it to roll erratically, which accounted for the frequent crashes. On the steeper slopes, however, it could really pick up speed.

"Come on," I said as I jogged along the course of the stream. Libby followed close behind, taking two steps for every one of mine. Glancing over my shoulder, I estimated the creature to be no more than two hundred feet behind us. After another two minutes of jogging, our lead had shrunk to half that.

"Faster," gasped Libby, as she pulled abreast of me. "It's gaining."

We broke into a full run, stealing backward glances every few paces. As fast as we ran, the Ball-Thing kept closing the distance. It was soon close enough for me to figure out why.

The tarbaby was no longer black. Instead, it appeared brown and fuzzy. It was plastered in a thick coat of pine needles, so its natural stickiness was no longer acting as a drag. At this point, it could roll downhill as fast as a soccer ball.

"We can't outrun it," I exclaimed when it was fifty feet away. "We've got to do something!"

Libby scanned the slope ahead, looking for something to hide behind. There were no boulders here, no uphill slopes, nothing that would slow the tarbaby's progress. Nothing but trees.

"We've got to get uphill of it," she said. "There!" she panted, sprinting furiously. "Those two birches!"

I stole another peek over my shoulder. The creature was forty feet away and still gaining. "What, climb them? There's no time!"

"No! Run between them! You go left—I go right!" Libby was almost out of breath. "Touchdown!"

Thirty feet.

"Touchdown?"

Twenty feet.

"You mean field goal?"

"Whatever!" wheezed Libby. "Run!"

With less than ten feet separating us from our pursuer, we put on a last desperate burst of speed. The birches were coming up fast, but the tarbaby was almost at our heels.

"On three!" cried Libby. "One!"

Libby was never a good judge of distance. We hit the trees before she had time to count to two. She hooked her arm around the one on the right and, without breaking stride, pirouetted neatly around to the other side. I attacked my side with the same enthusiasm, but less grace. Grabbing the leftmost tree, I defied the laws of inertia by failing to change direction in the slightest. Instead, my feet flew out straight in front of me.

Luckily, that was enough. The tarbaby rolled directly underneath my outstretched body, doing better than fifteen miles per hour. Had I let go of the tree at that point, I would have landed right on top of the creature. Instead, my grip held as my body continued outward, wrenching my shoulder severely. My momentum spent, I dropped like a stone, hitting the ground hard enough to drive the breath from my lungs.

Exhausted, fighting for breath, Libby and I lay motionless, listening to the continuing progress of the Ball-Thing. The creature had built up considerable momentum and was slow in figuring out how to arrest it. It was more than thirty feet away before it got the idea to untuck itself, returning to its less streamlined duck form. Freed from its ball shape, its roll turned to a bounce, then a series of flops and crashes until, another twenty feet later, it too lay still on the forest floor.

As I struggled to regain both my wind and my senses, Libby kept a close eye on the tarbaby. We both needed to get our breath back, so she didn't want to move again until she absolutely had to.

The creature was currently on its back, but was wasting no time in resuming the chase. It rocked methodically from side to side, attempting to right itself.

"Babe?" asked Libby. "You OK?"

"Unh," I replied groggily. "I fell on my butt."

"But are you OK?"

"I fell on my butt. How can anyone be OK after falling on their butt?"

Libby breathed a sigh of relief. If I was complaining, that generally meant I was fine.

"The duck's on its feet again," she reported.

"It's a duck again?"

"It's a duck again. But you know what's weird?"

"Do I know what's weird about being chased through the Catskills by a duck made out of sticky Jell-O? Nuh-uh. Seems fairly routine."

"What's weird," she continued, "is that it's shedding pine needles."

I raised my head. Sure enough, the coating of dried brown pine needles the thing had acquired during its roll down the hill was steadily falling off. It shook itself to expedite the process.

"Huh. So it doesn't have to be sticky. It can turn that off when it wants to?"

"And what's worse," added Libby, "is that it knows when to turn it off. It picked up needles when it needed to speed up, and now it's getting rid of them. It's a lot smarter than I thought it would be."

"And it keeps picking up new tricks. That rolling business was good. It almost had us."

"Do you think its learning?"

"It's definitely adapting," I mused, "and improvising."

"Which means we can't count on tricking it again."

"Not the same way. It's a good thing you're clever."

"It's on the move again," said Libby, as the Duck-Thing took its first exploratory step back up the hill. "What do we do?"

"We've got to stay level. We can't let it get upslope of us again."

"You ready?"

"I fell on my butt."

Groaning with the exertion, we regained our feet. We started moving perpendicular to our original path, and quickly put a respectable distance between ourselves and the Duck-Thing. Once we were satisfied the monster would not be able to repeat its previous strategy, we adjusted our course, angling slightly downhill.

I fished out my water bottle and sucked down a quarter of its contents at a single pull. Determined not to run out of water again, I looked for the stream we encountered previously, and spotted it off to our left. What piqued my interest was the fact that it was descending faster than we. Over the years, this modest little stream had carved an impressive gorge into the side of the mountain, dropping off at least ten feet from the hill above it. "You see that?" I asked Libby.

"The gully?"

"Yeah. If we could get the duck in there, it would take him a while to climb back out again."

"Do you think he'd fall for the same trick again?"

"Not really." I paused to scan the terrain, which was now comparatively flat. "He's not uphill of us this time. I don't think he'd be able to build up enough momentum to fall in there on his own."

We continued on as we considered the problem.

"The old Okey-Doke?" asked Libby.

I beamed with delight. "I love that you remember stuff like that."

"So who gets to raise the ruckus?"

I stopped, evaluating the ground again. "I do. Right now, you're faster than me, and a lot more surefooted. You've got the best chance of taking him by surprise."

"Is it worth the risk?"

"We've got to do something. If we stay on level ground, we're just going to end up circling the mountain. We've got to start going downhill again, and we can't do that until we've got a decent head-start."

Libby unslung her pack and took a seat on the ground. "All right then," she said, unwrapping a granola bar. "Looks like we've got time for breakfast."

25

For the moment, the Duck-Thing had run out of surprises. It caught up to us right on schedule, following precisely the same path that we had traveled ourselves. From her hiding spot behind a fallen maple, Libby wondered if it was tracking us by spoor, like a bloodhound. If that were true, it could seriously compromise our plan, since it would have an equally likely chance of turning upslope to her present location as it would of homing in on me.

If the creature relied on sound rather than smell, we were more than covered. I had been sitting at the edge of the gorge for the last quarter hour, gleefully crooning away in an attempt to lead the tarbaby as close to the edge of the crevasse as possible. Despite my current role as live bait, I was enjoying myself enormously.

"We're running with the shadows of the night!" I warbled, atonally but enthusiastically. "So baby take my hand, we'll be all right!"

The Duck-Thing paused, as if puzzled by what it was seeing, though I made an effort not to attribute human emotions to the creature. The only motivations these things had exhibited so far were pursuit and capture. Was it confused by our trail? I tried to remember exactly where we had first split up. I thought it was further on, but couldn't remember for certain.

"Surrender all your dreams to me tonight!" That did it. Apparently the tarbabies could hear well enough, for the Duck-Thing resumed its awkward waddle toward whatever was causing the horrible noise.

"You'll come through in the end!" I screeched, rising to my feet to ensure I had the monster's full attention. Leaving nothing to chance, I propped my foot up on a rock and began strumming an air mandolin—my signature dance move.

"Because we're running from the shadow of a duck!" I wailed, and Libby tightened her grip on the branch she had chosen as her weapon. The Duck-Thing waddled on.

"Not certain why we're being chased by a duck!" I keened, and Libby vaulted the fallen tree she had been hiding behind. The Duck-Thing waddled on.

"My wife is just about to whack a duck!" I yowled, and Libby closed the distance between herself and the creature, raising the makeshift club to her shoulder. The Duck-Thing stopped.

"She'll come through in the end!" I yelped, and the Duck-Thing turned. Libby swung the club in a smooth arc, smacking the creature dead center with a satisfying slap.

Libby's delight at making contact was immediately overwhelmed by the pain shooting through her forearms. Her expectation was that the Duck-Thing would career neatly off the end of her club like a ball being walloped by a field hockey stick. The creature turned out to be significantly heavier than she expected, and it had no intention of careening anywhere.

The Duck-Thing stuck to the end of her club like a marshmallow on a fondue fork, arresting her swing as abruptly as if she had struck the ground beneath it. Unprepared for the sudden stop, her grip failed, and her hands jolted off the club. She lost her footing and slid to the ground just inches from her target. The tarbaby appeared not to notice the impact at all, nor the three foot length of poplar currently sticking out of its back, as it stretched its neck toward the stunned woman lying by its side.

Josh Heaney was on the case. In a single motion, I grabbed the top of the club with both hands and spun. On my first revolution, the Duck-Thing lifted off the ground, just barely clearing Libby, who plastered herself to the earth as flat as she could. On my second turn, it was waist high, and I was building up speed. On my third turn, I let go.

The Duck-Thing-on-a-stick sailed into the gorge, landing with a shallow splash. Deprived of its weight as a counter-balance, I stumbled sideways, tripping over Libby. Ever the gentleman, I had the courtesy to land on my own backside instead of hers.

For the second time that day, the two of us lay side by side, struggling to catch our breath. After a minute devoid of any sound but our panting, Libby sat up. She cradled her hands in front of her face, and was not surprised to see they were bleeding. Rolling onto her stomach, she elbow-walked to the edge of the gorge and peeked over the side.

Still attached to the club, the Duck-Thing had not yet succeeded in righting itself. As Libby watched it thrash about in the water, I crawled to her side.

"They'll come true in the end," she said.

"Beg pardon?"

"You said *'you'll come through in the end.'* It's *'they'll come true.'* The dreams. The ones you surrendered. They'll come true in the end."

I took a moment to let the news sink in. "Didn't I make that song up?"

"Just the part about the duck. The first part is an actual thing."

"Oh."

With a thud, the poplar branch slipped free of the Duck-Thing. It had finally figured out where its feet were.

"I fell on my butt again."

"Where do you suppose Banjo got to?"

The Duck-Thing was inconvenienced by its new situation, but it would find its way out of there sooner or later. The goal now was to get far enough down the mountain that it wouldn't be able to catch up, even with its bowling ball trick. Since the most direct route we knew was now behind us, we jogged back the way we came, following the gorge. A bit over a half mile later, the gorge leveled out, and the stream was at ground level again. We located a shallow spot, hopped across, and were once again on our way downhill.

The sun had crested the mountain, giving us much better light to work with. Though still not on an official path, the ground was clear enough for us to proceed at a trot. After only five minutes, we had progressed far enough down the mountain that the sun was once again blocked, and the forest darkened. Less sure of the path ahead, we slowed to a walk.

"How are you feeling?" asked Libby. "Do you need a rest?"

Still feverish, I was sweating abundantly, and on the verge of hyperventilating. I just shook my head.

"Poor Snooky," said Libby. "You look exhausted."

I continued walking, mopping my face with the tail of my t-shirt. Libby followed a few paces behind, checking back every few steps to make sure we weren't being followed. "Can't run anymore," I said after a few minutes. "I'm OK to walk, but I don't think I can run for a while."

"That's fine, babe. We should be hitting level ground soon. We'll be safe then."

It took the better part of a half hour, but Libby was right. Eventually the slope began to level, until we found ourselves hitting brief uphill stretches again. The sun caught up to us as well, making it easier to navigate.

"Any idea where the road is?" I asked, mounting a tree stump in hopes of getting a better view of the terrain ahead.

"Your guess is as good as mine. Ordinarily, we could probably hear it by now. I doubt we can depend on much traffic today, though." Libby stopped and turned in a slow circle, looking for any clues as to where we were, or in what direction civilization might lie.

"What kind of tree is that?" I asked. Libby turned to see what I was looking at. Still on the stump, I was scanning the canopy of the forest off to our right.

"What," she asked, "the pines?"

"No, I don't think it's a pine."

"Maybe spruces? I never really knew the difference."

"It's not a spruce."

"I think it may have to do with the size of the needles, or whether they make cones…"

"That one," I said, pointing into the distance. "Right there. What is that?"

Libby stood in front of me, trying to follow my gaze, and saw nothing but what she assumed were pines and/or spruces.

"Come up here," I said, relinquishing my place on the stump. Libby stepped up and craned her neck, searching for anything out of the ordinary.

"Ummm, I'm still not seeing it."

I squatted down, wrapping my arms around her knees. Libby leaned back slightly, sitting on my shoulder. When I stood up again, she was now a yard higher than she had been on the stump. Even then, she almost missed it.

"Do you see it?" I asked. "It looks like this really cheap artificial Christmas tree we had when I was a kid."

The thing that we were looking at looked like a gray utility pole, but with a ring of branches some five feet from its crown. "Let me down," said Libby.

Once back on the ground, Libby unsnapped a pouch on her backpack and pulled out her cell phone. She flipped the phone open and pressed the power button, watched the screen for a few moments, then showed it to me.

"Four bars," I noted.

"That's a cell tower," she said, walking in the direction of our new discovery.

"So, what, they camouflaged it to look like a tree?" I trotted to catch up with my wife.

"Just not very well. But if it's camouflaged at all, that means it can be seen by people. Out here, I'm hoping that means it's near a road."

The trees were growing much closer together at this level, slowing our progress. Several times we had to walk dozens of yards out of our way in order to find gaps in the tree line wide enough to squeeze through. These maneuvers were disorienting, and the closer we got to the cell tower, the more difficult it was to find.

In the end, we never did find the tower. We stopped looking once we found the road. It wasn't big, but it was flat, and it was gray, and it probably led toward civilization.

"Sing hallelujah," I said. "We are delivered from the wilderness."

"So. Which way?"

"Do we have any idea where we are?"

"Not really."

"Any idea what's around here?"

"Not really."

I looked up the road—Libby looked down. Both ends curved within a half mile, making it impossible to tell what might lie in either direction. "Well," I said at last, "the plan was to go north. We may as well stick to that."

"And we were heading west."

"To the best of our knowledge."

"So north is... left?"

"Almost."

"Dammit," said Libby, turning right.

As the morning wore on, the hike began to border on pleasant again. We were both tired and hungry, and I was still streaming sweat, but the weather was cool, the walking was easy, and we hadn't seen the Duck-Thing in over an hour. It was beginning to feel like normalcy was just around the next bend.

The next bend came a mile and a half later, and normalcy followed in the form of Alan a'Dale's Resort Lodge and Cabaret Theater. The sign beside the driveway promised color TV and air conditioning in every room, as well as a kosher deli and bakery, and the lounge chairs arranged behind a chain-link fence promised an outdoor swimming pool. After wandering in the woods for two days, stumbling upon a full-service hotel out in the wilderness seemed a stroke of luck too good to be true.

The shadowy figure of a deer that now stood between us and the safety of that hotel seemed par for the course.

26

"Can we outrun that thing?" Libby asked, transfixed at the sight of the Deer-Thing standing between us and Alan a'Dale's Resort Lodge. It was big—taller than she was certainly, though probably not quite my height. If it had antlers, it would have easily topped six feet. Most unsettling was the length of its slender, black, translucent legs. Even if this thing wasn't as graceful as a normal deer, it certainly would not plod along like the Duck-Thing. It hadn't moved yet, but it looked like it could overtake us if it wanted to.

"Not for long. We need to get back into the woods. It might be too big to follow us."

"Maybe I can lead it away," Libby suggested. "Maybe you can…"

"Do you hear that?" We paused, and after a moment Libby heard it too—a low, mechanical sound that we hadn't heard in two days. A car was approaching.

We scanned the road in both directions, ready to move to the shoulder, but saw nothing. A few seconds later, we turned in unison back to the entrance of the hotel. A comically large, bone-white, 80s-vintage Chrysler LeBaron pulled out of Alan a'Dale's driveway. The driver had been courteous enough to put the turn signal on before rolling out of the entry road and pulling up to the Deer-Thing. The car could not have been going much above five miles per hour when they collided with a soft sucking sound like a refrigerator door opening. The Deer-Thing stuck tight to the car's shiny front grill.

The LeBaron pulled forward slightly, angling around Libby and me. The driver's window rolled down, revealing a heavyset, white-haired man wearing enormous tortoise-shell sunglasses. His left arm rested on the door, sporting what looked to me like an authentic Rolex Oyster.

"Hiya kids!" said the stranger, thrusting his right arm through the window. "Saul Gerber. Glad to meet you!" The car rolled forward a couple of inches, and the stranger chuckled an abashed "whoops!" before shifting into Park.

Once the car had come to a secure stop, the man put his hand out again, and it took me a moment to understand what he was doing. With an embarrassed grunt, I stepped forward and grabbed his hand, pumping it enthusiastically.

"Josh Heaney," I said at last. "My wife, Libby."

"We're obviously very happy to meet you, as well," added Libby. "Thanks for the rescue!"

"Happy to oblige," said Saul. "Let me just take care of this thing. You kids go on into the office there. Bitzy will take care of you." With that, he accelerated again, pulling off down the road and out of sight, and taking the Deer-Thing with him.

"Do you know what a Bitzy is?" I asked at length.

"Nuh-uh."

"Do we want one taking care of us?"

"At this point, I think we do." Checking back over our shoulders every few steps, we walked past the entry sign and down the driveway to Alan a'Dale's Resort Lodge. Contrary to what the sign wanted us to believe, none of the structures within the resort complex looked remotely lodge-like. Most of the buildings sported an aluminum, brick and glass façade typical of institutional design of the 1950s. Nothing, from the guest wings to the utility buildings to the offices, was more than a single story high.

The hotel lobby was a quarter mile from the main road, behind a circular turn-around wide enough to accommodate a tour bus. At the moment, there were three vehicles parked out front—a maroon Town and Country, a beige Cadillac, and a twelve-seat mini-bus with the Alan a'Dale logo painted on its side.

The lobby doors slid open at our approach. A woman who appeared to be in her sixties, but with hair the color of a ripe eggplant, leaned out of the office, exhaling a long plume of cigarette smoke. "Hey you two!" she called. "Come join the party!"

"Is Saul going to be all right?" asked Libby.

"He didn't start out all right, so I don't see why anything should change now!" The woman cackled at her own joke as she waved us in. "Bitzy Gerber. It's a pleasure."

As we walked into the lobby, we became a bit self-conscious of our current grimy state. Bitzy looked like she was ready to go to a matinee, dressed in a colorful silk blouse, tight black capris pants, open-toed sling-back sandals, and an impressive collection of large, noisy costume jewelry. An enormous beaded necklace, a half-dozen bracelets on each wrist, and hoop earrings the size of coasters each competed for attention with bright, candy-colored finger and toe polish. By contrast, Libby's clothes were plastered to her body with sweat, her teeth were unbrushed, and she had leaves in her hair.

"Libby Heaney. This is my husband, Josh."

"Aren't you adorable," said Bitzy, brushing something off Libby's head.

"I'm afraid you're not seeing us at our best," she answered. "We've spent the last two days on the mountain."

"Why would you do that? There's plenty of rooms available! Do you want a room?"

"The problem was getting here…" offered Libby, before I interrupted.

"We would love a room," I said.

"You don't look at all well," said Bitzy, laying a hand on my forehead. "You're burning up! We need to get you off your feet." She walked behind the counter, scanning the rack of keys. The hotel was working a half-hearted Robin Hood theme, and each key dangled from a large plastic arrowhead, designed to be uncomfortable in any pocket. After a brief deliberation, she plucked one off the bottom row.

"Here, let's keep you in the main building. It's not the best views, but I'll be able to keep an eye on you. Thank God they never got those awful electric key cards here. I don't think I would be able to figure out those things."

"So, you don't work here?" asked Libby.

"At the moment, no one works here. The season was supposed to start on Monday, but the staff deserted us days ago. Fortunately, Saul and I have a time share, so we've got our own keys." She emerged from behind the counter and walked past a seating area cluttered with chrome and vinyl chairs. Libby and I followed obediently.

"The kitchen's stocked, though, so we've been making the best of it."

"Are you the only ones here?" I asked.

"No, we were the first, but then the Perlmans and the Bambergers arrived. We know them from Boca."

"Florida?" Libby was amazed. "You traveled all the way from Florida in the middle of all this?"

"Have you ever tried to get a refund on a time share?" We arrived at Room 114, and Bitzy inserted the key into the door lock. A few jiggles later, the door opened onto a small suite, containing a seating area with a couch, chair and TV, a bedroom with a pair of twin beds, a bathroom, and a kitchenette with an antique mini-fridge and microwave.

"Here you go. It's not as good as our room, but then we're paying, and you're freeloading." Bitzy chortled at her joke. Libby smiled politely, while I salivated at the thought of a bed and toilet.

"It's beautiful," I said. "It's so much better than where I thought we'd be sleeping tonight."

"Bitzy," said Libby, "we cannot thank you enough. I'm a little worried about Josh's fever, though. I'd really like to get him to bed."

"You and me both, toots," she snorted. "And no offense, but you could both stand to freshen up a little. Lunch will be at Fryer Tuck's in a few hours. I'll leave you alone until then."

Bitzy closed the door as she left. Libby and I let our bags drop to the floor without concern. I stumbled to a bed and flopped down backward, sprawling out on top of the coverlet. Libby followed me into the bedroom and pulled off my sneakers and socks. She winced at the sight of the blisters on my feet, but I'm sure she had her own matching set.

"Golly gumbucks," I sighed. "That feels so good!"

"Get your pants off."

"Oh, you naughty minx." I unbuckled my belt and wriggled out of my jeans, then scooted up the bed and laid my grimy head on the crisp, clean pillow. Libby walked out to the kitchenette, where she deposited her own shoes and socks. She filled an ice bucket with tap water and fetched a washcloth from the bathroom. Returning to the bedroom, she soaked the cloth in the bucket and laid it gently over my face. I moaned my approval.

Libby returned to the bathroom, peeling off her soiled clothes and recoiling from the aroma. She opened the faucet on the tub and stuffed our crusty laundry into a plastic bag she found in the closet while she waited for the bath to fill. When she emptied a small bottle of bath gel into the tub, our room filled with the sweet scent of lilac. I heard Libby slip into the tub, but I couldn't tell you which of us fell asleep first.

27

Libby awoke to a leg spasm, and frothy scented water sloshed out of the tub onto the bathroom's white tile floor. She scanned the room frantically, unsure of what she was looking for, but certain that it had found us at last. When she realized she was alone, she sank back into the tub in relief.

The water had cooled, but it was still above her body temperature, and still felt wonderful. She allowed herself another few moments of blissful relaxation before it occurred to her to wonder what had awoken her. The answer came in the form of a light knock at the door of our room.

Libby clambered out of the tub, displacing more water than she had intended, and making a sloppy mess of the floor. She pulled a towel from the rack above the toilet and wrapped it around herself, then stepped out of the bathroom and peered through the peephole in the front door.

As she expected, Bitzy was standing out in the hallway, a lit cigarette by her ear. She was preparing to knock again when Libby opened the door.

The minor commotion was enough to wake me, but as Libby was unaware of this, she kept her voice at a whisper. "Sorry, Mrs. Gerber. I was asleep."

Not picking up on Libby's caution, Bitzy bellowed her response. "Good! Good! You two looked exhausted!" Libby winced, looking back toward the bedroom. Bitzy took the hint and switched to a broad stage whisper. "Oh, sorry. Is dreamboat still asleep?"

"I think so," said Libby, as she struggled to remember what she had done with her clothes. "What time is it?"

"Just past one," answered Bitzy, over-pronouncing her consonants to emphasize the fact that she was whispering. "I wanted to let you know we've got lunch ready in Fryer Tuck's Deli, if you want to join us."

"Five minutes." The moment the possibility of a real meal was floated, Libby realized how hungry she was. "We'll be there in five minutes."

She then remembered the current state of her wardrobe, and that most of her clothes were now festering in a damp laundry bag. "Maybe fifteen?"

I was not easily rousted, but once the idea of food solidified in my head, I was up and alert. Libby insisted I shower first, and we both treated ourselves to a brush and a gargle. I was still running a fever, but a few minutes under a stream of cool water helped immeasurably. A bigger concern was clothing. Neither of us wanted to put our filthy trail clothes back on, but our supplies were otherwise limited. We each had a spare set of underwear left, but had run through our last change of socks on the hike. I found a t-shirt that was only pretty dirty, and it was long enough to serve Libby as a makeshift dress. I resigned myself to putting my filthy jeans back on, but rejected the idea after getting a whiff of them.

"There is no way I'm subjecting people to that stink at the dinner table," I said.

"I suppose I could just bring a plate back to the room," Libby volunteered.

"No need. Inspiration has struck."

We left the room soon after, Libby bare-legged but otherwise respectably draped in an oversized Flash Gordon shirt. I looked notably more regal, having stripped the top sheet off of my bed and wrapping it around myself toga-style.

"And you said Latin Club was a waste of time," I admonished.

"You were in Latin Club?" asked Libby. "I married a man who was in Latin Club?" She shuddered theatrically. "I need another shower."

"Caveat emptor, Pixie."

Fryer Tuck's Deli had a posted notice requiring shirts and shoes. We were both barefoot, but were counting on the policy being laxly enforced. The Deli was cafeteria-style, with a self-serve soup and salad station at one end, a counter for ordering hot and cold sandwiches, and a drink and dessert bar leading up to a mechanical cash register. Like much of the equipment behind the counter, the register appeared to be at least three decades old.

Our interest in the décor vanished the moment we saw the spread that had been laid out. To be precise, it was the remains of a spread, since the other guests had taken the liberty of tucking in already. There were an even half dozen of them: the Gerbers plus two other older couples. A diminutive, wizened woman with a foot-high tower of hair sat at one end of the table, placidly chewing on an onion roll. At her side was an equally tiny old man who was busy tearing up pieces of pastrami and tossing them to the floor. I peeked around a chair to see where the meat was going, and found a familiar thumping tail.

"Banjo?"

"Hey, look who's up!" The voice of Saul Gerber boomed forth from behind a small mountain of carved meats and cheeses. Platters of sliced bread competed for precious tabletop real estate with bowls of chips, pretzels and potato salad. From an electric crock pot, the salty aroma of chicken soup wafted toward us, inviting us in metaphorically even as Bitzy Gerber rushed forward to do so literally.

"Kids! Get in here. Eat! Eat!" Bitzy's attentions were enthusiastic enough that we could not have refused even if we had wanted to, and we most definitely did not want to. Bitzy laid a hand on my forehead and frowned at the heat of my lingering fever. "You. Soup. Now." She ushered me by my elbow to the table, and ladled an enormous bowl full of a dense chicken soup.

"When did Banjo get here?" asked Libby.

"The flea circus? He stumbled in yesterday morning. Art there has been spoiling him ever since."

"Corky!" said Art, and Banjo yapped his agreement.

"Is he yours?" asked Saul.

I considered the question. "He's… with us. Or he was anyway, until he ditched us on the trail."

"His name's Banjo," added Libby.

"Corky!" insisted Art.

"Art has decided he's a Corky," said Saul. "That's Art Bamberger, by the way. And his lovely wife Doris."

"Corky's a good girl! Aren't you, Corky?"

"He's also decided he's a girl."

"That dog's half the reason I was out this morning," said Saul. "He looked too well fed to be a complete stray, so I figured there must be someone around looking for him. Since I was going out on patrol, anyway, I thought I'd see if I could find them."

"Patrol?" I asked.

"I'm Elliott," said a gentleman of advanced years at the center of the table. In checkered pants, a salmon polo shirt, and a cap of the type that I always associated with newsies from the 1940s, he looked like he was taking a short break from his golf game, and would any minute be excusing himself to go tackle the back nine, whatever that was. "Elliott Perlman."

Libby was heaping potato salad onto her plate, but put the spoon down long enough to make introductions. Elliott's wife Iris was seated across the table from him, wearing a sequined cocktail dress. Like her husband, Iris appeared to be in her seventies, while I doubted the Bambergers would ever see the south side of ninety again.

Our introduction to the Perlmans had put my previous question out of my mind, so instead I asked "I take it you had no problem getting rid of that deer?"

"It's not that big a deal, really," Saul replied, clearly pleased that someone had asked about his strategy. "At least, once you've figured out their weak spot."

"They have a weak spot?" I asked through a mouth full of broth and noodles. Libby fished a slice of rye bread out of the basket and piled it with a selection of cheeses.

"You kids get yourselves rested up, and I'll show you. We'll take a field trip."

"That's a very interesting dress you're wearing," Iris told Libby. "Couldn't Julius Caesar here spring for something couture?"

I clapped a hand over my mouth to avoid spitting out my soup. A carrot chunk the size of a bottle cap lodged in my windpipe, and I started coughing. Libby pounded me on the back to get me breathing again, while Bitzy fetched me a can of cream soda from the stand-up cooler by the register.

When I had calmed down somewhat, Libby explained our wardrobe choices. "We've been hiking for a few days now. Most of our clothes aren't fit for polite company."

"There's washing machines in the service wing," offered Bitzy. "I've never used them, but how hard can it be?"

"Why don't we get them some stuff out of Robin's Goods?" asked Elliott. "They've got clothes in there."

Saul agreed. "It's all covered with the Alan a'Dale logo, but it beats wearing a toga."

"The gift shop is open?" asked Libby.

"We've been making some amendments to our time share agreement."

"By which he means breaking and entering," added Bitzy. "We wouldn't be eating otherwise."

"Fortunately," Saul continued, "the security on the main office is older than me. Once we got in there, we had the keys to the kingdom." Saul unclipped an enormous ring from his belt, on which hung dozens of keys. "We'll check out Robin's Goods once you're done eating. You should really try that pastrami, by the way."

"I'm a vegetarian," said Libby.

"What about him?" asked Saul, indicating me.

"He'll eat your fingers if they're in front of his face"

Elliott pushed himself back from the table and rose to his feet. "Excuse me," he said to the gathering. "I need to... I'll, uh... I'll be back." He limped as he shuffled to the rest rooms in the back of the restaurant.

After the door had closed, Saul turned to Iris. "How's he doing?"

"He's fine. He just needs to stay close to a toilet."

"Prostate," Saul explained to us. "Don't get old."

"I'm not sure I like the alternative much."

28

As Robin's Goods was the only non-food related retail store in the Alan a'Dale resort complex, I was surprised at how little of its stock was in any way useful. Just inside the main entrance, which Saul had opened with his magic key ring, was a rack of CDs featuring New Age instrumental music, and another sporting large, mirrored sunglasses. Beyond that, the entire north wall was dominated by shelves of gift items inspired by Native American art, none of which matched the hotel's purported theme of medieval English legend. I picked up a scrimshaw grizzly bear from a shelf filled with a dozen more identical to it and confirmed the presence of the "Made in China" sticker hidden under the left rear paw.

For the kids, there were kaleidoscopes and sticker books and plastic dinosaurs. There was a barrel full of polished rocks that sold for five dollars a pound and a machine that stamped pennies with souvenir slogans. There were leather key fobs etched with the word "Catskills" and ceramic spoon rests with painted mountain scenes. There were plush toys in all sizes, including a life-sized coyote in a howling posture that looked like it had been part of the stock for a very long time.

Entirely absent was anything that a traveler stuck in an isolated location might actually need. I saw no toothbrushes or toothpaste, no deodorant, no fingernail clippers or shoelaces. There was a small rack of pharmaceuticals behind the register, but I saw neither painkillers nor cough remedies nor sunscreens. Instead, there were a half-dozen varieties of tablets and elixirs designed to aid in digestion and a box of flavored lip balms. There were no books, no magazines, no crossword puzzles, no sewing kits, no combs or cotton swabs. Apparently, the guests of Alan a'Dale's came prepared.

As promised, there was an assortment of clothing. All of it was embroidered with the official Alan a'Dale logo, with letters designed to look like woodcuts. A selection of t-shirts in pastel colors also sported the resort mascot, a cartoon merry man in a red leotard jauntily strumming a lute. The figure sported a dark Van Dyke beard and offered the viewer a roguish wink. Another rack held polo shirts featuring just Alan a'Dale's winking head.

Aside from some tennis visors and wide-brimmed sun hats (no baseball caps, I noted), this was the extent of the clothing selection in Robin's Goods. The shop offered no socks or underwear or shoes, and nothing resembling pants.

"Huh. I could'a swore they had Bermuda shorts in here last year," said Saul as he flipped through the shirt selection.

"They used to have swimsuits," added Bitzy. "The most god-awful hideous things you've ever seen. You're better off with bed sheets. Or skinny-dipping. You could get away with skinny-dipping," she told Libby with a conspiratorial nudge in the ribs. "You got the tush for it."

"These polo shirts are kind of nice," replied Libby, desperate to change the subject. "Are you sure no one would mind?"

"So let them mind. If they mind so much, let them get their butts up here and charge you for it." Bitzy hunted through the rack. "You're a small, right? You'll want the blue."

"I like the purple."

"No," said Bitzy, pulling a blue shirt off its hanger and holding it up against Libby's shoulders. "Not with your complexion, sweetheart. You need more color if you're going to wear purple." Unsure of what else to do, Libby accepted the shirt, and Bitzy turned her attention to me. "And what about you?"

"Um… I don't think they have my size."

"What are you talking about? You're a tall drink of water, but a large should do you. Here's one right here." She handed me a shirt from the far end of the rack.

"Oh. Uh, thanks, but…"

"But what? What's wrong with it?"

"It's… um… its pink."

"What's wrong with pink?" asked Saul. "I've got a beautiful pink shirt. Brooks Brothers. It's beautiful."

"I'm sure it is…"

"I gave him that shirt," beamed Bitzy. "It's beautiful."

"I just don't usually wear pink…"

"It don't mean nothing," protested Saul. "What, you think someone's gonna say something?"

"No…"

"Who's gonna say something? What are they gonna say?"

"No one. Nothing."

"So take the shirt."

"Um… OK."

"You're gonna thank me for that."

"Thank you."

"I meant later."

"It's a shame they don't have any pants," said Libby, who was now carrying a purple shirt, having discretely swapped out the blue one during the Great Pink debate. "Can we check out the laundry?"

"Oh sure," said Bitzy. "Your stuff's already in there."

Libby paused, uncertain she had heard correctly. "Our stuff?"

"Yeah, your clothes. I put in a load for you."

"You did?"

"Sure. When you were eating."

I held my new pink shirt to my bosom defensively. "I thought we had locked our room."

"Oh, it's OK, honey," said Bitzy, laying a reassuring hand on my arm. "We've got keys."

"Oh… good."

"Thanks?" added Libby.

"She's happy to do it," said Saul. "There's nothing she loves more than going through other people's bags."

"I've gotta tell you," continued Bitzy. "I don't think it could have waited much longer. Your clothes were in no kind of state!"

"The woods were not kind to us," said Libby. I noticed she was not lacking for color any more. Her face was several shades closer to matching her new shirt.

"It wasn't the woods that did that to this one's underpants," said Bitzy, jerking a thumb at me.

"Yeah... I didn't really think anyone would be doing my laundry," I stammered. "I would have washed them first, if I'd known."

"They're probably ready for the dryer by now. Come on, I'll show you where Housekeeping is."

While Saul perused the jigsaw puzzles, Bitzy escorted us back out to the main Reception area. She pulled a large ring of keys off of the main desk and unlocked a metal fire door concealed behind a row of potted fichus trees. "You can get more towels and soap in here, if you need them," she explained. "But I stocked up all the rooms in this building already, so you should be set for a while."

A phone on the reception desk reminded Libby that she hadn't had a chance to speak with her parents for several days. "Is it OK if I make a call?" she asked.

Bitzy shrugged. "Indulge. Come on sexy, let's go see how your underpants turned out." I shot a pleading look to my wife, but Libby was already dialing as Bitzy pulled me into the Housekeeping corridor.

Libby grimaced when she heard the chimes that signaled an engaged line. A pleasant but artificial voice came on to confirm that all circuits were busy. She sighed and disconnected the call. As she waited for the dial tone to come back so she could try again, she ran an idle finger along the rack of keys hanging behind the desk. She dialed again, and again she heard the message about busy circuits. She hung up and reminded herself to try her cell phone when we got back to our room. Even if the landlines were busy, there was a chance a cell signal might get through.

"Do not tell me you don't use dryer sheets," said Bitzy, in the same tone of voice she might use to accuse me of using heroin. "What do you do about static cling?"

"I like static cling," I replied as we emerged again from the Housekeeping corridor. "It makes me feel loved."

Bitzy rolled her eyes at Libby. "You went and married a funny man, huh?"

"No, I married *him*," replied Libby, waving a hand in my direction.

I ignored the dig. "Did you talk to your mom?"

"No, the circuits are all busy."

"Or they're dead," said Bitzy.

"That's a horrible thing to say!" protested Libby, who was doubly shocked when Bitzy laughed.

"Not your parents. The circuits! Phone service is spotty enough in these mountains in the best of times. I don't guess they're doing much maintenance with all these Jelly Babies on the loose."

"We've still got power," I noted.

"Knock wood," replied Bitzy, who did so. "I'm not counting on that lasting forever. So, what are you up for, Stretch? There's a billiards table in the bar…"

"I'm thinking Stretch needs to get back to bed," replied Libby, wrapping a proprietary arm around my waist. "Ew. And another shower. Would it be terribly rude if we went back to our room for a while?"

"Probably, but who's gonna know?" Bitzy cackled and retrieved her cigarettes from the front desk. "Go on, you kids get your rest. Tonight I'll teach Highpockets here how to Bossanova."

"I really hope she's talking about dancing," I said as soon as Bitzy was safely out of earshot. Before we left I studied the key rack behind the front desk. There were eighty hooks for this building, and a dozen of them were missing their enormous arrowhead key fobs. As far as I knew, only four of those rooms were currently occupied.

Our own room was not far from the main reception area, and in less than a minute I was wiggling our key in the lock of room 114, trying to persuade the aging mechanism to turn.

"Is there even a point to locking the room?" I muttered after a few seconds of frustration. "Bitzy has a master set, and it's not like we have anything worth stealing." I looked over my shoulder to gauge Libby's agreement and discovered I was talking to an empty hallway. I double-checked the number on the key fob with the tarnished brass numerals on the room door. "We are 114, aren't we?" I asked to no one in particular. In response, a low "shush" came from around the corner to my right, where the lower numbered rooms were.

I padded to the corner and glanced around the side to discover Libby standing on her tiptoes, attempting to peer through the peephole on the door of room 107. "They don't really work that way," I suggested, and Libby put a finger to her lips in reply.

"What are you looking for?" I whispered as I shuffled to her side.

"I'm trying to see if anyone's in this room," she answered, putting her ear against the heavy wood of the door. "This key was missing from the rack out front." Hearing nothing through the door, Libby tried the peephole again.

"Do you see anything?"

"No," she whispered, stepping back from the door. "I can see light, but I can't make out any shapes." She looked up and down the hall. "There must be some way of finding out if anyone's inside."

"This might work," I said as I rapped on the door.

"Ack! What are you doing?" hissed Libby, in a sharp whisper.

"Seeing if anyone's to home." I once again rapped my knuckles five times on the door, then called out, "Housekeeping! Do you need any tiny sewing kits?" I cupped an ear to the door, then knocked again. "Hello? Complimentary shoe shine?"

Libby had retreated around the corner, but poked her head out again. "Do you hear anything?"

"Nah. I don't think there's anyone…" I stopped and took a cautious step backward.

"What's wrong? What did you hear?"

This time it was my turn to shush. I leaned forward, cupping both hands around my right ear, and closed my eyes. I stood like that a full minute before shaking my head and rejoining my wife around the corner.

"Did you hear something?" she asked again.

"I can't be sure, but I may have heard a *splut*."

"Oh crap."

"It was a wet sound like those things make, but really soft. Like a cat licking its paw."

"Or like a tarbaby taking a step on thick berber weave carpeting?"

I flexed my toes against the hallway carpet, then nodded. "Yeah, kind of like that."

Libby put her shoulder against the door of room 114 and flicked the lock open.

"How did you do that?" I asked, as I hurried inside after her. When the door was safely shut behind us, I engaged the deadbolt and the security chain as well.

"Door's warped. You've got to lean into it."

"Great." I shrugged off my makeshift toga. "A finicky lock is just what you want when you're staying down the hall from a monster."

29

"Is there a tarbaby in room 107?"

I coughed up a bit of my cream soda, the bluntness of Libby's question having caught me in mid-swallow. We had been debating how best to broach the subject of the missing key, and as we sat down to dinner, freshly showered and neatly attired in laundered pants and matching Alan a'Dale polo shirts, it became apparent that she had opted for the direct approach.

"Hmm?" asked Bitzy, with a look of doe-eyed innocence. Ladling green beans from a ceramic serving bowl, she added, "what would make you ask a thing like that?"

"Yep," said Saul, "there sure is."

"Saul!" chastised Bitzy, scooping green beans onto his plate with an abruptness that made it clear he didn't deserve them.

"What? They're going to find out sooner or later." Saul helped himself to a spoonful of macaroni and cheese from a casserole dish in the center of the table. As I took another swig of soda to quell my coughing fit, Libby looked from Saul to Bitzy expectantly.

When it became clear that neither was about to volunteer any more details, Libby tried again. "So... why are you keeping a monster in your hotel?"

Bitzy rolled her eyes theatrically. "We're not 'keeping a monster' in the hotel," she exclaimed, putting special emphasis on the air quotes.

"The hotel came with its own monsters," added Saul, though a mouthful of macaroni and green beans. "They were here when we arrived."

"They?" I asked. "There's more?"

"Three or four. They're all confined. It's under control."

"I think 107 is Lupita," said Iris Perlman, who was waiting for her husband Elliott to finish slicing the pot roast Bitzy had selected for our dinner.

"Lupita was one of the chambermaids," explained Elliott, as he sawed at the meat.

"She was a plump girl," continued Iris, "but very sweet." After a brief pause, she whispered "I think she stole."

"Whoever is in 107 isn't fat enough to be Lupita," countered Art Bamberger, who had opted for a jacket and tie this evening. His wife Doris sat by his side, her full attention devoted to buttering an onion roll. In our entire stay at Alan a'Dale's, I don't believe I ever saw Doris eat anything but onion rolls. "I think it might have been the night manager, what's-her-name. The one with the stammer."

Libby took a moment to regroup. "So… you don't have a problem with a monster living in the hotel?"

"I don't see as we've got a lot of choice," said Saul. "The thing just turned up one day. Damned if I know where it came from. It was in a room already, so we locked the door and put the key away for safe-keeping."

"And you put us in the same wing with it?"

"I thought you'd like the privacy of your own wing," answered Bitzy. "It's not like those things make a lot of noise."

"But, what if it gets out?"

"It's been here three days now," said Saul. "If it was going to get out, it would have done it already."

I helped myself to some macaroni as I considered my next question. Libby beat me to it. "So you're not planning on feeding us to that thing?"

Saul smiled. "We'll see how things work out."

"We could try luring it out," I offered. "If we can get it outside, we could…"

"We'd like to keep it around a while," said Elliott. "We might… need it."

Libby sagged. "Oh, for crying out loud…"

"Don't judge," Bitzy protested.

"It's just that we've already seen our share of kooks who were eager to turn into one of those things."

I nodded. "We watched an entire nursing home line up to feed themselves to those creatures. Plus a busload of religious nuts."

"Dozens of them," added Libby. "They ended up driving us out of our home. Please don't tell me you're thinking of joining them."

Elliott fished a pickle out of a small tureen and pointed it at me. "How many times a night do you get up to pee?"

I paused, momentarily confused by the sudden change in the direction of our conversation. "How many… what?"

"Maybe once, around two o'clock? Twice, if you had a beer before bed?"

"I don't really... keep track..."

"Oh my Lord, its zero, isn't it? You sleep soundly the whole night through, and your bladder doesn't make a squeak until after your alarm goes off. Tell me I'm wrong."

"Josh sleeps late," offered Libby helpfully. "He doesn't usually set an alarm."

"You don't work?" asked Bitzy.

"Self-employed," I answered. "I do Search Engine Optimization." The table stared at me, so I continued. "You know when you do an Internet search how you usually find what you're looking for on the first page of results? Well, what I do is..." The table stared at me even more. "No, I don't work."

Elliott leaned back and took a bite out of his pickle. The crunch served as punctuation to his argument. "I can't go an hour and a half without a pee."

"It's his prostate," added Iris. She leaned forward conspiratorially and mouthed the word "Cancer" as though she were trying to prevent eavesdroppers from overhearing.

"You don't have to whisper," he husband chided. "We all know its cancer. If you don't believe the doctors, the blood I see in my urine four times a night is a good clue."

"We're sorry to hear that," said Libby. "Is it operable?"

"Absolutely. It's a routine procedure. They do it with robots now, I understand. And if the biopsy's clean, they tell me I've got a ninety-eight percent chance of staying cancer-free."

"Well that's great!" I said.

"My operation was scheduled for yesterday."

Elliott took another bite of his pickle, and for a long moment the only sound in the dining room was the enthusiastic crunch of his chewing. "Mount Sinai. In Manhattan," he added with a swallow.

Saul rested his meaty elbows on the table and sighed. "Elliott, we can find you another hospital. We've still got time."

Elliott nodded. "Possibly. It's possible we'll be able to get out ahead of these things and find a working hospital. It's possible the government will get the situation under control. It's possible we'll be able to do this before the cancer has spread to any other organs." Elliott laid a hand across his stomach, as if he could gauge the spread of his disease through touch alone. "It's also possible that the cancer has already spread. To my bladder maybe, or my pancreas."

Iris leaned across the table and whispered to Libby. "My aunt Rachel died of pancreatic cancer." She shook her head slowly and mouthed the words "Not Good."

"Of course, it's also possible that I can avoid rotting from the inside out. It's possible I can live free of pain. Maybe forever."

"If you call that living," muttered Bitzy.

"What else should I call it? They move around. They reproduce. That looks like life to me."

I felt compelled to state the obvious. "But they're not human."

"Lots of things aren't human. That dog's not human." Elliott gestured to Banjo, who was curled up on a blanket in the corner of the dining room, oblivious to the conversation as he gnawed on a strip of turkey jerky Art had found in the gift shop. "If you had a choice between living as a dog and dying as a man, wouldn't you at least think about it?"

I made no reply. What Elliott was saying was crazy, of course. I just couldn't articulate precisely *why* it was crazy.

"I always wanted to be a seal," offered Iris. "When I was a girl, I thought it would be such fun to swim around the world, just laughing and playing and eating. I had a horn on my bicycle that I used to try honking with my nose." She sighed. "Never got the hang of it."

"What about you?" Libby asked of Saul. "Have you given any thought to… you know?"

Saul scratched a chin which looked like it had not seen a razor in a week. "Not for me. I'm not wild about the thought of wandering around for eternity as an emotionless pile of goo."

"Where are you getting 'emotionless' from?" countered Elliott. "We don't know what those things feel. We don't know if they recognize their family, or if they know a sunset for what it is. But we know they'll live to see another one."

The rest of the meal passed in silence, broken only by the enthusiastic chewing of the dog in the corner. I took comfort in the conviction that Banjo, at least, didn't want to be anything other than Banjo.

30

Twelve feet of Detroit steel prowled Route 28, cruising lazily at the cost of a pint of gas every mile. Saul Gerber was hunting tarbabies, and Libby, Banjo and I were taking our first car ride since abandoning the Focus in New Paltz.

The LeBaron's normally embarrassing fuel efficiency was further sabotaged by the weight of the four tarbabies that were clinging to the exterior of the vehicle—one plastered to the passenger-side door, one sprawled diagonally across the front grill, and two stuck to the driver's side. Saul had picked up these extra passengers deliberately, as today's excursion was a teaching exercise as well as an opportunity to clear Alan a'Dale's driveway of a handful of stray monsters. Even if he had wanted to avoid them, the road leading to the resort was thick enough with the creatures that it would have been impossible for Saul to get the massive car through their midst without picking up at least a couple of hitchhikers. He could have easily nabbed half a dozen more if that had been his aim, but even four was taxing the LeBaron's acceleration, and he didn't feel comfortable risking more.

"They're getting thicker out here," said Saul as he maneuvered the mammoth vehicle around a fallen branch. "When you two showed up, I had to drive three miles before I could unload that deer you came across. That's a good distance, far enough that I don't worry about them following me back. I don't think we'll be able to get that far today." Saul threaded the car through a trio of tarbabies forming a perfect equilateral triangle, with at least twenty feet separating the creatures. He jerked his thumb back as we passed the shapes. "You see the way they spread themselves out?"

I nodded from the back seat. A couple days of rest and decent food had largely restored my strength, but I still suffered a chronic headache. Libby had taken the shotgun seat so that I could lie down across the LeBaron's enormous back seat. I was using Banjo as a pillow while the dog hung his head out the window and drooled down the side of the car. "Yeah, it makes it really difficult to avoid them all. It's pretty clever of them, when you think about it."

"It might be clever," Saul conceded. "It might. It could be some kind of instinctive, organized hunting tactic, I guess."

"But you don't think so?" asked Libby.

"I couldn't swear to it, but I think maybe they spread themselves out because they don't like each other very much."

I snorted a laugh, and Banjo looked back to see what the commotion was. A thin string of drool followed him into the car.

"Yeah, I might be whadyacallit... anthropomorphizing them. But watch what happens here." Saul nudged the gas pedal, urging the car to close in on a distant, dark shape a half mile down the road. When he was within a dozen yards of the creature, he gently applied the brakes, allowing the car to pull alongside his target. At the last possible moment, he cut the wheel sharply to the right.

Splut.

As the car came to a halt, the creature affixed to the passenger side door came into contact with the one in the road, its shoulder thumping lightly into the other tarbaby's chest. For a long moment, nothing happened.

"What now?" asked Libby, craning to see around the creature that was blocking her window.

"Give it a minute," replied Saul.

And indeed, less than half a minute later, the tarbabies began to move again. The one who had been in the road, whom I thought of as the Pedestrian, slowly raised its arms. Though it didn't seem to be threatening us directly, I pulled Banjo's slobbery snout back inside the car and rolled up the rear window as a precaution. But the creature did not seem interested in us. Instead, it placed its right hand on the shoulder of the Passenger tarbaby that was still clinging to the car and its left hand on the other creature's head. Almost imperceptibly, the Pedestrian began to lean backward. The pose was peculiar, like some strange wrestling stance, but as its arms straightened, the creature's true intentions became obvious.

"It looks like it's trying to push the other one off."

Libby's eyes widened. "Are they... stuck... to each other?"

"You better believe it," Saul confirmed.

"I didn't know they could do that."

"I've never seen it happen on its own. The way they space themselves out, they never run into each other by accident. You have to force them into it. But once one of the buggers touches another, they are stuck in every sense of the word."

We watched in rapt fascination as the Pedestrian tried to extricate itself from its colleague. It pulled its shoulders back farther and farther, and its arms began to elongate with the strain. They did not, however, pull free. Nor did the creature manage to separate its chest from the back of the Passenger.

"That's really weird," noted Libby as she watched the thing's sluggish efforts. "But how does it help us? Now we've got five of them stuck to us, instead of four."

Saul put the car in park and folded his arms with a satisfied smile. "Keep watching. It should be any minute now."

As the Pedestrian reached what appeared to be the limit of its ability to pull backward, the Passenger began to move as well. With a sound like cellophane tape being pulled off the roll, it yanked its left arm, which had been thrown over the car's roof, free of the vehicle. It then thrust its newly liberated limb backwards, until its elbow collided with one of the Pedestrian's outstretched arms.

"That's not going to help," I noted, and indeed the movement only seemed to allow the Pedestrian to lean back farther. Unable to push away, the Passenger was pulled back with it, and as it swiveled toward the other retreating tarbaby, it also peeled slowly away from the side of the LeBaron.

"Cohesion is stronger than adhesion," said Saul. "That's what my high-school chemistry teacher told us, anyway. They're sticking to each other stronger than they can stick to anything else, so now they're going to follow the path of least resistance."

It took somewhere in the neighborhood of two minutes for the Passenger to pull far enough away from the car so that only its right leg remained attached. Saul put the car back in gear and hit the gas hard. The two creatures were pulled along with the vehicle for a moment before ripping free with a noise that sounded vaguely painful. Saul pulled forward a single car length, then stopped again. We turned to watch the progress of the conjoined tarbabies.

Both were still trying in vain to push off the other. The Passenger had swiveled its waist to a grotesque degree in an effort to bring its right arm to bear on the Pedestrian. Despite the unnatural angle of its torso, it was unable to reach the other monster, which continued its attempts to pull back. Before long, the pair's center of balance had shifted to the point where gravity could not help but take over, and the tangled mess toppled over backward onto the pavement.

Saul put the car in gear again, and the LeBaron rolled forward, somewhat more sprightly than before. "That's one down. You up for three more?"

"Can't we do them all at once?" asked Libby. "If we drove these three into the other two, wouldn't they all stick together?"

"They might," said Saul, with a glance to the rear-view mirror. "But I'm not sure it's a good idea." Saul spoke with an uncharacteristic sharpness to his voice, as though the question made him nervous. "If you had four of five of them in a single clump, and just one of them decided to hang on to the car, I'm not sure we'd be able to shift that much weight."

His tone told me there was more to Saul's reluctance than simple engineering. "Have you ever tried it?"

"Once," Saul admitted. "It didn't turn out so good."

"What happened?"

Saul didn't answer for a long while, and I was beginning to wonder if I'd offended him when the older man finally said, "It's easier if I show you."

It took us fifteen minutes to dispatch two more of the tarbabies clinging to the car. Saul nudged the thing on the hood into a tar version of either a large dog or a small deer, then bumped the creature hanging on the driver's side door into a shape that had no doubt been human, but had been so fat that its gender could not be confidently guessed. It was also sagging significantly. Mass that had probably once been centered on its waist was now hanging down around its knees, giving the creature the overall shape of a chocolate kiss.

"Look at that," said Saul. "That thing's been a tarbaby for maybe a week now, and now it looks like its melting. In another week, that bag of goo it's hauling around is gonna be dragging on the ground." He shook his head and eased the car forward again. After a moment he pointed ahead and said, "Here's what I wanted to show you."

Off on the right side of the road was a small clearing, empty except for a large wooden bulletin board. It appeared to be a parking area for a hiking trail. Signs bearing multi-colored dots pointed back into the woods. Saul pulled the car even with the board and stopped. Libby and I traded a glance, unsure at what we were supposed to be looking at.

"There," said Saul, pointing at the ground. "Down in front of the sign."

I looked again, but was unable to discern anything in the shadow of the sign. I was about to ask Saul what he was looking at when Libby gave a sudden, sharp gasp. "Good God, what is that?"

With that, I understood. I had been looking for something in the sign's shadow, but now realized that the sign was not casting a shadow. The dark mass down at its base was something else entirely.

Saul put the car in Park. "Come on," he said. "I want to take another look at it." His own door was still partially blocked by our remaining passenger, so he motioned for Libby to open her door. She did so, but without much enthusiasm. Not counting the creature on our car, there were two other tarbabies visible on this stretch of road, though neither was closer than a quarter mile away. Of more immediate concern was the unknown shape in front of her. Banjo and I hopped out of the back seat and move forward cautiously, giving the thing a wide berth.

The dark mass was about eight feet long, and about half as wide. The appendages sticking out from the center area were no doubt limbs, but it was difficult to make sense of them. One shape that must have been a leg was scraping at the ground on the thing's right, while a thinner limb, probably an arm, waved above it without any clear purpose. I counted five distinct leg shapes, four stems that were probably arms, and a half dozen other protuberances that were too indistinct to identify.

"This is why I don't want to stick more than two together," said Saul, squatting down in front of the dark mass. "Every time I've gotten two of them stuck, they've always managed to sort themselves out again. There was one pair that took two days to get it together, but on the third day, they were gone." He stood up again, wincing at the stiffness in his knees. "This is what happened when I tried to stick three of them at once. They've been like this for five days now. No... six. This is the sixth day, and they only seem to be getting worse."

I saw what he meant. The shape being described by the mass was not simply that of three human beings joined together in an awkward position. The arrangement of the limbs was impossible in any kind of logical combination of parts.

"That arm over there was about two feet to the right yesterday," noted Saul. "And it looks like there's a head missing this time. It's getting more... blobby. Like it's forgotten what it's supposed to look like." Saul sighed and turned to look up the road at another of the tarbabies. The creature did not appear to be advancing. "It's like they literally can't tell where one ends and the next begins."

"So what are we going to do about it?" I asked.

"I don't know that there's anything that can be done. I'd shoot it in the head if I thought that would work. Or if I could tell for sure where its heads were. Hell, I'd shoot all of these miserable bastards if I thought it would make a dime's worth of difference." We stood in silence for a while, watching the shapeless thing's aimless scratching and flailing, while Banjo amused himself by sniffing around the entrance to the path.

Saul broke the silence with another sigh. "At this point the only thing I can think to do is to not make any more of these messes." He turned back to the car. "Come on, let's get rid of this last one. Then we can… Oh."

Libby and I turned to see why Saul had stopped. At some point while the three of us were distracted by the misshapen blob on the ground, the last tarbaby had pulled itself off of the car. But rather than take the opportunity to advance on us, it had instead retreated, and was now moving off of the shoulder of the road into the woods beyond.

"That's a first," muttered Saul as he watched the creature heading off through the weeds at the road's edge.

"Is it afraid of… this?" wondered Libby.

"It doesn't like it, that's for sure."

We took one last look at the wriggling mess on the ground, then returned to the car. The ride back to Alan a'Dale's was quiet as we reflected on the tarbaby's retreat into the woods. I had never seen one of these creatures display any kind of emotion prior to this and was reluctant to credit its actions to anything resembling fear. Was it possible that Saul had discovered the one thing that even these monsters were afraid of?

I remembered a story I had read in college from Plato's *Symposium*. The fable claimed that, in the beginning, every human being was actually two people joined together. Jealous of the happiness these duplex beings felt, the gods decided to take us down a few pegs, and literally cut us in half. As time went on, every half-person retained a faint memory of being part of a greater whole and spent its life looking for its lost other half. This was how the gods invented love, quite by accident.

I wondered if we had just invented terror for the tarbabies.

31

By the end of our first full week at Alan a' Dale's, we lost phone service entirely. Libby's cell phone was still getting four bars, but any attempts to call from it resulted only in silence. The hotel's landline gave us the encouragement of a dial tone, but nothing more. Calls to New York resulted in a recorded message indicating all circuits were busy. Calling our house yielded only a busy signal. The number Libby tried most frequently, her parents' house in Albany, was also the most disconcerting. From there we heard only a series of electronic clicks, punctuated by an occasional faint squeal. We tried dialing random numbers in west coast area codes, to see if we could gauge the extent of the problem. Nowhere could we establish a connection.

"That probably means the problem's here," suggested Saul. "The circuits must be screwed up in this area. You'll be fine once you get out of the county."

The TV wasn't any more helpful. The hotel was too far from any of the major hubs to receive a broadcast signal, and was dependent upon a satellite network. For a few days that operated normally, and we were able to track the epidemic's spread westward, as the tarbabies showed up first in Philadelphia, then Pittsburgh, then Cincinnati. CNN was chasing down the first rumors of the creatures appearing in Chicago when the satellite signal was lost. For the last three days, the antiquated CRTs peppering the hotel's rooms displayed only blue screens, indicating the system was busily attempting to reestablish a connection.

The Internet was the last of our lifelines to the outside world to fail. Though the computers at the hotel's reception desk were underpowered and out of date, the satellite afforded them a high-speed broadband connection. While we were able to access the major news outlets, we soon discovered that the frequency with which these sites were being updated plummeted as the week progressed. As a test, I posted comments on every user forum I could find, from news outlets to social networks to shopping sites. In many cases, my posts failed to show up on the message boards at all. In most others, they went unanswered.

After seven days of clean sheets and hot food, we felt confident enough to risk traveling again. Our assorted blisters, scrapes and abrasions were healing, and my digestive tract was finally working in a way I recognized. As I had not in fact transformed into a tarbaby from the inside out, I reluctantly concluded that my stomach problems had likely been the result of dehydration and a perfectly pedestrian form of bacteria, and not of microscopic tar bogeys. Properly provisioned, I felt strong enough to complete the trek to Albany.

"You're walking?" asked Saul, when we explained our intention to continue on to Libby's parents. "That's nuts. It'll take you two days, at least."

With a full stomach and a hundred working toilets to choose from, I was more optimistic. "I think we can make it in one. It can't be more than thirty miles."

"Follow," said Saul, who led us back to Robin's Goods. There he produced a New York State road atlas. It hadn't been for sale, of course—that would have conflicted with the store's theme of random uselessness. Instead it was tucked in a drawer beneath the cash register, dog-eared and decades out of date, but still suitable for our purposes. Without even checking the index, Saul flipped to the page he needed, then stabbed a thick forefinger down in the middle.

"That's us. Here's the Catskills, and here…" Saul flipped the page, "…is the thruway. That takes you here…" flipping the page again, "… then up to here." One more flip brought us to the page hosting the black star in the red circle—the state capital. "That's forty-five miles once you make it to the Thruway, and another five miles just to get there."

"That doesn't sound right," I said as I traced the route for myself. "We walked for close to two days. We must have made at least thirty miles in that time."

"You started at New Paltz?" asked Saul, to which I nodded. He flipped the pages again. "New Paltz is here. That's about…" Saul consulted the legend, "fifteen miles."

"No," I insisted, but without much enthusiasm. "We must have gone further than that."

"Over rough terrain? Over mountains? Don't bet on it." Saul closed the atlas and replaced it in its drawer. "You've gone fifteen miles. You've got three times that far left to go. You can walk it in two days, or you can drive it in an hour."

"But we don't have a car," observed Libby.

Saul did not look at us when he replied. "You can take Elliott's car. The Bonneville."

"Elliott's car? Won't he be needing it?"

Saul shook his head. "Elliott isn't going to be driving anymore. He's going to… do it."

"It?"

Saul nodded.

"Oh."

"And what are you going to do about it?" I asked.

"We're going to help him."

Lunchtime that day was more awkward than usual. Bitzy had assembled the usual selection of cold cuts and mayonnaise-drenched side dishes (macaroni salad held the pride of place today), but her usual bubbling hospitality had been replaced by thinly disguised hostility.

"I just don't understand what the rush is," she chided as she ripped into a bag of German-style hard pretzels. "These monsters will still be here a month from now. Why do you have to kill yourself now?"

Elliott's expression was impassive. He had been through this argument before, and was tired of it. "I'm not killing myself," he said with exaggerated calm. "The whole point here is that I don't have to die. And why not now? I'm already in pain. Am I morally obligated to suffer? Do I have to wait until Iris has to spoon-feed me and change my soiled sheets every hour?"

"Don't even pretend you're doing this for Iris!" spat Bitzy. "She's the real victim here. She's the one who's going to have to live with what you did, after you've left her behind."

Iris laughed. There was not a trace of irony in that laugh—it was the spontaneous, guileless laughter of someone who has finally gotten the joke. "Oh Bitzy, he's not leaving me behind."

Bitzy froze, the bowl of pretzels in her hand hovering above the table as she attempted to make sense of this. "Oh, you've got to be kidding me."

"I'm going with him," Iris confirmed, giving her husband's bicep a supportive squeeze.

"But… but you're not dying! You're not even sick!"

"And now I get to keep it that way."

Bitzy looked to Elliott, her mouth agape. "You're going to let her do this? You're going to let her throw her life away for you?"

"I'm going to let her spend her life *with* me. Just like she has for the last thirty-five years. Hell, for all we know, we might get to be together forever."

"It's really kind of romantic, when you think about it," added Iris, with just the faintest touch of a quaver in her voice.

"It's obscene!"

"Bitzy, come on. Enough," said Saul. "They're adults. They've made up their minds. We can either support them or stay out of their way." Libby and I had been discretely keeping our peace during the argument, but now Saul turned his attention to us. "Which reminds me. There's something I'd like your help with before you go."

It took us a few hours to notice that the power had gone out. When we lost satellite service, we had fallen back on more pastoral entertainments to pass the time, like reading, napping or learning to play something called "pinochle." It wasn't until Bitzy started planning the dinner menu that she noticed the walk-in cooler was off. We spent most of the afternoon packing the perishables into coolers. At Fryer Tuck's, most of the food items were perishable, and it was clear we could not count on the free lunch lasting much longer.

The horizon was tinged a brilliant pre-twilight orange by the time we assembled outside Room 107. The silver ring that held the keys to the Bonneville was already in my pocket—a thank-you gift for the service I was about to perform for Elliott and Iris.

"Why can't you do this outside?" complained Bitzy. "There's hundreds of monsters out there. Why does it have to be this one?"

"Because outside, we couldn't be confined," explained Elliott for the third time. "If you decided to leave the hotel, we'd be in your way. Here, you can just close the door and not have to worry about us."

"After we've gotten the other one out," added Libby.

"That's right."

"I know it's silly, all things considered," said Iris. "But if we're going to be locked in a hotel room for eternity, I'd prefer it was just the two of us. Shacking up with a stranger just seems… dirty."

"Lupita's hardly a stranger," noted Elliott.

"We don't know its Lupita," countered Iris. "And even if it is, I don't need her sharing a bedroom with us."

"So what's the plan?" I asked.

"It's simple," Saul explained. "Elliott and Iris go in, get comfortable, and then… change. Once they're finished, you're going to help me lure Lupita out of this room, and into the one across the hall. We lock her in that one, them in the other, and we're done."

There was silence as we considered the finality of this statement. Libby broke it by asking, "are you sure you want to do this?"

Elliott smiled. "No. But I'm sure I don't want to die." He turned to the assembled group, but could find no words for us. In the end, he simply kissed his wife, and squeezed her hands. "All right then."

Elliott took the room key out of his pocket, the enormous arrowhead keychain snagging on the fabric of his jacket. Then he unlocked the door, pushed it open a crack, and peeked inside. "Lupita?"

The hand was upon him far too quickly. The tarbaby had been at the door. *Right* at the door. Had it been waiting for us to open it, and if so, for how long?

The hand was indeed fast, but not graceful. It flailed at Elliott's exposed face, but an involuntary flinch on his part caused it to miss its target and fall instead on the lapel of his jacket. He would only need to shrug the garment off, and he would be free.

Except once again, instinct trumped good sense. Elliott's impulsive reaction to an unwanted hand pawing at his jacket was not to remove the jacket, but rather to swat the intruder away. Without considering what he was doing, Elliott swept his hand upward.

Splut.

And that's how Elliott came to be standing in the hallway during his transformation, rather than inside Room 107. With the thing that had been Lupita inside, and Elliott outside, he was unable to enter the room, and the door between them could not be closed.

"My goodness," said Elliott in bemused astonishment, as he watched the sticky blackness of the tarbaby's hand begin to overspread his own. He looked around to see if anyone else appreciated the humor in what was happening. "I guess this isn't according to plan, huh?"

"I guess not," agreed Saul, taking this complication with an admirable degree of calm.

"Sorry about that."

"Don't worry about it."

Elliott peeked back inside. "I don't remember her being that fast when she was still Lupita." He looked back down at his hand and laughed. "I don't have to pee. For the last six months, I've felt like I had to pee twenty-four hours a day. And just like that, it's gone." He looked to his wife. "This is going to be amazing."

32

Libby eyed the faux-brass hardware that was now visible through the crack in the open door. "We could take the door off its hinges," she suggested. "Then we could at least get Elliott inside the room."

Saul examined the hinge plates skeptically. "The door's got to be open all the way to get to the screws. And even if we could get the door off, I don't think we could get him in far enough to put it back on again."

"We'd have to push Lupita back a few feet as well."

"It's hard enough shoving these things around with a car. I don't think we'd have much luck trying it by hand."

"We were able to move them back home," noted Libby. "We couldn't exactly push them around, but we managed to pick them up and carry them. Josh did, anyway."

"That we did," I agreed. "But those guys were standing on a lawn." I knelt down and took a tentative tug at the industrial-grade carpet. "This stuff is pretty tough. It's not going to come up as easy as grass."

Iris was standing across the hall, watching the activities with a sincere but nervous fascination. "Can't you get her inside?" she asked her husband. "Won't she follow you, Honey?"

"Hmm?" said Elliott, coming to attention as though he had been caught dozing. "Oh, we're fine, Sugar. We'll go in when we're finished."

The absorption process had been especially slow. Elliott was fully dressed, including a long-sleeved shirt and sport coat, and the only exposed flesh on his person was his head and hands. The tarlike goop had already oozed over his right hand, which was pinned to his chest, and was now spreading inside his coat sleeve and over his shirt, searching for skin.

"You're going to love this, Sugar," added Elliott. "You don't realize how many little aches and pains you've accumulated over your lifetime until they're taken away."

Iris nodded and smiled. "It sounds wonderful."

Elliott beamed back an ear-to-ear grin. "Wonderful it is! That's the word for it all right! Yes sir, a wonder is exactly what it is!" His gaze returned to the creature holding him. He peered deep into the shadows of the room's interior, to where the thing's face must surely be. I could see nothing but the monstrous black arm and the goopy mass that was now seeping upward, in defiance of gravity, toward Elliott's exposed face. "You've all got to try this," the older man whispered.

"Soon, darling. Soon," Iris promised. She stepped beside her husband and laid a tender hand on his shoulder, following his gaze into the room. The thing that may have been Lupita seemed to be watching her, though it made no attempt to come into the light of the hallway.

"Why wait?" Elliott replied, and with a single deft movement, brought his free left arm across his body, and gripped Iris' hand in his own.

"Oh," said his wife, who instinctively tried to step back. But Elliott's grip was firm. "Honey, let go."

"Three chairs, no waiting!" exclaimed her husband, a broad, joyful grin still dominating his face. Then he pulled, dragging Iris' hand toward the Lupita-creature's arm.

"No. Wait." Iris was pulling now as well. Her right hand gripped the door jamb and her feet dug into the industrial carpet below. Her left hand inched forward nonetheless. "Elliott, stop it!"

"Really! It's OK!" If Elliott's grin were any wider, it would have met in the back, and the top of his head would have slid off. For a moment I stood paralyzed, uncertain as to whether I should intervene. Then I heard a faint crackling sound from Iris' hand, like pretzels snapping, and the decision was made for me. I grabbed Elliott's wrist and struggled to pull both it and Iris away from the doorway.

Saul also leapt to Iris' aid, but while his intentions were admirable, his capacity for multi-tasking was not. As he stepped forward to encircle Elliott in his powerful arms, he thought only of the danger the man posed to his wife. In that short moment, Saul forgot that the real threat was still lurking behind the door. Had he been permitted time to consider his actions, he surely would not have thrown his arms around Elliott's chest, which was now thick with probing black muck.

Splut.

"Hey!" said Elliott, and it was neither a Hey of outrage, nor of frustration. It was not the kind of Hey that is followed by "what's the big idea" or "get your hairy monkey mitts off of me." This was a Hey of camaraderie—the gentle interjection of surprise you might exclaim when you run into someone you work with at the movies. It was not the Hey of someone who felt the slightest bit threatened.

There was absolute silence in the hallway following the sticky sound that marked the end of Saul's human existence. The large man blinked three times, then laughed. This was no embarrassed chuckle—it was a violent, spasmodic guffaw that shook Saul hard enough to rattle the door in its frame. As I watched the older man's face grow red from the effort of drawing breath, I realized that this was the first time I had seen Saul laugh.

"Oops," he said between convulsions. "Oops! I sure… Wow. I sure…" But the rest would not come out. Elliott appeared to be the only one who got the joke, and he too joined in the party. His laughter was not quite as violent as his friend's, but it distracted him enough to allow me to relax his grip and free Iris' hand without being noticed. I backpedaled quickly, and Iris sagged to the floor, clutching her injured hand to her chest.

"What the hell!" Bitzy shrieked. She ran to her husband, nearly stepping on the prostrate Iris, and grabbed him by the shoulders. "Saul! What the hell!" She tired pulling him back, which just sent her husband into a stronger fit of hysterics. Saul tightened his grip on Elliott, threw back his head, and let out a piercing *WHOO-HOO* of unabashed joy.

"Let go of him!" commanded Bitzy, though it wasn't immediately clear at whom this was directed. She turned her beet-red fact to me, and hissed, "Make them let go!"

I looked at Bitzy, at Saul, at Libby, and at Bitzy again. When that accomplished nothing, I looked back down the hall to the diminutive figures of the Bambergers, who had been watching the proceedings in silence as Art stroked Banjo's head. "I don't know how," I conceded at last.

Bitzy thrust an accusing finger in Iris' face. "This is your fault! You and your idiot husband! Make them let go... right now!" But the woman on the floor only shook her head as tears welled in her eyes.

"I don't... I can't... We need to do it over..."

Bitzy lunged forward, raising an awkward fist in preparation for what surely would have been an ineffectual blow. But Libby stepped calmly between the women, looking Bitzy directly in the eyes.

"We need another one."

Bitzy stopped, her arm still raised. She wasn't certain what it was that Libby had just said, but the assured, certain tone in which she said it spoke of hope—and a plan. "Another one?"

"There are more in the hotel, aren't there? Where are they?"

Bitzy turned uncertainly, looking back up the hallway toward the reception area.

"Yes!" I cried, as I caught up to what my wife was doing. "We can get another one!"

Having caught Bitzy's full attention, Libby continued her explanation. "When two of the monsters touch each other, they let go of anything else they're touching. Saul taught us that." Bitzy slowly lowered her fist. "They don't like touching each other. If they let go of the car, they'll let go of Saul."

Bitzy closed her eyes, and her lower lip quivered. For a moment, I thought the older woman was going to faint. Then she opened her eyes, and shouted, "134! There's one in room 134!" Without looking to see if anyone was joining her, she sprinted down the hallway toward the hotel's entryway.

"You're brilliant," I said, and kissed my wife on the forehead. A moment later, we were running after Bitzy, leaving behind the sound of two old men cackling like hyenas.

33

The door to room 134 would not budge. Just as with 107, the thing inside had been standing immediately behind the door, as if waiting for someone to open it. It did not appear to understand that the door needed room to swing open. Each time I tried to push it open, the creature lurched forward, slamming it shut again.

"I don't know if I can get this one out. Should we try one of the others?"

The Sherwood Lodge, Alan a'Dale's primary building, sported four wings, jutting out from the main reception area in an ornate H pattern. Each of these wings hosted twenty guest rooms. Room 107 was in the southeast wing, as was the room Libby and I had been occupying. We were presently in the southwest wing.

"138," sighed Bitzy. "This way." She carried an enormous red leather shoulder bag that had been squirreled away behind the main desk. There was a moment of frenetic jingling as she fished around inside. "Dammit anyway!" she shouted, then upended the bag, dumping its contents onto the hallway carpeting. A dozen keys spilled onto the floor, all still attached to merry arrowhead fobs. Bitzy kicked some aside, then pounced on the one labeled 138.

"Saul said there were only three or four of those things in here," I noted, staring at the pile of metal on the floor.

"Yeah, well, Saul lies," replied Bitzy, cramming the key into the lock on 138. Her hand slipped, banging heavily against the door jamb, and she dropped the key. "Dammit anyway!" she repeated, pounding the door for emphasis. She took a deep breath, then picked up the key again. "He didn't want to worry you kids."

Slowly, with deliberate caution, Bitzy slid the key into the brass lock on the door. After a couple of experimental jiggles, the lock slid open. Bitzy nudged the door forward, but it stopped after swinging inward less than two inches. "Dammit dammit dammit!"

"All right," I said. "Let me try again." As Bitzy stepped aside, I put my shoulder to the door and shoved. The door gave another inch. "Good. This one's moving."

The hallway was barely six feet wide, but it was all the room I had to work with. I backed up as far as I could, then jumped at the door. The attempt was half-hearted, but even so I could feel the door rock when I hit it. On my second effort, I aimed for a spot two feet beyond the door. My head thumped hard against the wood, leaving a peephole-sized dimple in my right temple, but I was rewarded with a faint sound like Velcro from within. The door swung inward, and I collapsed backward into the hallway.

The thing inside was slender and tall. From my vantage point on the floor, I judged it must have been just shy of seven feet tall when it was human. It appeared to have settled somewhat since then. Its arms were longer than they should have been, and its calves and feet were exceptionally thick, as though the liquid goop that comprised its body were pooling down there. The thing swayed momentarily, as if trying to recover its balance, then took a long step forward, swinging its arms at a preposterous angle. Behind it, I could see another patch of black silhouetted against the curtains.

"There's two of them!" I shouted, then rolled out of the doorway. Libby and Bitzy had already retreated away from the door, and as I scrambled to my feet, I could see that this was going to present a problem. For while Libby was moving back toward the reception area, Bitzy had stationed herself further down the hall.

"Bitzy! This way!" But my warning was too late. The Long Man was already swinging its awkward shape through the doorway and into the hall. It stood still for a moment and did not bother to look left or right. With whatever senses were left to it, it found prey waiting on both sides and instinctively chose the target that had the fewest options for retreat. It swiveled toward Bitzy and lumbered forward, swinging its ropy arms toward her face.

With remarkable speed for a woman of her years, Bitzy did some lunging of her own. She still held the large leather bag that had contained the room keys, and she thrust that forward into the creature's grasp. The tarbaby hit the bag with both hands, and Bitzy shoved forward again, rocking her attacker back far enough for her to slip past it.

"Catch me if you can, you freak!" she screamed as she sprinted down the hall toward Reception. Libby and I followed, keeping our eyes fixed on the tall, skinny creature loping clumsily after us.

The Long Man was not as slow as the average tarbaby, but it was still a long way from spry. For Bitzy, Libby and I, most of the chase through the hotel consisted of waiting. The reception area was peppered with furniture, decorative columns and potted plants, all of which proved difficult obstacles for the Long Man to maneuver around. Upon encountering an obstruction, the creature would stop dead, as if weighing its options, then shuffle sideways until the way ahead was clear again. There was always a brief delay before the thing swung itself forward again to continue its pursuit.

This tortuous manner of walking slowed the Long Man, which gave its roommate sufficient time to catch up. The second tarbaby in room 138 turned out to be much smaller than the first, and of an indistinct form. It might have been an adolescent when it was still human, though something about its manner of walking gave the impression of a small-framed woman. Unlike the loping Long Man, this one kept its arms primly at its sides at all times, and advanced with small, precisely measured steps. It did not walk with the speed of its mate, but it maneuvered better, and did not need to pause when it encountered something in its path.

I did some mental calculations as I watched the creatures' progress, as we needed only one of them at Room 107. It would be risky if we had to avoid both of them in that narrow corridor. The Prim-Thing seemed like the more viable option at first. Even with the tarbabies' additional mass, I was confident I could lift the petite creature by myself. On the other hand, the Long Man was naturally awkward and had a higher center of gravity. It would be easier to topple over, which is what I had in mind.

Having settled on a plan, I commenced redecorating. I cleared a path between the Long Man and the southeast hallway as best I could, sliding the furnishings across the lobby and piling them in front of the Prim-Thing instead. By the time the taller creature had reached the Reception Desk, its cohort was a dozen feet behind it, struggling to get around an overturned armchair.

A thought occurred to me then, and before I could fully process it, I found myself bolting for the Front Desk. The Long Man hesitated, then swiveled to follow me. "What's opposite 107?" I shouted. Neither Bitzy nor Libby had an answer for me, so I ripped half a dozen keys off the rack behind the desk—everything from 104 to 110. As the skinny tarbaby was reaching its exaggerated arms out toward me, I ducked and scrambled away. I trotted down the southeast corridor, and the women followed after me.

It was Room 108 that stood directly opposite 107, and I slipped that key into the door's lock, discarding the rest on the floor of the hallway. One of them bounced off of Iris, who was still sitting quietly on the floor, watching her husband's silent transformation. Both Elliott and Saul had stopped laughing, though in the case of the former, this was because the lower half of his face was encased in a thick coating of tar. Saul's arms were still wrapped around his friend, Lupita's goo now covering them to the elbows, and his head now rested on Elliott's shoulder, as though they were sharing a quiet snuggle. He was no longer smiling, but was instead enraptured by the inky, viscous gel that was spreading over Elliott's face.

I opened the door to 108 cautiously, uncertain what I might find waiting inside. The room was empty of anything except the expected assortment of bland hotel furniture, and I risked a glance back down the hallway. The Long Man had not yet entered the corridor, but I could hear movement in the lobby.

I stepped to the room's queen-sized bed and peeled off the thin comforter. "I'm going to wait in here. You two keep going down the hall, and holler out when it's about to pass the room. I'll try to knock it into the doorway there. If we get lucky, it'll hit Lupita, and she'll stop what she's doing to untangle herself."

"Are we going to get lucky?" asked Libby.

"Of course. We're lucky people." I gave my wife a peck on the lips, and she and Bitzy helped Iris up off the floor. The three of them retreated down the hall to where the Bambergers were keeping Banjo entertained.

"Good girl, Corky," I heard Art say, and he was wrong on all three counts.

I wrapped the comforter around my arms and prepared for a quick lunge out the door. Seconds later, Libby called out, "It's coming!" I suppressed my first instinct, which was to call back, trusting my wife to give me the information I needed without betraying my location. As expected, half a minute later she called out again. "It's at Room 116! Four doors to go!"

I retreated half a step. The last light of the setting sun was streaming through the room's windows, and I didn't want to risk my shadow peeking out through the doorway. It was dark in the hallway, and I couldn't actually see where my shadow ended, but I had no idea what kind of spectrum the tarbabies saw the world in.

"114!" I shifted my weight back and forth between my feet. My muscles were tense enough to constrict blood flow, and I didn't want my feet falling asleep now.

"112!"

"Knock him on his sticky ass, Slim!" hollered Bitzy. "But be careful about it!" she added after a moment's thought.

"110! Get ready!" I wanted to shout something brave and manly, just to cut the tension, but didn't want to alert the approaching creature to my presence. I settled for bobbing my head enthusiastically. At the rate it had been traveling, it would be passing the doorway in three... two...

"Something's wrong!"

I was so keyed up that my wife's voice almost triggered me to sprint out of the room. I did in fact take a lunging step forward before catching myself. Now my balance was off, and I teetered uncertainly as I debated what to do.

"Josh, it's stopped!"

I craned my neck forward, trying to see around the corner into the hallway. The floor beneath me let out a muffled creak, and

I froze. I leaned back again, concerned that the Long Man might now be trying to peek around at me.

"It's moving again. It... Hey! Hey, down here!"

The patter of Libby's feet on the hallway carpet coincided precisely with the appearance of the tar on the door jamb. It was high off the ground, nearly at eye level, that the dark flipper-like appendage oozed its way around the corner. The creature no longer had distinct fingers, but the goopy mass that used to be its hand still moved as if it did. After the hand was secured to the door frame, the Long Man's head poked into view, nearly perpendicular to the floor. The tarbaby and I considered one another for a long moment, then the creature stumbled forward, its shoulder crashing into the open door. The thing was coming in.

I backed up to the window, figuring I could get out that way and double-back through the lobby. I risked turning my back on the advancing creature in order to flip open the latch and slide the window open. It was a superb plan, impeded only by the fact that the windows had no latches, and did not slide open. The large center sections of the windows were fixed sheets of plate glass, and could not be opened. On either side were thin casement windows which swiveled open by means of a small crank at the bottom of the frame, but as these were less than a foot wide, they were not a viable escape route.

Fighting the urge to panic, I looked around for something heavy enough to smash the window. The phone on the bedside table was a flimsy plastic affair, while the desk appeared to be too heavy to throw. By the time I spotted the small wooden chair parked underneath the desk, I was out of time. The Long Man was upon me.

With no time to consider my actions, I attacked. I threw the comforter over my head and charged, hoping to shove the creature back into the hallway by brute force alone. I hit the monster low, wrapped my arms around its midsection, and simultaneously pushed and lifted with all the strength I could muster.

If I had a longer run-up—if I had time to build up more momentum—it might have worked. As it was, the creature's mass stopped me dead in my tracks. I dug my feet into the carpet and shoved for all I was worth, but only found myself sliding backward. The Long Man, heavier than me and with a huge advantage in traction, leaned forward. As I was doubled over backward, I felt my balance slip. In another moment, I would fall to the floor, and the Long Man would be on top of me.

I could not see what saved me, but I could hear it. A pair of roars bellowed from the direction of the hallway—one low and throaty, with a texture derived from several thousand cigarettes too many, and the other high, shrill, and entirely unaccustomed to demonstrations of rage. Bitzy and Libby had thundered into the room like the Valkyrie, and were hauling the Long Man back into the hall.

At least they were trying to. The creature's height, the narrowness of the doorway and their reluctance to get too close to their quarry robbed them of any chance of getting a proper position of leverage. Still, they wrapped their hands in the sheet with which they had covered the dark shape and pulled with every ounce of strength they could summon, and this was enough. As the creature's weight fell off of me, I reared up once again and shoved.

For a moment, the ripping sound that ensued convinced me that I had herniated myself. But when I looked down, I discovered a large, oval-shaped bare patch in the carpeting. We had succeeded in knocking the Long Man off balance, and were now moving him back. I dug my feet deeper into the rug and pushed again.

Had the Long Man been human, this would have worked. A man would have instinctively attempted to keep his balance in the face of an assault. But the tarbaby did not share this impulse and made no effort to replant its dislocated foot. Instead, the free leg swung up toward me, and the creature went down on its back. Libby plastered herself against the open door to avoid its fall, while Bitzy stumbled back into the hallway.

That's where she was reminded that the Long Man was not alone.

The struggle with the Long Man had been short, but it was enough time for the Prim-Thing to maneuver its way past the crude maze of furniture I had thrown together. In their haste to come to my aid, neither Bitzy nor Libby had noticed the small creature's silent advance down the darkened hallway, and when the older woman stumbled out of the room again, the thing had been in perfect position to tag her.

Splut.

The impact was harsh. In its enthusiasm, the Prim-Thing had swung its right hand up in a short, fierce swipe, catching Bitzy squarely on the cheek. From the sound of the slap, I'm certain it would have left a vivid red welt, if the hand had ever left the woman's face. But, true to form, the dark appendage simply hung from Bitzy's cheek, hiding the look of utter shock and outrage that was now gripping her features. In a last act of defiance, capping off a lifetime that had no doubt been full of acts of defiance, Bitzy pulled back her right hand and delivered a healthy slap of her own, smack dab across the center of the Prim-Thing's dark, goopy head.

SPLUT!

The woman and the monster stood in the doorway in silence, each with a hand plastered to the other's face. Bitzy coughed gently, then again. Then she threw her head back as far as her situation allowed, and she laughed. She laughed without grace, in big hiccupping gulps, and the sound set Saul off again into his own laughing fit.

"Look at me!" she chortled, fighting for the breath to form the words. "Have you ever... HUH... seen a worse... HUH HYUH... plan... HAH... in all... HUH... in all..." She could not finish the sentence.

While Bitzy appeared delighted beyond words at her current predicament, Libby was less enthusiastic about her own situation. The cackling madwoman to her right was the least of her worries. Bitzy and the Prim-Thing were blocking the doorway, with the tarbaby's right arm crossing the exit at chest height. If she gave Bitzy a healthy shove, she could probably squeeze through, but the monster's left arm was still free and dangerous. To her left, the Long Man was still prostrate, though it was now struggling to find its feet. It was still mostly covered by the sheets we had thrown over it, which made this the path of least resistance. Libby placed her left foot delicately in the center of the creature's chest, then pushed off the door and hopped over the Long Man and into the room.

"Nicely done," I said as we backed into the far corner, away from the wriggling form in the entryway.

"Are we still going to be able to free them?"

It had taken three of us to budge the Long Man a single step, and that had ended disastrously. With three of the creatures on the loose, we would need help. I cupped my hands over my mouth and shouted. "Mister Bamberger? Missus Bamberger?"

There was movement from the hallway, the metallic click of a lock snapping into place, then silence. A moment later, we heard a faint, querulous whine.

"Banjo?"

The dog poked its snout through the open doorway and let out a single excited yap. He put one exploratory paw inside the room, but retreated when he saw the Long Man.

"Come on, Banjo!" encouraged Libby. "If I can do it, you can too!" Her logic was flawed, of course. Libby could drive a car, cook spaghetti, build a PowerPoint slide, and do a hundred other things for which Banjo had yet to display the slightest aptitude, but in this case she happened to be correct. Banjo sized up the wriggling mass of fabric in front of him, reared back, and leapt.

At that same moment, Bitzy grabbed at the dog. Her positioning was awkward, and she only managed to touch his tail, but it was enough to startle him. Banjo yelped and flinched as he jumped, causing him to misjudge his trajectory. Midway through his leap, it was clear to us that he was going to land on the exposed right foot of the Long Man.

This was also clear to Banjo, who had no intention of cooperating. As he descended, the dog rolled in mid-air. While this maneuver did not allow him to clear the creature entirely, it did mean that he caught the foot on his haunch, rather than his belly. As he hit the floor, Banjo scrabbled his claws against the carpet, yelped again, and rolled under the bed. From our corner, I could see a tuft of light brown hair stuck to the Long Man's toe.

It seemed a very long time before Banjo's nose emerged from under the bed. He looked up with the canine equivalent of "Now what?" in his eyes.

I called out for the Bambergers once again, and after receiving no reply, Libby and I said at precisely the same moment, "We need to get out of here." We had hoped to leave in the morning, as the thought of traveling in the dark held no appeal. But the sun was now gone, and the notion of waiting around Alan a'Dale's with as many as half a dozen monsters roaming about was even less attractive.

I picked up the small wooden chair by the desk and motioned for Libby to stay back. The chair was much lighter than I had hoped, but it was the only item to hand that looked like it had a chance of breaking glass. I turned my back to my target, then spun as quickly as I could, smashing the chair into the window. Its leg glanced off the center strip dividing the glass down the middle and splintered into half a dozen fragments. The glass remained intact.

I stared at the shattered stump of chair leg that remained in my hand.

"That's one tough window," observed Libby.

"That's one cheap-ass chair," I corrected. I gripped the chair leg tightly in both hands, raised it above my head, and then plunged it into the center of the right-hand window as though I were staking a vampire. The glass exploded outward into the night in a thousand shining fragments.

Not all of which hit the ground.

As the cool evening air flooded into the room, I found myself staring at an eerily beautiful field of stars hanging motionless in the air just outside the window. My first thought wasn't really a thought at all—just a vague sense of wonderment at the sight of a hundred sparkling points of light dangling directly in front of me. My second thought was that I was merely looking at my own distorted reflection, fractured by the splintered glass of the window. My third thought was that my second thought was preposterous, as the glass in that particular pane was now gone, and the only reason I thought it was my reflection was because the star-field pattern was human shaped. There had been a tarbaby standing directly behind the window when I smashed it, perhaps attracted by the commotion of our struggle with the Long Man, and it was now coated in tiny, round fragments of safety glass.

My fourth thought was that this sucked, so I hit it with a pillow.

I was not surprised when the creature failed to react. That which can survive gunfire and immolation without complaint is all too seldom fazed by a bag of feathers. It is fortunate then that my intention was not to harm the thing, but only to give us a way to get past it. Despite the coating of glass covering much of the tarbaby's upper body, the pillow stuck fast to its head and shoulders. I pulled a second pillow off the bed and slammed it into the monster's belly, providing me with a reasonably safe landing zone. I launched myself through the window feet first, hitting the tarbaby square in the chest and gut and driving it back. Not by much—the creature staggered backward just a single step, but it was enough room for me to squeeze past. After scooping up Banjo from beneath the bed, Libby followed.

It was Banjo who saved us from the second monster in the night. We had been so focused on staying outside the Glitter Man's reach that we missed the shape clinging to the building itself. Only when the dog began barking hysterically in Libby's arms did we see the fat black ball hanging just above eye level beside the broken window pane. So well camouflaged was it among the natural shadows on this side of the building that its exact shape was difficult to determine, but I settled on Possum.

Libby lingered at the window for a moment longer than was strictly prudent under the circumstances. As I opened my mouth to ask her what she was waiting for, she cupped her hands around her mouth, stuck her head in the window, and bellowed "Iris!!"

There was no response from inside the lodge, but both the Glitter Man and Possum-Thing appeared to take an interest. I grabbed my wife by the arm, and the two of us bolted for a small parking lot tucked nearly out of sight on this side of the main building with Banjo still cradled in Libby's arms. I fished the keys Saul had given me from my pocket, then stared at them, confused by their lack of volume.

"Where's the remote?"

Libby glanced at the key ring in my hand and confirmed that it was indeed missing the big plastic keyless entry fob we were accustomed to. "Maybe it doesn't have one."

"How the devil are we supposed to find it?" I surveyed the four cars in this lot. I remembered seeing three more at the hotel's entrance, and another lot on the opposite side of the building. "What kind of car doesn't have a remote?"

"A Bonneville?"

I studied the cars in front of me. "What do you suppose a Bonneville looks like?"

"Big and boxy. Landau roof. Lighted curb feelers."

"Really?"

"I'm guessing."

One of the cars in the lot was a Volkswagen, so that was out. Two more were late model SUVs, which would certainly come with keyless entry. The last was a compact sedan, and though it felt wrong, I approached it to get a closer look. Two tarbabies sprang up directly in front of me.

Not really. But that's what it looked like. What actually sprang up were our own shadows, projected on the pavement and car ahead of us by the sudden appearance of a pair of headlights approaching from behind. A white Lexus SUV had just turned the corner from the rear parking lot and was approaching at an unsettling speed. It looked like the car wasn't going to stop for us, but then at the last minute, it didn't. Libby dropped Banjo as she scrambled to get out of the way, while I hopped up onto the curb on the opposite side.

"Dammit, Bamberger!" I yelled as the car lurched to a stop ten feet past the point where we had been standing. When the driver's head turned, her profile illustrated my error.

"Iris?" asked Libby, but the driver made no reply. Instead she put her left hand against the side of her face as if shielding it from the paparazzi, and put the car in gear again.

"That was Iris?" asked Libby. "She just… left?"

"So where the hell are the Bambergers?" I marched to the side doors of the Sherwood wing. The doors themselves were locked, but there were narrow strips of glass on either side. Through cupped hands I peered through these windows for any trace of the older couple. It was too dark to make out any details, and there was no sign of movement. I banged on the door a few times.

"Josh!" called Libby from the curb.

"I don't see them. They may be holed up in one of the guest rooms."

"Josh! Be quiet!"

I froze. I froze, and I listened, and I heard it.

Splut.

The sound was coming from the north, where the Lexus had emerged. The lot in that direction was a tangle of shadows that could have hidden anything. A rustling in the bushes to my left told me the Glitter Man was still advancing. Of the Possum-Thing there was no sign, but I now found myself scrutinizing every shadow for movement.

"Josh, we need to go."

If I held very still, I could hear them. More of those soft sucking sounds, coming from a dozen different directions—from all around us.

Without any clear idea of where we were going, we headed toward the rear lot. It was too dark to run with any confidence, so we took our time and let Banjo take the lead. Even in the dark we could follow the sound of his toenails clicking on the pavement and the occasional growl when he came too close to one of the shadows.

I wished that I had thought to bring our flashlights, but our Go-Bags remained unpacked in our room. We were leaving with only what was in our pockets. In my case, that was my cell phone, fully charged but useless without a signal, and my wallet, which currently contained a little under forty dollars. I'm guessing Libby probably had some Chapstick, because Libby always had Chapstick.

With Banjo's help we made it safely to the rear parking lot, where we could just barely make out the silhouettes of three vehicles.

One of those was a pickup truck, leaving two possible candidates "What was Iris driving? Was that the Bonneville?"

"It had a slanty L on the front. Is that a Lexus?"

"So where did she get a Lexus?" I trotted over to a large sedan parked beneath a non-functioning lamppost. "You don't think that was the Bamberger's car, do you?"

Libby considered the question. "You think she would just strand them?"

I tapped the Pontiac arrowhead on the car's trunk. "This is it." I walked to the driver side door and slid the key into the lock. When the latch popped, I opened the door and thumbed the switch to open the passenger side lock. Banjo hopped in and settled in the driver's seat. I shooed him into the back, and he and Libby nestled into the spacious leather-trimmed seats. When the doors closed, electric shoulder and lap restraints whirred back into position automatically. I took a few seconds to get the feel of the console. The turn signal lever was cluttered with switches for cruise control, and I had trouble locating the headlights. I tried twisting the lever, and twin jets of light blue liquid spurted out over the windshield. The wiper blades started up, and as I watched them clear the fluid from the glass, I noticed the car's unorthodox hood ornament for the first time.

"You've got to be kidding me," I said as I watched the Duck-Thing watching me through the glass.

"Is that..." said Libby, not entirely sure of what she was seeing. "Is that... the same duck?"

"Couldn't be," I replied, absolutely certain that it was. "There's no way that thing followed us all the way here," I added, knowing that this was exactly what it had done. "And it sure as hell wouldn't know what car we were driving," I concluded without much conviction.

If the Duck-Thing recognized us, it gave no sign. It stood on the Bonneville's hood, head swaying slightly on its goopy neck as it stared back at us. It made no attempt to approach, and I wondered if whatever bizarre senses it relied upon could see the glass of the windshield.

"How are we going to get rid of it?" asked Libby.

I switched on the ignition, and the car surged to life without a sound. The cabin was so well insulated that I had to check the tachometer to confirm that the engine was in fact on. "We're not. Not here anyway. Not now." I pulled the headlight knob, and the gloom in front of the car retreated. As I feared, there were traces of movement in the direction the car was facing. It could have been simply tree branches swaying with the wind, but I didn't think so. There were now four confirmed tarbabies in the parking lot, and my instincts told me there would soon be more.

I put the car in gear and pulled around to the side lot. When I was even with the southeast exit, I swung the enormous sedan toward the doors and stopped. I flicked on the high beams and leaned on the horn for half a minute. There was no sign of movement within, though I could see the Possum-Thing waddling along the building's side. After another minute had passed, I put the car in gear again and weaved toward the exit. The car steered like a boat, so I took it slow and made the turns wide.

In the driveway leading out to Route 28, we passed two more human-shaped tarbabies and had to drive on the grass to avoid them. When we reached the main road, I aimed the car north.

"How are we on gas?" asked Libby.

I scanned the dashboard, and was amused to discover I had accidentally put the turn signal on. Like the rest of the car, the directional made no sound. "A little over half a tank. Should be plenty." The clock on the radio indicated it was a quarter past ten.

"Looks like we'll be in Albany by midnight."

34

We were still on the road at two in the morning. The drive had been frustrating from the outset. Route 28 was peppered with monsters, and we couldn't drive more than a quarter mile without having to swerve around a dark shape in the road. There were few streetlights in that region under the best of circumstances, and with the power out the visible world had shrunk to whatever lay within the reach of our headlights. And while I soon grew accustomed to the Bonneville's laissez faire steering, I still didn't trust the brakes. The distance required to bring the massive pile of metal to a stop was far greater than I was used to in the Focus. Under these conditions, I never felt comfortable coaxing the car much over twenty miles an hour.

We were also driving blind. The Bonneville had neither GPS nor compass, and a search of the cabin revealed no maps either. We knew that Albany was due north, but the only road we knew that went there directly was the thruway, and the thought of returning there made us nervous. So we stuck to the local roads and trusted to our own sense of direction. Whenever we were offered a choice of directions, I always bore right, on the assumption that heading east would at worst bring us back to the thruway, where we could at least get our bearings again. If we started drifting west, we could end up in Syracuse before realizing our mistake.

We were surprised to find that we were not the only car on the road. On half a dozen occasions we spotted lights in the distance and wondered if we had finally escaped the blackout area. In each case, they turned out to be the lights of other travelers picking their weary way through the night. None of our fellow journeymen made any attempt to approach us, and eventually we lost sight of each of them. Our only constant companion was the Duck-Thing perched on our hood. The creature itself could not be seen in the darkness, but at the right angle we could pick its shape out against the illuminated road in front of us.

When midnight rolled around, my mind was alternately occupied with two things. The first was our fuel supply. Half a tank should have been more than enough to get us the forty or fifty miles we needed to go, but the mammoth car was drinking an extraordinary amount of gas. By midnight the needle had dipped below the quarter tank level, and we still had no idea how far we had to go. At times I thought I could actually see the needle on the gas gauge drifting to the left, though this may have been a side effect of my second problem.

I was finding it increasingly difficult to stay awake. It was not yet my usual bedtime, but we had been rising earlier than we were accustomed to during our stay at Alan a'Dale's. The comfort of the car's interior conspired with the lack of visual stimulation outside our windows to lull us into a drowsy stupor. Banjo had put up no fight at all. The dog had spread himself out over the plush back seat as soon as we had hit the road, and had been snoring steadily for two hours.

Libby had been a trooper, gamely forcing herself to stay awake to keep me company, but I knew that was a losing battle. There were two things that always put Libby out faster than a bottle of cough syrup—moving vehicles and, for some reason, puppet shows. Sooner or later, I knew I was going to lose her, and when her chin finally slumped down to her chest and her breathing deepened, I made no attempt to keep her awake.

Keeping myself awake was a more serious problem. At the speed we were going, I wasn't worried about rolling off the road or hitting another car, but every so often a tarbaby would loom within the range of our headlights, and I didn't want to pick up any more hitchhikers. So I stretched, and I pinched my face, and I shook every available extremity to keep the blood flowing to my brain. I tried the radio, but the only thing I could tune in was a French news station from Montreal. The sonorous tones of the newsreader's voice, speaking softly in a language I did not understand, only made me drowsier.

Around one o'clock it started to rain. This was not a problem at first, but after twenty minutes of sporadic spotting, the drops began to fall with a heavy, monotonous rhythm. I turned on the wipers, and the regular back-and-forth motion was like the swing of a hypnotist's pocket watch. By two, it was pouring. A thick cascade of water beat ferociously against the hood of the car, and even the otherwise stoic Duck-Thing found its head bowing under the weight of the water. I was surprised to find myself feeling sorry for the creature.

At twelve minutes past two, I conceded defeat. After navigating a curve at just a hair over five miles an hour, I found myself in the left lane, drifting toward a sidewalk with no idea of how I had gotten there. I panicked momentarily, searching the road for any excuse to avoid admitting to myself that I had fallen asleep. There was no harm done, and even if I had gone off the road, the damage at this speed would have been trivial, but waking up behind the wheel was one unsettling experience too many for one day. I tightened my grip on the wheel and scanned the side of the road for any breaks in the curb that would indicate a parking lot. A mile and a half later, I found it and pulled in.

The lot belonged to a bowling alley. The front of the building was windowless, and oversized banners indicated that Summer Leagues were now forming. I let the car coast to a stop wherever it wanted, then shoved the gearbox into Park and killed the engine. I pushed the button for the lights, and the world outside vanished except for the thundering sound of rain on metal. With sincere delight, I took my foot off the brake, laid my head back on the overstuffed leather headrest, and closed my eyes.

From the backseat came a long, unabashed yawn. Banjo stirred to see where we were, but it was dark and warm, and there was only so far he was willing to raise his head.

"Wuzzat?" said Libby.

"Dog. S'nothin."

"Oh gosh. I fell asleep. I'm so sorry!"

"Sokay."

"Why didn't you wake me?"

"You're sleep… sleepy."

Libby stretched and peered out the window into the darkness. "Where are we?"

"Dunno. Bolnalley.. S'raining. Can't drive anymore."

"Bowling Alley?" Libby reached across my lap and pulled the knob for the headlights. She squinted through the driving sheets of rain to make out the words painted across the front windows. "Penny Lanes? Is this Penny Lanes?"

The sound of the car door opening to the roar of raindrops slapping on the pavement was enough to get Banjo's attention, but I still found myself unable to open my eyes.

"It is!" cried a small voice from somewhere outside my small, comfortable bubble. "Josh, this is Penny Lanes!"

"S'good." A half-dozen wet, slapping sounds were punctuated by cold and damp, as Libby yanked open the driver side door and poked her head inside. She had pulled the hood of her sweatshirt up to ward off the worst of the storm, but it was already soaked through.

She shook me hard. "Josh, this is Penny Lanes! I know where we are!"

I opened my heavy eyes and blinked at her without comprehension.

"We're only five miles from my parent's house! I know how to get us there!"

Banjo yawned. I closed my eyes again.

"Come on!" she yelled, poking me hard on the shoulder. "Scoot over! I can drive from here!" I looked to my right and tried to slide into the passenger seat, but the gearbox was in the way. I pulled my leg up to crawl over, but even in the Bonneville's spacious cabin this was a difficult maneuver for someone of my height.

Libby snagged me by the elbow and pulled. "Come on! Out you go! Chinese Fire Drill!" I looked at the cold dark wet that awaited me outside and shivered. Still, experience had taught me that I got to bed faster if I did what Libby told me, so when my wife threw open the door and stepped back, I unfolded myself from my seat and stepped out into the night.

It was every bit as unpleasant as I had imagined. The rain was cold and stabbed at my skin like a thousand tiny acupuncture needles. As I shuffled around the front of the car, I had the limited presence of mind necessary to give the Duck-Thing a wide berth. Its head was still drooping from the weight of the water, and I could see a hundred tiny beads of moisture clinging to its skin.

By the time I got around to the other side and slumped into the passenger seat, my hair was already plastered to my forehead. I shook my head as I slammed the door shut, then scooped wet hair away from my face. I was still bone-tired, but the rain and the cold had shocked me awake again. I was fully alert when I turned to Libby and said, "so how long…"

The sentence hung in the air unfinished. The driver's seat was empty, and the door was still wide open.

From the back seat, I heard a low rumbling noise. Banjo was standing on the soft leather upholstery with his nose pressed against the tiny triangular vent window on the driver's side of the car. The hair on his back was standing straight up in a perfect Mohawk, and he was trembling from snout to tail. The rumbling turned into a growl, and the growl turned into a steady, mournful howl.

I was no longer tired, but I was suddenly colder than I'd ever been. Part of this was the rain that had plastered my pink Alan a'Dale's polo shirt to my body, but most of it was the realization that I knew exactly what I would find if I were foolish enough to ever get out of the car. My worse judgment prevailed. Less than a second after Banjo started howling, I had ripped open the passenger door and rolled back out into the rain.

The darkness was no longer absolute. The Bonneville's headlights still stabbed through the falling rain to illuminate the front of the Bowling Alley, while the car's interior dome light allowed a puddle of feeble yellow light to spill out past the driver's side door, but I still could see nothing beyond the car's roof. I could, however, hear something. To be more precise, I could hear the absence of something. All around the rain clattered down heavily on the pavement. In front I heard a thousand tiny clangs of water hitting the car's hood and trunk. But in a space just beyond the car's rear left tire, the slapping sounds stopped. Something there was keeping the rain from hitting the ground.

I took a small, careful step toward the rear of the car, with my eyes fixed on the spot where the rain wasn't falling. I longed for my night vision to kick in, and tried to force my pupils open through willpower alone. A moment later, that was no longer necessary. A bolt of lightning streaked across the sky to my left, and for the barest fraction of a second, the entire world stood revealed.

There was Libby, right where I thought she would be, just beyond the rear wheel well, barely outside the glow spilling from the open door. Behind her was nothing—a black hole where the rain should be falling. A black hole that had already begun wrapping its arms around her. When she ordered me out of the car, Libby had stepped right back into a tarbaby that had been attracted by the arriving vehicle. Her hooded sweatshirt should have insulated her from this initial contact, but I could see her left arm was bent backwards. In her delight at discovering she was almost home, Libby forgot herself, and reflexively tried to push off from whatever she had walked into. Her left hand touched the creature at hip-level, and if she had time to call out, the driving rain had swallowed the sound.

There were others. The lightning flash was gone almost as soon as it arrived, but it was enough for me to see that the monster that held Libby was not alone. There were shapes in the rain, dark patches where there should have been only sheets of glittering silver. When the lightning had gone, I could still sense them. Just as I could see them as the vacant space where the rain wasn't, so too could I hear the sound of where the rain was not hitting the pavement. I couldn't tell exactly how many there were, but I knew we didn't have much time to act.

But acting is what I was determined to do. The monsters had taken the Spillers, and I let them be. They took Big Tobacco, and I did not complain. They took Brandon Mathis, they took Roscoe Carson, they took the residents of Friendly Haven and the Church of the Most Precious Blood, and I moved on. And they could have Elliott Rosenthal, and they could have the Gerbers, and they could even have the Bambergers, if they had a use for them.

But they couldn't have my Pixie.

I needed to get one in close enough to touch the thing that had my wife. Back at Alan a'Dale's it had taken three of us to budge one of the creatures. Even as angry as I was, there was simply no way I'd be able to lift and carry one of the things on my own. Especially without a bed sheet to protect myself. Especially when I couldn't see them.

I considered my options. If I could lure one in, I might be able to take a running leap at it, and maybe my momentum would be enough to knock them together. Even better—the car. I could use Saul's trick with the car. It would be delicate work. The parking lot was not without obstacles, including light posts and enormous concrete planters, and if I ran into more than one of those monsters, I might find steering difficult. And if I drove into one of them, I'd have to be careful that it didn't touch…

My breath caught in my throat. Listening carefully for the sound of sloshing footsteps, I circled back to the front of the car. And there it was, looking sodden and bedraggled and absolutely perfect.

There was little hope of lifting a full-grown humanoid tarbaby, but by damn I could lift the Duck-Thing.

I remembered Carrie Spiller, and Brandon Mathis, and Saul and Bitzy. None of them had given themselves to the tarbabies. They had all been taken as the result of a single careless misstep. I needed to act swiftly, but rushing this could prove disastrous.

First, I needed to protect myself. I had no sheets this time, nor even a jacket. Was there anything of use in the car? Floor mats, maybe. In the bowling alley? Perhaps if I could see, but not with a squadron of those creatures encircling us. With no other resources to hand, I peeled off my shirt. It was the pink one with Alan a'Dale winking on the breast, and I was not sorry at the prospect of losing it. Without it, the rain pummeled my bare skin. I hunched my shoulders against the pounding and the cold.

I laid the shirt gingerly across the Duck-Thing's back as though I were setting a very small table. I made sure the body and tail were covered, but left the neck and head exposed. I was tempted to simply swaddle the creature in fabric from head to tail, but once the material was stuck to it, there was no guarantee I would be able to unwrap it. Some part of the thing's body would have to remain exposed.

I folded the shirt around the Duck-Thing's tail feathers, then again around its breast. Laying my head against the car's hood, I confirmed that, accepting the feet and neck, every inch of the creature was covered. Once satisfied, I slid my right hand under the Duck-Thing's breast, my left under its butt, and pulled. I was not surprised when the creature refused to budge.

I tightened my grip, wrapping my arms around the creature up to the elbows. I pulled again, and again the Duck-Thing refused to move. Another flash of lightning spiked through the sky, and this time I counted four dark shapes in the rain before the glow faded. Distance was impossible to judge, but I didn't have long.

Hoping to improve my leverage, I released the Duck-Thing and climbed up onto the car's front fender. I wrapped my arms around the sodden bundle again, then tried to stand up, but could not rise above a low crouch. I tried to straighten my legs, but only found my feet sliding farther apart on the wet metal of the fender.

Unable to stand, I squatted back down on my haunches and tried leaning backward. Though this pose was precarious, being able to bring my body weight into play felt promising. I leaned back further, and the Duck-Thing leaned with me. Its feet were still plastered to the hood, but its legs were now at an angle, forcing its head up toward the sky. I secured my feet against the car's front grill and slowly pushed off. I still couldn't straighten my legs very far, but I was in a far more stable position, and when I tensed the muscles in my legs, the creature began to move with me.

The movement was almost imperceptible, but once I was confident that I was not going to fall off the bumper, I dug in. Leaning back to a fully horizontal pose, I looked skyward into the storm that was now pelting my exposed face. I pushed again, and at first my legs did little more than tremble, but after a moment I could feel myself straightening out. Yet still the Duck-Thing would not release its grip on the car.

A third bolt of lightning struck, this one almost directly overhead. I whipped my head from side to side, trying to catch a glimpse of the shapes in the rain, but in my current position I could tell nothing before the flash faded. I braced myself for another pull.

As I was readjusting my stance, the thunder from the last bolt exploded around us like a bomb. I flinched, my legs and back spasming as my reptile brain tried to convince my body to leap for safety. Having no better plan, I accepted the advice and leapt, and found myself catapulted free of the car, unsure of what was happening until I hit the ground more than four feet from where I started.

Where I hit the ground is not the same as where I stopped. I slid for another foot-and-a-half, my naked skin hydroplaning across the lubricated pavement. A few pebbles dug painful gouges into the flesh of my back, but a thin film of water prevented the concrete from flaying the flesh off my back entirely. I barely noticed these injuries, as the impact had knocked the wind out of me. I fought to breathe and struggled to sit up, desperate to get back up on the car for another attempt at prying the Duck-Thing loose.

I raised my head and winced in pain. Something was pulling on my hair. I opened my eyes, certain I would find myself in the clutches of one of the shadows that had been stalking me through the rain. Instead, I saw only pink. I tightened my grip tentatively and realized I was still holding the shirt. Even more surprising, the shirt was still holding the Duck-Thing. The entire bundle had come with me when I leapt from the car, and was now covering my face. I lifted it experimentally, and my phantom assailant pulled at my hair again.

I rolled my eyes upward, and discovered that my problem was not behind me, but on top of me. Most of the Duck-Thing remained safely swaddled in my Alan a'Dale polo shirt, but in the fall from the car, its exposed neck and head had flopped backward, striking me on the top of my head. The thickness of my hair had prevented immediate skin contact, but that wouldn't last long. I had only seconds before the creature spread its goopy, viscous form onto my scalp and forehead.

Kicking my legs hard against the pavement, I rolled onto my belly, then fought my way up to a kneeling position, never taking my hands off the creature affixed to my head. I yanked the bundle down toward the ground and winced at the audible ripping sound that resulted. The Duck-Thing came free with a thick tuft of my hair still attached. A moment later the pain caught up, and for a moment my howls drowned out Banjo's.

The sound of rain not falling was very close now. I stumbled to my feet and saw that the nearest of the tarbabies had entered the pool of illumination thrown by the car's headlights. Two more shadows were outlined just behind it. Holding the bundle containing the Duck-Thing high above my head, I stepped around to the side of the car, idly observing two triangular patches on the hood where the paint had torn away from the metal.

Libby's eyes were open, and she was beaming a warm smile of greeting. "Hiya handsome," she giggled. "What happened to your hair?"

I smiled back. "Got attacked by a duck. Again. You ready to go home?"

Libby shook her head. "There's no need, silly goose." She leaned forward slightly and whispered conspiratorially. "You've got to try this."

With a grunt loud enough to distract Banjo from his singing, I hefted the Duck-Thing high above my head, then slammed it down on top of the creature holding Libby.

SPLUT!

Almost immediately, nothing happened.

Banjo looked to me, then back to Libby, then to me again. Libby looked mildly puzzled, but still ridiculously happy. I held my breath and waited. The Duck-Thing had hit the other tarbaby square on, and their heads were now solidly stuck together. The rest of its body, still wrapped in my shirt, dangled down onto the other creature's shoulder.

Slowly, the pink bundle began to slide further to the side. Then it stopped and rolled a few inches onto the larger tarbaby's back. Then back to the side again as the thing holding Libby shook its head in a tentative attempt at knocking its new burden loose.

My eyes were fixed on the creature's right arm—the one draped across Libby's chest. If I could get that arm out of the way, I had a chance. I ignored the rain pelting my wounded scalp and back. I ignored the things that were slowly advancing toward us through the parking lot. I ignored Banjo's querulous whines. I waited, and I watched the arm.

And the arm moved. The creature raised the limb up toward its head, as if intending to swat the Duck-Thing away. And as the arm moved, the hem of Libby's sweatshirt rose with it, as the fabric clung tight to the tarbaby. When I could finally see the purple of Libby's Alan a'Dale polo shirt, I moved.

I stepped in close and tucked my hands under the sweatshirt, grabbing the creature's arm through the fabric from below. I shoved the arm upward as far as I could, and the thing did not resist. With the arm out of the way, I tugged the sweatshirt up over Libby's head.

"Well hi there!" laughed Libby as her face was revealed again. I wrapped my arms around her and stepped backward. Libby's right arm slid free of the sweatshirt sleeve, which deflated and plastered itself against the tarbaby's side. She threw her liberated arm around my neck and kissed me on the mouth. She remained trapped only by her left hand, the fingers of which were coated up to the second knuckle in her attacker's inky goo.

With Libby's face so close to my own, I did not see the second tarbaby enter the dim circle of illumination thrown by the car's interior lights. Even when it had placed one gelatinous hand on the frame of the open door and eased it open, I was oblivious to its movements. It was the growling that alerted me. While Libby mashed her mouth against mine, I glanced inside the car and saw Banjo crouched on the back seat, the hair on his back standing at full attention, and the most vicious snarl I had ever seen on the dog aimed right at me.

In fact, his growls were actually directed past me at something that was still out in the rain, and it wasn't difficult to guess what that might be. With no more time to consider my options, I raised my right fist high, then slammed it down onto Libby's elbow.

A second later, I was shoving my wife into the car, then rolling on top of her into the driver's seat. A second after that, Libby was screaming. With my left leg still on the pavement I fired up the ignition, heaved Libby across the gear box into the passenger's seat, and slammed the transmission into Drive. The car lurched forward, and the only thing that prevented my exposed leg from being caught in the closing door was the newly arrived tarbaby that held it open. In a single movement, I yanked my left leg inside the car and stamped onto the gas pedal with my right. The car lurched again, the tires screeched in protest, and we stopped. Then I went blind.

At first I thought the door had finally slammed shut, turning off the interior dome lights. But I could still hear the rain, and felt it drumming down on my left arm and knee. But if the door was open, why was it so hard to breathe?

I waved my arms in front of my face, and Banjo yelped. When the car surged forward the dog had leapt into the front seat, and his hairy butt was now plastered against my face as he tried to crawl on top of Libby. She was sprawled across the front seat, one foot still in my lap, clutching at her bloodied left hand and wailing in a mixture of pain and either terror, outrage, or something else I didn't understand.

Peeking around the dog's bottom, I discovered why we were not moving. There were two man-sized shadows plastered to the Bonneville's front grill, and a third was still holding the door open. I groped under the pile of dog beside me until I found the gear shift again, and forced the car into Reverse. The tires squealed again, and the Bonneville retreated a dozen feet. The door sprang open again to the full extent that its hinges allowed, and then beyond. With a sharp BANG that prompted Banjo to scramble into the floor space in front of Libby, the door's hinge snapped, and the window shattered in an explosion of glass.

I hit the brakes. The creature that had attacked Libby was right outside my door, though it paid no attention to the car as it struggled to rip the Duck-Thing off its head. I pounded the accelerator again, and the car lurched back another three feet—just enough to slam the creature holding onto our door into its neighbor. The monster released its grip on the doorframe, and I was able to coast back another ten feet.

I turned the wheel just slightly, bringing the tarbabies into the glow of his headlights. What I could see of the creatures no longer made any sense—they were just a mass of shadow thrashing about in the dark. I looked at the figures plastered to the grill of the car. They were moving as well, though their movements were more purposeful. They were reaching for me.

I held my breath, straightened out the steering wheel, and put the car in Drive. I resisted the urge to hit the gas. This was going to be a short trip, but I wanted to be able to drive away from it. The car was already chastising me several different ways, with an urgent pinging alerting me to the "Fasten Seatbelt" and "Door Ajar" lights on the dashboard. I noted with chagrin that the Low Fuel warning was also adding to the glow. I had no idea how long that had been on.

I eased my foot off the brake, and the car rolled forward at a sluggish speed. It was only a matter of seconds before we closed the distance to our target, but I was certain I saw the tarbabies on the grill straighten up slightly, as if aware of their predicament. If so, they were nowhere near fast enough to avoid it.

Splut.

Minutes later, the Bonneville backed out of the Penny Lanes parking lot, leaving behind a writhing mass of shadow and confusion. I took one last look at the creatures as they struggled to free themselves from themselves before turning the car back onto the road heading north. I was too tired to pity them.

35

I drove much too fast for the conditions. The streets were wet, visibility was poor, I was exhausted, and the road was peppered with monsters. But I was also desperate for this trip to end. Libby had said we were close to her parent's house, but I had been too groggy to pick up any particulars. I tried to ask her for directions, but she had curled into a tight ball in the passenger seat and could do nothing more than tremble. Banjo was trying to fix her with dog spit, but it didn't seem to be taking.

It didn't help that the car's dome light kept winking on, robbing me of my night vision. Something very bad had happened to the driver-side door's hinge, and the door refused to close fully. It kept drifting open as we drove, then banging shut again, and I had been unable to find a switch that would prevent the interior lights from coming on each time that happened. In those fleeting seconds when the cabin was illuminated, all I could see were streaks of my wife's blood on every surface in the car's interior.

A few minutes after we leaving Penny Lanes, the engine began coughing. I knew that sound—the Bonneville's gas tank was bone dry. I scoured the roadside for any promising landmarks. The problem wasn't that nothing looked familiar, but rather that *everything* looked familiar. The area we were in now was not quite suburban, and not quite rural. The houses we passed were uniformly old, mostly two or three-story colonials with detached garages, and they all felt right. I was certain that something identifiable would be just around each corner, yet each corner came and went with me just as lost as when we started.

"Pixie?" I tried. "Is that the road there? Is that where we need to go?" I shook Libby's shoulder a bit harder than I intended, trying to bring her out of her stupor.

"Back," she mumbled.

I had not really expected a reply. "Back? We need to go back? How far?"

"It felt so nice," she said, trailing off, and I understood. She didn't know where we were any more than I did. She only knew she wanted to go back to Penny Lanes.

Having no better plan, I made the turn anyway. The engine coughed again, and when I straightened out the wheel the car stalled. I shifted into Neutral and let the car drift under its own inertia. We rolled past several more houses, each of them at once familiar and noncommittal. I was beyond merely scanning for landmarks, and was now looking for a place to shelter. With a broken door, the car was no longer safe, and I didn't want to risk spending the night in it. We could try getting into a house, but at this hour it would be difficult to tell if any of them were occupied. There was an old barn off to my left, but the rotting timbers on its roof didn't promise much in the way of weatherproofing. Maybe that shed off to the side would be unlocked…

I cut the wheel to get the shed into my headlights, then hit the brakes. On the side nearest the street was a small window, above which was a tin sun, decorated with a smiling face, its once bright yellow paint now faded to a dull mustard. I knew that happy sun.

I closed my eyes and summoned up a mental map. Just up the street on the right would be a small Raised Ranch. There would be a Christmas Wreath hanging on the front door, visible through the rusted screen door. It would be there even though it was June, because it had always been there.

Then what? The Feed Store. Again, on the right. Not even a quarter mile, I guessed. Then there's the traffic light. And once we were at the traffic light...

I put the car in Park and closed my eyes. I turned the key in the ignition. The engine clicked and whirred, but did not engage. I turned the key again, this time putting just the barest whisper of pressure on the accelerator. The engine clicked and whirred and clicked and whirred, and then rumbled. The Bonneville came back to life.

The car may have been alive again, but it was not at all well. It continued to sputter and ping, and it was only a matter of moments before it would stall again. I put the car in Drive and hit the gas hard, trying to force whatever last fumes of petroleum still lingered in the system into the dying carburetor.

The car surged ahead. Within moments we passed a white Raised Ranch with a brown Christmas Wreath taking pride of place on the front door. The Bonneville coughed and choked, and still we rolled on. There ahead was the Feed Store that did double-duty as a Dog Grooming Salon. And there, hanging across the intersection just beyond, was the traffic light. It was dark now, as were all the other traffic lights we had passed that evening, but it didn't need to be lit to tell me what I needed to know. We had reached Iroquois Street, and that's where Libby's parents lived.

To avoid stalling out on the turn, I took my foot off the gas, shifted the car into Neutral and eased around the corner. Libby's house was only two miles from this intersection—maybe only a mile and a half. And even with the engine coughing like it was, I knew now we were going to make it.

We didn't make it. The moment we straightened out from the turn, I put the car back into gear. It stalled immediately. I shifted back into Neutral and turned the key, but the engine only clicked and whirred and failed to catch. The car drifted along another fifty yard or so, then stopped.

And so we walked. Banjo didn't understand this. Even with the rain pounding on the roof and the thunder crashing around us, the Bonneville was still warm and reasonably dry. When I stepped out of the car and called for him to follow, the dog assumed he must have misheard me. But when the tall human who gave him cookies opened the other door and scooped out the short human who smelled nice, Banjo knew he had to follow.

He ended up leading. I had to carry my unresponsive wife, and while she was lighter than a bag of kitty litter, I was still exhausted. The rain was still pounding us mercilessly, and I still could see nothing. And there were still monsters out in the night. So Banjo trotted ahead, his soaked fur heavy against his skin, and I followed, my arms growing numb, and my back and shoulders aching from the drumming of the rain against my bare skin.

To assure myself that I was making progress, I counted my steps. I heard that the Romans defined a mile as a thousand paces, so I figured that once I had counted off fifteen hundred steps, I would be there. But pain and exhaustion made it difficult to focus, and I found myself losing count. Every now and then I heard a low growl from directly ahead, then the soft sound of toenails clacking across the pavement to the other side of the street. I limped behind Banjo as best I could. Other than the dog, I saw and heard only rain.

After a half-hour of sodden, aching trudging, lightning flashed, and I saw the gnome. It was a jauntily painted ceramic statue of a white-bearded dwarf pushing a wheelbarrow full of plastic flowers at the base of a mailbox. I knew that gnome. Indeed, at this moment I loved that gnome, because it meant we had arrived. In fact, we had gone too far. The gnome belonged to the house two doors beyond the Rimbeau house. In the dark, I had walked right past our destination.

Suddenly dizzy and finding it difficult to breathe, I nearly dropped Libby to the pavement. I stooped, gently lowering my wife onto the neighbor's lawn, then sank to my hands and knees beside her. "Pixie? You ready to go home?" I wheezed. "You ready to see Mom and Dad?"

In the dark I couldn't be sure, but when she spoke, Libby sounded like she was smiling. "That'll be nice," she replied. "We can take them to Penny Lanes with us."

Out in the street, Banjo barked. I couldn't see exactly what had caught the dog's attention, but I knew we needed to keep moving. I struggled to my feet and, legs trembling, hooked my hands under Libby's arms and pulled. She moved not so much as an inch. From my fingers to my elbows, I felt nothing but pins and needles, and I knew I would not be carrying Libby again anytime soon.

I tried the soft approach. "Coming, Pixie?" To my astonishment, she stood up at once, even taking my arm as I led her back across the neighbor's lawn to her parents' house. I called to Banjo, and the dog followed obediently, though he was still growling at something out in the darkness. Now I just needed to figure out how to wake up Libby's parents. I wasn't sure if doorbells would work with the power out. I suspected not, but then I realized that getting in the house wouldn't be a problem.

The front door stood wide open.

Libby has always been terrible about locking doors, so it was possible that there was a perfectly innocent explanation. In the storm, it was possible the door had simply blown open. With the power out, it was possible that…

I was too tired to hope. None of that was possible. Either Libby's parents weren't here or the tarbabies had got them. Either way, an open door meant there was a monster inside the house waiting for us.

But we had nowhere else to go. And I was so very tired.

The darkness outside the house was nothing compared to the absolute blackness inside. I had been in the house a dozen times before, but once the front door was shut behind us, I had trouble remembering where anything was. My first task was to find light. There would be candles in the dining room, but where would I find matches? In the kitchen, probably. Better yet, by the fireplace. The living room was just ahead and to the left, and the fireplace was at the far end. There would surely be matches nearby.

Unable to see anything ahead of me, I raised my hands and took a single step forward. Banjo growled, and I stopped dead. Stumbling about the house blindly with my hands flailing about suddenly seemed like a very bad idea. Surely there must be something…

My phone. My phone was in my pocket, useless for the last few days, but still more or less fully charged. I flipped the lid open and thumbed the power button. A bright white welcome screen lit up, and suddenly I could see. Not much, to be sure. Just shapes, and none of those were more than a few feet away, but it would be enough to let me know if anything was lurking in front of my face.

I sidled forward slowly, pushing random keys every couple of steps to keep the phone's display from going to sleep. Half a dozen feet from the front door was the entrance to the living room. There I would find a pair of arm chairs on the near wall, a sofa against the opposite side, and a heavy coffee table carved from a tree stump between them. The fireplace would be just beyond.

I took Libby's hand and guided her to the nearest chair, then snapped my fingers. Banjo trotted forward and crouched by her side. The dog was staring intently into the living room and whining, but I could not see what he was looking at. "Stay here, Pixie," I whispered. "I'm just going to get a candle."

I took a step toward the fireplace, and jumped another two feet when Banjo barked. "Dammit dog!" I hissed, and then I saw it. There, directly in front of me, a shape was coalescing out of the darkness. It hovered in the air before my face, then reached out for me. Though I knew it would not save me, I threw my hands up to ward the creature off.

When nothing claimed me, I pressed the keypad on my phone. The feeble light stabbed out once again, revealing absolutely nothing. The creature I had seen had been nothing more than a combination of darkness and nerves. Still, there was something near. Banjo was sure of that, at least. I squinted into the darkness, vigilant for any indication of movement. I held my breath and listened. Aside from Banjo's sporadic whines, I heard nothing.

I let out my breath in a slow stream, then took four decisive steps forward. My hands found the mantle, and my shin found the rack of fireplace tools. The collection of pokers, tongs and shovels clanged together, and I winced at the sudden noise. I ran the phone's light over the mantle and found a small glass bowl with a votive candle inside. It smelled faintly of pine, and I wondered if it had been overlooked when the Christmas decorations had been put away. A few feet down was a small tin box featuring an illustration from an old laundry soap ad. I pried open the lid and was rewarded with a dozen random matchbooks collected from area restaurants.

My hands shook as I opened the first book and plucked out a match. I pinched the tiny stick tightly in my fingers to steady them, but only succeeded in breaking off the match head when I tried to strike it. I shook my right hand vigorously to relax it, and on my second attempt the match flared to life. I held the flame to the candle wick, which took several seconds to light. Cradling the candle in both hands, I turned to face the room, and saw the monsters.

This time there was no doubt as to their reality, even though the things on the couch looked like an optical illusion. On the sofa sat two shadows without anyone to cast them. Both were short and both were slight, just like Libby. The thing on the right was slightly larger, with a small pot belly. That would have been Donald, Libby's father. That would make Miriam the one on the left—the one sitting directly opposite her daughter and looking at once like both her reflection and her shadow. The two shapes sat in perfect stillness, with their heads just slightly tilted toward one another. Twin tendrils of darkness jutted out from the sides of the figure, joining between them into a perfect V shape.

"They're holding hands," said Libby. "That's so sweet."

I snatched the fire poker from the rack by my side and brandished it like a sword. The shadows on the sofa did not react, though Libby covered her face with a hand and snickered. Banjo looked confused. The moment I felt more foolish than frightened, I replaced the poker in the rack.

I walked to my wife's side. "Are you OK, Pixie?"

Libby smiled, but did not look at me. "They look so happy. Do you see how happy they are?"

I studied the things on the couch. I had no idea how long it had been since they had been Donald and Miriam Rimbeau, but I wondered if they had changed position at all in that time. "They sure seem content," I admitted, thinking there was something wrong about the scene in front of me. They're not supposed to touch each other, I thought. They're supposed to avoid each other, not hold hands like school kids in love. Something was going on here that was beyond everything I had seen before, and I did not know what that was.

An involuntary yawn slipped out before I could squelch it. "You should go to bed," said Libby, looking at me for the first time. "You must be tired."

I took my wife's hand in my own. "We're both tired. We should both go to bed." I gently pulled Libby to her feet, and steered her toward the staircase.

"Goodnight, Mom and Dad," she said, and gave them a little wave with her injured left hand.

Banjo bolted up the stairs ahead of us, which I took as a good sign. There was no way to be sure there weren't more tarbabies inside the house, but the dog's eagerness to get upstairs led me to believe the coast was more or less clear.

I led Libby into her childhood bedroom and fetched a pair of towels from the adjoining bathroom. I tried drying my hair and winced when I touched the bald spot where the Duck-Thing had ripped out a clump. I tried drying my back and winced again at the gouges that had been carved there by the asphalt in the Penny Lanes parking lot. Libby would have to help me clean and bandage those wounds in the morning.

I had planned to help Libby shed her soaked clothing, but she had already collapsed face down atop her old twin bed, and appeared to have fallen asleep. I carefully held her injured left hand up to the candle. It didn't look good. The nails on her two smallest fingers were gone, having been ripped out when I pulled her away from the tarbaby in the parking lot, and the pinky was bent at an unnatural angle. I didn't know exactly what to do about a broken finger, but I didn't want to leave it untreated. At the very least, I thought I should wash the wound.

I returned to the bathroom and turned the hot water spigot in the sink. Nothing happened. Libby's parents were off the municipal water lines, I remembered, and relied on a well. With no power to run the well pump, we would have no running water. I hunted around the medicine cabinet until I found a bottle of rubbing alcohol. I was hoping for some gauze as well, but there didn't seem to be any. I found a washcloth hanging from a hook beside a threadbare bathrobe on the bathroom's other door and settled for it instead.

Returning to the bedroom, I knelt by Libby's side and poured a capful of alcohol over her injured fingers. She winced and clenched her hand protectively, but did not wake up. I wound the washcloth loosely around her hand and resolved to do a better job in the morning. I pulled her damp sneakers off her feet and called it good enough.

Libby's tiny twin bed was not big enough for the both of us, so I pulled some pillows and blankets out of the closet and made a nest on the floor. I was about to drop into it when I considered the door to the room. There was no lock on it, and while the Parent-

Things downstairs did not seem eager to pursue us, there was no point in taking chances. I slid a dresser in front of the door to block it shut.

By the time I turned around again, Banjo had taken my bed. Not having the strength to argue, I peeled off my sopping wet jeans and curled myself around the dog, facing the door. I could not remember ever being so tired, but it was nearly sunrise by the time I fell asleep.

36

Arf!

Once again, Norman Spiller couldn't shut his damn dog up. The dizzy beast wasn't doing his usual non-stop, adrenaline-fueled tirade, just the occasional yap every minute or two. But it was enough to keep me from getting back to sleep. And I didn't hear Norman making any attempt at all to quiet the animal.

Arf!

I had a pounding headache and no desire to get out of bed to look out the window. There was a natural rhythm to these things. The dog barked. Norman yelled. The dog ignored him. Norman dragged the dog back inside. It was a horrible system, but it worked.

Arf!

So where the hell was Norman?

Arf!

Oh. That's right.

"Banjo?" I tried to sit up and regretted it at once. My arms and back howled in protest at their treatment the night before, and I could not move my neck. Only after wiping away a thick layer of crust was I able to open my eyes. There appeared to be a similar shell coating the corners of my mouth. I dragged the back of my hand over my lips and rolled onto my stomach.

Arf!

"What's up there buddy?" The volume of the dog's barks indicated Banjo was not far away, but I could not see him from my position on the floor. The chest of drawers was still blocking the door to the room, so there's no way he could have gotten out.

Arf!

"Cool it, Banjo." Bathroom. The dog had to be in the bathroom. But what was he looking for there? Was Libby in there? She must be. Taking a shower maybe.

Arf!

Only there was no water.

"Libby?" With considerable effort, I pushed up off the floor until I could see the top of the bed. It was empty.

So Libby had to be in the bathroom, even if there was no water. Maybe she was brushing her teeth in that immaculate way of hers. Maybe she was hanging her wet clothes up to dry. Maybe she was changing into that bathrobe I had seen hanging on the other door.

Arf?

The other door.

I was up on my feet in a second, then back down on the floor again just as quick. In my haste to get to the bathroom I had stepped on a discarded shoe, which slipped out from under me. I kicked the offending footwear under the bed and cursed as I rose, more cautiously this time.

It was an idiotic mistake. I knew the door was there—I had complained about it a dozen times before. It made no sense to have two doors in a bathroom that small, I had explained to Libby. What you lose in wall space isn't justified by the minor convenience of having exits on both the bedroom and the hallway. Libby, of course, had humored me. That's the way the house was. That's the way it had always been.

I had seen the other door last night, but was too bone-weary to make the connection that it was a way in past my barricade.

Or a way out.

The door was shut now, though the bathrobe was gone. Libby had been considerate enough to close it behind her when she left. And I knew that after she had closed it, she had gone down to visit the folks. That's where she would be now, curled up on the couch with her head in the Mother-Thing's lap.

I didn't want to go downstairs. I knew what I would find there, and I didn't want to find it. All I wanted was to curl back up into my nest, try to ignore the reek of wet Banjo, and go back to sleep.

But that wasn't even true. I didn't want to sleep. Yes, I desperately needed to rest, but what I *wanted* was my Pixie back, and while I knew in my heart that I was too late, that I had lost her due to my own exhaustion-induced carelessness, I also knew that I would never be able to rest again until I had done everything in my power to bring her back.

My hand trembled as I turned the knob and slipped out into the hallway.

I ached. My back and shoulders felt like solid blocks of wood, and I could not stand fully upright. A streak of fur came thundering up the stairs and deposited itself at my feet. Banjo yapped at me from the center of the hallway as if admonishing me for my stupidity, and I had to step over him to get to the stairs. I gripped the banister with all the strength my outraged arms were willing to offer and made the slow descent to the living room.

The Mom-and-Dad-Things remained on the sofa, their gooey fingers still lovingly intertwined, and their featureless heads still tilted just slightly toward one another. Though my guts had turned to water, I had to admit the image was every bit as sweet as Libby had declared it to be last night. Or rather, this morning. Notably absent from the scene was any sign of the Rimbeaus' daughter.

"Libby?" I looked to the front door. It was closed, and both deadbolts were engaged. Had I done that last night? Or this morning? I certainly would have wanted to, but couldn't remember thinking that clearly.

The back door was through the kitchen. As I stepped in that direction, I realized I was dizzy from a combination of pain, hunger and thirst. I opened the refrigerator, and was rewarded with a potent sour-milk smell. The power had doubtless been out here for several days. There were a half-dozen bottles of an imitation orange-flavored drink on the top shelf. I didn't know what it was, but it didn't look like it contained anything natural enough to spoil. I twisted the cap off one and brought the bottle to my lips. It was a foul, chalky concoction, thicker than fruit juice and piss-warm, and I drained the bottle in a single long gulp. I promised myself I would never drink this stuff again as I finished off a second bottle.

With a third drink in hand, I opened the kitchen door and stepped out onto the back lawn. The day was warm, the sky was clear, and the sun was almost directly overhead. I had neglected to check any of the clocks inside, but it felt like it must be somewhere in the neighborhood of noon. What shadows I could see were short.

There was still one place, however, where the shade was thick. The Rimbeaus' neighbors had an ancient willow on their property, though a quarter of its canopy now extended over the

Rimbeau yard. The tree's branches were still heavy from the weight of last night's rain, and the longest of them dragged on the ground. As thick as they were, the branches could not entirely blot out the sunlight, so I could easily see the figure pacing within the tree's shaded canopy—the short, slender, waif-like figure, the color of India ink from head to toe.

I was too tired to do this standing up. I dragged a canvas folding chair off of the Rimbeaus' patio and carried it over to the neighbor's yard. I noted with admiration that the chair had a cup caddy molded into the right arm, and I deposited my bottle of orange-colored syrup there as I sat down. Because that's what it was for.

"Hi Pixie," I said to the Pixie-Thing beneath the willow tree. "I forgot about the other door. Sorry about that."

The Pixie-Thing made no reply, which I took to mean my apology was accepted.

"It's just ridiculous to have it there! You could fit a double sink in there if you got rid of one of those doors. Or a linen closet!"

The thing beneath the tree humored me.

"But I should have remembered it was there, and I didn't, and I'm sorry." I popped the top on my orange drink and, from force of habit, tilted the bottle toward the tree to offer the Pixie-Thing a sip.

"So, is it as wonderful as you thought it would be?" I took a drink, then realized I was no longer anywhere near thirsty enough. I capped the bottle again.

"Josh."

The voice was small and hesitant, but it was unmistakably Libby's. The bottle slipped from my fingers and bounced on the lawn.

"Pixie?" I asked the thing under the willow. "You can talk?"

"Josh."

Of course she couldn't talk. She's got no vocal cords. No lips. No lungs to draw air. A five foot pile of jello salad just didn't have the equipment to form words.

"Josh!"

So it had to be some kind of telepathy. The tarbaby's mind was reaching directly into mine. That would explain how the creature could talk without making any movement. And why the voice sounded so far away.

"Josh, what the buggery bollocks are you doing?"

And why it sounded like it was coming from behind me.

The latch on the Rimbeaus' back door clicked shut, and with a great deal of pain and effort, I turned. Libby was crossing the lawn to me, wearing her old high-school gym clothes, the bathrobe that had been hanging on the other door, and an expression of concerned puzzlement. "Babe, are you all right?"

"Guarding!" I shouted as I struggled to my feet. The folding chair offered me no leverage, and I was only able to extricate myself by leaning forward and grabbing handfuls of lawn. "I was... the thing... guard."

Libby looked to the creature under the tree. "Were you... talking to it?"

"No, nuh-uh," I replied as I fought for balance. "A little bit."

"Oh good Lord, you thought that was me!"

"No! Not at all! What?"

Libby looked at the Pixie-Thing critically. "My chest is not that small, Josh. Do you really think my chest looks like that?" She pointed, and I dutifully examined the creature's chest. Though it was painful, I shook my head vigorously, hoping it was the reaction she wanted.

"And look at those hips! Josh, that's a boy! Are you telling me you can't tell the difference between your wife..." She continued her thought, but it was directed into my chest. I had wrapped my weary arms around her and was holding her as close as my arthritic muscles would allow.

"I thought you were gone, Pixie."

Libby stopped complaining and returned the embrace. She didn't say, "Don't be silly." She didn't say, "I could never leave you." She didn't say, "The thought never crossed my mind." She did nothing but hold her husband, and that would do.

I could have happily stayed there forever, basking in the smell of Libby's not-very-clean hair and feeling the warmth of her body pressed up against those few parts of me that didn't ache. But there were monsters about, and the sun would not keep them at bay forever. We had no electricity, no running water, and questionable shelter. With Libby's parents... indisposed... the closest family either of us had was in Indiana, and without television or Internet access, we had no way of determining how far the contagion had spread. Also, I was in my underpants. This last was the only problem I had a clue of how to fix.

When we finally stepped apart, Libby held up her hand for my inspection.

"I was in my parent's bathroom. They had bandages in there." She had cleaned and wrapped her two injured fingers in gauze. The hand still looked unhealthy—each finger was red and swollen from the first knuckle down. But at this point red and swollen was still preferable to black and sticky. If we could avoid infection, Libby would heal.

We stood and watched the thing under the willow, and the thing under the willow stood and watched us. When the sun began to sink, it would come for us. When Libby's parents finally noticed our presence, they might come for us too. But inside there were doors to close, so we went inside.

Libby took my hand and led me back to the house. "Come on," she said, "let's see if there's anything good in the pantry."

There wasn't.

Also Available From Spore Press

LYKAIA
by Sharon Van Orman

"I'm afraid I won't be able to properly express my fascination with *LYKAIA*. It was such an awesome read I would definitely recommend it to all who'd love to spend some quality time with a really well-written book.

The main character, forensic pathologist Sophia Katsaros gets a phone call from Greece and finds out that her brothers have been missing for two months. She goes there to start an investigation of her own that might not end well for her."

　　　-　Amazon Review

WAITING IN THE SILENCE
by Rosalyn W. Berne

"Praise is due for this debut novel set in post-apocalyptic Nantucket in the USA, The complexity is dynamic between nano-enhanced humans who have access to universal knowledge and the independents whose access is limited. Oriana, our heroine, dangles between them, sometimes condemned and sometimes praised. The virtual mysterious intelligence, which rules the community, must control Oriana for she is the source of fertility for many barren women. Suspense. Drama. And the ending is a delightful surprise."

　　　-　Louise Meriwether, author, "Daddy Was A Number Runner"

SEASON OF THE DEAD
by Lucia Adams, Paul Freeman,
Gerald Johnston, & Sharon Van Orman

"It is said that unto everything there is a season...these are the stories of a group of survivors during the season of the dead."

Four individuals fight to survive as the zombie apocalypse crashes over the world in a wave of terror and destruction. Color, creed, and social standing mean nothing as the virus infects millions across the planet.

<u>Sharon</u>: a zoologist from Nebraska, USA, has worked with the virus, and has seen the effects on the human mind. She knows more about the virus than nearly anybody alive, and far more than she wants to. <u>Gerry</u>: from Ontario, Canada, he gets his first taste of the virus from inside a prison cell. Locked up after an anti-government riot, his prison guard transforms before his eyes into a flesh craving zombie. <u>Lucia</u>: a chemist from Pittsburgh, USA, flees from a furry convention dressed as a giant squirrel, and escapes from the city in a Fed-Ex van. She's a girl who knows when to run and when to fight. <u>Paul</u>: thinks he can sit out the apocalypse in his apartment block in Dublin, Ireland, until the virus comes to visit, bursting his bubble and leaving him with no choice but to face reality or perish.

All four begin perilous journeys in mind and body as they face daily trials to survive: Four threads, four different parts of the world, one apocalypse!